"Let me advise you to leave Miss Bolderwood alone!"

Gervase said nothing, but kept his eyes on his brother's face, their expression amused, yet watchful.

"You may think you can come into Lincolnshire, flaunting your title and your damned dandified airs, and amuse yourself by trifling with Miss Bolderwood, but I shall not permit it and so I warn you!"

Gervase still looked amused and instead of answering, he lifted the second foil from where he had laid it on the table, set both hilts across his forearm and offered them to Martin.

Martin stared at him. "What's this tomfoolery?"

"Don't you fence?"

"Fence? Of course I do!"

"Then choose a foil. All these wild and whirling words don't impress me, you know. Perhaps your swordplay may command my respect!" Gervase paused and added softly: "No? Do you think you can't creditably engage with such a dandified fellow as I am?"

Martin's eyes flashed; he grasped one of the hilts. "We'll see about that!"

SHOWCASE

HEYER
GEORGETTE

THE QUIET GENTLEMAN

With a foreword by
Karen Hawkins

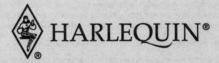

HARLEQUIN®

TORONTO • NEW YORK • LONDON
AMSTERDAM • PARIS • SYDNEY • HAMBURG
STOCKHOLM • ATHENS • TOKYO • MILAN • MADRID
PRAGUE • WARSAW • BUDAPEST • AUCKLAND

ISBN 0-373-83684-8

THE QUIET GENTLEMAN

Copyright © Georgette Heyer 1951

Copyright renewed © 1979 by Richard George Rougier

Foreword copyright © 2006 by Harlequin Books S.A.

THE QUIET GENTLEMAN

Foreword by
Karen Hawkins

KAREN HAWKINS

is a *USA TODAY* bestselling author. She has published nine historical romance novels, a young adult book and two novellas. A double RITA® Award finalist and winner of the Maggie Award for Outstanding Romantic Fiction, Karen began writing after getting a bit bored while working on her Ph.D. in political science. When she received the call that she'd sold her first book, Karen did what all good students would do; she promptly burned her stats book on the front lawn and dropped out of school.

For more information on Karen, her latest release or pictures of her doing sit-ups, visit her Web site at www.karenhawkins.com.

FOREWORD

MY GRANDMOTHER WAS partially responsible for introducing me to the works of Georgette Heyer.

When I was fourteen, each and every Sunday at 2:00 p.m. I was brutally forced—I still shudder to think of it—to visit my grandmother.

Before you break out your memories of sugar cookies and milk, lace doilies and Lawrence Welk, you should know that my grandmother had a violent aversion to noises (of any kind) and children who breathed. I qualified on both counts. By various hissed threats from my mother and stern glares from my father, I was forced to sit quietly, to be "seen and not heard" for *hours*.

My parents finally took pity on me, and one week my father stopped at the library on the way to my grandmother's. He handed me a library card and said, "Pick out a book. Any book. Just be quick."

Thus began my life as a reader. The library was tiny and had only one small room for fiction. But each Sunday I'd pick up a stack of books, and the next Sunday I'd bring them back and get another stack. I read every one I checked out.

Some books were great, some were just good, some

were merely okay, but none of them were bad. There are no bad books, only less good ones.

Suddenly Sundays weren't so terrible anymore. In fact, Sunday became the best day of the week.

After several months of reading, I'd worked my way through most of the books in that tiny room. One day, library card in hand, I suddenly realized that the shelves went all the way to the floor. Somehow I'd never looked at the very bottom shelf. Not even once.

In order to see that elusive shelf, I would have to bend over until my head almost touched my shoes. Fortunately I was fourteen and quite limber. I put a hand on a middle-level shelf to steady myself, bent over… and found Georgette Heyer.

To this day, I can still picture the row of books with her name on them. I can still feel the slick plastic of the library-issue bindings and smell the old paper. I could even draw that shelf for you *and* list the order of her books—it is *that* clear a memory.

It was also the beginning of a very long, very rich, very passionate love affair. I do not like Georgette Heyer's books; I love them.

To say that her books changed me would be a gross understatement. It was a love affair that would grandly escort me out of the world of reading and into the world of writing. From that day on my reading, and eventually my writing, had the same purpose—I wanted warmth and humor, intelligent characters and witty conversations, glamorous clothes and places, all written with a faultless sense of pacing. Those are the qualities I found in Georgette Heyer's writing. I have been such a fan that when my first book, *The Abduction of Julia,* was published, the dedication began, "To the incomparable Georgette Heyer, who stands as a shining example of perfection." I wrote that book, my initial foray into fiction, in 1996.

One of the first Heyer books I read was *The Quiet Gentleman.* It is an honor to be able to write a foreword for that same book almost thirty years later. It was, and still is, one of my favorites.

Ms. Heyer's sense of humor and her love for a good mystery make *The Quiet Gentleman* a delicious read. The heroine is the not-so-beautiful, painfully pragmatic yet always humorous Miss Drusilla Morville—only Heyer could name a heroine "Drusilla" and make it work!—who is the companion to the irascible Dowager Countess of St. Erth.

The entire St. Erth family—which consists of hard-working cousin Theo, the grumpy dowager and her spoiled son, Martin—are anxiously awaiting the arrival of the new earl, Gervase. The dowager and Martin are not happy to see Gervase, the seventh earl of St. Erth, after he disobliged them by surviving the dangers of Waterloo unscathed and returning home hale and hearty to assume his duties. They would much rather have received a terse note telling them of his death and Martin's inheritance of the title and lands. Alas, Gervase has not been so obliging as to fall upon the field of battle.

Gervase himself is no wilting flower of a man. Though quiet by nature and not given to dramatics, he meets his unhappy family with an urbane humor and wit that makes one love him the instant he steps foot onto the page. Cousin Theo and Drusilla seem to be Gervase's only allies, especially when his stepmother and Martin become unhappy that Gervase has not only inherited the family lands and title, but has captured the attention of the local beauty who once favored Martin.

Things heat up swiftly after that as several "accidents" befall Gervase. He narrowly manages to escape them all, though each effort seems to bring him closer to death. Is Martin trying to kill his own stepbrother in order to inherit the title and lands and secure the local beauty's interest? Has the irritable dowager decided to clear the way for her own son? Or is some other dastardly hand at work?

One of the delights of Ms. Heyer's writing is her sense of surprise. You might *think* you know the answer to her mysteries or have a good idea as to what a character might say next, but she always manages to surprise.

Though Martin is the most likely suspect, he is not the only one. As Gervase attempts to discover the person out to murder him, he finds himself and Miss Morville thrown together. Something about our heroine, Drusilla, captures both his attention and his fancy. But the question remains—has she captured his affections, as well?

One of the things I love about Heyer's heroines is their endearing humanity. Drusilla is normally the most prosaic of women, but like all of us, she finds herself wishing the new earl felt something more for her than mere friendship. As she tells herself at one point, "Depend upon it, you are just the sort of girl a man would be glad to have for his sister! You don't even know how to *swoon,* and I daresay if you tried you would make wretched work of it, for all you have is common sense, and of what use is that, pray?"

Yet Gervase is a true Heyer hero. There is far more to his character than a handsome face and a romantic disposition. He is also brave, charming and utterly capable of falling in love with a woman whose practical and dryly humorous observations are, as he says at the first opportune moment, "the delight" of his life!

The Quiet Gentleman is a magical, marvelous, thoroughly captivating book and one of Heyer's best.

I could go on and on about Georgette Heyer's writing and her delightful characters, though perhaps the best tribute I can give her is to keep writing. While no mere mortal writer can attain the heights she has already reached, we'll all be the better for trying.

CHAPTER ONE

IN THE guide-books it figured as Stanyon Castle; on the
tongues of the villagers, it was the Castle; the Polite
World spoke of it as Stanyon, as it spoke of Woburn, and
of Cheveley. It was situated in Lincolnshire, not very
many miles from Grantham, rather nearer to Stamford:
a locality considered by those who were more interested
in the chase than in any particular grandeur of scenery
to be admirable. It had more claim to be called a Castle
than many another nobleman's seat. A mediaeval
fortress, of which various not very interesting records
were to be found in the muniment room, now used by
Mr. Theodore Frant as an office, had previously stood
upon the site; and such portions of the ancient building
as had survived the passage of time had been incorpo-
rated into the Tudor manor which had succeeded the
fortress. Later generations had enlarged and beautified
the structure much as their fancies dictated, any difficulty of adding to the mansion being overcome by the
designing of another court. The Frant who survived
friendship with Bluff King Hal scandalized his generation by the lavish use of oak for wainscoting; his
grandson, having enjoyed the advantages of travel, built
a new wing, and embellished the old with gildings and

painted ceilings; a later Frant, succumbing to the prevailing fashion, ran riot in the rococo style, created the Fountain Court, and was prevented only by death from attempting something of a still more grandiose conception; his heir, one of Mr. Walpole's more fervid adherents, reverted to the Gothick, and by the time an unlucky fall at a regular stitcher, when out with the Old Club, put a period to his career, nowhere in England could have been found such massive doors of oak, such ponderous iron latches, so many pointed, narrow windows, as at Stanyon.

The sixth Earl of St. Erth, possibly thinking that his principal seat already sprawled over too much ground, more probably prevented from adding a wing in the Palladian style by the straitened times in which he had the ill-fortune to live, contented himself with rebuilding the stables, papering a great many of the rooms, and installing a closed-stove in the enormous kitchen. This was declared by an embittered valet to be the only sign of modern civilization in the entire pile; but the head-cook, mistrusting modernity, allowed it to be used merely for the boiling of vegetables by one of his underlings, while he himself continued to preside over his furnace, with its antiquated ovens, its huge spits, and its iron cauldrons. Unaccustomed guests, wandering distractedly down ill-lit galleries, discovering stairs that led only to uncharted domestic regions, and arriving, flustered and exhausted, where they had been for long attended, had been known to express astonishment that anyone should choose to live in such a rabbit-warren when he owned two other and more convenient country residences. Neither of these, it was true, could boast of

Great Halls, Minstrels' Galleries, Armouries, Towers, or Moats: on the other hand, no draughts whistled down their passages; no creeping chill arose from damp walls; and their chimneys very rarely smoked.

Neither the sixth Earl nor his second wife perceived anything amiss with Stanyon: the Earl because it was the home of his childhood, his lady because she had been bred in an even more inconvenient mansion in the bleak north, and would, in any event, have unhesitatingly bartered comfort for pomp, had she been offered a choice in the matter. The Earl's first wife had hated Stanyon. But the Earl's first wife, though admittedly a lady of birth and quite remarkable beauty, had proved herself to have been quite unworthy of the high position she was called upon to fill. Before her son was out of leading-strings, she ran away with a notorious rake. Her lord, cuckolded, betrayed, and turned into a laughing-stock, expunged her name from the family records, permitted no mention of her to be made within his walls, and scarcely thought himself avenged when he learned that she had died, three years after her flight, in conditions of distress and hardship. His steward and his housekeeper, both persons of sentiment, hoped that upon his death-bed he would remember her, and speak of her with a forgiving tongue, for it seemed to them incredible that so gentle and lovely a lady should hold no place in his heart or memory. They even indulged their fancies by supposing that his overt dislike of his elder son was caused by the secret pangs the sight of the fair boy, who was indeed the image of his mother, caused him to feel. But if the Reverend Felix Clowne, my lord's Chaplain, was to be believed, the Earl's last coherent speech, forcibly phrased if feebly uttered, was a complaint that the wine he had commanded his valet to bring to his room was corked. He had earlier bestowed his blessing upon Martin, his younger son; he had had a kind word for Theodore, his nephew; he had taken punctilious leave of his lady; he had sent proper messages to his married daughter; but the names of his first wife and of his heir had not passed his lips. Nor had his heir arrived at Stanyon to attend his deathbed, although it was certain that Mr. Theodore Frant had sent a letter express to him in Flanders, warning him that his father's demise was imminent. Captain Viscount Desborough, as he then was styled, was at Mons, with his regiment, and it was conceivable that a high sense of his military duties had prevented him from applying for furlough at a moment when Napoleon was almost hourly expected to cross the frontier. But the seventh Earl, surviving a minor, but rather bloody, engagement at the village of Genappe, and a major engagement at Waterloo, still showed no disposition to return to the home of his ancestors. He sold out, but he remained on the Continent, reposing the fullest confidence in his cousin's ability to administer his estates. Not until twelve calendar months had passed since his father's death did his cousin, and the Dowager Countess, receive tidings from him that he was in England, and about to take possession of his inheritance. He wrote a very civil letter to his mother-in-law, informing her of the proposed date of his arrival at Stanyon, and enquiring in the politest way after her health, and the healths of his half-brother and sister. It was a very pretty letter, the Dowager allowed, but, she added, in unhopeful accents, his mother had had just such caressing ways, and had shown herself to be a Snake in the Bosom.

"I should perhaps warn you, ma'am, that my cousin will not relish animadversions upon the character of his mother," said Mr. Theodore Frant, a little tight-lipped. "In his presence, such remarks should be spared."

"My dear Theo," responded the Dowager, "it would be odd indeed if I were to be obliged to consult you on the observances of civility!" He bowed, and, because she cherished no ill-will towards him, she said graciously: "Or anyone else, I am sure! In *this* house, Desborough—or, as I must learn to call him, St. Erth—may be sure of every attention called for by his consequence."

"Just so, ma'am," Mr. Frant said, bowing again.

"Providence has decreed that he should succeed to his dear father's honours," pronounced the Dowager, thinking poorly of Providence. "One might have supposed that military service in the Peninsula—a very unhealthy locality, I understand, setting aside the chances of Violent Death in an engagement, which cannot be altogether precluded—might have rendered the present occasion unnecessary. But it was not to be! Had my advice been sought, I should have considered myself bound to state that a military career, for one whom I should have had no hesitation in declaring to be far from robust, could be little short of Fatal! That, my dear Theo, I must have said, for, whatever must be my maternal feelings, if there be *one* thing upon which I pride myself it is my observance of my duty as a Christian! Happily, as it then seemed (though, according to the workings of an inscrutable fate, it now appears to be a circumstance of little moment), my advice was *not* sought. Since Lady Penistone chose to interest herself so particularly in her grandson, and my dear husband saw nothing objectionable in the connection, it was not for me to raise my voice. On her head, I said at the time, be the outcome! No doubt her ladyship is a good enough sort of a woman in her way: I do her the justice to acknowledge that she did *not,* as one might have feared she would, from the incurable levity of her behaviour, condone her unhappy daughter's misconduct: but if she petted and indulged Desborough from any other motive than a malicious desire to tease my poor husband I shall own myself astonished! A spiritless boy, I always thought him, with too much reserve to be pleasing. His career at Eton, you know, was quite undistinguished: a very odd sort of a soldier he must have been!"

"It is some years since you have seen my cousin, ma'am," Mr. Frant interposed, in a measured tone.

"I hope," said the Dowager, "I am not to be blamed for that! If Lady Penistone chose to invite the boy to stay with her during his school-vacations, and my lord to acquiesce in the arrangement, I take heaven to witness that it was by no expressed wish of mine that Desborough ceased to regard Stanyon as his natural home! On every head my conscience is easy: while he was a child I did my duty towards him; and I am determined now that as no word of censure for his conduct in absenting himself from a beloved parent's obsequies shall be permitted to pass my lips, so also no mark of the respect due to the Head of the Family shall be unobserved. I shall receive him in the Hall."

This momentous decision being faithfully adhered to, a chilly afternoon in spring saw five persons assem-

bled in what had once been the Great Hall of the Castle.
The artistic energies of several generations had largely
obliterated most of its original features, but the hammer-
beams in its lofty roof remained, and a vast fireplace,
made to accommodate the better part of several tree-
trunks. The carved screens, having been discovered to
have become worm-eaten, had been removed in a
previous age, the apartment being thrown open to the
vestibule, or entrance-hall, situated at right-angles to it.
From this smaller apartment the Grand Staircase,
erected in the latter half of the seventeenth century on
a scale designed to allow some dozen persons to walk
up it abreast, rose in one imposing flight to a broad half-
landing, whence it branched to right and left, thus at-
taining the main gallery of the Castle. Several massive
doors strengthened by applied iron-straps, besides the
great front-door opposite to the staircase, opened on to
the vestibule, a circumstance which added nothing to
the comfort of the Hall, in itself a passage to a series of
saloons beyond it. The heat thrown out by the logs
burning in the fireplace was considerable, but was unavailing to prevent the draughts sweeping through the
room. These seemed to come from all quarters, even the
heavy curtains which had been drawn across the
windows composing almost the entire long wall
opposite the fireplace being continually stirred by them.
It was dusk, and candles had been lit in the sconces as
well as in the several candelabra which stood on the
various tables. The little tongues of flame flickered continually, causing the wax to melt unevenly, and making
it impossible for one of the persons assembled in the
Hall to set the stitches in her embroidery with any

degree of accuracy. Having twice changed her seat to no purpose, she folded the work, and replaced it in a tapestry-bag, drawing forth, in its stead, a prosaic piece of knitting, with which she proceeded to occupy herself, in the manner of one prepared to make the best, without comment, of adverse conditions.

The furnishing of the Hall might have been taken as an example of the heterogeneous nature of the whole Castle, few of the pieces which it contained having been chosen with any nicety of judgment. A fine refectory table, pushed under the windows, and several carved oak chairs with wooden seats, were the only objects which bore any particular relation to their surroundings, the rest of the furniture consisting of pieces representative of every age and style, and including a modern and very ugly side-table, with a marble top, supported by brazen gryphons' heads. Two suits of armour of the surcoatless period guarded the entrance, and several shields, pikes, halberds, and gisarmes were arranged upon the wall above the high plaster mantelpiece. These were flanked by a full-length portrait of the late Earl, leaning negligently with one leg crossed over the other, against the shoulder of his horse; and a fine Battle-piece, of which the most noticeable features were the arresting figure of the commanding officer in the foreground, and the smoke issuing in woolly balls from the mouths of innumerable cannons.

Only one of the five persons gathered round the fireplace in expectation of the Earl's arrival seemed to be conscious of the discomfort of her situation, and she made no complaint, merely shifting her chair so that the leaping flames should not scorch her face, and pinning her shawl securely across her shoulders to protect them from the cold blast from the vestibule. The Dowager Countess, regally enthroned in a wing-chair, with her feet upon a stool, was indifferent to draughts; neither her son, Martin, moodily standing before the fire, and kicking at a smouldering log, nor Mr. Theodore Frant, engaged in snuffing a candle in the branch set in the centre of the refectory table, was aware of any unusual chilliness; and the Chaplain, seated at her ladyship's left hand, had long since become inured to the Spartan conditions prevailing at Stanyon, and had pronounced the gathering to be very snugly placed. This tribute earned him a gracious smile from the Dowager, who said that it had frequently been remarked that few fires gave out so fierce a heat as this one. She then desired Miss Morville, in a voice of mingled civility and condescension, to be so good as to run up to the Crimson Saloon, and to fetch from it a little hand-screen. Miss Morville at once laid aside her knitting, and departed on her errand; and, as though her absence released him from constraint, Martin looked up from his scowling scrutiny of the fire, and exclaimed: "This is a curst business! I wish it were well over! Why must we kick our heels here, waiting on *his* pleasure? The lord knows we don't want him! I have a very good mind to ride over to eat my mutton with Barny!"

His cousin looked frowningly at him for a moment, but said nothing. Another candle needed attention, and he dealt with it methodically. He was a powerfully built man, nearing his thirtieth birthday, with a resolute, rather square countenance, and a good deal of reserve in his manner. The cast of his features bore a certain re-

semblance to that of his young cousin's, but the likeness
existed merely in the aquiline trend of the nose, the
slightly heavy line of the jaw, and the set of the eyes
under brows which overhung them enough to give a for-
bidding look to the face. The colour of his eyes was a
clear, light gray, as cool and as inexpressive as lake-
water; his mouth, with its firmly closed lips, betrayed
no secrets, but seemed to show that its owner, besides
possessing resolution of character, knew how to keep
his own counsel. His address was good, and his manner
had all the quiet assurance of his breeding.

With Martin, it was otherwise. Every change of
mood was reflected in his eyes, so dark a brown as to
appear almost black, and in the sensitive curves of his
full mouth. Six years younger than his cousin, he had
not altogether thrown off the boy; and, from having
been the idol of his mother and the pet of his father, he
was a good deal spoiled, impatient of restraint, thrown
into the sulks by trifling causes, and into wild rages by
obstacles to his plans. Treated from his earliest youth
as though he, and not his half-brother, had been his
father's heir, it was not to be expected that he could face
with equanimity the succession of the seventh Earl. A
vague belief that his brother would not survive the
rigours of the campaign in Spain had fostered in him
the unexplored thought that he would one day step into
his father's shoes; the emergence of the seventh Earl,
unscathed, from the war found him unprepared, and
filled him, when his first shocked incredulity had
passed, with a sense of burning resentment. He had
only a slight recollection of the brother seven years his
senior, his memory retaining little beyond the impres-

sion of a fair, quiet boy, with a gentle manner, and a very
soft voice; but he was sure that he would dislike him.
He said, with a defiant glance cast in the direction of
his impassive cousin: "I daresay it is past six o'clock
already! When are we to dine? If he thinks to bring town
ways to Stanyon, I for one won't bear it!"

"Do not put yourself about, my dear!" recommended
his parent. "Dinner must for this once await his convenience, but with all his faults his disposition was always
compliant. I assure you, I do not expect to find our style
of living overset by any fashionable nonsense which he
may have learnt in Lady Penistone's establishment.
That would not suit me at all, and I am not quite nobody
at Stanyon, I believe!"

This announcement, being plainly in the nature of a
pleasantry, caused Mr. Clowne to laugh a little, and to
say: "Indeed your ladyship is not nobody! Such a whimsical fancy must really quite startle anyone unacquainted with those flashes of wit *we* know so well!"
He encountered a sardonic look from Theodore, and
added hastily: "How many years it is since I have had
the pleasure of meeting his lordship! How much he will
have to tell us of his experiences! I am sure we shall all
hang upon his lips!"

"Hang upon his lips!" exclaimed Martin, with one of
his fiery looks. "Ay! toad-eat him to the top of his bent!
I shall not do so! I wish he were underground!"

"Take care what you say!" interposed his cousin
sternly.

Martin flushed, looking a little conscious, but said in
a sullen tone: "Well, I do wish it, but of course I don't
mean anything! You need not be so quick to take me up!"

"Military anecdotes are never acceptable to me," said the Dowager, as though the brief interchange between the cousins had not occurred. "I have no intention of encouraging Desborough to enlarge upon his experiences in Spain. The reflections of a General must always be of value—though I fancy we have heard enough of the late war: those of a junior officer can only weary his auditors."

"You need feel no alarm on that score, ma'am," said Theodore. "My cousin has not altered so much!"

This was uttered so dryly that the Chaplain felt himself impelled to step into a possible breach. "Ah, Mr. Theodore, you remind us that you are the only one amongst us who can claim to know his lordship! *You* have frequently been meeting him, while *we*—"

"I have met him occasionally," interrupted Theodore. "His employment abroad has not made *frequent* meetings possible."

"Just so—precisely as I was about to remark! But you know him well enough to have a kindness for him!"

"I have always had a great kindness for him, sir."

The reappearance of Miss Morville, bearing a small fire-screen set upon an ebony stick, which she handed to the Dowager, created a timely diversion. The Dowager bestowed a smile upon her, saying that she was very much obliged to her. "I do not know how I shall bear to relinquish you to your worthy parents when they return from the Lakes, for I am sure I shall miss you excessively. My daughter—Lady Grampound, you know—is for ever advising me to employ some genteel person to bear me company, and to run my little errands for me. If ever I should decide to do so I shall offer the post to *you,* I promise you!"

Miss Morville, not so swift as Mr. Clowne to recognize her ladyship's wit, replied to this pleasantry in a practical spirit. "Well, it is very kind in you to think you would like to have me to live with you, ma'am," she said, "but I do not think it would suit me, for I should not have nearly enough to do."

"You like to be very busy, don't you?" Theodore said, smiling at her in some amusement.

"Yes," she replied, seating herself again in her chair, and resuming her knitting. She added thoughtfully: "It is to be hoped that I shall never be obliged to seek such a post, for my disposition is *not* meek, and would render me ineligible for any post but that, perhaps, of housekeeper."

This prosaic observation appeared to daunt the company. A silence fell, which was broken by the ubiquitous Mr. Clowne, who said archly: "What do you think of, Miss Morville, while your hands are so busy? Or must we not seek to know?"

She looked rather surprised, but replied with the utmost readiness: "I was wondering whether I should not, after all, make the foot a little longer. When they are washed at home, you know, they don't shrink; but it is sadly different at Cambridge! I should think the washerwomen there ought to be ashamed of themselves!"

Finding that this reflection evoked no response from the assembled company, she again applied herself to her work, and continued to be absorbed in it until Martin, who had quick ears, jerked up his head, and ejaculated: "A carriage! At last!"

At the same moment, an added draught informed the initiated that the door beyond the Grand Staircase had been opened; there was a subdued noise of bustle in the vestibule, and the sound of trampling hooves in the carriage-drive. Miss Morville finished knitting her row, folded the sock, and bestowed it neatly in the tapestry-bag. Though Martin nervously fingered his cravat, the Dowager betrayed by no sign that she had heard the sounds of an arrival. Mr. Clowne, taking his cue from her, lent a spuriously eager ear to the platitude which fell from her lips; and Theodore, glancing from one to the other, seemed to hesitate to put himself forward.

A murmur of voices from the vestibule indicated that Abney, the butler, had thrown open the doors to receive his new master. Several persons, including the Steward, and a couple of footmen, were bowing, and falling back obsequiously; and in another instant a slim figure came into view. Only Miss Morville, seated in a chair with its back turned to the vestibule, was denied this first glimpse of the seventh Earl. Either from motives of good manners, or from lack of interest, she refrained from peeping round the back of her chair; and the Dowager, to mark her approbation, addressed another of her majestic platitudes to her.

All that could at first be seen of the seventh Earl was a classic profile, under the brim of a high-crowned beaver; a pair of gleaming Hessians, and a drab coat of many capes and graceful folds, which enveloped him from chin to ankle. His voice was heard: a soft voice, saying to the butler: "Thank you! Yes, I remember you very well: you are Abney. And you, I think, must be my steward. Perran, is it not? I am very glad to see you again."

He turned, as though aware of the eyes which watched him, and stood foursquare to the Hall, seeing his stepmother, her imposing form gowned in purple satin, a turban set upon her gray locks, her Roman nose elevated; his half-brother, standing scowling before the fireplace, one hand gripping the high mantelshelf, the other dug into the pocket of his satin breeches; his cousin, standing a little in the background, and slightly smiling at him; his Chaplain, torn between curiosity and his allegiance to the Dowager. He regarded them thoughtfully, while with one hand he removed the beaver from his head, and held it out, and with the other he relinquished his gloves and his cane into the care of a footman. His hat was reverently taken from him by Abney, who murmured: "Your coat, my lord!"

"My coat, yes: in a moment!" the Earl said, moving unhurriedly towards the Hall.

An instant Theodore hesitated, waiting for the Dowager or for Martin to make some sign; then he strode forward, with his hands held out, exclaiming: "Gervase, my dear fellow! Welcome!"

Martin, his affronted stare taking in the number of the capes of that drab coat, the high polish on the Hessian boots, the extravagant points of a shirt-collar, and the ordered waves of guinea-gold hair above a white brow, muttered audibly: "Good God! the fellow's nothing but a curst *dandy!*"

CHAPTER TWO

THE FLICKER of a quizzical look, cast in Martin's direction, betrayed that his half-brother had heard his involuntary exclamation. Before the ready flush had surged up to the roots of his hair, Gervase was no longer looking at him, but was shaking his cousin's hand, smiling at him, and saying: "How do you do, Theo? You see, I *do* keep my promises: I have come!"

Theo held his slender hand an instant longer, pressing it slightly. "One year past! You are a villain!"

"Ah, yes, but you see I must have gone into black gloves, and really I could not bring myself to do so!" He drew his hand away, and advanced into the Hall, towards his stepmother's chair.

She did not rise, but she extended her hand to him. "Well, and so you have come at last, St. Erth! I am happy to see you here, though, to be sure, I scarcely expected ever to do so! I do not know why you could not have come before, but you were always a strange, whimsical creature, and I daresay I shall not find that you have changed."

"Dear ma'am, believe me, it is the greatest satisfaction to me to be able to perceive, at a glance, that *you* have not changed—not by so much as a hairsbreadth!" Gervase responded, bowing over her hand.

So sweetly were the words uttered, that everyone, except the Dowager, was left in doubt of their exact significance. The Dowager, who would have found it hard to believe that she could be the object of satire, was unmoved. "No, I fancy I do not alter," she said complacently. "No doubt, however, you see a great change in your brother."

"A great change," agreed Gervase, holding out his hand to Martin, and scanning him out of his smiling, blue eyes. "Can you be my little brother? It seems so unlikely! I should not have recognized you." He turned, offering hand and smile to the Chaplain. "But Mr. Clowne I must certainly have known anywhere! How do you do?"

The Chaplain, who, from the moment of the Earl's handing his hat to Abney, had stood staring at him as though he could not drag his eyes from his face, seemed to be a trifle shaken, and answered with much less than his usual urbanity: "And I you, my lord! For one moment it was as though— Your lordship must forgive me! Memory serves one some strange tricks."

"You mean, I think, that I am very like my mother," said Gervase. "I am glad—though it is a resemblance which has brought upon me in the past much that I wish to forget."

"It has frequently been remarked," stated the Dowager, "that Martin is the very likeness of all the Frants."

"You are too severe, ma'am," said Gervase gently.

"Let me tell you, St. Erth, that if I favour the Frants I am devilish glad to hear it!" said Martin.

"Tell me anything you wish, my dear Martin!" said Gervase encouragingly.

His young relative was not unnaturally smitten to silence, and stood glaring at him. The Dowager said in a voice of displeasure: "I have the greatest dislike of such trifling talk as this. I shall make you known to Miss Morville, St. Erth."

Bows were exchanged; the Earl murmured that he was happy to make Miss Morville's acquaintance; and Miss Morville, accepting the civility with equanimity, pointed out to him, in a helpful spirit, that Abney was still waiting to relieve him of his driving-coat.

"Of course—yes!" said Gervase, allowing the butler to help him out of his coat, and standing revealed in all the fashionable elegance of dove-coloured pantaloons, and a silver-buttoned coat of blue superfine. A quizzing-glass hung on a black riband round his neck, and he raised this to one eye, seeming to observe, for the first time, the knee-breeches worn by his brother and his cousin, and the glory of his stepmother's low-cut gown of purple satin. "Oh, I am afraid I have kept you waiting for me!" he said apologetically. "Now what is to be done? Will you permit me, ma'am, to sit down to dinner in all my dirt, or shall I change my clothes while your dinner spoils?"

"It would take you an hour, I daresay!" Martin remarked, with a curling lip.

"Oh, more than that!" replied Gervase gravely.

"I am not, in general, an advocate for a man's sitting down to dine in his walking-dress," announced the Dowager. "I consider such a practice slovenly, and slovenliness I abhor! In certain cases it may be thought, however, to be allowable. We will dine immediately, Abney."

The Earl, taking up a position before the fire, beside his brother, drew a Sèvres snuff-box from his pocket, and, opening it with a dexterous flick of his thumb, took a pinch of the mixture it contained, and raised it to one nostril. An unusual signet-ring, which he wore, and which seemed, at one moment, dull and dark, and at another, when he moved his hand so that the ring caught the light, to glow with green fire, attracted his stepmother's attention. "What is that ring you have upon your finger, St. Erth?" she demanded. "It appears to me to be a signet!"

"Why, so it is, ma'am!" he replied, raising his brows in mild surprise.

"How comes this about? Your father's ring was delivered to you by your cousin's hand I do not know how many months ago! *All* the Earls of St. Erth have worn it, for five generations—I daresay more!"

"Yes, I prefer my own," said the Earl tranquilly.

"Upon my word!" the Dowager ejaculated, her bosom swelling. "I have not misunderstood you, I suppose! You prefer a trumpery ring of your own to an heirloom!"

"I wonder," mused the Earl, pensively regarding his ring, "whether some Earl of St. Erth as yet unborn— my great-great-grandson, perhaps—will be told the same, when he does not choose to wear this ring of mine?"

A high colour mounted to the Dowager's cheeks; before she could speak, however, the matter-of-fact voice of Miss Morville made itself heard. "Very likely," she said. "Modes change, you know, and what one generation may admire another will frequently despise. My Mama, for instance, has a set of garnets which I consider quite hideous, and shan't know what to do with, when they belong to me."

"Filial piety will not force you to wear them, Miss Morville?"

"I shouldn't think it would," she responded, giving the matter some consideration.

"Your Mama's garnets, my dear Drusilla—no doubt very pretty in their way!—can scarcely be compared to the Frant ring!" said the Dowager. "I declare, when I hear St. Erth saying that he prefers some piece of trumpery—"

"No, no, I never said so!" interrupted the Earl. "You really must not call it trumpery, my dear ma'am! A very fine emerald, cut to my order. I daresay you might never see just such another, for they are rare, you know. I am informed that there is considerable difficulty experienced in cutting them to form signets."

"I know nothing of such matters, but I am shocked—excessively shocked! Your father would have been very glad to have left his ring to Martin, let me tell you, only he thought it not right to leave it away from the heir!"

"Was it indeed a personal bequest?" enquired Gervase, interested. "That certainly must be held to enhance its value. It becomes, in fact, a curio, for it must be quite the only piece of unentailed property which my father did bequeath to me. I shall put it in a glass cabinet."

Martin, reddening, said: "I see what you are at! *I'm* not to be blamed if my father preferred me to you!"

"No, you are to be felicitated," said Gervase.

"My lord! Mr. Martin!" said the Chaplain imploringly. Neither brother, hot brown eyes meeting cool blue ones, gave any sign of having heard him, but the uncomfortable interlude was brought to a close by the entrance of the butler, announcing that dinner was served.

There were two dining-rooms at Stanyon, one of which was only used when the family dined alone. Both were situated on the first floor of the Castle, at the end of the east wing, and were reached by way of the Grand Stairway, the Italian Saloon, and a broad gallery, known as the Long Drawing-room. Access to them was also to be had through two single doors, hidden by screens, but these led only to the precipitous stairs which descended to the kitchens. The family dining-room was rather smaller than the one used for formal occasions, but as its mahogany table was made to accommodate some twenty persons without crowding it seemed very much too large for the small party assembled in it. The Dowager established herself at the foot of the table, and directed her son and the Chaplain to the places laid on her either side. Martin, who had gone unthinkingly to the head of the table, recollected the change in his circumstances, muttered something indistinguishable, and moved away from it. The Dowager waved Miss Morville to the seat on the Earl's right; and Theodore took the chair opposite to her. Since the centre of the table supported an enormous silver epergne, presented to the Earl's grandfather by the East India Company, and composed of a temple, surrounded by palms, elephants, tigers, sepoys, and palanquins, tastefully if somewhat improbably arranged, the Earl and his stepmother were unable to see one another, and conversation between the two ends of the table was impossible. Nor did it flourish between neighbours, since the vast expanse of napery separating them gave them a sense of isolation it was difficult to overcome. The Dowager indeed, maintained, in her penetrating voice, a flow of very uninteresting small-talk, which consisted largely of exact explanations of the various relationships in which she stood to every one of the persons she mentioned; but conversation between St. Erth, his cousin and Miss Morville was of a desultory nature. By the time Martin had three times craned his neck to address some remark to Theo, obscured from his view by the epergne, the Earl had reached certain decisions which he lost no time in putting into force. No sooner had the Dowager borne Miss Morville away to the Italian Saloon than he said: "Abney!"

"My lord?"

"Has this table any leaves?"

"It has many, my lord!" said the butler, staring at him.

"Remove them, if you please."

"*Remove* them, my lord?"

"Not just at once, of course, but before I sit at the table again. Also that thing!"

"The epergne, my lord?" Abney faltered. "Where— where would your lordship desire it to be put?"

The Earl regarded it thoughtfully. "A home question, Abney. Unless you know of a dark cupboard, perhaps, where it could be safely stowed away?"

"My mother," stated Martin, ready for a skirmish, "has a particular fondness for that piece!"

"How very fortunate!" returned St. Erth. "Do draw your chair to this end of the table, Martin! and you too, Mr. Clowne! Abney, have the epergne conveyed to her ladyship's sitting-room!"

Theo looked amused, but said under his breath: "Gervase, for God's sake—!"

"You will not have that thing put into my mother's room!" exclaimed Martin, a good deal startled.

"Don't you think she would like to have it? If she has a particular fondness for it, I should not wish to deprive her of it."

"She will wish it to be left where it has always stood, and so I tell you! And if I know Mama," he added, with relish, "I'll wager that's what will happen!"

"Oh, I shouldn't do that!" Gervase said. "You see, you don't know me, and it is never wise to bet against a dark horse."

"I suppose that you think, just because you're St. Erth now, that you may turn Stanyon upside down, if you choose!" growled Martin, a little nonplussed.

"Well, yes," replied Gervase. "I do think it, but you must not let it distress you, for I really shan't quite do that!"

"We shall see what Mama has to say!" was all Martin could think of to retort.

The Dowager's comments, when the fell tidings were presently divulged to her, were at once comprehensive and discursive, and culminated in an unwise announcement that Abney would take his orders from his mistress.

"Oh, I hope he will not!" said Gervase. "I should be very reluctant to dismiss a servant who has been for so many years employed in the family!" He smiled down into the Dowager's astonished face, and added, in his gentle way: "But I have too great a dependence on your sense of propriety, ma'am, to suppose that you would issue any orders at Stanyon which ran counter to mine."

Everyone but Miss Morville, who was studying the Fashion Notes in the latest Ladies' periodical, waited with suspended breath for the climax to this engagement. They were disappointed, or relieved, according to their several dispositions, when the Dowager said, after a short silence, pregnant with passion: "You will do as you please in your own house, St. Erth! Pray do not hesitate to inform me if you desire me to remove to the Dower House immediately!"

"Ah, no! I should be sorry to see you do so, ma'am!" replied Gervase. "Such a house as Stanyon would be a sad place without a mistress!" Her face showed no sign of relenting, and he added, in a coaxing tone: "Do not be vexed with me! Must we quarrel? Indeed, I do not wish to stand upon bad terms with you!"

"I can assure you that no quarrel between us will be of *my* seeking," said the Dowager austerely. "A very odd thing it would be if I were to be picking quarrels with my son-in-law! Pray be so good as to apprise me, in the future, of the arrangements which you desire to alter at Stanyon!"

"Thank you!" Gervase said, bowing.

The meekness in his voice made his cousin's brows draw together a little; but Martin evidently considered that his mother had lost the first bout, for he uttered a disgusted exclamation, and flung out of the room in something very like a tantrum.

The Dowager, ignoring, in a lofty spirit, the entire incident, then desired Theo to ring for a card-table to be set up, saying that she had no doubt St. Erth would enjoy a rubber of whist. If Gervase did not look as though these plans for his entertainment were to his

taste, his compliant disposition led him to acquiesce
docilely in them, and, when a four was presently made
up, to submit with equanimity to having his play ruth-
lessly criticized by his stepmother. His cousin and the
Chaplain, after a little argument with Miss Morville,
who, however, was resolute in refusing to take a hand,
were the other two players; and the game was continued until the tea-tray was brought in at ten o'clock. The
Dowager, who had maintained an unwearied commen-
tary throughout on her own and the other three players'
skill (or want of it), the fall of the cards, the rules which
governed her play, illustrated by maxims laid down by
her father which gave Gervase a very poor opinion of
that deceased nobleman's mental ability, then stated
that no one would care to begin another rubber, and rose
from the table, and disposed herself in her favourite
chair beside the fire. Miss Morville dispensed tea and
coffee, a circumstance which made the Earl wonder if
she were, after all, one of his stepmother's dependents.
At first glance, he had assumed her to be perhaps a poor
relation, or a hired companion; but since the Dowager
treated her, if not with any distinguishing attention, at
least with perfect civility, he had come to the conclusion that she must be a guest at Stanyon. He was not
well-versed in the niceties of female costume, but it
seemed to him that she was dressed with propriety, and
even a certain quiet elegance. Her gown, which was of
white sarsnet, with a pink body, and long sleeves,
buttoned tightly round her wrists, was unadorned by the
frills of lace or knots of floss with which young ladies
of fashion usually embellished their dresses. On the
other hand, it was cut low across her plump bosom, in

a way which would scarcely have been tolerated in a hired companion; and she wore a very pretty ornament suspended on a gold chain round her throat. Nor was there any trace of obsequiousness in her manners. She inaugurated no conversation, but when she was addressed she answered with composure, and readily. A pink riband, threaded through them, kept her neat curls in place. These were mouse-coloured, and very simply arranged. Her countenance was pleasing without being beautiful, her best feature being a pair of dark eyes, well-opened and straight-gazing. Her figure was trim, but sadly lacking in height, and she was rather short-necked. She employed no arts to attract; the Earl thought her dull.

Family prayers succeeded tea, after which the Dowager withdrew with Miss Morville, charging Theo to conduct St. Erth to his bedchamber. "Not," she said magnanimously, "that I wish to dictate to you when you should go to bed, for I am sure you may do precisely as you wish, but no doubt you are tired after your journey."

It did not seem probable that a journey of fifty miles (for the Earl had travelled to Stanyon only from Penistone Hall), in a luxurious chaise, could exhaust a man inured to the rigours of an arduous campaign, but Gervase agreed to it with his usual amiability, bade his stepmother good-night, and tucked a hand in Theo's arm, saying: "Well, lead me to bed! Where have they put me?"

"In your father's room, of course."

"Oh dear! *Must* I?"

Theo smiled. "Do my aunt the justice to own that to

have allotted any other room to you would have been quite improper!"

The Earl's bedchamber, which lay in the main, or Tudor, part of the Castle, was a vast apartment, rendered sombre by dark panelling, and crimson draperies. However, several branches of candles had been carried into the room, and a bright fire was burning in the stone hearth. A neat individual, bearing on his person the unmistakable stamp of the gentleman's gentleman, was awaiting his master there, and had already laid out his night-gear.

"Sit down, Theo!" said St. Erth. "Turvey, tell someone to send up the brandy, and glasses!"

The valet bowed, but said: "Anticipating that your lordship would wish it, I have already procured it from the butler. Allow me, my lord, to pull off your boots!"

The Earl seated himself, and stretched out one leg. His valet, on one knee before him, drew off the Hessian, handling it with loving care, and casting an anxious eye over its shining black surface to detect a possible scratch. He could find none, and, with a sigh of relief, drew off the second boot, and set both down delicately side by side. He then assisted the Earl to take off his close-fitting coat, and held up for him to put on a frogged and padded dressing-gown of brocaded silk. The Earl ripped the intricately tied cravat from about his throat, tossed it aside, and nodded dismissal. "Thank you! I will ring when I am ready for you to come back to me."

The valet bowed, and withdrew, bearing with him the cherished boots. St. Erth poured out two glasses of brandy, gave one to his cousin, and sank into a deep chair on the other side of the fire. Theo, who had blinked at the magnificence of the dressing-gown, openly laughed at him, and said: "I think you must have joined the dandy-set, Gervase!"

"Yes, so Martin seemed to think also," agreed Gervase, rolling the brandy round his glass.

"Oh—! You heard that, then?"

"Was I not meant to hear it?"

"I don't know." Theo was silent for a moment, looking into the fire, but presently he raised his eyes to his cousin's face, and said abruptly: "He resents you, Gervase."

"That has been made plain to me—but not why."

"Is the reason so hard to seek? You stand between him and the Earldom."

"But, my dear Theo, so I have always done! I am not a lost heir, returning to oust him from a position he thought his own!"

"Not lost, but I fancy he did think the position might well be his," Theo replied.

"He seems to me an excessively foolish young man, but he cannot be such a saphead as that!" expostulated Gervase. "Only I could succeed to my father's room!"

"Very true, but dead men do not succeed," said Theo dryly.

"Dead men!" Gervase exclaimed, startled and amused.

"My dear Gervase, you have taken part in more than one engagement, and you will own that it could not have been thought surprising had you met your end upon a battlefield. It was, in fact, considered to be a likely contingency."

"And one that was hoped for?"

"Yes, one that was hoped for."

The Earl's face was inscrutable; after a moment, Theo said: "I have shocked you, but it is better to be plain with you, I think. You cannot have supposed that they loved you!"

"Not Lady St. Erth, no! But Martin—!"

"Why should he? He has heard no good of you from my uncle, or from his mother; he has been treated in all things as though he had been the heir; so much indulged and petted—well, talking pays no toll, or there is much I could say to you! To him, you are a usurper."

Gervase finished his brandy, and set down the glass. "I see. It is melancholy indeed! Something tells me that I shall not be at Stanyon for very long."

"What do you mean?" Theo said sharply.

Gervase looked at him, a little bewildered. "Why, what should I mean?"

"Martin is rash—his temper is uncontrollable, but he would not murder you, Gervase!"

"Murder me! Good God, I should hope he would not!" exclaimed the Earl, laughing. "No, no, I only meant that I think I should prefer to live at Maplefield, or Studham—ah, no! Studham was not entrailed, was it? It belongs to Martin!"

"Yes, it belongs to Martin, along with the Jamaican property," said Theo grimly. "And your mother-in-law has the London house and the Dower House for the term of her life!"

"I grudge her neither," replied the Earl lightly.

"When I can bring you to pay a little heed to the way in which things are left, you may well grudge the pair of them a great deal of what they do not stand possessed!" retorted Theo. "I have sometimes thought that my uncle had taken leave of his sense! You have me to thank for it that the estate is not cut up even more!"

"I think I have you to thank for more than you would have me guess," St. Erth said, smiling across at him. "You have been a good friend to me, Theo, and I thank you for it."

"Well, I have done what lay in my power to keep the property intact," Theo said gruffly. "But I am determined you shall be made to attend to your affairs, and so I warn you!"

"What a fierce fellow you are, to be sure! But you wrong me, you know! I did read my father's will, and I fancy I know pretty well how things stand."

"Then I wonder that you will be so expensive, Gervase!" said Theo forthrightly. "The charges you have made upon the estate this past twelvemonth—!"

"Oh, won't it bear them? I shall be obliged to marry an heiress!"

"I wish you will be serious! Things have not come to such a pass as that, but you will do well to be a little more careful. When I have shown you how matters stand, I hope you may be persuaded to take up your residence here. It will not do to leave Stanyon masterless, you know."

"Stanyon has a very good master in you, I fancy."

"Nonsense! I am nothing but your agent."

"But I should find it a dead bore!" objected Gervase. "Only consider the dreadful evening I have spent already! I have not the remotest guess where Martin went to, but I am sure he was not to be blamed for his flight. I wish I had had the courage to follow his example! And who, pray, is that little squab of a female?

Was she invited for my entertainment? Don't tell me she is an heiress! I could not—no, I really *could* not be expected to pay my addresses to anyone with so little countenance or conversation!"

"Drusilla! No, no, nothing of that sort!" smiled Theo. "I fancy my aunt thinks she would make a very suitable wife for me!"

"My poor Theo!"

"Oh, she is a very good sort of a girl, after all! But my tastes do not run in that direction. She is a guest at Stanyon merely while her parents are visiting in the north. They live at Gilbourne: in fact, they are your tenants. Her ladyship has a kindness for Drusilla, which is not wonderful, for she is always very obliging, and her lack of countenance, as you have it, makes it in the highest degree unlikely that she will ever be a danger to Lady St. Erth's schemes for Martin." He rose from his chair, and added, glancing down at the Earl: "We can offer you better entertainment, I hope! There is the hunting, remember, and your coverts should afford you excellent sport."

"My dear Theo, I may have been abroad for a few years, but I *was* reared in England, you know!" expostulated Gervase. "If you will tell me *what* I am to hunt, or shoot, at this moment—!"

Theo laughed. "Wood-pigeons!"

"Yes, and rabbits. I thank you!"

"Well, you will go to London for the Season, I daresay."

"You may say so with the fullest confidence."

"I see it is useless for me to waste my eloquence upon you. Only remain at Stanyon for long enough to understand in what case you stand, and I must be satisfied! Tomorrow, I give you warning, I shall make you attend to business. I won't tease you any more tonight, however. Sleep sound!"

"I hope I may, but I fear my surroundings may give me a nightmare. Where are you quartered, Theo?"

"Oh, in the Tower! It has come to be considered my particular domain. My bedchamber is above the muniment room, you know."

"A day's march to reach you! It must be devilish uncomfortable!"

"On the contrary, it suits me very well. I am able to fancy myself in a house of my own, and can enter the Tower by the door into the Chapel Court, if I choose, and so escape being commanded to furnish my aunt with the details of where I have been, or where I am going!"

"Good God! Will it be my fate to endure such examinations?"

"My aunt," said Theo, with a lurking twinkle, "likes to know all that one does, and why one does it."

"You terrify me! I shall certainly not remain at Stanyon above a week!"

But his cousin only smiled, and shook his head, and left him to ring for his valet.

When the man came, he brought with him a can of hot water, and a warming-pan. The Earl, staring at this, said: "Now, what in thunder are you about?"

"It appears, my lord," responded Turvey, in a voice carefully devoid of expression, "that extremely early hours are kept in this house—or, as I apprehend I should say, Castle. The servants have already gone to bed, and your lordship would hardly desire to get between cold sheets."

"Thank you, my constitution is really not so sickly as you must think it! Next you will bring me laudanum, as a composer! Set the thing down in the hearth, and don't be so foolish again, if you please! Have they housed you comfortably?"

"I make no complaint, my lord. I collect that the Castle is of considerable antiquity."

"Yes, parts of it date back to the fourteenth century," said the Earl, stripping off his shirt. "It was moated once, but the lake is now all that remains of the moat."

"That, my lord," said Turvey, relieving him of his shirt, "would no doubt account for the prevailing atmosphere of damp."

"Very likely!" retorted Gervase. "I infer that Stanyon does not meet with your approval!"

"I am sure, a most interesting pile, my lord. Possibly one becomes inured to the inconvenience of being obliged to pass through three galleries and seven doors on one's way to your lordship's room."

"Oh!" said the Earl, a trifle disconcerted. "It would certainly be better that you should be quartered rather nearer to me."

"I was alluding, my lord, to the position of the Servants' Hall. To reach your lordship's room from my own, it will be necessary for me to descend two separate stairways, to pass down three corridors; through a door permitting access to one of the galleries with which the Castle appears to be—if I may say so!—somewhat profusely provided; and, by way of an antechamber, or vestibule, reach the court round which this portion of the Castle was erected." He waited for these measured words to sink into his master's brain, and then added, in soothing accents: "Your lordship need have no fear, however, that I shall fail to bring your shaving-water in the morning. I have desired one of the under-footmen—a very obliging lad—to act as my guide until I am rather more conversant with my surroundings." He paused. "Or, perhaps I should say, until your lordship decides to return to London!"

CHAPTER THREE

NEITHER the Dowager nor Miss Morville appeared at the breakfast-table next morning; and although a place was laid for the Chaplain, he had not emerged from his bedchamber when Gervase joined his brother and his cousin in the sunny parlour. His entrance disconcerted Martin, who was fairly embarked on a scathing condemnation of the clothing which he apparently considered suitable for country-wear. Since Gervase was impeccably attired in riding-breeches, top-boots, and a serviceable, if unusually well-cut, frock-coat, Martin's scornful animadversions became, even in his own ears, singularly inapposite. Theo, who had listened to him in unencouraging silence, smiled slightly at sight of the Earl, and said to his younger cousin: "You were saying?"

"It don't signify!" snapped Martin, glowering at him.

"Good-morning!" said Gervase. "Oh, don't ring the bell, Theo! Abney knows I am here."

"I trust no nightmares, Gervase?" Theo said quizzically.

"Not the least in the world. Do either of you know if my horses have yet arrived?"

"Yes, I understand they came in early this morning,

your groom having stayed at Grantham overnight. An old soldier, is he?"

"Yes, an excellent fellow, from my own Troop," replied Gervase, walking over to the side-table, and beginning to carve a large ham there.

"I say, Gervase, where did you come by that gray?" demanded Martin.

The Earl glanced over his shoulder. "In Ireland. Do you like him?"

"Prime bit of blood! I suppose you mean to take the shine out of us Melton men with him?"

"I haven't hunted him yet. We shall see how he does. I brought him down to try his paces a little."

"You won't hack him during the summer!"

"No, I shan't do that," said the Earl gravely.

"My dear Martin, do you imagine that Gervase does not know a great deal more about horses than you?" said Theo.

"Oh, well, I daresay he may, but troopers are a different matter!"

That made Gervase laugh. "Very true!—as I know to my cost! But I have been more fortunate than many: I have only once been obliged to ride one."

"When was that?" enquired Theo.

"At Orthes. I had three horses shot under me that day, and very inconvenient I found it."

"You bear a charmed life, Gervase."

"I do, don't I?" agreed the Earl, seating himself at the table.

"Were you never even wounded?" asked Martin curiously.

"Nothing but a sabre-cut or two, and a graze from

a spent ball. Tell me what cattle you have in the stables here!"

No question could have been put to Martin that would more instantly have made him sink his hostility. He plunged, without further encouragement, into a technical and detailed description of all the proper high-bred 'uns, beautiful steppers, and gingers to be found in the Stanyon stables at that moment. Animation lightened the darkness of his eyes, and dispelled the sullen expression from about his mouth. The Earl, listening to him with a half-smile hovering on his lips, slipped in a leading question about the state of his coverts, and finished his breakfast to the accompaniment of an exposition of the advantages of close shot over one that scattered, the superiority of the guns supplied by Manton's, and the superlative merits of percussion caps.

"To tell you the truth," confessed Martin, "I am a good deal addicted to sport!"

The Earl preserved his countenance. "I perceive it. What do you find to do in the spring and the summertime, Martin?"

"Oh, well! Of course, there is nothing much to do," acknowledged Martin. "But one can always get a rabbit, or a brace of wood-pigeon!"

"If you can get a wood-pigeon, you are a good shot," observed Gervase.

This remark could scarcely have failed to please. "Well, I can, and it *is* true, isn't it, that a wood-pigeon is a testing shot?" said Martin. "My father would always pooh-pooh it, but Glossop says—you remember Glossop, the head-keeper?—that your pigeon will afford you as good sport as any game-bird of them all!"

The Earl agreed to it; and Martin continued to talk very happily of all his sporting experiences, until an unlucky remark of Theo's put him in mind of his grievances, when he relapsed into a fit of monosyllabic sulks, which lasted for the rest of the meal.

"Really, Theo, that was not adroit!" said the Earl, afterwards.

"No: bacon-brained!" owned Theo ruefully. "But if we are to guard our tongues every minute of every day—!"

"Nonsense! The boy is merely spoilt. Is that my mother-in-law's voice? I shall go down to the stables!"

Here he was received with much respect and curiosity, nearly every groom and stableboy finding an occasion to come into the yard, and to steal a look at him, where he stood chatting to the old coachman. On the whole, he was approved. He was plainly not a neck-or-nothing young blood of the Fancy, like his half-brother; he was a quiet gentleman, like his cousin, who was a very good rider to hounds; and if the team of lengthy, short-legged bits of blood-and-bone he had brought to Stanyon had been of his own choosing, he knew one end of a horse from another. He might take a rattling toss or two at the bullfinches of Ashby Pastures, but it seemed likely that he would turn out in prime style, and possible that he would prove himself to be a true cut of Leicestershire.

He found his head-groom, Sam Chard, late of the 7th Hussars, brushing the dried mud from the legs of his horse, Cloud. Chard straightened himself, and grinned at him, sketching a salute. "'Morning, me lord!"

"You found your way here safely," commented the Earl, passing a hand down Cloud's neck.

"All right and tight, me lord. Racked up for the night at Grantham, according to orders."

"No trouble here?"

"Not to say trouble, me lord, barring a bit of an *escaramuza* with the Honourable Martin's man, him not seeming to understand his position, and passing a remark about red-coats, which I daresay he done by way of ignorance. *Red-coats!* The Saucy Seventh! But no bones broken, me lord, and I will say he didn't display so bad."

"Chard, I will have no fighting here!"

"*Fighting,* me lord?" said his henchman, shocked. "Lor', no. Nothing but a bit of cross-and-jostle work, with a muzzler to finish it! Everything very nice and *abrigado* now, me lord. You're looking at that bay: a rum 'un to look at, but I daresay he's the devil to go. One of this Honourable Martin's, and by what they tell me he's a regular dash: quite the out-and-outer! Would he be a relation of your lordship's?"

"My half-brother—and see that you are civil to him!"

"Civil as a nun's hen, me lord!" Chard responded promptly. "They do think a lot of him here, seemingly." He applied himself to one of the gray's fore-legs. "Call him the young master." He shot a look up at the Earl. "Very natural, I'm sure—the way things have been." Before the Earl could speak, he continued cheerfully: "Now, that well-mixed roan, in the third stall, me lord, he belongs to Mr. Theo, which I understand is another of your lordship's family. A niceish hack, ain't he? And a very nice gentleman, too, according to what I hear. Yes, me lord, *on* the whole, and naming no exceptions, I think we can say that the natives are *bien dispuesto!*"

The Earl thought it prudent to return an indifferent answer. It was apparent to him that his groom was already, after only a few hours spent at Stanyon, fully conversant with the state of affairs there. He reflected that Martin's feelings must be bitter indeed to have communicated themselves to the servants; and it was in a mood of slight pensiveness that he strolled back to the Castle.

Here he was met by Miss Morville, who said, rather surprisingly, that she had been trying to find him.

"Indeed!" Gervase said, raising his brows. "May I know in what way I can serve you, Miss Morville?"

She coloured, for his tone was not cordial, but her disconcertingly candid gaze did not waver from his face. "I shouldn't think you could serve me at all, sir," she said. "*I* am only desirous of serving Lady St. Erth, which, perhaps, I should have made plain to you at the outset, for I can see that you think I have been guilty of presumption!"

It was now his turn to redden. He said: "I assure you, ma'am, you are mistaken!"

"Well, I don't suppose that I am, for I expect you are used to be toad-eaten, on account of your high rank," replied Drusilla frankly. "I should have explained to you that I have no very great opinion of Earls."

Rising nobly to the occasion, he replied with scarcely a moment's hesitation: "Yes, I think you should have explained *that!*"

"You see, I am the daughter of Hervey Morville," disclosed Drusilla. She added, with all the air of one throwing in a doubler: "*And* of Cordelia Consett!"

The Earl could think of nothing better to say than that he was a little acquainted with a Sir *James* Morville, who was a member of White's Club.

"My uncle," acknowledged Drusilla. "He is a very worthy man, but not, of course, the equal of my Papa!"

"Of course not!" agreed Gervase.

"I daresay," said Drusilla kindly, "that, from the circumstance of your military occupation, you have not had the leisure to read any of Papa's works, so I should tell you that he is a Philosophical Historian. He is at the moment engaged in writing a History of the French Revolution."

"From a Republican point-of-view, I collect?"

"Yes, certainly, which makes it sometimes a great labour, for it would be foolish to suppose that his opinions have undergone no change since he first commenced author. That," said Drusilla, "was before I was born."

"Oh, yes?" said Gervase politely.

"In those days, you may say that he was as ardent a disciple of Priestley as poor Mr. Coleridge, whom he knew intimately when very young man. In fact, Papa was a Pantisocrat."

"A—?"

She obligingly repeated it. "They were a society of whom the most prominent members were Mr. Coleridge, and Mr. Southey, and my Papa. They formed the intention of emigrating to the banks of the Susquehanna, but, fortunately, neither Mrs. Southey nor Mama considered the scheme practicable, so it was abandoned. I daresay you may have noticed that persons of large intellect have not the least common-sense. In this instance, it was intended that there should be no servants, but everyone should devote himself—or herself, as the case might be—for two hours each day to the performance of the necessary domestic duties, after which the rest of the day was to have been occupied in literary pursuits. But, of course, Mama and Mrs. Southey readily perceived that although the gentlemen might adhere to the two-hour-rule, it would be quite impossible for the ladies to do so. In fact, Mama was of the opinion that although the gentlemen might be induced, if strongly adjured, to draw water, and to chop the necessary wood, they would certainly have done no more. And no one," continued Miss Morville, with considerable acumen, "could have placed the least reliance on their *continued* performance of such household tasks, for, you know, if they had been engaged in philosophical discussion they would have forgotten all about them."

"I conclude," said Gervase, a good deal amused, "that your Mama is of a practical disposition?"

"Oh, no!" replied Miss Morville serenely. "That is why she did not wish to form one of the colony. She has no turn for domestic duties: Mama is an Authoress. She has written several novels, and numerous articles and treatises. She was used to be a friend of Mrs. Godwin's—the *first* Mrs. Godwin, I should explain—and she holds views, which are thought to be very advanced, on Female Education."

"And have you been reared according to these views?" enquired Gervase, in some misgiving.

"No, for Mama has been so fully occupied in prescribing for the education of females in general that naturally she has had little time to spare for her own children. Moreover, she is a person of excellent sense, and, mortifying though it has been to her, she has not hesitated to acknowledge that neither I nor my elder brother is in the least bookish."

"A blow!" commented the Earl.

"Yes, but she has sustained it with fortitude, and we have great hopes that my younger brother, who is now at Cambridge, will become distinguished. And, after all, there must be someone in a household who does not dislike domestic management."

"Is that your fate, Miss Morville?" the Earl asked, rather touched. "Is your life spent in these rural fast-nesses, performing a housekeeper's duties? I pity you!"

"Well, you need not," returned Miss Morville un-romantically. "We are only to be found in Lin-colnshire when Papa requires quiet for the per-formance of his labours. In general, we reside in London, so that Mama may enjoy the benefits of literary society."

"Forgive me, ma'am, if I say that it sounds to me like a dead bore!"

"Oh, yes, to those who are not bookish, it is!" agreed Miss Morville. "When in London, I spend much of my time in the company of my aunt, Lady Morville, and my cousins. Parties, and theatres, you know, for they are always very gay, and most good-natured in including me in their schemes. My aunt even undertook my Presenta-tion last year, which, when you consider that she had three daughters of her own to bring out, you must allow was very handsome in her. Particularly when Mama had declared herself ready to sink her scruples, and to perform the duty herself. Neither Mama nor Papa approves of Royalty, of course. But neither, I assure you, is an advocate of the more violent forms of Jacobinism."

"I am relieved. They would not, you think, wish to see such heads as mine fall under the knife of the guillotine?"

"I shouldn't think they would wish to see any head do so."

While they had been talking, they had mounted the Grand Stairway, crossed the hall at the head of it, and now entered the Long Drawing-room. The Earl enquired: "Where are you taking me, Miss Morville?"

"To the Small Dining-room, if you please. I wish you to inform me whether you approve of what I have done with the epergne, or whether you would prefer some other arrangement."

"What *you* have done with it? Pray, why should you be called upon to do anything with it?"

"Well, I was not precisely called upon, but *someone* had to decide what was to be done, when all you would say was that it should be stowed away in a dark cupboard!" she pointed out. "Poor Abney was quite bewildered, you know, for he could not suppose that you meant it; and as for Lady St. Erth, she says that after what has passed nothing will prevail upon her to raise her voice in the matter."

"I am delighted to hear it. A dark cupboard seems to be the only place for such a hideous object. Do not tell me that you admire it!"

"No, not at all, but I don't consider myself a judge, and what I might think ugly other people, perhaps, would consider a very handsome piece."

"Let me make it plain to you, Miss Morville, that I will not sit down to dinner with that thing in the middle of the table!"

"You could not, for now that the table has been reduced, which, I must say, was a very good notion, there is no room on it for the epergne. But now and

again, I daresay, you will wish the table enlarged to accommodate more persons, and the epergne can be set
upon it for the occasion. It is certainly very disagreeable to be obliged to crane one's neck to see round it,
when one dines informally, and it may be thought allowable to converse with persons seated on the opposite
side of the table; but on more state occasions that would
be a sadly ill-bred thing to do, and the epergne need be
an annoyance to no one."

"I hesitate to contradict you, ma'am, but it must
always be an annoyance to me," said Gervase.

"Not," said Miss Morville, "if it were turned so that
you were not confronted by a snarling tiger. When Abney
brought me here this morning, to consider what was to
be done, I instantly perceived that you had been obliged,
throughout the meal, to look at this creature; and, naturally, I realized that the spectacle of a ferocious beast, in
the act of springing upon its prey, could not be thought
conducive to conviviality, and might, indeed, be offen-
sive to a person of sensibility. But on the reverse side,"
pursued Miss Morville, preceding the Earl into the Small
Dining-room, "there are a group of natives gathered
beneath a palm tree, two peacocks and an elephant, with
trunk upraised. *Quite* unexceptionable, I think!" She
halted inside the Dining-room, and indicated a Buhl
table, placed in the window embrasure. "You see, I
desired Abney to have that table from the Crimson Saloon
carried into the room, and have caused the epergne to be
set upon it; but if you do not like it, it can be moved."

"A dark cupboard!" said the Earl obstinately.

"Recollect that you will be seated with your back
turned to it!" begged Miss Morville.

"I should suppose the tiger to be leaping upon me."

"Oh, no, indeed you could not, for it is facing the window!"

"Unanswerable! Pray, why are you so anxious to preserve the epergne, ma'am?"

"Well, I think Lady St. Erth might be a little mollified, if it were still in the room; and it would be quite improper, you know, to consign all your heirlooms, which you do not like, to dark cupboards," said Miss Morville reasonably. "I daresay there are several changes you will wish to make at Stanyon, but it is a favourite saying of my brother Jack's—my *military* brother—that one should always try to get over heavy ground as light as one can."

He smiled. "Very true! In what regiment is your military brother?"

"A line regiment: I daresay you would not know," said Miss Morville. "*You,* I collect, were in the 7th Hussars—one of the *crack* cavalry regiments!"

The Earl, a little shaken, admitted it.

"The Lilywhite Seventh," said Miss Morville indulgently, shepherding him out of the room. "*I* know!"

"And the devil of it is," said the Earl, twenty minutes later, to his cousin, "that I have let that wretched chit talk me into permitting the continued existence of that abominable epergne in my dining-room!"

CHAPTER FOUR

THE EARL SPENT the rest of the morning in the muniment room, docilely permitting his cousin to explain the management of his estates to him, and to point out to him the various provisions of his father's will. Besides the very considerable property which had been left to Martin, personal bequests were few, and included no more than a modest legacy to the nephew whose diligence and business ability had made it possible for him to spend the last years of his life in luxurious indolence.

Theodore Frant was the only offspring of the late Earl's younger brother, who, in the opinion of his family, had crowned a series of youthful indiscretions by marrying a penniless female of birth considerably inferior to his own. His tastes had been expensive, and a passion for gaming had made him swiftly run through his patrimony. His wife survived the birth of her child only by a few weeks; her place was filled by a succession of ladies, ranging from an opera-dancer to a fruit-woman, according to the fluctuating state of his finances; and the Earl, upon the only occasion when he was constrained to visit his disreputable relative, finding his youthful nephew engaged in bearing a quartern of

gin upstairs to the reigning mistress of the establishment, acted upon the impulse of the moment, and bore
the sturdy boy off with him, to be reared with his own
two sons at Stanyon. His brother, though he had hoped
for more tangible relief, raised no objection, reflecting
that in moments of acute stress the Earl's purse must
always be untied for him, his lordship having the
greatest objection to allowing any scandal to be attached
to his name. Happily for the Earl's peace of mind, an
inflammation of the lungs, contracted during a wet
week in Newmarket, carried the Honourable John off
three years later.

It was not to be expected that the second Lady St. Erth
would immediately greet with approbation the inclusion
into her home of the son of so unsteady a man; but even
she was soon brought to acknowledge that Theo inherited none of his father's instability. He was a stolid, even-
tempered boy, and he grew into a taciturn but dependable
young man. The Earl, who sent his own sons to Eton, in
the tradition of his family, caused Theo to be educated at
Winchester. He did not, like his cousins, go to Oxford,
but instead, and by his own choice, applied himself to the
task of learning the business of his uncle's agent. So apt
a pupil did he prove to be, that when the older man
resigned he was able and ready to succeed him. In a very
short space of time he was managing the Earl's estates
better than they had been managed for many years, for
he was not only capable and energetic, but his subordi-
nates liked him, and he was devoted to the Frant interests. His uncle relinquished more and more of his affairs
into his hands, until it became generally understood that
Mr. Theo must be applied to for whatever was needed.

Gervase, knowing this, had expected his father to have left him more handsomely provided for. He said as much, looking at his cousin in a little trouble, but Theo only smiled and said: "You may be thankful he did not! I had no expectation of it."

"He might have left you an estate, I think."

"Studham, perhaps?"

"Well, I had as lief you had it as Martin," said Gervase frankly. "I was really thinking of the property he bought towards Crowland, however. What's the name of the manor?—Evesleigh, is it not? Shall I make it over to you?"

"You shall not! There has been enough cutting-up of the estate already."

'But, Theo, you cannot spend all your life managing my property!"

"Very likely I shall not. I have a very saving disposition, you know, and you pay me a handsome wage, besides housing me in the first style of elegance, so that I am not put to the expense of maintaining an establishment of my own!"

Gervase laughed, but shook his head. "You cannot like it!"

"I like it very well indeed, thank you. Stanyon has been as much my home as yours, recollect!"

"Much more," said the Earl.

"Yes, unfortunately, but you will forget the past. Do you mean to allow Martin to continue here?"

"I had not considered the matter. Does he wish to?"

"Well, it will certainly not suit him to remove to Studham!" replied Theo. "I do not know how he is to continue hunting with the Belvoir from Norfolk! He would be obliged to put up at Grantham throughout the winter, and I own it would be uncomfortable. There is, moreover, this to be considered: when Cinderford died, your father permitted our aunt to take up her residence there, and it would be hard, I daresay, to prevail upon her to remove."

"Impossible, I imagine. He may remain at Stanyon, if only he can be persuaded to treat me with the semblance at least of civility. There appears, at the moment, to be little likelihood, however, of his doing so."

But when the Earl presently joined the rest of his family in one of the parlours on the entrance floor, where a light luncheon had been set out on the table, he found the Dowager and her son apparently determined to be amiable. That he had been the subject of their conversation was made manifest by the conscious silence which fell upon them at his entrance. The Dowager, recovering first from this, said with the utmost graciousness that she was glad to see him, and invited him to partake of some cold meat, and a peach from his own succession-houses. These, which had been installed at her instigation, were, she told him, amongst the finest in the country, and could be depended on to produce the best grapes, peaches, nectarines, and pines which could anywhere be found.

"The gardens, of course, cannot be said to be at their best this early in the year," she observed, "but when you have had time to look about you, I trust you will be pleased with their arrangement. I spared no pains, for I dote upon flowers, and I fancy something not altogether contemptible has been achieved. Indeed, the Duchess of Rutland, a very agreeable woman, has often envied me my show of choice blooms. Martin, pass the mustard to your brother: you must perceive that it is beyond his reach!"

This command having been obeyed, she resumed, in the complacent tone habitual to her: "Unless you should prefer to speak with Calne yourself, St. Erth, which I cannot suppose to be very likely (for gentlemen seldom interest themselves in such matters), I shall request him to devise one or two elegant bowls for the State saloons. It is not to be supposed that people will care to be backward in paying their morning-calls, now that it is known that you are in residence; and very few families, you know, have as yet removed to the Metropolis. We must not be found unprepared, and, I do not by any means despair of Calne's achieving something creditable."

"Am I to understand, ma'am, that I must expect to receive visits from all my neighbours?" asked Gervase, in some dismay.

"Certainly!" said the Dowager, ignoring a muffled crack of laughter from her son. "It would be very odd in them not to render you the observances of civility. It will be proper for you to hold a few dinner-parties, and now that I have put off black gloves I shall not object to performing my duties as hostess. Stanyon has ever held a reputation for hospitality, and I fancy that my little parties have not been, in the past, wholly despised. I am sure nothing is further from my thoughts than a disposition to meddle, but I would advise you, my dear St. Erth, to allow yourself to be guided in these matters by me. *You* cannot be expected to know who should be honoured by an invitation to dine with you, and who may be safely fobbed off with a rout-party, or even a Public Day."

"A Public Day!" repeated Gervase. "You terrify me, ma'am! What must I do upon such an occasion?"

"Oh, you have merely to move about amongst the company—your tenants, you know!—saying something amiable to everyone!" said Martin. "The most tedious affair! *I* have always contrived to be a couple of miles distant!"

"What admirable good sense! Pray, into which class may Miss Morville, and her peculiar parents, fall, ma'am?"

"That," responded the Dowager, "is a question that has frequently exercised my mind. There can be no denying that the Morvilles—they are able, you know, to trace their lineage back to the time of the Norman Conquest—must be thought to rank amongst those of the best blood in the country; but there can be no denying that the opinions held by Mr. Hervey Morville—and, I feel compelled to say, by his lady, though she too is of excellent birth, so that one is quite in a puzzle to determine what circumstances can have prevailed upon her to turn to the pen—that these opinions, as I have observed, must cause the most liberally-minded person to hesitate before including him in any select invitation. A shocking thing for his family, you know! He was actually acquainted with Horne Tooke! However, the late Earl was used to say that he had a well-informed mind, and we have been used to invite him, and his lady, to dine with us from time to time. His daughter is quite a favourite with me; a delightful girl!"

At this point, the eyes of the half-brothers met. The Earl was able to command his features, but Martin choked over a mouthful of cold beef. The Dowager said indulgently: "I do not assert that she is beautiful, but she is a very pretty-behaved young female, and one that will do very well for poor Theo. I have a great regard for Theo, and I should be happy to see him comfortably established."

"Where," asked Gervase, with only the slightest tremor in his voice, "is Miss Morville now? She does not care for a nuncheon?"

"The dear child has walked through the Park to Gilbourne House," answered the Dowager. "A letter from her Mama desired her to forward some small matters to Greta Hall, for she and Mr. Morville, you must know, are spending a few days as the guests of Mr. and Mrs. Southey—the Laureate, I need scarcely remind you. I believe he and Mr. Morville were once intimate, but Mr. Southey, one is thankful to say, has long since abandoned those Revolutionary tendencies which must, previously, have rendered him quite ineligible for the distinguished position which he now adorns. *The Curse of Kehama!* His *Life of Nelson!* I am no great reader myself, but I am sure I must have heard the late lord speak favourably of these works I daresay a dozen times!"

"We must certainly invite him to dinner," murmured Gervase.

"I believe it will be proper for us to do so," acknowledged the Dowager. "His brother, Sir James Morville, is a distinguished man; and they are related, one must remember, to the Minchinhamptons. We must wait, however, to see whether a suitable party may be arranged, though, to be sure, I have no doubt that we might, if we chose, arrange a dozen such! I should not think it marvellous if we were to receive as many as fifty visits from our neighbours this sennight."

"I sincerely trust you may be wrong, ma'am!" said Gervase.

The next few days, however, showed that the Dowager had not misjudged the civility, or the curiosity, of the neighbouring gentry. Chaises, barouches, curricles, and even, when old Lady Wintringham decided that it behoved her to leave cards upon the new Earl, an antiquated coach bowled up the avenue to the imposing front-doors of Stanyon, and set down passengers dressed in all the finery of silk and velvet, or the natty elegance of yellow pantaloons and best Bath suiting. The Earl found most of his visitors as tedious as they were well-disposed; and, after enduring three consecutive days of almost continuous civilities, the sight of a carriage drawing up under his window was enough to send him stealthily down one of the secondary staircases to a vestibule whence it was possible for him to escape from the Castle, into the Fountain Court. From here it was an easy matter for him to reach the stables without being intercepted by an over-zealous servant; and while the Dowager entertained the morning-guests with one of her powerful monologues, her undutiful stepson was enjoying a gallop on the back of his gray horse, Cloud, having speedily put several miles between himself and the Castle.

He had already, once or twice, ridden out with his cousin, and the Bailiff, but his way led him on this occasion in a direction hitherto unvisited by him. It was a fine day towards the close of March, the ground rather heavy from recent rains, but fast drying under a strong wind, blowing from the east. The hedgerows were bursting into new leaf, and the banks were starred with primroses. The Earl, having, as he would have said, galloped the fidgets out of Cloud, was hacking gently down a narrow lane when he came, round a bend, upon an unexpected sight. A lady was seated on the bank, engaged in gathering primroses from a clump within her reach. This in itself, however imprudent in such damp and blustery weather, would not have attracted more than the Earl's fleeting attention had he not perceived that the lady was attired in a riding-habit. Here, plainly, was an equestrienne in distress. He brought Cloud trotting up and caused him to halt alongside her.

The lady had lifted her head at the first sound of Cloud's hooves, and Gervase, raising his beaver, found himself looking down into a charming, wilful countenance, framed by the sweep of a hat-brim, and a cascade of pale, wind-tossed ringlets. A pair of large blue eyes, lighter and merrier than his own, met his with a rueful twinkle; a roguish dimple hovered at the corner of a kissable mouth striving unavailingly to preserve its gravity.

"I beg pardon!" Gervase said, his gaze riveted on the fair face upturned to his. "Can I be of assistance, ma'am? Some accident, I apprehend! Your horse—?"

He dismounted, as he spoke, and pulled the bridle over Cloud's head. The fair Diana broke into a ripple of laughter. "Depend upon it, the horrid creature is by now standing snugly in her stall! Was ever anything so vexatious? Papa will so roast me for *parting company* at such a paltry fence! Only the mare pecked, you know, and over her head I went, and perhaps I was foolish, or perhaps I was stunned—shall I declare that I was stunned?—and I released the bridle. You would have thought, after all the carrots and the sugar I have bestowed on her, that Fairy would have come to me when I coaxed her! But no! Off she set, thinking of nothing but her comfortable stable, I daresay!"

"Ungrateful indeed!" Gervase said, laughing. "But you must not sit upon that bank, ma'am, perhaps catching your death of cold! Is your home far distant?"

"No, oh, no! But to be walking through the village in my muddied habit, advertising my folly to the countryside—! You will allow it to be unthinkable, my lord!"

"You know me, then, ma'am? But we have not previously met, I think—I am sure! I *could* not have forgotten!"

"Oh, no! But a stranger in this desert: one dressed, moreover, in the first style of elegance! I could be in no doubt. You are—you must be—Lord St. Erth!"

"I am St. Erth. And you, ma'am? How comes it about that this is our first encounter?"

She replied, with the most enchanting primming of her face, wholly belied by the mischievous look in her eyes: "Why, you must understand that one would not wish to appear *pushing,* by too early a visit, nor *uncivil,* by too late a one! Mama has formed the intention that Papa shall pay a morning-call at Stanyon next week!"

He was very much amused, and said: "I could not receive *that* morning-call too early, I assure you! It will be quite unnecessary, however, for Papa to be put to the trouble of a formal visit, for I shall forestall him. If I were to lift you on to Cloud's back, ma'am, will you permit me to lead him to your home?"

She jumped down from the bank, catching up the

skirt of her voluminous habit, and casting it over her arm. "Oh, yes! Will you do that? I shall be so very much obliged to you!"

On her feet, she was seen to be a slim creature, not above the average height, but exquisitely proportioned. Her movements, though impetuous, were graceful, and the Earl was permitted a glimpse of a neatly-turned ankle. She tucked her primroses into the buttonhole of her coat, where, mingling with her curls, they seemed almost exactly to blend with them. The Earl lifted her on to the saddle; she contrived to arrange one leg over the pommel, and declared herself to be perfectly safely established.

"Now, where am I to take you?" asked Gervase, smiling up at her.

"To Whissenhurst Grange, if you please! It is only a mile from where we stand, so you will not be obliged to trudge so *very* far!"

"I should be glad if it were twice as far. But did you mean to sit upon that bank for ever, ma'am?"

"Oh, they would have found me in a little while!" she said airily. "When Fairy reached the stables, you know, they would be thrown into such a pucker! I daresay everyone may already be searching the countryside for me."

She spoke with all the unconcern of a spoiled child; and it was easy for him to guess that she must be the pet of her father's establishment. With some shrewdness he asked her if her parents were aware of her riding out without a groom, and glanced quizzically up in time to see her pouting prettily.

"Oh, well, there can be no objection, after all, in the

country! In town, of course, I could not do so. If only I had not jumped that wretched little hedge! Nothing was ever so mortifying! Indeed, I am not in the habit of tumbling off my horse, Lord St. Erth!"

"Why, the best of riders must take a toss or two!" he reassured her. "It was used to be said of the Master of the Quorn, when I was living at Stanyon previously, that he would have as many as fifty falls in a season!"

"Ah, you are talking of Mr. Assheton Smith, I collect! His name, you must know, is for ever on the tongues of the Melton men! You must have heard your brother deplore his leaving Quorndon Hall, I daresay! This has been his last season with the Quorn: he is coming into Lincolnshire, to hunt the Burton, and that will put him many miles beyond poor Martin's reach!"

"I have indeed heard of it from Martin," said Gervase, with a droll look. "Not all his calculations and his measurements will bring Reepham closer to Stanyon than fifty miles. He sees nothing for it but to put up at Market Rasen, if he should wish for a day with the Burton."

"Martin is one of Mr. Smith's upholders. A great many of the sporting gentlemen, however, complain that he draws his coverts too quickly, and will not lift as often as he should in Leicestershire."

"You hunt yourself, ma'am?"

She threw him one of her roguish looks. "Yes, when hounds meet in the vicinity, and I will faithfully promise to do just as Papa bids me!"

"I hope you keep your promises!"

"Yes, yes, in general I am very good!"

"You will think me abominably stupid, I fear, but I

think I can never have met your Papa, and thus do not know what I shall call him when we meet."

"Papa is Sir Thomas Bolderwood," she replied at once. "Very likely you might not have encountered him, for we came to live at Whissenhurst only a few years ago, and you have all the time been abroad."

"I must be grateful to whatever lucky chance it was that brought Sir Thomas into Lincolnshire," said Gervase.

She received this with a laugh, and a little shake of her head. She was young enough to feel embarrassment at broad compliments, but she betrayed none: plainly, she was accustomed to being very much admired, although the coming London Season, as she presently confided to the Earl, was to be her first. "For one does not count *private* parties, and although I was *almost* seventeen last spring, Mama could not be prevailed upon to present me, though even my Aunt Caroline, who is so strict and stuffy, counselled her most strongly to do so. However, this year I am to be presented, and I shall go to Almack's, and the Opera, and *everywhere!*"

The Earl, concluding from this artless prattle that Miss Bolderwood moved in unexceptionable circles, began to wonder why no mention of her family had been made to him by his stepmother. In all her consequential enumerations of the persons likely to leave their cards at Stanyon he could not recall ever to have heard her utter the name of Bolderwood. But as he led Cloud into the village through which they were obliged to pass on their way to Whissenhurst Grange, an inkling of the cause of this omission was conveyed to him by an unexpected encounter with his half-brother.

Martin, who was hacking towards them in the company of a young gentleman who sported a striped waistcoat, and a Belcher tie, no sooner perceived who was the fair burden upon Cloud's back than he spurred up, an expression on his brow both of astonishment and anger. "Marianne!" he exclaimed. "What's this? How comes this about? What in thunder are you doing on St. Erth's horse?"

"Why, that odious Fairy of mine, having thrown me into the mire, would not allow me to catch her!" responded Marianne merrily. "Had it not been for Lord St. Erth's chivalry I must still be seated miserably by the wayside, or perhaps plodding along this very dirty road!"

"I wish I had been there!" Martin said.

"I wish *I* had been there!" gallantly echoed his companion.

"I am very glad you were not, for to be seen tumbling off my horse could not at all add to my consequence! Oh, Lord St. Erth, are you acquainted with Mr. Warboys?"

Martin, interrupting the exchange of civilities between his friend and his brother, said: "You might have been killed! I do not know what Lady Bolderwood will say! You must let me escort you home!" He seemed to become aware of the fatuity of this utterance, and added awkwardly, and with a rising colour: "You will wish to be going on your way, St. Erth!"

"I *am* going on my way," replied the Earl, who was looking amused. "I must tell you, Martin, that I find you very much *de trop!*"

"By Jove, yes!" agreed Mr. Warboys, with even more gallant intention. "Anyone would! Would myself!" He encountered a fiery glance from Martin, which flustered him, and added hastily: "That is to say—what I meant was, that's a devilish good-looking hunter you have there, St. Erth! Great rump and hocks! Splendid shoulders! Not an inch above fifteen-three, I'll swear! The very thing for this country!"

"Oh, he is the loveliest creature!" Marianne said, patting Cloud's neck. "He makes no objection to carrying me in this absurd fashion: I am sure he must be the best-mannered horse in the world!"

"My Troubadour would carry you as well!" Martin muttered.

Mr. Warboys was moved to contradict this statement. "No, he wouldn't. Wouldn't carry her as well as my Old Soldier! Got a tricky temper, that tit of yours."

"He is better-paced than that screw of *yours!*" retorted Martin, firing up in defence of his horse.

"Old Soldier," said Mr. Warboys obstinately, "would give her a comfortable ride."

"You must be besotted to think so."

"No, I ain't. Old Soldier has often carried m'sister. Your Troubadour has never had a female on his back."

"That can soon be mended!"

"I wonder," said the Earl diffidently, "if you would think it rude in us to be proceeding on our way while you thrash the matter out between you? Miss Bolderwood will be in danger of contracting a chill, I fear."

Martin cast him a smouldering look, but Mr. Warboys at once responded: "By Jupiter, so she will! Nasty wind blowing! No sense in standing about—silly thing to do!"

"I'll accompany you!" Martin said, wheeling his horse about.

"Yes, pray do!" said Marianne, thoroughly enjoying

this rivalry for her favours. "Papa and Mama will be so glad to see you! And you too, Mr. Warboys!"

"If I and not St. Erth had found you," said Martin, "we would soon have seen whether Troubadour would have carried you or not!"

"Well, since the matter appears to trouble you, why should you not at once put it to the test?" suggested Gervase. "You will not object to changing horses, Miss Bolderwood? I very much fear that nothing less will satisfy poor Martin."

Martin looked to be at once surprised and scornful. He had no great opinion of his brother's mettle, but he had not expected him to relinquish his advantage so very tamely. He smiled triumphantly, and dismounted, but not in time to forestall Gervase in lifting Marianne down from Cloud's back. She was installed on Troubadour's saddle; the Earl swung himself on to Cloud again; and Martin, preparing to lead his horse along the street, realized too late that between the horseman and the pedestrian the advantage lay with the former. The Earl, riding easily beside the lady, was able to engage her in conversation, while his brother, plodding along at Troubadour's head, was obliged, whenever he wished to claim her attention, to turn his head to look up at her, and to repeat his remark several times. The playful nature of her exchanges with Gervase considerably exacerbated his temper; nor was he mollified to observe that the Earl's gallantry seemed to be very much to Marianne's taste. After one or two unsuccessful attempts to draw her into conversation with himself, he relapsed into sulky silence; and was very nearly provoked, at journey's end, into giving his friend, Mr.

Warboys, a leveller. Mr. Warboys, a mournful witness of his discomfiture, was ill-advised enough to say to him, as Marianne led the Earl up the steps to the door of Whissenhurst Grange: "Rolled-up, dear boy! Very shabby stratagem! Fellow must have been on the Staff, I should think!"

Marianne's safe arrival was greeted by her mother, her father, the butler, the housekeeper, and her old nurse with the most profound thanksgiving. The news of Fairy's riderless return to the stables had only just been brought up to the house, so that there was time yet to send one of the footmen running to stop the grooms and the stableboys setting forth to scour the countryside in search of her. Sir Thomas, who had been shouting for his horse, pulling on his boots, and issuing instructions, all in one breath, was only induced to cease shaking and hugging his daughter by the necessity of thanking her preserver. His wife, though very much more restrained in her expressions, was equally obliged to the Earl; and it was hard to imagine how either of them could have been more grateful to him had he rescued Marianne from some deadly peril. As for Marianne, she laughed, and coaxed, and begged pardon, and was very soon forgiven her imprudence. Her Mama bore her upstairs to put off her muddied habit; Sir Thomas shouted for refreshment to be brought to the saloon, whither he led the Earl; and Martin, fairly gnashing his teeth, said stiffly that he would take his leave, now that he had seen Marianne restored to her parents.

"Yes, yes, there is no occasion for you to kick your heels, my boy!" said Sir Thomas genially. "To be sure, we are always glad to see you at Whissenhurst, and you too, Barny, but you will be wanting to go about your business now! This way, my lord! To think I had been meaning to wait on you next week, and here you are, making it quite unnecessary for me to do so! I am glad of it: I am no hand at doing the punctilio, you know!"

Thus dismissed, Martin bowed grandly, and left the house, closely followed by Mr. Warboys, who said helpfully, as they mounted their hacks: "No sense in getting into a miff, dear boy! Come about again presently, I daresay! Very unlucky chance your brother should have been riding in this direction, but not a bit of good staying there to outface him! Corkbrained thing to do! The devil of it is he's a dashed handsome fellow. Good address too, besides the title."

"If he thinks I will permit him to trifle with Marianne—!" said Martin, between his teeth.

"No reason to think he means to do so," said Mr. Warboys soothingly. "Seemed very taken with her!"

Martin turned his head sharply to look at him, so menacing an expression in his dark eyes that he was thrown into disorder. "What do you mean?"

"Well, now you come to ask me," said Mr. Warboys, with the air of one making a discovery, "I don't know what I mean! Spoke without thinking! Often do! Runs in the family: uncle of mine was just the same. Found himself married to a female with a squint all through speaking without thinking."

"Oh, to hell with your uncle!" Martin said angrily.

"No use saying that, dear boy. The old gentleman took a pious turn years back. Won't go to hell—not a chance of it! Aunt might—never met such a queer-tempered woman in my life!"

"*Will* you stop boring on and on about your relatives?" said Martin savagely.

"Don't mind doing that: no pleasure to me to talk about them! But if you think you're going to have a turn-up with me, old fellow, you're devilish mistaken!"

"Saphead! Why should I?"

"There ain't any reason, but whenever you take one of your pets," said Mr. Warboys frankly, "it don't seem to signify to you whose cork you draw! All I say is, it ain't going to be mine!"

Meanwhile, Sir Thomas, having ushered the Earl into one of his saloons and furnished him with a comfortable chair, and a glass of Madeira, had arrived at a more precise understanding of the service which had been rendered to his daughter. He chuckled a good deal over it, rubbing his hands together, and ejaculating: "Cow-handed little puss! I shall roast her finely for this, I can tell you! All's well that ends well—though I'll wager her Mama will have something to say to her giving her groom the slip! But there! she is our only chick, my lord, and we don't care to be too strict, and that's the truth! Yes, the Almighty never saw fit to give us another, and though I shan't deny we did wish for a son—for there will be no one to inherit the baronetcy when I'm gone, you know—it was not to be, and, damme, we wouldn't exchange our naughty puss for all the sons in creation!"

Gervase said what was proper, and sipped his wine, watching Sir Thomas, as he bustled about, casting another log on to the fire, altering the position of a screen to exclude a possible draught, tugging at the bell-rope to summon a servant to bring in the ratafiawine for Miss Marianne. He was a stout little man, with a shrewd pair of eyes set in a round face whose original ruddy complexion had been much impaired by a tropical climate. He was dressed without much pretension to fashion in a blue coat and buckskin breeches, but he wore a large ruby-pin in his neckcloth, and another set in a ring upon his finger, so that he was clearly a person of affluence, if not of taste. The Earl was at a loss to decide from what order of society he had sprung, for although the cast of his countenance was aristocratic, with its aquiline nose, and finely-moulded lips, and his voice that of a well-bred man, his manners lacked polish, and he had a rough colloquial way of expressing himself. His wife, on the other hand, had the appearance and the manners of a gentlewoman, and the style in which his house had been furnished was as elegant as it was expensive. That he had at some period during his lifetime visited the East was indicated by various specimens of Oriental art which were scattered about the room. He saw the Earl glancing at the ornaments on the mantelshelf, and said: "Ay, you are looking at my ivories, my lord. I bought them for the most part in Calcutta, and a pretty sum they cost me, I can tell you! You won't find any finer, for although I don't know much about art, I won't buy trumpery, and I'm a hard man to cheat."

"You have resided in India, sir?"

"Spent the better part of my life there," replied Sir Thomas briskly. "If you hear anyone speak of the Nabob, that's me, or, at any rate, it's what they call me here at home, and I won't deny it's true enough, though I could name you a good few men who made bigger fortunes in India than ever I did. Still, I'm reckoned to be a warm man, as they say. Queer world, ain't it? I often wonder what my poor father would think if he had lived to see the Prodigal Son come home only just in time to save the family from landing in the basket! Ay, I was a wild young fellow, I can tell you, and caused my father a deal of trouble, God forgive me! The end of it was I was shipped off to India, and I daresay they all hoped I should be heard of no more. I don't say I blame them, but it was a desperate thing to do, wasn't it? I wouldn't serve a son of mine so, but it all turned out for the best; and when I came home, with a snug fortune, and my girl just six years old, and as pretty as a picture, the tables were turned indeed! For what should I find but that brother of mine that was always used to have been as prim and as *tonnish* as the starchiest nob of them all regularly under the hatches! The silly fellow had been speculating, and he hadn't the least head for it. A bubble-merchant, that's what I called him! I found him as near to swallowing a spider as makes no matter, and what he found to squander his money on, with never a chick nor a child to call his own, is more than I can tell you. I daresay it was my lady who spent it, for it was always my lady who must have this, and my lady who was used to have that, till I told him to his head his lady might go hang for all of me! For ever prating about her grand family, she was, but she came to the wrong shop, for I married a girl who was better-born than she, and never any fine-lady nonsense about her, bless her! Well, the long and the short of it was that poor George was never so glad to see anyone in his life as he was to see me, for he actually had an execution in the house! And the worst set of Jeremy Diddlers hanging round him—well, well, I soon sent them packing, you may be sure! The joke of it was that George wasn't pleased above half, because he had been always in the way of thinking himself much above my touch! Ah, well, he's dead now, poor fellow, and I should not be laughing at him! Ay, he died a matter of six years ago, leaving no one but me to succeed him. He felt it, and so, I warrant you, does Caroline, though between you and me that don't by any means stop her expecting me to drop my blunt into her purse every now and then!" He laughed heartily at this reflection, and his guest, considerably taken aback by these revelations, and scarcely knowing what to say in reply to them, was thankful when the door opened just then to admit the two ladies.

Marianne, who had changed her habit for a dress of sprigged muslin, tied with blue ribbons, was looking lovelier than ever; and the Earl found that he had not been mistaken in his first reading of Lady Bolderwood's character. A fair, slender woman of considerable beauty, she was affable without being effusive. Without assuming any airs of consequence, or seeming to deprecate her husband's free manners, she had a quiet dignity of her own, and talked very much like a sensible woman. While Sir Thomas boisterously rallied his daughter on her lack of horsemanship, she sat down beside the Earl, and conversed amiably with him. He decided that he liked both her and Sir Thomas. He was made to feel at home, and although both, in their several degrees, were grateful to him for the service he had rendered Marianne, neither showed the least disposition to toad-eat him. As for Marianne, he could not suppose that a lovelier or a sunnier-tempered girl existed. She bore all her father's roasting with laughter, and coaxing pleas to be forgiven for having caused him anxiety; and when she saw that he had finished his wine, she jumped up to set down his glass for him.

"I hope that now we have been so unceremoniously introduced, you will visit us again, Lord St. Erth. We do not pretend to entertain in any formal style while we are in the country, for Marianne cannot be considered to be out, you know, until we remove to London next month; but if you don't disdain a game of lottery-tickets, or to stand up to dance in a room with only perhaps half a dozen couples, I shall be very happy to welcome you whenever you should care to come."

"That's right!" said Sir Thomas, overhearing. "No state or flummery! We reserve all that for Grosvenor Square. If I had my way—but, there! this little puss of mine is determined to drag me to all manner of routs and soirées and balls, aren't you, my pretty?"

She was seated on the arm of his chair, and at once bent to lay her cheek against his, and to say caressingly: "Dear Papa! Now, confess! You would not forgo any of it for the world!"

"Ay, I know you! You are a rogue, miss, and think you may twist me round your finger! Come and eat your mutton at Whissenhurst when you feel so inclined, my lord! You know your way, and if you did not, young Martin would show it to you fast enough. No offence, but I've a pretty good notion of the way things are at Stanyon, and although I'm sure her ladyship is a very good sort of a woman, I'll go bail you are yawning till your jaws crack six days out of the seven!"

The Earl laughed, thanked him, and rose to take his leave. As he shook hands with Marianne, she smiled up at him in her innocent way, and said: "Do come again! We sometimes have the merriest parties—everyone comes to them!"

"I shall most certainly come," Gervase said. "And you, I hope—" his glance embraced them all "—will honour Stanyon with a visit. My mother-in-law is planning one or two entertainments: I believe you must shortly be receiving cards from her."

"Oh, famous!" Marianne cried, clapping her hands. "Will you give a ball at Stanyon? Do say you will! It is the very place for one!"

"Miss Bolderwood has only to give her commands! A ball it shall be!"

"My love, it is time and more that you ceased to be such a sad romp!" said Lady Bolderwood, with a reproving look. "Pray do not heed her, Lord St. Erth!"

She gave him her hand, charged him to deliver her compliments to the Dowager, and Sir Thomas escorted him to the front-door, and stayed chatting to him on the steps, while his horse was brought round from the stables.

"There is no need for you to be giving a ball unless you choose," he said bluntly. "Puss will have enough of them in another month, and I daresay her Mama don't care for her to appear at any bang-up affair until after our own ball in Grosvenor Square. We'll send you a card. But come and visit us in a friendly way when you choose! I like to see young people round me, enjoying themselves, and I remember my old Indian ways enough still to be glad to keep open house." He chuckled. "No fear of *our* being dull in the country! If there's any young spark for twenty-five miles round us whom you won't find at Whissenhurst, one day or another, I wish I may meet him! But what I say to Mama is, there's safety in numbers, and I can tell you this, my lord, we ain't anxious to see our girl married too young! Sometimes I wonder what will become of us, when she sets up her own establishment! There were plenty of people to advise us to bring her out last Season, but, No, we said: there's time and to spare! Hallo! is this your horse! Now, horseflesh is something I flatter myself I *do* understand! Ay, grand hocks! forelegs well before him! You'll hear men praising cocktails, but what I say is, the best is always the best, and give me a thoroughbred every time!"

CHAPTER FIVE

IT WAS SOME TIME BEFORE Martin returned to Stanyon, his friend having persuaded him, with the best intentions possible, to accompany him to his parental home. Mr. Warboys, inured by custom to Martin's tantrums, formed the praiseworthy scheme of allowing that young gentleman's wrath time to cool before he again encountered his half-brother. In itself, the scheme was excellent, but it was rendered abortive first by the encomiums bestowed by Mrs. Warboys, a fat and very nearly witless lady of forty summers, on the very pronounced degree of good-looks enjoyed by the Earl; and second by a less enthusiastic but by far more caustic remark uttered by Mr. Warboys, senior, to the effect that Martin, his own son, and almost every other young aspirant to the Beauty's favours could be thought to stand no chance at all against a belted Earl.

"Unless Bolderwood is a bigger fool than I take him for," he said, "he will lose no time in securing St. Erth for that chit of his!"

Shocked by such a display of tactlessness on the part of his progenitors, Mr. Warboys, junior, said: "Shouldn't think St. Erth has any serious intentions, myself!"

It was perhaps not surprising that the cumulative

effect of these remarks should have sent Martin Frant
back to Stanyon in a mood of smouldering anger.

Although he could not have been said to have
received any particular encouragement from Sir
Thomas, or from Lady Bolderwood, he was generally
acknowledged to have been, before the arrival of his
half-brother at Stanyon, the most likely candidate for
Marianne's hand. He had first known her when she was
a schoolroom miss, and he a freshman at Oxford, his
thoughts far removed from matrimony. Long before he
had thought more about her than that she was a very
good sort of a girl, pluck to the backbone, even if lacking
in judgment, he had captured her maiden fancy. He was
a handsome young man, whose magnificent background
lent his careless, imperious ways a romantic aura. He
was a stylish cricketer, a good shot, and a bruising rider
to hounds, and his patronage could not but give consequence to a schoolgirl. Lady St. Erth, whose discreet enquiries had early established the fact that the Beauty was
heiress to something in the region of a hundred thousand
pounds, from the outset smiled upon the friendship. Sir
Thomas might have eaten his dinner at Stanyon every
day of the week had he chosen to do so; and not only
were his manners pronounced to be refreshingly natural,
but he provided her ladyship with a subject for a pious
lecture on the value of golden hearts that were hid under
rough exteriors. Sir Thomas, cherishing no illusions on
the substance of the Dowager's heart, and unimpressed
by her rank, visited Stanyon as seldom as common
civility permitted, but was perfectly ready to extend his
hospitality to Martin, whom he thought of as a wild
colt, not vicious, but in need of breaking to bridle.

By the time Martin awoke to the realization that his little madcap friend had become the toast of the neighbourhood, Marianne, courted on all sides, was no longer hanging admiringly upon his lips, or gazing worshipfully up into his face. Instead, she was flirting in the prettiest, most unexceptionable way with several other young gentlemen. The knowledge, not only that he was in love with her, but that she unquestionably belonged to him, then burst upon Martin, and caused him to conduct himself in a style which made one poetically-minded damsel, who would not have objected to finding herself the object of his jealous regard, say that he reminded her of a black panther. Mr. Warboys, without putting himself to the trouble of deciding which of the more ferocious animals his friend resembled, stated the matter in simple, and courageously frank terms. "Y'know, old fellow," he once told Martin, "if you had a tail, damme if you wouldn't lash it!"

The tail, if not lashing, was certainly on the twitch when Martin reached Stanyon, but although some part of the time spent on his solitary ride home from Westerwood House had been occupied by him in dwelling upon his grievances, he also had time to reflect on the extreme unwisdom of quarrelling openly with his brother, and had no real intention of forcing an issue. Unfortunately, he had occasion to go into the Armoury, which was one of the broad galleries which flanked the Chapel Court, and was also used as a gunroom, and he found the Earl there.

Gervase was in his shirt-sleeves, trying the temper of a pair of foils. He seemed to have been engaged in oiling his pistols, for these lay in an open case on a table near him, with some rags and a bottle of oil standing beside them. He looked up as Martin entered through the door at one end of the gallery, and it occurred to Martin for the first time that he was indeed a damnably handsome man—if one had a taste for such delicate, almost womanish features.

"Oh! You here!" Martin said, in no very agreeable voice.

Gervase regarded him meditatively. "As you see. Is there any reason why I should not be here?"

"None that I know of!" Martin replied, shrugging, and walking over to a glass-fronted case which contained several sporting guns.

"I am so glad!" said Gervase. "So much that I do seems to anger you that I am quite alarmed lest I should quite unwittingly cause you offence."

The gentle irony in his tone was not lost on Martin. He wheeled about, and said trenchantly: "If that is so, let me advise you to leave Marianne Bolderwood alone!"

Gervase said nothing, but kept his eyes on Martin's face, their expression amused, yet watchful.

"I hope I make myself plain, brother!"

"Very plain."

"You may think you can come into Lincolnshire, flaunting your title, and your damned dandy-airs, and amuse yourself by trifling with Miss Bolderwood, but I shall not permit it, and so I warn you!"

"Oh, tut-tut!" Gervase interrupted, laughing.

Martin took a hasty step towards him. "Understand, I'll not have it!"

Gervase seemed to consider him for a moment. He still looked amused, and, instead of answering, he lifted the second foil from where he had laid it on the table, set both hilts across his forearm, and offered them to Martin.

Martin stared at him. "What's this foolery?"

"Don't you fence?"

"Fence? Of course I do!"

"Then choose a foil, and see what you can achieve with it! All these wild and whirling words don't impress me, you know. Perhaps your sword-play may command my respect!" He paused, while Martin stood irresolute, and added softly: "No? Do you think you can't creditably engage with such a dandified fellow as I am?"

Martin's eyes flashed; he grasped one of the hilts, exclaiming furiously: "We'll see that!"

"Gently! Don't draw the blade through my hand!" Gervase said, allowing him to take the foil he had chosen. "How does the length suit you?"

"I have frequently fenced with this pair!"

"You have the advantage of me, then: I find them a trifle overlong, and not as light in hand as I could wish. However, that is a common fault."

He moved away to the centre of the Armoury as he spoke, and waited there while Martin flung off his coat. Martin swiftly followed him, torn between annoyance and a desire to demonstrate his skill to one whom he suspected of mocking him. He knew himself to have been well-taught, and was, indeed, so much above the average at most forms of sport that he expected to give a very good account of himself. But after a few minutes he was brought to realize that he had met his master. The Earl fought with a pace and a dexterity which flustered him a little, and never did he seem to be able to break through that unwavering guard. Every attack was baffled by a close parade, and when he attempted a feint, Gervase smiled, his wrist in no way led astray, and said as he delivered a straight thrust: "Oh, no, no! If you must feint, you should oppose your forte, moving your point nearer to my forte, or you won't very easily hit me."

Martin returned no answer. He was panting, and the sweat was beginning to stain his shirt. Had his adversary been any other man he would have been delighted to have found himself matched with a swordsman so much superior to himself, and would not in the least have resented his inability to score a hit. But it galled him unspeakably to be unable to break through the guard of so effeminate a person as Gervase, who never seemed at any moment to be hard-pressed, or even to be exerting himself very much. He was obliged to acknowledge a number of hits, his choler steadily rising. A return from the wrist, which caught him in mid-thrust, destroyed the last rags of his temper; he parried a carte thrust half-circle, his weight thrown on to his left hip, and swiftly turned his wrist in tierce, inclining the point on the left, with the intention of crossing the Earl's blade. But just as he was about to do so, Gervase disengaged, giving way with the point, so that it was Martin's blade, meeting no opposition, which leaped from his hand, and not his brother's.

"So your master taught you that trick!" Gervase said, a little out of breath. "Very few do so nowadays. But it's dangerous, you know, unless you have very great swiftness and precision. Try again! Or have you had enough?"

"No!" Martin shot at him, snatching up his foil, and dragging his shirt-sleeve across his wet brow. "Damn you, I'm not so easily exhausted! I'll hit you yet! I'm out of practice!"

"You might hit me out of practice; you won't do it out of temper," said Gervase dryly.

"Won't I? *Won't* I?" gasped Martin, stung to blind rage by this merited but decidedly provocative rebuke.

He closed the Earl's blade, and on the instant saw that the button had become detached from his point. Gervase saw it too, and quickly retired his left foot, to get out of distance. "Take care!" he said sharply.

"*You* may take care!" Martin panted, and delivered a rather wild thrust in prime. It was parried by the St. George Guard; and even as he became conscious of the enormity of what he had done, he found himself very hard-pressed indeed. He would have dropped his point at a word, but the word was not spoken. Gervase was no longer smiling, and his eyes had narrowed, their lazy good-humour quite vanished. Martin was forced to fight. A careless, almost mechanical thrust in carte over the arm was parried by a sharp beat of the Earl's forte, traversing the line of his blade, and bearing his wrist irresistibly upwards. The Earl's left foot came forward; his hand seized the shell of Martin's sword, and forced it out to the right; he gripped it fast, and presented the button of his foil to Martin's face.

"The Disarm!" he said, holding Martin's eyes with his own.

Martin relinquished his foil. His chest was heaving; he seemed as though he would have said something, but before he could recover his breath enough to do so an interruption occurred. Theo, who, for the past few minutes, had been standing, with Miss Morville, rooted on the threshold, strode forward, ejaculating thunder-ously: "Martin! Are you *mad?*"

Martin started, and looked round, a sulky, defensive expression on his flushed countenance. His brother laid down the foils. Miss Morville's matter-of-fact voice broke into an uncomfortable silence. "How very careless of you, not to have observed that the button is off your point!" she said severely. "There might have been an accident, if your brother had not been sharper-eyed than you."

"Oh, no, there might not!" Martin retorted. "I couldn't touch him! There was no danger!"

He caught up his coat as he spoke, and, without looking at Gervase, went hastily out of the gallery.

"I expect," said Miss Morville, with unruffled pla-cidity, "that swords are much like guns. My Papa was used to say, when they were boys, that he would not trust my brothers with guns unless he were there to keep an eye on them, for let a boy become only a little excited and he would forget the most commonplace precautions. I came to tell you, Lord St. Erth, that your Mama-in-law wishes you will join her in the Amber Drawing-room. General Hawkhurst has come to pay his respects to you."

"Thank you! I will come directly," he replied.

"Drusilla, you will not mention to anyone—what you saw a moment ago!" Theo said.

She paused in the doorway, looking back over her shoulder. "Oh, no! Why should I, indeed? I am sure Martin would very much dislike it if anyone were to roast him for being so heedless."

With this prosaic reply, she left the Armoury, closing the door behind her.

"Gervase, what happened?" Theo said. "How came Martin to be fencing with a naked point?"

"Oh, he tried to cross my blade, but since I am rather too old a hand to be caught by such a trick as that, it was his sword, not mine, which was lost," Gervase said lightly. "The button was loosened, I daresay, by the fall."

"Are you trying to tell me that he did not perceive it?"

Gervase smiled. "Why, no! But the thing was, you see, that he was so angry with me for being the better swordsman that his rage quite overthrew his judgment, and he tried to pink me. I was never in any danger, you know: he has not been so badly taught, but he lacks precision and pace."

"So I saw! You had him clearly at your mercy, but that cannot excuse his conduct!"

"As to that, perhaps I was a little at fault," Gervase confessed. "But, really, you know, Theo, he is such an unschooled colt that I thought he deserved a set-down! I own, I said what I knew must enrage him. No harm done: he is now very much ashamed of himself, and that must be counted as a gain."

"I hope you may be found to be right. But—" He broke off, his brows contracting.

"Well?"

"It happened as you have described, of course, but—" he raised his eyes to his cousin's face, and said bluntly: "Gervase, be a little more careful, I beg of you! You might not have noticed it, but I saw, in his face, such an expression of fury—I had almost said, of hatred—!"

"Yes, I did notice it," Gervase said quietly. "He

would have been happy to have murdered me, would he not?"

"No, no, don't think it! He is, as you have said, an unschooled colt, and he has been used to being so much petted and praised— But he would not murder you!"

"It was certainly his intention, my dear Theo!"

"Not his intention!" Theo said swiftly. "His impulse, at that instant!"

"The distinction is too nice for his victim to appreciate. Come, Theo! Be plain with me, I beg of you! You tried to put me on my guard, I fancy, that first evening, when you came to my bedchamber, and drank a glass of brandy with me there. Was it against Martin that you were warning me?" He waited for a moment. "I am answered, I suppose!"

"I don't know. I dare not say so! Only be a little wary, Gervase! If some accident were to befall you—why, I dare swear he himself would admit to being glad of it! But that he would contrive to bring about such an accident I have never believed, until I saw his face just now! The suspicion did then flash into my mind—but it must be nonsensical!"

"Theo, I *do* think you should have rushed in, and thrown yourself between us!" Gervase complained.

"Yes, and so I would have done had I wished to startle you into dropping your guard!" Theo retorted, laughing. "What I might have felt myself impelled to do had you appeared to me to be hard-pressed I know not! Something heroic, no doubt! But stop bamming, Gervase! What have you been doing to make Martin ready to murder you?"

"Why, I have been flaunting my title and my dandified airs in the eyes of his inamorata, and he fears she may be dazzled!"

"Oh! I collect that you have somehow contrived to meet Miss Bolderwood?"

"Yes, and I wish you will tell me why no one has ever told me of her existence! She is the sweetest sight my eyes have alighted upon since I came into Lincolnshire!"

Theo smiled, but perfunctorily, and turned a little aside, to lay the foils in their case. "She is very beautiful," he agreed, in a colourless tone.

"An heiress too, if I have understood her father! Shall I try my fortune?"

"By all means."

Gervase glanced quickly at his averted profile. "Theo! You too?"

Theo uttered a short laugh. "Don't disturb yourself! I might as well aspire to the hand of a Royal Princess!" He shut the sword-case, and turned. "Come! If General Hawkhurst has honoured you with a visit, you had better make yourself a little more presentable."

"Very true: I will do so at once!" Gervase said, rather glad to be relieved of the necessity of answering his cousin's embittered words. From the little he had seen of both, he could not but feel that the staid Drusilla would make a more suitable bride for Theo than the livelier and by far more frivolous Marianne; he must, moreover, have been obliged to agree that there could be little hope that Sir Thomas would bestow his only child on a man in Theo's circumstances.

He did not again see Martin until they met at the dinner-table. There was then a little constraint in Martin's manner, but since he was so much a creature of moods this caused his mother no concern. Her mind was, in fact, preoccupied with the startling request made to her by her stepson, that she should send out cards of invitation for a ball at Stanyon. Since her disposition generally led her to dislike any scheme not of her own making, her first reaction was to announce with an air of majestic finality that it was not to be thought of; but when the Earl said apologetically that he was afraid some thought would have to be spent on the project, unless a party quite unworthy of the traditions of Stanyon were to be the result, she began to perceive that his mind was made up. An uneasy suspicion, which had every now and then flitted through her head since the episode of the Indian epergne, again made itself felt: her stepson, for all his gentle voice and sweet smile, was not easily to be intimidated. From her first flat veto, she passed to the enumeration of all the difficulties in the way of holding a ball at Stanyon at that season of the year. She was still expatiating on the subject when she took her place at the foot of the dinner-table. "Had it been Christmas, it might have been proper for us to have done something of that nature," she said.

"Hardly, ma'am!" said Gervase, in a deprecating tone. "You had not then, I am persuaded, put off your blacks."

This was unanswerable; and while she was thinking of some further objection, Martin, who had not been present when the scheme was first mooted, demanded to be told what was going forward. When it was made known to him, he could not dislike the project. His eyes brightened; he turned them towards Gervase, exclaiming: "I call that a famous notion! We have not had such an affair at Stanyon since I don't know when! When is it to be?"

"I have been explaining to your brother," said the Dowager, "that a ball held in the country at this season cannot be thought to be eligible."

"Oh, fudge, Mama! No one removes to town until April—no one we need care for, at least! I daresay we could muster as many as fifty couples—well, twenty-five, at all events! and that don't include all the old frights who will come only to play whist!"

"I fear that my state of health would be quite unequal to entertaining so many persons," said the Dowager, making a determined bid for mastery.

As she had never been known to suffer even the most trifling indisposition, this announcement not unnaturally staggered her son. Before he could expostulate, however, Gervase said solicitously: "I would not for the world prejudice your health, ma'am! To be sure, to expect you to receive and to contrive for so many people would be an infamous thing for me to do! But I have been considering, you know, whether, if I sent my own chaise to convey her, my Aunt Dorothea might not be prevailed upon to drive over from Studham, to relieve you of those duties which might prove too much for your strength. I daresay, if we invited her to stay at Stanyon for a week or so, she would not altogether object to it."

There was a pregnant silence. Theo's firm lips twitched; the Chaplain gazed in deep absorption at the bowl of spring flowers which had replaced the epergne in the centre of the table; and Martin directed a glance of awe, not untinged with respect, at the Earl. Only Miss Morville continued to eat her dinner in complete unconcern.

"Lady Cinderford," said the Dowager, referring to

her widowed sister-in-law in accents of loathing, "will act as hostess at Stanyon over my dead body!"

"That would be something quite out of the ordinary way," murmured the Earl.

Miss Morville raised her eyes from the portion of fricandeau of beef on her plate, and directed a quelling look at him. She then turned her attention to her hostess, saying: "Should you find it too much for you, ma'am, if I were to write all the invitations for you, and, in general, undertake the arrangements?"

The Dowager, snatching at this straw, bestowed one of her most gracious smiles upon her, and gave the assembled company to understand that under these conditions she might be induced to sink her personal inclinations in a benevolent desire to oblige her stepson. After that, she entered in a very exhaustive way, which lent no colour to her previous assertion that she was in failing health, into all the preparations it would be necessary to make for the ball. Long before dinner was at an end, she had talked herself into good-humour; and by the time she rose from the table she had reached the felicitous stage of saying how happy she would be to welcome the dear Duchess of Rutland to Stanyon, and how happy a number of persons of quite inferior rank would be to find themselves at Stanyon.

While the inevitable card-table was being set up in the Italian Saloon, the Earl found himself standing beside Miss Morville, a little withdrawn from the rest of the party. He could not resist saying to her, with an arch lift of his brows: "I have incurred your censure, ma'am?"

She seemed surprised. "No, how should you? Oh, you mean that *most* ill-advised remark you made! Well,

I must say, it was the outside of enough! However, it is not my business to be censuring you, my lord, and if I seemed to do so I have only to beg pardon."

"Don't, I entreat! I will own my fault. Shall you dislike my ball?"

"Dislike it! No, indeed! I daresay I shall enjoy it excessively."

"I am afraid you will be put to a great deal of trouble over it."

He expected a polite disclaimer, but she replied, candidly: "I shall, of course, because whatever I suggest Lady St. Erth will not like, until she has been brought to believe that she thought of it herself. I wish very much that she would let me contrive the whole, for there is nothing I should like better. But that would be rather too much to expect her to do, and one should never be unreasonable!"

"You would like nothing better than to order all the arrangements for a large party? I can conceive of nothing more tiresome!"

"Very likely you might not, for I think gentlemen do not excel at such things." She looked across the room, to where Martin was discussing with his mother the various families it would be proper to invite to the ball. "I expect he will ask her particularly to send a card to the Bolderwoods," she said sagely. "If I were you, I would not mention to her that you wish them to be invited, for it will only put up her back, if you do, and you may depend upon Martin's good offices in *that* cause."

"May I ask, ma'am," he said, a trifle frigidly, "why you should suppose that I wish to invite the Bolderwoods?"

She raised her eyes to his face, in one of her clear,

enquiring looks. "Don't you? I quite thought that it must have been Marianne who had put the notion of a ball into your head, since you were visiting at Whissenhurst this morning."

He hardly knew whether to be amused or angry. "Upon my word, Miss Morville! It seems that my movements are pretty closely watched!"

"I expect you will have to accustom yourself to that," she returned. "Everything you do must be of interest to your people, you know. In this instance, you could not hope to keep your visit secret (though I cannot imagine why you should wish to do so!), for your coachman's second grand-daughter is employed at the Grange."

"Indeed!"

"Yes, and she has given such satisfaction that they mean to take her to London with them next month, which is a very gratifying circumstance." She fixed her eyes on his face again, and asked disconcertingly: "Have you fallen in love with Miss Bolderwood?"

"Certainly not!" he replied, in a tone nicely calculated to depress pretension.

"Oh! Most gentlemen do—on *sight!*" she remarked. "One cannot wonder at it, for I am sure she must be the prettiest girl imaginable. I have often reflected that it must be very agreeable to be beautiful. Mama considers that it is of more importance to have an informed mind, but I must own that I *cannot* agree with her."

At this moment the Dowager called to Gervase to come to the card-table. He declined it, saying that he had letters which must be written, upon which Miss Morville was applied to. She went at once; and Martin, after fidgeting about the room for a few minutes, drew near to his brother, and said awkwardly: "You know, I didn't mean it! That is—I beg your pardon, but—but it was you who made me fight on! And it would have been the sheerest good luck if I *had* pinked you!"

Gervase was in the act of raising a pinch of snuff to one nostril, but he paused. "You are very frank!" he remarked.

"Frank? Oh—! Well, of course I didn't mean—what I meant was that it would only be by some accident, or if you were careless, or—or something of that nature!"

"I see. I was evidently quite mistaken, for I formed the opinion that you had the very definite intention of running me through."

"You made me as mad as fire!" Martin muttered, his eyes downcast, and his cheeks reddened.

"Yes, I do seem to have an unhappy trick of offending you, don't I?" said the Earl.

CHAPTER SIX

MISS BOLDERWOOD'S NAME was not again mentioned between the half-brothers, Martin apparently being conscious of some awkwardness in adverting to the subject of his late quarrel with Gervase, and Gervase considering himself to be under no obligation to account to his brother for his visits to Whissenhurst Grange. These were more frequent than could be expected to meet with the approval either of Martin, or of the numerous other gentlemen who paid court to the beautiful heiress; for the Earl, driving over to Whissenhurst on the day after his first encounter with Marianne to enquire politely after her well-being, after such a misadventure as had befallen her, was able to persuade her, without much difficulty, to accompany him on a drive round the neighbourhood. Informed by some chance observation that she had never yet handled a pair of high-bred horses, he conceived the happy notion of offering to instruct her in this art. It took well; Sir Thomas, having early perceived, from his handling of his cattle, that the Earl was no mean whip, raised no objection; and on several mornings thereafter those of Miss Bolderwood's admirers who happened, by some chance, to find themselves in the vicinity of Whissenhurst were revolted by the spectacle of their goddess bowling smartly along the lane under the tuition of her latest and most distinguished swain. On more than one occasion they had the doubtful pleasure of meeting him at a Whissenhurst tea-party. These informal entertainments, where tea, quadrille, and commerce were followed by an elegant supper, just suited the Earl's humour, for his prolonged service in the Peninsula, with its generally happy-go-lucky way of life, had rendered him unappreciative of the formal tedium obtaining at Stanyon. Sir Thomas was a genial host, his lady was a notable housewife; and nothing delighted either of them more than to see a number of young persons enjoying themselves at their expense. As for Marianne, it would have been hard to have guessed which of her swains she was inclined to prefer, for she seemed equally pleased to see them all, and if one gentleman was the recipient of her particular favours one day, the next she would bestow these sunnily upon another. Nor did she neglect the members of her own sex: she had even been known to leave a hopeful and far from ineligible cavalier disconsolate merely because she had promised to go for a walk with another damsel, and would on no account break her engagement. The gentlemen said she was the most beautiful girl they had ever beheld; the ladies, for the most part, bestowed on her an even more striking testimonial: they were sure there could not anywhere be found a more good-natured girl. She had her detractors, of course; and it was not long after his arrival at Stanyon that the Earl learned from several mothers of pretty daughters that Miss Bolderwood, though well-enough, had too short an upper lip to be considered a Beauty, and was sadly deficient in accomplishments. Her performance upon the pianoforte was no more than moderate, and she had never learnt to play the harp. Nor had Lady Bolderwood ever called upon morning-visitors to admire her daughter's latest water-colour sketch, from which it was to be apprehended that Miss Bolderwood's talent did not lie in this direction either.

Martin was nearly always to be found at the Whissenhurst tea-parties; and once, having received a particular invitation from Lady Bolderwood, Theo drove over with the Earl to bear his part in an informal dance. Gervase, watching how Theo's eyes followed Marianne, could only be sorry: it did not appear to him that she held him in greater regard than himself, or Martin, or the inarticulate Mr. Warboys.

Cards of invitation were sent out from Stanyon; Marianne was in transports, and if it did not quite suit Lady Bolderwood's sense of propriety to permit her to appear at a regular ball before she had been brought out in London at a ball of her own parents' contriving, Sir Thomas could not be brought to see that such niceties mattered a jot. Lady Bolderwood's scruples were overborne, and Marianne could be happy, and had only to decide between the rival merits of her white satin dress with the Russian bodice, fastened in front with little pearls; and one of white crape, trimmed with blonde lace, and worn over a satin slip.

Her happiness, with that of every other lady who had been honoured with an invitation to the ball, very soon became alloyed by anxiety. The weather underwent a change, and in place of bright spring days, with the wind blowing constantly from the east, a stormy period threatened to set in. A gay little party of damsels, seeking violets in the woods about Whissenhurst, were caught in such a severe downpour that they were soaked almost to the skin; and when anxious questions were put to such weather-wise persons as gardeners and farmers, these worthies would only shake their heads, and say that it showed no sign of fairing-up. The date of the ball had been carefully chosen to coincide with the full moon, but not even so indulgent a parent as Sir Thomas would for a moment consider the possibility of driving some six miles to a party of pleasure if the moon were to be obscured by clouds, and the coachman's vision still further impaired by driving rain.

"Do we despair, Miss Morville?" asked the Earl.

"No, but if the weather continues in this odious way, I fear you will find your rooms very thin of company," she replied. "The people who are coming from a distance, and are to sleep here, will come, because they will set out in daylight, you know, and they will hope that the rain won't come on, or that they may drive away from it. I should think you may be sure of the party from Belvoir, but I do feel that you should perhaps fortify your mind to the likelihood of your immediate neighbours not caring to set forth in wet, cloudy weather."

"I will endeavour to do so," promised the Earl gravely.

Three days before the ball, the weather, so far from showing signs of improvement, promised nothing but disaster. The prophets said gloomily that it was banking up for a storm, and they were right. The day was tempestuous; and when the Stanyon party assembled for dinner even Martin, who had hitherto refused to envisage the possibility of the inclement weather's persisting, took his place at the table with a very discontented expression on his face, and announced that he thought the devil had got into the skies.

"Well, if it continues in this way, we must postpone the ball," Gervase said cheerfully.

"Yes! And find everyone gone off to London!" retorted Martin.

He could talk of nothing but the probable ruin of their plans; and since no representation sufficed to make him think more hopefully of the prospects, not even his mother was sorry when, shortly after the party rose from the table, he said, after a series of cavernous yawns, that he rather thought he would go to bed, since he had the head-ache, and everything was a dead bore.

The usual whist set had been formed, and so fierce were the battles fought over the table that none of the four players noticed that the wind was no longer rattling the shutters, and moaning round the corners of the Castle, until Miss Morville, who sat quietly stitching by the fire, lifted her head, and said: "Listen! the wind has dropped!"

"I rather thought it would," observed the Dowager, gathering up her trick. "Indeed, I said as much this morning. 'Depend on it,' I said to Abney, 'the wind will drop, and we shall have it fine for our party.' I flatter myself I am seldom at fault in my calculations. Dear me, St. Erth, I am sure if I had known you had the King of Diamonds in your hand we might have taken a couple of tricks more!"

"I am very much afraid, ma'am, that this is the lull before a storm," said Theo.

So indeed it proved. After a brief period of quiet, a

distant but menacing rumble of thunder was heard; and the Dowager instantly said that she had suspected as much, since nothing so surely gave Martin the head-ache as a thunderstorm.

After half an hour, during which time thunder grumbled intermittently, Miss Morville announced that she too would go to bed. She said that she could wish that, if a storm there must be, it would lose no time in bursting into full force, and thus be the more quickly finished.

"Poor Drusilla!" said Theo, smiling. "Do you dislike it so very much?"

"I *do* dislike it," she replied, with dignity, "but I am well aware that to be afraid of the thunder is unworthy of any person of the *least* intelligence. The noise is certainly disagreeable, but it cannot, after all, harm one!" With these stout words, she folded up her needlework, bade good-night to the company, and went away to her bedchamber.

"I fear we must expect to spend a disturbed night," said Mr. Clowne, shaking his head. "There has been a feeling of oppression in the atmosphere throughout the day which presages a very considerable storm. I trust you ladyship's rest will not be impaired."

"I have no apprehension of it," she responded. "I do not fear the elements, I assure you. Indeed, I should think it a very remarkable circumstance if I were to lose my sleep on account of them. We have very severe storms at Stanyon: I have often observed as much. Ah, here is the tea-table being brought in at last! What a pity Drusilla should not have waited, for she might have dispensed the tea, you know, and now I shall be obliged to do so myself."

As the evening wore on, the storm increased in violence, the reverberations of one crash of thunder hardly dying away before another, and even more severe clatter, seeming to roll round the sky above the Castle, succeeded it. Powerful gusts of wind buffeted the windows, and drove the smoke downwards in the chimneys; the howl of the gusts, sweeping round the many angles of the Castle, rose sometimes to a shriek which could be heard through the loudest peals of the thunder.

The Chaplain having meekly retired to bed when his patroness sought her own couch, the Earl and his cousin were left to amuse themselves as best they might. The Earl lit one of his cigarillos, but Theo declined joining him. "And I wish you may not repent your temerity, when my aunt detects—as I promise you she will!—the aroma of tobacco in this room tomorrow!" he added.

Gervase laughed. "Will she give me one of her tremendous scolds, do you think? I shall shake in my shoes: she is the most terrifying woman!"

His cousin smiled. "What a complete hand you are, St. Erth! Much you care for her scolds! All this mild compliance is nothing but a take-in: you engage her at every turn!"

"Military training, Theo: a show of strength to deceive the enemy!" said Gervase firmly. "But the room will reek of wood-smoke in the morning, and my iniquity may be undiscovered. It is a very bad habit, however: one that I learned in Spain, and have tried in vain to abandon. I don't find that snuff answers the purpose at all. Good God, what a gust! You will be blown out of your turret!"

"Not I! The walls are so thick I shall spend the night very much more snugly than you will, I daresay."

"Don't think it! I became inured to this kind of thing in Spain, and very soon learned to sleep peacefully through a veritable tornado—in a draughty billet, too, with no glass in the windows, but only a few boards nailed across them to protect us from the worst of the weather. I have taken the precaution, too, of telling Turvey to let the fire die down in my room, and thus need not fear to be smothered by smoke. Like her ladyship, I guessed how it would be!"

"At all events, there is a very good chance that it will blow itself out, and we may expect better weather after it. You need not despair of your ball! But it is not, I fancy, so violent a storm as you might suppose from the way the wind screeches round us. *I* am accustomed to it, but, after so long an absence, *you,* I imagine, might well believe yourself to be listening to the screams of souls in torment."

"No, I well recall the discomforts of Stanyon in inclement weather. I shall go to bed. I am sure I know not how it is, but an evening spent in the company of my Mama-in-law fatigues me more than a dozen cavalry charges!"

"To that also I am accustomed," Theo said gravely.

They left the Saloon together, the Earl's hand tucked lightly into his cousin's arm. The candles and the lamps were still burning in the galleries and on the Grand Staircase, the Earl having, in the gentlest manner possible, informed his household that, since it was not his habit to retire at ten o'clock, he did not wish to find the Castle plunged in darkness at this hour. A couple of footmen were hovering about in a disinterested way, their purpose being to extinguish the lights as soon as he should have shut his bedchamber-door. The Earl smiled faintly, and murmured: "My poor Turvey! He cannot reconcile himself to the rigours of life in the country, and wonders that he should be required to grope his way to bed by the light of a single candle. I wish he may not leave my service, as a result of all these discomforts! He understands my boots as no other valet has ever done."

"And your neckcloths?" said Theo quizzically.

"No, no, how can you do me such an injustice? Mine is the only hand employed in their arrangement! But you have set my doubts at rest, Theo! This Oriental style, which you so rightly deprecate, is too high—by far too high! You shall see tomorrow how beautifully I am able to tie a *trône d'amour!*"

"Go to bed! It is by far too late for your funning!" Theo said, laughing at him. "Sleep well!"

"No fear I shall not: I have been yawning this hour past! Good-night!"

The Earl passed into his bedchamber, where Turvey awaited him by the embers of a dying fire. "A rough night!" he remarked.

"Extremely so, my lord."

"My cousin, however, believes that we may not indulge our optimism too far in expecting a period of better weather after the storm."

"Indeed, my lord?"

"I daresay," said the Earl, drawing the pin from the over-tall Oriental-tie, and laying it down on his dressing-table, "that if you were to step out into the open you would not find the storm to be so severe as you might suppose."

"Unless your lordship particularly desires me to do so, I should prefer not to expose myself to the elements."

"My unreasonable demands of you fall short of that," said Gervase gravely.

Turvey bowed; it was plain that he was not to be won over, and his master abandoned the attempt, permitting himself to be undressed in silence. When he had been assisted to put on his dressing-gown, he told the man he might go, and sat down at his dressing-table to pare his nails. Turvey gathered up the discarded raiment, bade him a punctilious good-night, and withdrew into the adjoining dressing-room, where he could be heard moving about for some minutes, opening and shutting drawers, and brushing coats. Gervase, having critically regarded his slender fingertips, extinguished the candles in the brackets beside the mirror, forced a wedge of paper in the door on to the gallery, which showed a disagreeable tendency to rattle, and climbed into his formidable bed. It was hung with very heavy curtains of crimson velvet, fringed and tasselled with gold, but Gervase, in whom several years of campaigning had engendered a dislike of being shut in, would never permit his valet to draw these. He disposed himself on his pillows, shifted the position of his bedside candle, and, with some misgiving, opened the book which had been pressed on him by the Dowager, after he had very unwisely owned that it had never come in his way. It was entitled *Self-Control,* and since the Dowager had described it to him as a very pretty and improving book, and one which would do him a great deal of good to read, he had not much expectation of being amused. The thunder went on rumbling and crackling overhead, and the wind was now driving rain against the windows, but this continuous noise had as little power as Mrs. Brunton's moral tale to keep him awake. He very soon found that the printed words were running into one another, tossed the book aside, blew out his candle, and within ten minutes was soundly asleep.

He awoke very suddenly, he knew not how many hours later, as though some unusual sound, penetrating his dreams, had jerked him back to consciousness. The room was in dense darkness, the fire in the hearth having died quite away; and he could hear nothing but the rain beating against the windows, and the howl of the wind, more subdued now, round the corner of the building. Yet even as he wondered whether perhaps he had been awakened by the fall of a tile from the roof, or the slamming of a door left carelessly open, he received so decided an impression that he was not alone in the room, that he raised himself quickly on to one elbow, straining his eyes to see through the smothering darkness. He could hear nothing but the wind and the rain, but the impression that someone was in the room rather grew on him than abated, and he said sharply: "Who is there?"

There was no answer, nor was there any sound within the room to betray the presence of another, but he could not be satisfied. Grasping the bed-clothes, he flung them aside in one swift movement, and leaped up. As his feet touched the floor, something creaked, and his quickened ears caught a sound which might have been made by a softly closing door. He reached the windows, grazing his shin against the leg of the dressing-table, and dragged one of the curtains back. A faint, gray light was admitted into the room. He could perceive no one, and strode back to the bedside, groping on the table for his tinder-box. His candle lit, he held it up, keenly looking about him. He noticed that his wedge was still firm in the door leading to the gallery; he glanced towards the door to his dressing-room, and saw that that too was shut. He set the candle down, thrust his feet into a pair of gay Morocco slippers, and shrugged himself into his dressing-gown, aware, as he did so, of the unlikelihood of anyone's entering his room at such an advanced hour of the night, but still convinced that he had not imagined the whole.

A board cracked outside the room. He picked up the candlestick, and wrenched open his door, stepping out on to the gallery. He found himself staring at Martin, who, fully dressed, except for his shoes, and carrying a lantern, had halted in his tracks, just beyond his door, and was looking in a startled, defensive way over his shoulder. "Martin!" he exclaimed. "What the devil—?"

"Don't kick up such a dust!" Martin begged him, in a savage but a lowered voice. "Do you want to wake my mother?"

"What are you doing?" Gervase demanded, more softly, but with a good deal of sternness in his tone. "Where have you been?"

"What's that to you?" Martin retorted. "I suppose I need not render *you* an account of my movements! I have been out!"

"Out?" Gervase repeated incredulously. "In this hurricane?"

"Why shouldn't I go out? I'm not afraid of a paltry thunderstorm!"

"Be so good as to stop trying to humbug me!" Gervase said, with more acidity in his voice than his brother had ever heard. "You had the head-ache! You went early to bed!"

"Oh, well!" Martin muttered, reddening a little. "I—I recalled that—that I had an appointment in the village!"

"An appointment in the village! Pray, in which village?"

"Cheringham—but it's no concern of yours!" said Martin sulkily.

"It appears to me to be raining, but I observe that you are not at all wet!" said Gervase sardonically.

"Of course I am not! I had my driving-coat on, and I left it, with my boots, downstairs! There is no need for you to blab to my mother that I was out tonight—though I daresay that is just what you mean to do!" He cast his brother a look of dislike, and said: "I suppose that curst door woke you! The wind blew it out of my hand."

"Which door?"

"Oh, the one into the court, of course!" He jerked his head towards a door at the end of the gallery, which, as the Earl knew, led to a secondary flight of stairs. "I came in by that way: I often do!"

Gervase looked at him under slightly knit brows. "Very well, but what brought you to my room?"

"Well, I am bound to pass your room, if I come up by that stairway!"

"You are not bound to enter my room, however."

"Enter your room! That's a loud one! As though I should wish to!"

"Did you not, in fact, do so?"

"Of course I did not! Why should I? I wish you will

be a little less busy, St. Erth! If I choose to go to Cheringham on affairs of my own—"

"It is naturally no concern of mine," interposed Gervase. "You choose wild nights for your intrigues!"

"My—?" Martin gave a crack of laughter, hurriedly smothered. "Ay, that's it! Old Scrooby's daughter, I daresay!"

"I beg pardon. You will allow that if I am to be expected to swallow this story some explanation should be vouchsafed to me."

"Well, I ain't going to explain it to you," said Martin, scowling at him.

A glimmer of light at the angle of the gallery in which they stood and that which ran along the north side of the court, caught the Earl's eye. He took a quick step towards it, and Miss Morville, who, shrouded, lamp in hand, had been peeping cautiously round the corner of the wall, came forward, blushing in some confusion, but whispering: "Indeed, I beg your pardon, but I thought it must be house-breakers! I could not sleep for this horrid storm, and it seemed to me that I heard footsteps outside the house, and then a door slammed! I formed the intention of slipping upstairs to wake Abney, only then I heard voices, and thought I could recognize yours, my lord, so I crept along the gallery to see if it were indeed you." She looked at Martin. "Was it you who let the door slam into the court? Have you been out in this rain and wind?"

"Yes, I have!" said Martin, in a furious undervoice. "I have been down to the village, and pray, what have either of you to say to that?"

"Only that I wish you will be more careful, and not

give me such a fright!" said Miss Morville, drawing her shawl more securely about her. "And, if I were you, Martin, I would not stand talking here, for if you do so much longer you will be bound to wake Lady St. Erth."

This common-sense reminder had the effect of sending him off on tiptoe. Miss Morville, conscious of her bare toes, which her nightdress very imperfectly concealed, and of the neat cap tied under her chin, would have followed him had she not happened to look into the Earl's face. He was watching Martin's retreat, and, after considering him for a moment, Miss Morville asked softly: "Pray, what has occurred, sir?"

He brought his eyes down to her face. "Occurred?"

"You seem to be a good deal put-out. Is it because Martin stole away to the village? Boys will do so, you know!"

"That! No!—if it was true!"

"Oh, I expect it was!" she said. "I thought, did not you? that he had been drinking what my brother Jack calls Old Tom."

"I know of no reason why he must go to the village to do so."

"Oh, no! I conjecture," said Miss Morville, with the air of one versed in these matters, "that it was to see some cocking that he went."

"Cocking!"

"At the Red Lion. To own the truth, that was what I thought he meant to do when he said he had the head-ache and would go to bed."

"But, in God's name, why could he not have told me so?"

"They never do," she replied simply. "My brothers

were just the same. In general, you know, one's parents frown upon cocking, on account of the low company it takes a boy into. Depend upon it, that was why he would not tell you."

"My dear ma'am, Martin can hardly regard me in the light of a parent!"

"No—at least, only in a disagreeable way," she said. "You are so much older than he, and have so much more experience besides, that I daresay the poor boy feels you are a great distance removed from him. Moreover, he resents you very much at present. If I were you, I would not mention his having gone out tonight."

"I shall certainly not do so. How deep is his resentment, Miss Morville? You seem to know so much that perhaps you know that too!"

"Dear me, no! I daresay he will recover from it when he is better acquainted with you. I never heeded him very much, and I expect it will be better if you do not either."

"You are full of excellent advice, ma'am!"

"Well, I am not clever, but I am thought to have a great deal of common-sense, though I can see that you mean to be satirical," she replied calmly. "Good-night! I think the wind is less, and we may perhaps be able to sleep at last."

She flitted away down the gallery, and the Earl returned to his bedchamber. Sleep was far from him, however, and after drawing the curtain across the window again he began to pace slowly about the room, thinking over all that had passed. The creak he had heard might, he supposed, have been caused merely by

the settling of a chair; but he could not charge his nerves
with having led him to imagine the closing of a door.
He could have sworn that a latch had clicked very softly,
and this sound was too distinctive to be confused with
the many noises of the storm. He glanced towards the
door into his dressing-room, and took a step towards it.
Then he checked himself, reflecting that his silent
visitor would scarcely return to his room that night.
Instead of locking the door, he bent to pick up his handkerchief, which had fallen on the floor beside the bed,
and stood for a moment, kneading it unconsciously
between his hands, and wondering whether the click he
had heard had not been in the room after all, but had
been caused by Martin's closing of the door leading to
the stairway down the gallery. He could not think it, but
it was useless to cudgel his brain any further at that hour.
He tossed the handkerchief on to his pillow, and took
off his dressing-gown. Suddenly his abstracted gaze
became intent. He picked the handkerchief up again,
and held it near the candle, to perceive more clearly the
monogram which had caught his eye. Delicately em-
broidered on the fine lawn were the interlinked initials,
M and F.

CHAPTER SEVEN

A BRIGHT DAY succeeded the storm, with a fresh wind blowing, but the sun shining, and great cumulus clouds riding high in a blue sky. Some of the havoc wrought from the night's tornado could be observed from the windows of the breakfast-parlour; and when Martin strode in presently, he reported that at least one tree had been struck in the Home Wood, and that shattered tiles from the roof of the Castle littered the courts.

"I trust your lordship's rest was not too much disturbed?" Mr. Clowne said solicitously. "It was indeed a tempestuous night!"

"His lordship will tell you, sir," said Theo, "that, having bivouacked in Spain, an English thunderstorm has no power to disturb his rest. He was boasting of it to me last night. I daresay you never enjoyed a quieter sleep, eh, Gervase?"

"Did I boast? Then I am deservedly set-down, for I must own that my rest was not quite undisturbed." He met his brother's wary, kindling glance across the table, and added, meeting those dark eyes smilingly, but with irony in his own lazy gaze: "By the by, Martin, I fancy this must be yours!"

Martin caught the handkerchief tossed to him, and

inspected it casually. "Yes, it is. Did you find it amongst your own?"

"No," said Gervase. "You dropped it."

Martin looked up quickly, suspicion in his face. "Oh! I daresay I might have: it can easily happen, after all!" He turned away, and began to tell his cousin about the damage caused by the storm which had so far been reported.

"Then, as I really mean to ride towards Hatherfield this morning," observed the Earl, "I shall no doubt be besieged with demands for new roofs and chimney-stacks. What shall I say to my importunate tenants, Theo?"

"Why, that they must carry their complaints to your agent! Do you indeed mean to go there? I had abandoned hope of bringing you to a sense of your obligations! Mind, now, that you don't deny old Yelden the gratification of receiving a visit from you! He has been asking me for ever when he may hope to see you. You have no more devoted a pensioner, I daresay! He swears it was he who taught you to climb your first tree!"

"So he did, indeed! I will certainly visit him," Gervase promised.

Martin, who had become engaged in conversation with the Chaplain, seemed not be paying any heed to his interchange; nor, unless some direct enquiry obliged him to do so, did he again address his brother while the meal lasted. He strolled away, when the party rose from the table; and, upon Mr. Clowne's excusing himself, Theo looked shrewdly at his cousin, and said: "Now what's amiss?"

The Earl raised his brows. "Why do you ask me that? Do I seem to you to be out of humour?"

"No, but it's easy to see that Martin has taken one of his pets."

"Oh, must there be a reason for his pets? I had not thought it! Are you very busy today? Go with me to Hatherfield!"

"Willingly. I shall be glad to see what damage may have been done to the saplings in the new plantation, Cheringham way. I daresay we may meet Hayle there, and I must have a word with him about fencing. You might care to talk to him yourself!"

"Pray hold me excused! I know nothing of fencing, and should infallibly betray my ignorance. It will not do for my bailiff to hold me cheap!"

His cousin laughed, but shook his head at him. He went off to transact some trifling matter of business, but in less than twenty minutes he rejoined the Earl, and they set forward on their ride.

The most direct route to the village of Hatherfield lay through the Home Park and across a stream to Cheringham Spinney. The ground on either side of the stream was marshy, and a long wooden bridge had been thrown across it by the Earl's grandfather. No more than a footbridge, it was not wide enough to permit of two horsemen riding abreast across it. After the storm, the stream was a miniature torrent, with evidences of the night's havoc swirling on its churned-up flood. The nervous chestnut Gervase was riding jibbed at the bridge, but, after a little tussle with his rider, stepped delicately on to the wooden planks. "*You* would not do for a campaign, my friend!" Gervase chided him gently, patting his sweating neck. "Courage, now!"

"Take care, Gervase!" Theo ejaculated, hard on his heels, but reining back. "Gervase, *stop!*"

"Why, what is it?" Gervase said, obediently halting, and looking over his shoulder.

"It won't hold! Back!" Theo said, backing his own horse off the bridge. He dismounted quickly, thrust his bridle into the Earl's hand, and went squelching through the boggy ground to the edge of the swollen stream. "I thought as much!" he called. "One of the supports is scarcely standing! Good God, what a merciful thing that Hayle was speaking to me about the supports only five days ago, and I recalled it in time! One of those great branches must have been hurled against it: it is cracked almost right through!"

"No wonder, then, that Orthes refused to face it!" said Gervase. "Poor fellow, I maligned you, didn't I? You are wiser by far than your master, and would have spared him an ignominious wetting!"

"A wetting!" Theo exclaimed, coming back to dry ground. "You might think yourself fortunate to escape with no worse than that! There are boulders in the stream-bed: if you had ridden this way alone, and been stunned perhaps—! I blame myself: I should have had this bridge attended to when Hayle first spoke to me of it! My dear Gervase, it is very well to laugh, but you might have sustained an ugly injury—if not a fatal injury! Now what are we to do?"

"Ford the stream of course. Orthes won't like it, so this well-mannered roan of yours shall give him a lead."

Theo took the bridle from him again, and remounted. "Very well, but take care how you go! The water has risen so much that you can't perceive the rocks—and, I assure you, there are several!"

Though the muddied water did indeed hide the rocks,

it was not very deep, scarcely rising above the horses' knees. Gervase was obliged to acknowledge, however, that a fall from the bridge might have resulted in a broken limb or a concussion, for the boulders were numerous, making it necessary for them to pick their way very slowly across the stream. Once Orthes stumbled, but his master held him together, and the passage was accomplished in safety. "An adventurous ride!" remarked Gervase merrily. "I am glad you were with me, Theo. A tumble into this dirty water would not have suited me at all. And what my poor Turvey will have to say to my boots when he sees them I shudder to think of! Ah, now, behold the guardian of the bridge—a trifle late, but you can see how zealous!"

He pointed with his riding-whip down the rough track that lay before them to where a ruddy-cheeked urchin in a smock and frieze breeches was striding importantly towards them with a red handkerchief attached to a hazel-wand carried in the manner of a standard before him.

"Well, Ensign, and who may you be?" the Earl enquired, smiling down at the boy. "Horatius, I fancy!"

"That's Parson," disclaimed the urchin. "I'm nobbut Tom Scrooby, come to mind the bridge, and see no one don't come acrost, your honour, because it's clean busted." His round eyes, having thoroughly taken in the Earl, travelled to Theo. He pulled his sandy forelock. "Mr. Martin said as how he would tell Mr. Hayle, sir, and Father said when he come home that I could mind the bridge till Mr. Hayle come down to see it."

"Mr. Martin—!" Theo checked himself. "Very well! See you mind it carefully, Tom! Mr. Hayle will be here presently."

The Earl flicked a shilling to Master Scrooby, and set his horse in motion down the ride. Orthes was encouraged to break into an easy canter, but in a moment or two the roan caught up with him. Theo said in his quiet way: "You had better tell me what it is that troubles you, Gervase. If you are thinking that Martin should have warned you, I daresay he might not have heard you say that you would ride to Hatherfield this morning."

"Is that what you think?"

"No," said Theo bluntly.

"Nor do I think it. Do you know, I am becoming a little tired of Martin? Perhaps he would be happier at Studham after all. Or, at any rate, I should be."

His cousin rode on beside him in silence, frowning slightly. After a pause, the Earl said: "You don't agree?"

"That he would be happier there? No. That doesn't signify, however, If you wish him to leave Stanyon, so be it! It will mean a breach, for he will not leave without making a deal of noise. Lady St. Erth, too, will not be silent, nor will she remain at Stanyon. What reason will you give for banishing Martin when he and she publish their wrongs to the rest of our relations?"

The Earl let Orthes drop to a walk. "Must I give any?"

"Unless you wish it to be thought that you have acted from caprice, or—which perhaps might be said by those who do not know you well—from rancour."

There was a pause. "How very longheaded you are, Theo!" Gervase complained. "You are quite right, of course. But what is the boy about? Does he hope to drive me away from Stanyon? He cannot be so big a clodpole!"

Theo shrugged. "There is no saying what he may

hope. But you cannot, I believe, shut your doors to him merely because he fenced once with the button off his foil, and did not warn you that a bridge was unsafe."

"Ah, there is a little more than that!" Gervase said.

"What more?"

Gervase hesitated. "Why, I did not mean to tell you this, but I woke last night to the conviction that someone was in my room."

Theo turned his head to stare at him under his brows. "In your room? Martin?"

"I can't tell that. I have certain reasons for suspecting it may have been he, but by the time I was up, and could pull back my curtain, there was no one there."

"Good God! Gervase, are you sure of this?"

"No, I am not sure, but I think that someone entered my room through the dressing-room. I heard what sounded to me like the click of a lock."

"I cannot think it! Why, if— But what reason have you to think it was Martin?"

"I found him on the gallery outside my room."

"What?"

"He said that he had been out—to Cheringham, a statement which I was disinclined to believe. Miss Morville, however, who was roused by the slamming of a door, considers that he may well have been speaking the truth. She seems to think he went there to see a cockfight."

"Very likely. But I had no idea of this! I thought he had had the head-ache! And you believe—"

"No, no I believe nothing! But I have a strong notion I shall take my pistols to bed with me while I remain at Stanyon! It will be quite like Peninsular days."

Theo smiled. "You have brought some desperate habits home with you! Only don't rouse the household by firing at a mouse which is unlucky enough to disturb your rest!"

"Nothing less than a rat, I promise you!" Gervase said gravely.

They proceeded on their way without further mishap. The Earl faithfully visited his old friend, Yelden; his cousin inspected the new plantation; and they returned to Stanyon at noon, by way of the main avenue, which traversed the Home Park from the seventeenth-century lodge, with its wrought-iron gates, to the original Gate-tower of the Castle, still in remarkably good preserva-tion, but no longer guarding a drawbridge. The moat having been filled in, the tower served no particular purpose, but figured in the guide-books as a fine example of fourteenth-century architecture. Through its vaulted archway the east, and main, entrance to the Castle was reached, which opened on to what had once been the outer bailey, and was now a handsome court, laid out with a broad gravel drive, and formal flower-beds.

As the cousins rode through the archway, a sporting curricle came into sight, drawn up by the steps leading to the front-door. A smart-looking groom was standing at the heads of the wheelers; and the equipage plainly belonged to someone aspiring to the highest crack of fashion, since it was drawn by four horses. This made Theo exclaim that he could not imagine who could have come to visit Stanyon in such a turn-out. He sounded scornful, but Gervase said in mock-reproof that he showed a shocking ignorance. "A curricle-and-*four,* my dear Theo, is the mark of the Nonesuch, let me tell you!

Now, whom have you in Lincolnshire who— Good God! I should know those horses!" He spurred forward as he spoke, and a gentleman in a driving-coat of white drab, and a hat with a high, conical crown and beaver brim, who had been conferring with Abney at the head of the wide stone steps, turned, saw him, and came down the steps again, calling out: "Hallo, there, Ger! Turn out, man! The enemy is upon you!"

"Lucy, by all that's wonderful!" the Earl ejaculated, sliding from the saddle, and gripping both his friend's hands. "My dear fellow! Where have you sprung from?"

"Been staying with the Caldbecks, dear old boy," explained his visitor. "Couldn't leave the country without seeing you! Now don't, *don't* think yourself bound to invite me to put up here! My man is following me with all my baggage, but I see how it is—you have no room!"

An airy gesture indicated the sprawling pile behind the speaker; a pair of bright eyes quizzed the Earl, who laughed, and retorted: "An attic—we will find room for you in an attic! Theo, can we house this fellow, do you think? My cousin, Lucy—Theo, this is Captain Lucius Austell—oh, no! I beg pardon! It is Lord Ulverston! When did you sell out, Lucy?"

"Not so long after you," replied Ulverston, exchanging a cordial handshake with Theo. "M'father felt, when m'grandfather died, that he couldn't have the three of us serving, so it fell to me to sell out. I told him I might as easily be killed in the streets of London as on any military service—never saw such a rabble of traffic in my life! Lisbon's nothing to it, dear boy!—but nothing would do for him but to have me in England!"

By this time, Theo had grasped that his cousin's friend was the heir to the Earl of Wrexham, who had lately succeeded to his father's dignities. He enquired civilly after his youngest brother, Cornelius, whom he had once met in the house of a common acquaintance, and the Viscount replied, with the insouciance which characterized him: "Haven't a notion how he is! Think he's on the West Indian station, but these naval fellows, you know, jaunter about the world so that there's no keeping up with them at all! Corney means to be a Rear or a Vice, or some such thing, but with the Frogs rompé'd, and poor old Boney sent off to some curst island or another, devil a bit of promotion will there be! Said so to Freddy, when I sold out, but he's just got his company, and thinks he'll command the regiment in a brace of shakes. D'you know my brother Freddy? No? Very dull dog: ought to have been the eldest! Often thought so!"

The Earl, who had been inspecting the horses, interrupted, saying over his shoulder: "How do you like 'em, Lucy?"

"Why, you old horse-chaunter, didn't you sell 'em to me with a warranty they were sixteen-mile-an-hour tits? Not a second above fifteen-and-a-half—word of a gentleman! Now, Ger, why *did* you sell 'em to me? Four good 'uns—complete to a shade!"

"Oh, my cousin preached economy to me! You may say they are my breakdowns!"

"Economy!" exclaimed Theo. "Pray, what did you give for your grays?"

"Grays?" said the Viscount. "Ger, not Bingham's grays? Well, by God, if I had known he had a mind to sell them—!"

His cloak-bag having been unstrapped from the back of the curricle, and borne into the house, the Viscount waved dismissal to his henchman, saying: "Take 'em away, Clarence! Take 'em away!" and tucked a hand in the Earl's arm. "Well, old fellow, how does it suit you after all? You look pretty stout!"

Theo took his bridle from Gervase, saying that he must go to the stables, and would lead Orthes. Gervase smiled his thanks, and led the Viscount into the Castle.

"I hope you mean to stay at Stanyon for several weeks, Lucy," he said. "I warn you, however, that it is a dreadful place! I daresay my mother-in-law will dislike it excessively that you have come to visit me— and in *such* a rig!"

"Ger! The Four-Horse Club!" protested the Viscount, shocked.

"I am aware. She will think you a coxcomb, and you will leave Stanyon tomorrow, routed by her Roman nose!"

"Parrot-faced, is she?" said the Viscount, interested. "Lay you a monkey she don't peck me! Dear boy, did you ever *see* my aunts? Three of 'em, all parrot-faced, and all hot at hand! Father's frightened of 'em—m'mother's frightened of 'em—Freddy won't face 'em! Only person who can handle 'em's me! No bamming—true as I stand here! Ask anyone!"

Whatever his success might have been in captivating his aunts, it seemed, for the first few minutes after his presentation to the Dowager, as though she must be reckoned amongst his failures. He had shed his driving-coat, a preposterous garment of inordinate length and a superfluity of shoulder-capes, but whatever might have been gained by this was lost, Gervase informed him, by the consequent revelation of a single-breasted coat with a long waist, a kerseymere waistcoat of blue and yellow stripes, white corduroy small-clothes, and short boots with immensely long tops. A black-spotted muslin cravat, and a Stanhope Crop to his brown locks added the final touches to his appearance, and did nothing to recommend him to his hostess. Her instinct led her to eye with revulsion any friend of her son-in-law, and her consequence was offended by his having awaited no invitation to visit Stanyon. On the other hand, his rank could not but make him acceptable to her; and it very soon transpired that she had once stood up for two dances at a Harrogate Assembly with his Uncle Lucius. By the time she had discovered, by a series of exhaustive questions and recollections, that a connection of hers, whom she traced through several marriages, had actually married the Viscount's cousin Amelia, the enormities of his dress and his lack of ceremony were alike forgiven, and she was ready to declare him to be a very pretty-behaved young man, and one whom she was glad to welcome to Stanyon. His man arriving at Stanyon during the course of the afternoon, in a hired post-chaise piled high with his baggage, he was able, before dinner, to change the insignia of the Four-Horse Club for the propriety of knee-breeches and a dark coat, and thus to confirm himself in her good graces. She hoped he might be persuaded to remain at Stanyon for the ball. He was all compliance and good-nature; led her in to dinner, sat on her right hand at the table, and regaled her with the details, with which she had long desired to be furnished, of the extraordinary circumstances leading to his Aunt Agatha's second marriage. Since his conversation was freely embellished with such cant terms as never failed to incur rebuke from her when they passed the lips of her son and her stepson, these gentlemen had nothing to do, according to their separate dispositions, but to admire the address which could carry off such unconventionalities, or to wonder at the unpredictability of elderly ladies.

Martin, who had sustained a painful interview with his cousin, sat down to dinner in a mood of offended hauteur. The table having been rearranged to accommodate the unexpected guest, he was seated on his half-brother's left hand; and he took advantage of an animated discussion on the rival merits of Brighton and Scarborough as watering-places to say to Gervase in an angry undervoice: "I collect that you rode to Hatherfield this morning, and found the bridge unsafe! I daresay you may have said that you had that intention, but I was not attending! In any event, I had warned Hayle already that the bridge had been damaged!"

"In fact," said Gervase, "had I broken my neck you would have been inconsolable."

"No, I shouldn't," said Martin bluntly. "But to say that I tried to contrive that you should is the outside of enough! Break your neck indeed! In *that* paltry stream!"

"Don't lie to me, but own that you *did* hear me say I would ride to Hatherfield, and hoped that I might tumble into a very muddy river!"

"Oh, well—!" Martin said, reddening, but grinning in spite of himself. He found that Gervase was regarding him thoughtfully, and added, in a defensive tone: "It's no concern of mine where you choose to ride! Of course, if

you had *asked* me—! However, you did not, and as for
there being the least danger of your being drowned—
pooh!" He appeared to find some awkwardness in continuing the discussion, and said: "You won't have forgot
that we are to go to Whissenhurst this evening. I have
ordered the carriage; for Drusilla goes too. Do you care
to accompany me, or shall you drive yourself?"

"No, I don't go. Present my compliments and my
excuses to Lady Bolderwood, if you please!" Gervase
turned from him, as he spoke, to address some remark
to Miss Morville, who, never having visited Scarborough, had retired from the argument still being carried
on by the other persons seated at the table.

When the ladies presently withdrew, Martin also left
the table, saying that he must not keep Miss Morville
waiting. Theo, suggesting that his cousin might wish to
be alone with Lord Ulverston, engaged himself to keep
the Dowager tolerably well amused with a few rubbers
of piquet. This good-natured scheme for the Earl's relief
was rendered abortive, however, by her having previously extorted a promise from the Viscount to join her
presently for a game of whist. This was kept up for
some time after the appearance of the tea-table, the
Dowager declaring that she scarcely knew how to tear
herself away from the cards. "Twenty minutes to
eleven!" she said, consulting the clock on the mantelshelf. "I shall be worn-out with dissipation. In general,
you must know, I do not care to play after ten o'clock:
it does not suit me; but this evening I have so much
enjoyed the rubbers that I am not conscious of the hour.
You play a very creditable game, Ulverston. I am no flat-
terer, so you may believe me when I say that I have been

very well entertained. My dear father was a notable card-player, and I believe I have inherited his aptitude. Dear me, it will be wonderful if I am asleep before midnight! I shall not wait for Miss Morville to return, for if they are engaged in dancing, or speculation, at Whissenhurst, you know, there is no saying when she and Martin will come back. We will go to prayers immediately."

Before this programme could be enforced on the company, the door opened to admit the two absentees. Their early return was explained, composedly by Miss Morville, and with great discontent by Martin. They had arrived at Whissenhurst to find Sir Thomas indisposed; and although his lady apprehended no cause for serious anxiety, he had gone to bed with a sore throat and a feverish pulse, and she had sent a message to Dr. Malpas, desiring him to call at the Grange in the morning. Her fear was that Sir Thomas had contracted influenza; and in these circumstances Miss Morville had not thought it proper to remain after tea had been drunk.

"If only Marianne does not take it from him!" Martin exclaimed. "One would have thought he need not have chosen this moment of all others to be ill! He might have caught influenza last month, and welcome—and, to be sure, I don't know why he could not have done so, when half the countryside was abed with it! But no! Nothing will do but for him to be ill just when we are to hold our ball! I shouldn't be at all surprised if the Bolderwoods do not come! It is all of a piece!"

"Shabby fellow!" said Ulverston, looking amused. "But so it is always with these crusty old men! They delight in plaguing the rest of us!"

"Oh, well, as to that, I would not call him *crusty!*" Martin owned.

"Ah, now you are being over-generous, I feel!"

"Sir Thomas is a very respectable man," pronounced the Dowager. "We will send to enquire at Whissenhurst tomorrow, and I have no doubt that we shall receive a comfortable account of him. He would be very sorry not to be able to come to Stanyon, I daresay."

"What," demanded the Viscount, a little later, when Gervase had borne him away to the library on the entrance floor of the Castle, "is the peculiar virtue of Sir Thomas, which makes his presence indispensable to the success of your ball?"

Gervase laughed. "A daughter!"

"A daughter! Very well! I don't need to ask, is she beautiful?"

"Very beautiful, very engaging!"

"What a shocking thing it would be, then, for Sir Thomas to cry off! I shall certainly remain with you for a long visit, Ger!"

"Nothing could please me more, but take care you don't tread upon Martin's corns!"

"How can you, after watching my conciliatory manners this night, think such an event possible? What is the matter with that halfling?"

"Indulgence!"

The Viscount stretched out his hand for the glass of wine Gervase had poured for him. "I see. And is he in love with Sir Thomas's daughter?"

"Calf-love. He is ready to murder me for—" Gervase stopped, his hand arrested in the act of pouring a second glass of wine. "For flirting with her," he ended lightly.

The Viscount's countenance was cherubic, but his eyes held a good deal of shrewdness. He said: "I perceive, of course, that he is ready to murder you, my Tulip. Tell me about the damaged bridge!"

"Oh, so you heard that, did you? I had thought you absorbed in the attractions of the Steyne!"

"Very sharp ears, dear boy!" apologized the Viscount.

"There is nothing to tell. The storm last night cracked one of the supports to a wooden bridge thrown over a stream here, and Martin neglected to warn me of it. He is jealous of me, you see, and I think he felt it would do me good to be ducked in muddy water."

"But what a delightful young man!" commented the Viscount. "*Were* you ducked?"

"No, my cousin was with me, and had some apprehension that the bridge might not be safe. In justice to Martin, he had already given instructions that the bridge should be barred. A schoolboy trick: no more."

"Your cousin gave him a fine dressing for it: I heard him," said Ulverston, sipping his wine.

"Did he? A pity! It was not worth making a noise about it."

"Well, he seemed to think there was more to it than a schoolboy's trick. Is there?"

"Of course there is not! Now, Lucy, what's all this?"

"Beg pardon! It's these ancestral walls of yours," explained the Viscount. "Too dashed mediaeval, dear boy! They put the oddest notions into my head!"

CHAPTER EIGHT

IT WAS MARTIN WHO offered to be the bearer, on the following morning, of polite messages of condolence from his mother to Lady Bolderwood. He returned to Stanyon with no very encouraging tidings. Dr. Malpas had given it as his opinion that Sir Thomas's disorder was indeed the influenza, and since Sir Thomas was of a bronchial habit he had strictly forbidden him to leave his bed for several days, much less his house. Marianne did not despair, however, of being able to attend the ball, for her Mama had promised that she would not scruple, unless Sir Thomas should become very much worse, to leave old Nurse in charge of the sick-room while she chaperoned her daughter to Stanyon.

But the following morning brought a servant from Whissenhurst to Stanyon, with a letter for the Dowager from Marianne. It was a primly-worded little note, but a blister on the sheet betrayed that tears had been shed over it. The writer regretted that, owing to the sudden indisposition of her Mama, it would be out of her power to come to Stanyon on the following evening. In fact, Lady Bolderwood had fallen a victim to the influenza.

The Dowager, in announcing these tidings, said that it was very shocking; but it was plain that she considered the Bolderwoods more to be commiserated than the Stanyon party. They would no doubt soon recover from the influenza, but they would have missed being amongst the guests at Stanyon, which she thought a privation not so readily to be recovered from. "How sorry they will be!" she said. "They would have liked it excessively."

"It is the most curst thing!" Martin cried. "It ruins everything!"

"Yes, indeed, my dear, I am extremely vexed," agreed the Dowager. "We shall now have *two* more gentlemen than ladies, and I daresay it will be quite uncomfortable. I warned your brother how it would be."

It was not to be expected that this point of view would be much appreciated by either of her sons. Each felt that if Marianne were not to grace it the ball might as well be cancelled. Nothing but languor and insipidity could now lie before them.

"I wonder," said Miss Morville, after glancing from Martin's face to St. Erth's, "if the difficulty might not perhaps be overcome?"

"I am sure, my dear Drusilla, I do not know whom we could prevail upon to come to the ball at such short notice," replied the Dowager. "No doubt the Dearhams would accept an invitation with alacrity, and bless themselves for their good fortune, but I consider them pushing and vulgar, and if St. Erth expects me to entertain them I must say at once that it is out of the question that I should do so."

"I have not the slightest desire to invite the Dearhams, whoever they may be," said the Earl, rather impatiently.

"I should think not indeed!" Martin said. "The

Dearhams in place of Miss Bolderwood! That would be coming it a little too strong, ma'am! Nobody cares if there are too many men: the thing is that if Marianne doesn't come I for one would rather we postponed the ball!"

Miss Morville made herself heard again, speaking with a little diffidence, but with all her usual good sense. "I was going to suggest, ma'am, that, if you should not dislike it, Marianne might be invited to stay at Stanyon for a day or two, while her parents are confined to their beds. It must be sad work for her at Whissenhurst with no one to bear her company all day. You may depend upon it she is not even permitted the comfort of being able to attend to her Mama. They take such care of her, you know, that I am very sure she is not allowed to enter the sick-room."

"By Jupiter, the very thing!" Martin exclaimed, his face lighting up.

"Miss Morville, you are an excellent creature!" Gervase said, smiling gratefully at her. "I don't know where we should be without your sage counsel!"

The Dowager naturally saw a great many objections to a scheme not of her own devising, but after she had stated these several times, and had been talked to soothingly by Miss Morville and vehemently by her son, she began to think that it might not be so very bad after all. The Earl having the wisdom not to put forward any solicitations of his own, it was not long before she perceived a number of advantages to the plan. Martin would have the opportunity to enjoy Marianne's society, Drusilla would have the benefit of her companionship, and the Bolderwoods would doubtless think themselves very much obliged to their kind neighbour. Such benevolent reflections put her ladyship into good-humour, and she needed little persuasion to induce her to say that she would drive to Whissenhurst that very day, and bring Marianne back with her.

It then became necessary to discuss exhaustively the rival merits of her ladyship's chaise and her landaulet as a means of conveyance. From this debate the gentlemen withdrew in good order; and the Dowager, having weighed the chances of rain against the certainty of one of the passengers being obliged to sit forward, if she went to Whissenhurst in her chaise ("For there will be the maid to be conveyed, you know, and I should not care to go without you to bear me company, my dear Drusilla!"), decided in favour of the landaulet. Martin then very nobly offered to escort the ladies on their perilous journey, riding beside the carriage; and all that remained to be done was to decide whether the Dowager should wrap herself in her sables, or in her ermine stole. Even this ticklish point was settled; and midway through the afternoon the party was ready to set out, the only delay being caused by the Dowager's last-minute decision to carry a genteel basket of fruit from the succession-houses to the sufferers. "One would not wish to be backward in any attention," she explained. "To be sure, we have very little fruit at this period of the year, but I daresay St. Erth will not miss *one* each of his peaches and apricots and nectarines. I have directed Calne to fill up the basket with some of our apples, which I daresay Lady Bolderwood will be very glad to have, for the Stanyon apples, you know, are particularly good."

Miss Morville encouraging her to suppose that St. Erth would be only too happy to sacrifice his fruit to the

Bolderwoods, she was then ready to depart. The two ladies took their seats in the landaulet; a footman tenderly laid a rug about the knees; the basket of fruit was disposed upon the forward seat; Martin swung himself into the saddle of his good-looking bay hack; and the cavalcade set forth.

The way was beguiled by the Dowager in extolling her vicarious generosity in giving away her son-in-law's fruit, in calling upon Miss Morville to admire her son's admirable appearance on horseback, and in discovering that the bulbs in the various gardens which they passed on the road were not as far forward as those at Stanyon. They arrived at Whissenhurst in good time, without having been obliged to rely upon Martin's gallantry to rescue them from footpads or highwaymen, and were received there by Marianne, who came running out of the house at sight of the landaulet, and expressed her sense of obligation for the condescension shown her in such warm terms as served to convince her ladyship that she was a very pretty-behaved young woman, worthy to match with her son. A brief explanation of her purpose in coming to Whissenhurst Grange was enough to throw Marianne into ecstasies. It was as Miss Morville had supposed: solicitude for her well-being had compelled Lady Bolderwood to forbid her most strictly to enter either sick-room. She had nothing to do but to regret the misfortune which prevented her from gracing the Stanyon ball.

The only difficulty was, how to obtain Lady Bolderwood's consent to so delightful a scheme? Nurse was so cross she would be of no assistance: Marianne did not know what was to be done. Happily, Miss Morville was unafraid of the dangers attaching to sick-rooms, and she alighted from the landaulet with the express purpose of visiting Lady Bolderwood. The Dowager then permitted Marianne to escort her to the shrubbery, which she had the happiness of discovering to be not so extensive as that at Stanyon; and in a little while Miss Morville rejoined her with the welcome intelligence that Lady Bolderwood was most grateful to her for her kind thought, and would be pleased to allow her daughter to sojourn at Stanyon while she was confined to her chamber.

This was not strictly accurate. It did not quite suit Lady Bolderwood's nice sense of propriety that Marianne should make her first appearance at a formal ball unattended by herself, but against the decree of her husband she was powerless to resist. *He* could perceive nothing in the invitation that was not agreeable. They might entrust their treasure to Lady St. Erth's care with quiet minds; and how shocking a thing it would be to deny her this pleasure from some nonsensical scruple! He did not like to think of her moping about the house in solitude; he would be happy to know that she was being so well entertained, and in such unexceptionable hands. To find herself amongst a company of exalted persons would put her into excellent training for her coming London Season: he could not imagine what his Maria could find amiss in such a scheme. Lady Bolderwood acquiesced, therefore, her maternal agitation finding its only expression in the urgent messages which she charged Nurse to deliver to Marianne. These ranged from reminders of the conduct to be expected of débutantes, to the sum of money it would be proper to bestow upon the maidservant who waited on her, and the ornaments which she should wear with her ball-dress. Marianne's maid, overjoyed at such an enlargement to her horizon, began to pack a number of trunks and band-boxes, the only alloy to her delight being the gloomily expressed conviction of Sir Thomas's second footman that her pleasure had its root in the expectation of receiving the addresses of all the libertines employed at the Castle.

Marianne's own happiness knew no other bounds than regret that her Mama could not make one of the party. Had she been permitted to do so, she would have rendered her parents' malady still more hideous by smoothing their pillows, coaxing them to swallow bowls of gruel, and begging them to tell her, just as they were dropping into sleep, if there was anything she could do for them to make them more comfortable; but this solace had been denied her, so that she could not believe herself to be necessary to them. Her Papa bade her go to Stanyon and enjoy herself; her Mama, endorsing this command, only added a warning that she should conduct herself modestly; and as she had not the smallest inclination to go beyond the bounds of propriety she had nothing to do but to thank Lady St. Erth again and again for her exceeding kindness, and to prepare for several days of unsullied amusement. Her transports led her to embrace the Dowager, an impulsive action which, though it startled that lady, by no means displeased her. "A very good-hearted girl," she told Miss Morville, when Marianne had run away to put on her hat and her pelisse. "I am glad that I had the happy notion of inviting her to stay at Stanyon."

Miss Morville assented to it with great calmness. She did not feel it incumbent upon her to disclose to the Dowager the anxious qualms with which Lady Bolderwood parted from her daughter; but the truth was that the invitation was by no means welcome to Lady Bolderwood. While agreeing with Sir Thomas that her indisposition condemned Marianne to several days of solitary boredom, she still could not like her going alone to such a party as was contemplated at Stanyon. Sir Thomas said that their little puss could be trusted to keep the line; she could place no such dependence on the discretion of an eighteen-year-old girl, nor had she much faith in the Dowager's capabilities as a chaperon. "Lady St. Erth," she said, "is *not* the woman I should choose to entrust Marianne to!"

Miss Morville said that she would be at Stanyon, and would take care of Marianne.

"My dear," said Lady Bolderwood, pressing her hand, "if it were not for *that* circumstance I could not bring myself to consent to such an arrangement! I should not say it, but I have no great liking for Lady St. Erth! Then, too, it has to be remembered that Marianne is an heiress, and if there is *one* thing above all others which I do not wish, it is to see her exposed to every gazetted fortune-hunter in England! She is too innocent to detect mere flattery; and even were Lady St. Erth the best-natured woman alive, which I do not scruple to assert she is *not,* it would be unreasonable to expect her to guard a young girl as her own mother would!"

Miss Morville, who had written all the invitations for the Dowager, said that she did not think that Marianne would encounter any fortune-hunters at Stanyon. She added that the ball would be quite a small one, and that the guests, for the most part, were already known to Lady Bolderwood. With this assurance the anxious mother had to be content. She sent a loving message of farewell to Marianne; and Marianne, who anticipated no attacks, either upon her expectations or upon her virtue, danced out to the landaulet, with her eyes and her cheeks aglow with happiness. She looked so pretty, in a swansdown-trimmed bonnet and pelisse, that Martin caught his breath at sight of her.

So, too, a little later, did Lord Ulverston.

After his first rapture at the thought of having Marianne to stay at Stanyon had abated a little, it had occurred to Martin that the visit would afford his half-brother many undesirable opportunities for flirtation. It had not occurred to him that he might find a rival in Lord Ulverston, for although his lordship certainly drove a magnificent team of horses, wore the coveted insignia of the Whip Club, and showed himself in all respects a man of fashion, he was not handsome, and his figure, seen beside any one of the three Frants, was not imposing. Martin, who stood over six foot in his bare feet, thought of him as a little on the squat. He was, in fact, of medium height and compact build; and if his features were not classical his smile was engaging, and his address considerable. It almost deserted him at the dazzling sight which met his eyes, but he made a quick recovery, and sprang forward to hand Marianne out of the carriage before Martin had dismounted, and long before the Dowager had performed the proper introductions.

Since the dinner-hour at Stanyon was at half-past six, Miss Morville lost no time in escorting Marianne to her bed-chamber, a pleasant room next to her own, with a modern, barred grate, and a comfortable tent-bed. Marianne, looking about her at the flowered wallpaper, and all the evidences of up-to-date taste, seemed a little disappointed, and confided that she had expected to find herself in a panelled room, with a four-poster bed, and a powder-closet.

"Well, it *could* be arranged for you to sleep in one of the panelled rooms," said Miss Morville. "Only it will set you at a little distance from me, and I had thought you would prefer to be near me."

Marianne assured her that she would not change her room for the world. "I thought all the rooms were panelled!" she explained. "Is not the Castle of vast antiquity?"

"Oh, not this part of it!" said Miss Morville. "I think it was built at the time of Charles II. I fancy that not much of the original Castle still remains. If you are interested in antiquities, you should ask Theo Frant to take you over the whole building: he knows all about it."

"Is it haunted?" breathed Marianne, in delightful trepidation.

"Oh, no, nothing of that sort!" Miss Morville said reassuringly. She then perceived that she had given the wrong answer, and added: "At least, it may be, but I am not at all fanciful, you know, and I daresay I might not be conscious of the supernatural."

"Oh, but, Drusilla, if a spectre without a head were to walk the corridors, or a female form in gray draperies, *surely* you would be conscious of it!" cried Marianne, much shocked.

"If I saw a female form in gray draperies I should

take it for Lady St. Erth," said Miss Morville apologetically. "She has a gray dressing-gown, you see. However, a headless spectre would certainly surprise me very much. Indeed, it would very likely give me a distaste for the Castle, so I hope I never shall see such an apparition."

"Give you a distaste for the Castle! Oh no, how can you be so unromantic?" protested her youthful friend.

"To own the truth," replied Miss Morville candidly, "I can perceive of nothing romantic in a headless spectre. I should think it a very disagreeable sight, and if I did fancy I saw such a thing I should take one of Dr. James's powders *immediately!*"

Marianne was obliged to laugh; but she shook her head as well, and was persuaded that her friend could not be serious.

Miss Morville then went to her own room, to change her dress, promising to discover from Theo if they might reasonably expect to see a horrid apparition in any part of the Castle. She returned presently to escort Marianne to the Long Drawing-room, and, finding her charmingly attired in sprigged muslin, strongly recommended her to wrap a shawl round her shoulders. Though the Castle might lack a ghost, she said, it was well-provided with draughts.

"Provoking creature!" Marianne pouted. "You are determined to be prosaic, but I shan't attend to you!"

They found the rest of the party already assembled in the Long Drawing-room, gathered about a noble fire. The Earl came forward to draw the young ladies into the circle, and Marianne, with a droll look, complained of Drusilla's insensibility. "But she says that I must ask *you,* Mr. Frant, for the history of Stanyon, and you will tell it all to me—all about the secret dungeons, and the oubliette, and the ghost!"

Theo smiled, but replied ruefully that he could offer her neither ghost nor oubliette. "And I hardly dare to tell you that the dungeons were converted many years ago into wine cellars!" he confessed. "As for ghosts, I never heard of one here, did you, Gervase?"

"None beyond the shade that flits across the Fountain Court, weeping, and wringing its hands," the Earl replied, with a composed countenance.

Marianne clasped her own hands together, and fixed her eyes on his face. "Oh, no! Do you mean it? And is that the only ghost? Does it not enter the Castle?"

"I have never known it to do so," he said truthfully. "Of course, we have not put you in the Haunted Room—*that* would never do! The noise of clanking chains would make it impossible for you to sleep, and the groans, you know, are dreadful to hear. You will not be disturbed by anything of that nature, I hope. And if you *should* happen to hear the sound of a coach-and-four under your window at midnight, pay no heed!"

"For shame, Gervase!" exclaimed Theo, laughing, as Marianne gave an involuntary shudder.

"What is it that you are saying, St. Erth?" called the Dowager, breaking off her conversation with Ulverston. "You are talking a great deal of nonsense! If any such thing were to happen I should be excessively displeased, for Calne has orders to lock the gates every night."

"Ah, ma'am, but what can locked gates avail against a phantom?"

"Phantom! Let me assure you that we have nothing of that sort at Stanyon! I should not countenance it; I do not approve of the supernatural."

Her disapproval was without its effect, the gentlemen continuing to tease Marianne with accounts of spectres, and Martin achieving a decided success with a very horrid monkish apparition, which, when it raised its head, was seen to have only a skull under its cowl. "It is known as the Black Monk of Stanyon," he informed Marianne. "It—it appears only to the head of the house, and then as a death-warning!"

She turned her eyes involuntarily towards Gervase. "Oh, no!" she said imploringly, hardly knowing whether to be horrified or diverted. "You are not serious!"

"Hush!" he said, in an earnest tone. "Martin should not have disclosed to you the Secret of Stanyon: we never speak of it! It is a very dreadful sight."

"Well, I don't know how you should know *that*," remarked Miss Morville, a good deal amused. "You cannot have seen it, after all!"

"My dear Miss Morville, what makes you think so?"

"You are not dead!" she pointed out.

"Not *yet!*" struck in Ulverston, in sepulchral accents. "We cannot tell, however, when we may find him stiff in his bed, his fingers still clutching the bell-rope, and an expression on his face of the greatest terror!"

"No, no! Oh, you are roasting me! I do not believe it!" Marianne said faintly.

Her cheeks were quite blanched, and she could not resist the impulse to look over her shoulder. The Earl judged it to be time to have done, and to assure her that the Black Monk existed only in Martin's imagination. The Dowager set Lord Ulverston right on a little misapprehension, telling him that the bell-rope in the Earl's bedchamber hung beside the fireplace, and was out of reach of the bed. This was an inconvenience which she continued to deplore until dinner was announced; and as Miss Morville, rallied on her lack of sensibility, said that she could not be terrified by tales of skeletons, since these could only be produced by human contrivance, Marianne's alarms were soon sufficiently dispelled to enable her to eat her dinner with a good appetite, and not to suppose that if she glanced behind her at the footman about to present a syllabub to her she would discover him to be a fleshless monk.

The Dowager's benevolence had not led her to make any plans for the entertainment of her young guest, but when she discovered that the party numbered eight persons, she directed that a second card-table should be set up, so that those who did not play whist with herself might enjoy a rubber of Casino. "Mr. Clowne, and my nephew, Mr. Theo Frant, will make up our table," she informed Lord Ulverston. "You, I know, will prefer to play whist!"

The grace with which the Viscount accepted this decree was only equalled by the dexterity with which he convinced her ladyship that she would be better amused by a game of speculation. To her objection that she had never played the game, he responded that it would afford him delight to teach her. He seated himself on her right hand; and not even Martin, whose jealous disposition made him at all times suspicious, could decide whether it was by chance, or deep stratagem, that

Marianne was placed on his other side. To her he largely
devoted himself, cheating himself to enable her to win
fish, and keeping her in a ripple of laughter with his in-
consequent chatter. Fortunately for the Dowager, Mr.
Clowne, who sat on her left, considered that it behoved
him to direct bids; and since she was acquisitive by
nature it was not long before she grasped the principles
of the game, and was making some pretty shrewd bids
on her own account.

Seldom had an evening at Stanyon passed more
merrily. No one noticed the appearance of the tea-tray,
and it was very nearly midnight before the party broke
up.

On the following morning, an exercise in manoeu-
vres was won by the Earl, not, as his indignant friend
told him, so much by superior strategy as by inner
knowledge. The Viscount, suggesting that a riding-party
should be formed, was countered by the Earl, who said
that there was no horse in the stables accustomed to
carrying a lady, and followed up this advantage by
offering to let Miss Bolderwood drive his famous grays.
Martin, only deterred from pressing the claims of his
Troubadour as a safe lady's hack by the recollection that
the only lady's saddle at Stanyon was of an antiquated
design, quite unsuitable for Marianne's use, owned
himself to be very much obliged to Miss Morville, who
ventured to suggest that her own riding-horse could
easily be brought to Stanyon from Gilbourne House
for Miss Bolderwood's use.

It was of no avail. "Your horse shall of course be
fetched, ma'am," said the Earl, "but it is you who must
ride him! I know Miss Bolderwood too well to indulge

myself with the thought that she will set forth on any expedition while you remain at home!"

It was enough. Marianne declared that nothing would induce her to do so at the expense of her friend, and Miss Morville, who would have been happier to have attended to all the last-minute preparations for the evening's ball, was obliged to form one of the party bound for Whissenhurst, to enquire after the progress of the invalids there.

The expedition, after a vain attempt to persuade Theo into joining it, consisted of Marianne and the Earl, in the curricle, accompanied by Miss Morville, Lord Ulverston, and Martin, upon horseback. Martin's infatuation led him to stay as close to the curricle as the narrowness of the lanes permitted, but Lord Ulverston's manners were too well-bred to allow of his following this example. He devoted himself to Miss Morville, and, through the accident of his having once read one of her Mama's excellent novels when he was confined to bed with a bad chill and could find nothing else to his hand, contrived to maintain an animated conversation with her all the way to Whissenhurst.

Comfortable tidings having been received from old Nurse, every qualm was assuaged in Marianne's breast. She need not think herself a renegade; she could be happy in the knowledge that her parents were much amended, and wished her well.

"You show great aptitude as a whip, Miss Bolderwood," the Viscount told her, upon their leaving Whissenhurst Grange. "I have been observing you closely, and have derived no inconsiderable pleasure from the sight. But St. Erth is not the man to teach you those niceties which you should know! Ger, dear boy, take my horse, and relinquish your place beside Miss Bolderwood to me! I will show her how to feather-edge a corner."

"Yes, pray do!" Marianne said eagerly. "I collect that you are a member of the Four-Horse Club, and only think how I shall astonish Papa when I tell him that I have had a lesson from one of the first whips in the country!"

"*My* trick, I fancy, Ger!" murmured the Viscount, giving his bridle into St. Erth's hand.

"The treachery of one's friends affords food for much melancholy reflection," retorted St. Erth. "I warn you, I shall come about, and my revenge may well terrify you!"

"*I* would not have yielded so tamely!" muttered Martin, as the Viscount mounted lightly into the curricle.

"I can believe it, but I think myself very well-placed," replied his brother, swinging himself into the saddle. "That is a nice hack of yours, Miss Morville, and I fancy you have light hands. Do you hunt at all?"

She could not but be pleased with the good-breeding which not only kept him at her side, but prevented his emulating Martin's example in trying to ride as close to the curricle as possible. He continued to converse with her like a man satisfied with her company; and upon finding an open farm gate, suggested that they should leave the lane for the refreshment of a canter through the fields. The crops, which were so far forward that year as to have put an early end to the hunting season, made it necessary for them to skirt the fields rather than to cross them, but they enjoyed an agreeable ride, and reached Stanyon some time before the rest

of their party. The Earl hoped that the exertion would
not have made Miss Morville too tired to stand up for
every dance that evening, a civility which amused her,
since she meant to spend the afternoon, not, as he
seemed to suppose, in recruiting her energies for the
night's festivity, but in attending to all the details attaching to the entertainment of a large number of guests with
which her hostess was a great deal too indolent to
concern herself. Neither she nor the late Earl had been
fond of entertaining, and since the marriage of their
daughter no ball had been held at Stanyon. The housekeeper and the steward were thrown into a fluster by so
rare an event, and although they enjoyed all the consequence of being called upon to provide for the accommodation of the ducal party from Belvoir, besides
catering for the refreshment of some twenty persons at
dinner, and forty more at supper, they were unaccustomed to such grand doings, and depended on Miss
Morville, in default of their mistress, to advise on the
number of rout-cakes it would be proper to bake; the
propriety of serving tea and coffee at supper, as well as
lemonade and champagne; and what apartments ought
to be allotted to the several guests who were to spend
the night at Stanyon. Then there were the musicians to
be thought of: where they should be lodged, and whose
duty it was to wait upon them; the arrangement of the
flowers to superintend; the number of card-tables to be
set up in the Italian Saloon to be decided on; and sufficient chairs to be disposed about the ballroom for those
either desirous of watching the dancing, or unfortunate
enough to have no partners.

The Earl, finding Miss Morville in conference with

Abney, was a little conscience-stricken. "My dear ma'am, had I dreamed that all the labour of the ball was to fall upon you I would not have suggested we should give a ball at all! I should think you must bear me a considerable grudge!"

"No, indeed! I am happy to be of service, and this sort of contriving, you know, is exactly what I like."

"You do it very well," he said, looking about him at the flowers, and at the clean packs of cards laid ready on the several tables. "You remember all the details which I am very sure I must have forgotten."

"Very likely you might," she agreed. "Now, if you will excuse me, I must leave you. Lady St. Erth received an express from your sister this morning, informing her that she and Lord Grampound would be pleased to come to the party, and I find she has not told Mrs. Marple of it. I daresay her ladyship would wish to be given her former apartments, and we had arranged, you know, to put the Ashbournes in them."

"Louisa coming!" he exclaimed. "Good God, what folly! Who can have invited her to undertake a journey of eighty miles for a ball of no particular consequence?"

"I don't think anyone invited her," replied Miss Morville, "but I expect Lady St. Erth may have mentioned that a ball was to be held here. That, if you will not mind my saying so, would be enough to bring her."

"More than enough! She is the most tiresome, inquisitive woman of my acquaintance, I believe!"

"Her understanding is not powerful," said Miss Morville, "nor are her manners such as must universally please, but she is *not*, I think, ill-natured, and although she may *regret* your existence, I fancy she does not dislike you, or even hold you to blame for being older than her brother."

"I am very much obliged to her! This is something indeed!" he said sardonically.

She smiled, but would say no more; and upon the housekeeper's looking into the room, went away to confer with her on the necessary alteration in the bedchambers.

CHAPTER NINE

NONE OF THE GUESTS was expected to arrive at the Castle before five o'clock, at which hour it was thought that those who had been invited to stay the night at Stanyon might be looked for; but at a little after three Miss Morville, who happened to be in one of the saloons which overlooked the main entrance-drive, saw to her dismay that two large travelling-coaches were drawing up below the terrace. A stockily-built gentleman, just dismounted from his horse, chanced to look round, and Miss Morville recognized, with a sinking heart, the commonplace features of Lord Grampound. The servants were letting down the steps of the two coaches, and in another instant Miss Morville's worst fears were realized: Lord and Lady Grampound had brought their interesting offspring with them to Stanyon.

The reason was soon explained. As soon as all the bustle of greeting the visitors had abated, Lady Grampound, a young woman in her twenty-sixth year who already showed promise of closely resembling her mother, disclosed that the entire party was on its way to visit old Lady Grampound in Derbyshire. "She has been wanting for ever to see the children, you know, Mama, and since I was determined to come to your ball, it seemed an excellent scheme to bring them, for it is all on our way, or very little out of it, I am sure."

The Dowager was perfectly ready to accept her daughter's geography, nor could she conceive that two dear little boys of four and three years old could be the smallest trouble to her. In this she spoke nothing but the truth, for she made no attempt to arrange for their accommodation, and when they became too noisy for her comfort their nurses removed them from her vicinity. Their mother said complacently that she did not know when she had seen them in such high spirits. "It is coming to Stanyon which has occasioned it. I am sure if Harry has asked me once when we are to set forward on the journey he has asked me a hundred times. I knew St. Erth would be happy to see them: I told Grampound we need not scruple to bring them with us."

The Earl, admirably concealing his transports, asked his half-sister how long they were to have the pleasure of entertaining her at Stanyon. She replied regretfully that she would be obliged to continue her journey upon the following day. Everyone but the Dowager began to look more cheerful, but a damper was cast on the spirits of one of the company when her ladyship added: "It is a vast pity, to be sure, and poor little Harry screamed for half an hour at least when I told him we should not remain at Stanyon above a night. Dear little fellow! He has never forgot his Uncle Martin's kindness in taking him up before him on his horse, and riding with him round the Park, and now Johnny is wild for the treat too! However, I assured them they should have the indulgence of a ride with their uncle tomorrow morning, and, indeed, I do not know how I should contrive to tear them away unless this was granted them!"

Their fond Uncle Martin looked anything but gratified, but managed to control his feelings until he found himself out of earshot of his sister. He then declared that if Louisa imagined that he meant to waste his time in amusing her children she would find herself very much mistaken.

"Good God, Martin, are you mad?" demanded Gervase. "You will take those brats for rides as soon as they have swallowed their breakfasts, if Theo and I have to tie you to the saddle! Did you not hear Louisa say that she could not tear them from us until they had been granted this indulgence?"

Martin grinned, but said with considerable aplomb that he thought the boys would prefer to ride upon Cloud's back.

"Nothing," said Gervase instantly, "would afford me greater delight than to set them up before me on Cloud, but the melancholy truth is that though he is in general perfectly docile, he cannot abide the sight of small boys. I do not know how it is, but—"

"No, nor anyone else!" interrupted Martin indignantly. "You are the most complete hand!"

"I am, and I give you fair warning that you will leave Stanyon tomorrow, never to return, unless you oblige your nephews in this small matter!"

An expression of deep cunning entered Martin's eyes; he said in a conspiratorial tone: "I say, Gervase, could we not prevail upon *Theo*—?"

"The very thing!" exclaimed Gervase. "For anything we know, he dotes upon young children!"

"Who does?" enquired the subject of this plot,

entering the room in time to overhear this observation. He laughed, when the stratagem was disclosed to him, and said that nothing but their kind Uncle Martin would satisfy the boys. "And since Martin was so foolish as to set up such a precedent it is only right that he should bear the consequences," he added. "Do either of you know where Drusilla is to be found? Some arrangements must be made for the boys' supper, and I believe she is the best person to employ in approaching the head-cook."

"Unfortunate Drusilla!" commented the Earl. "What havoc are my little nephews creating now? When I left her ladyship's dressing-room they had done nothing more than set fire to the hearthrug."

"Have no fear! Miss Bolderwood has taken them to the Crimson Saloon, to play at spillikins!" said Theo.

This intelligence had the instant effect of sending the Earl and his brother off to participate in a sport for which each discovered in himself a forgotten, but strong, predilection.

Lady Grampound, meanwhile, was enjoying a *tête-à-tête* with her Mama, while her husband, himself a landowner, was wandering about the stables and the Home Farm, observing every improvement there since his last visit, and contrasting them all unfavourably with those on his own estate.

Lady Grampound's object in coming to Stanyon was to meet Marianne rather than to dance at the ball; and since Marianne's good-manners led her to say that she had never seen stouter or more intelligent children than Harry and John, and her sunny good-nature made it no hardship to her to play with them, her ladyship had no hesitation in declaring her to be a delightful girl, and one to whom she would be happy to see her brother married.

"It is such a shocking thing that poor Martin should be cut out of the succession!" she said. "I was never more grieved than when I heard that Gervase had come through the engagement at Genappe without a scratch, for, you know, the Seventh were heavily engaged there, and one might have supposed— But it was not to be, and, to be sure, I wish him no harm, if only he were not older than Martin. Indeed, I am excessively attached to him, and I shall never forget that he sent dear little Johnny a most handsome christening-gift. But if poor Martin is to be cut out he must marry well, and I do believe Miss Bolderwood is the very girl for him. She seems quite un-exceptionable, and they say, Mama, that Sir Thomas must be worth every penny of a hundred thousand pounds, and very likely more. The only thing I do not quite like is to find Ulverston visiting at Stanyon. To be sure, I never heard that he was hanging out for a wife, but now that his Papa has succeeded to the Earldom he must be desirous of seeing his son established, and there is no denying that Ulverston has considerable address. However, he is a man of easy fortune, so that to marry an heiress cannot be an object with him."

This observation caused the Dowager to suffer a qualm. It was but momentary. Her mind was not receptive of new ideas, nor could she suppose that there existed a young man more capable of engaging a maiden's fancy than her own son. He was tall, handsome, and well-born; and such faults of temper as he showed she regarded in much the same light as her daughter looked on the disobedience of her two little boys: every defect was due to high spirits.

Not being concerned to any very great degree with anything beyond the bounds of her immediate family, Lady Grampound soon passed to topics of more interest to her, and in recounting to her parent little Harry's progress in ciphering, Johnny's tendency to bronchial colds, and her own difficulties in finding a second footman who combined smartness with respectability, comfortably whiled away the time until it became necessary for her to change her dress for the ball.

It had been decided by Lady Bolderwood that Marianne should wear her white satin ball-dress with the Russian bodice, and pearls as her only ornaments. Miss Morville, visiting her room to enquire if she had all she needed for the completion of her toilet, privately considered that her ladyship was a good deal to be pitied for being unable to see how lovely her daughter appeared in this festal raiment; but as it was not in her nature to go into raptures she merely admired the dress, reassured Marianne on the vexed question of her curls, which Betty had arranged with charming simplicity, *à l'anglaise,* and placed a prettily spangled gauze scarf about her shoulders, showing her to a nicety how to dispose its folds to the best advantage. She herself, having already enjoyed several London Seasons, was not obliged to wear white, a colour which had never showed her off to advantage, but was dressed in a crape slip of her favourite soft pink, worn under a figured lace robe. Her pearl necklet was more modest than Marianne's, but she wore a pair of diamond drops in her ears, and carried an antique fan, and a pair of very long French gloves of a delicate shade of pink which instantly awoke Marianne's envy. "They *are* pretty," acknowledged Miss Morville. "My brother Jack was so obliging as to send them to me, when he was stationed near Paris last year, and I have never yet worn them."

"Do you know," confided Marianne, rather shyly, "I had thought that you did not care very much for such things?"

"On the contrary," replied Miss Morville, "my besetting sin is a great inclination towards finery. Unfortunately—or perhaps *fortunately*—my figure is not good, and my complexion rather brown, so that it suits me best to dress simply, and *never* in such colours as make you, my dear Marianne, appear quite ravishing!"

Marianne blushed, and disclaimed, and marvelled silently that her friend could so calmly refer to her own lack of beauty.

Together, they traversed the several galleries and ante-chambers which lay between their apartments and the Long Drawing-room. Here they found many of the dinner-guests already assembled, those who were to spend the night at Stanyon having arrived some time previously, and being now gathered to await the appearance of those persons living in the immediate neighbourhood of Stanyon whom the Dowager had thought it proper to honour with an invitation to dinner. She herself, formidably attired in purple grosgrain and velvet, and wearing the famous Frant diamonds, which comprised a tiara, necklet, and elaborate corsage, all of which would have been the better for cleaning, was assisting her daughter to bore the Duchess of Rutland with an account of the recent attack of measles suffered by Harry and Johnny. The Duchess was herself the mother of a young family, but only her strict training in the formal household of her Papa, the Earl of Carlisle, enabled her to support her part in this interchange with the appearance of complaisance. However, she was upborne by the reflection that her rank must make it a certainty that St. Erth would take her in to dinner, and for him she had no hesitation in declaring that she had a strong *tendre*.

He was looking particularly handsome, in a dark coat made for him by the first tailor in town, and a most intricately tied cravat. His glowing locks, brushed into the Brutus style made fashionable by Mr. Brummell, shone like new-minted guineas in the light of the candles; and his stockings, like Miss Morville's gloves, had been bought in Paris. So exactly were his coat and satin knee-breeches moulded to his figure that Martin was conscious of a sudden regret that he had not commissioned Weston to make his own evening-dress.

The entrance of the two young ladies was productive of a sensation in which Miss Morville realized, without rancour, that she had no part. Lord Ulverston was heard to mutter, "By Jupiter!" by the high-born damsel to whom he had been talking; and the Duchess, having rapidly assimilated Miss Bolderwood's charms, demanded of her hostess in an urgent whisper to be told the name of the newest Beauty.

But although Marianne might be first in beauty, she was not first in consequence, and not all the Dowager's concern for her son's success with an heiress could blind her to the impropriety of his leading a mere baronet's daughter in to dinner when other, and more important, ladies were present. To Mr. Warboys was the task of partnering Marianne allotted, and if his intellect

was not of a powerful order at least he contrived to
keep her very well-entertained throughout the meal.
Lord Grampound sat upon her other side, and since his
attention was pretty well divided between his other
neighbour, a matron with an inexhaustible flow of
small-talk, and his dinner, which he pronounced to be
uncommonly good, Marianne's notice was not often
claimed by him. At the head of the table, the Earl and
her Grace of Rutland were seen to be entertaining one
another creditably; rather lower down, Martin did his
duty by a chatty Countess; and in the centre of the table,
Miss Morville and Theo Frant conversed together with
all the ease and comfort of old friends.

Hardly had the gentlemen joined the ladies after
dinner than the rest of the guests began to arrive, and in
a very short space of time the musicians had struck up
for the first country-dance. Here again, propriety forbade
either the Earl or his brother to lead Miss Bolderwood to
the head of the set that was forming. To the Duchess
must belong the honour of opening the ball; and it was
Lord Ulverston who had the good fortune to secure Marianne's hand for the first two dances. Not all Martin's ma-
noeuvring served even to place him beside Marianne in
the set, a circumstance which Miss Morville, who had
that happiness, considered to be a merciful dispensation
of providence. The most dispassionate observer must
have been obliged to own that between the lively Viscount
and Marianne there already flourished an excellent understanding; and no one at all acquainted with Martin
could have placed the least dependence on his comport-
ing himself with composure under the trial of seeing her
responding so artlessly to Lord Ulverston's advances.

Her hand was presently claimed by Gervase for the first quadrille. She performed her part correctly, but since she had never danced it but under the guidance of her instructor, she was nervous of making some mistake in its various figures, and had little leisure for attending to the Earl's attempts to amuse her. He, as was to be expected of an officer under the Duke of Wellington's command, was an excellent dancer, performing all the most difficult steps with ease and grace. She exclaimed naively at the assurance with which he led her into the *grande ronde;* he told her that she wanted only practice to make her an unimpeachable exponent of the art: a compliment which emboldened her to attempt the *pas d'été* with more confidence than she might otherwise have felt.

But a severe set-back awaited the Earl. When the musicians, under his private instructions, struck up for a waltz, no persuasions could prevail upon Marianne to stand up to dance. Her Mama's instructions had been explicit: she might, if solicited to do so, dance the quadrille, but on no account must she waltz. Neither the Earl nor Lord Ulverston could induce her to contravene this prohibition: to be seen to waltz before she had received the accolade of the approval of the hostesses of Almack's must set upon any débutante the indelible stigma of being a fast girl. Lady Bolderwood had foreseen the danger, and had guarded against it: although some license might be permitted to a young lady making her appearance at a private ball, she was too shrewd not to know that there would be jealous matrons enough to report in influential circles that Miss Bolderwood was not quite the thing.

Marianne's docility might disappoint her male

admirers, but it did her no disservice in the eyes either
of Lady St. Erth or of her ladyship's acquaintance. She
was held to be a very modest girl by at least three
mothers of promising daughters; and the most delightful, unaffected girl possible by those ladies anxious to
marry their younger sons creditably.

Since Miss Morville happened to be standing beside
Marianne when the Earl begged for the honour of her
hand in the waltz, good manners compelled him to turn
next to her. She accepted the offer with her usual composure, curtseying slightly, and allowing him to lead her
on to the floor. Here she surprised him by proving
herself to be an experienced dancer, very light on her
feet, and so well-acquainted with the various steps that
she performed them as though by instinct, and was able
to converse sensibly while she did so. Under no illusions as to the value of the compliment paid her by her
host in asking her to stand up with him while many
ladies of more consequence awaited that honour, she
said seriously: "If only you had mentioned the matter
to me, I could have told you that there was no possibility of Miss Bolderwood's waltzing, my lord, and then,
you know, you need not have commanded the musicians
to strike up for one."

"How do you know that I did so command them,
ma'am?" he asked, smiling in spite of himself.

"Well, *I* did not, because Lady St. Erth does not like
to see it danced; and I am very sure Martin did not,
because he has never learnt the steps."

"You are correct in your surmise," he acknowledged.
"And I am going to bespeak another waltz. You dance
delightfully, Miss Morville!"

"I have had a great deal of practice," she said. "I am very much obliged to you for the courtesy, but I believe you ought rather to invite Lady Firth to dance with you."

"Miss Morville, you may manage the arrangements for the ball, but you shall not manage my conduct at it!" he told her. "I have already stood up with Lady Firth for the boulanger, and I consider myself now at liberty to please myself. I hope you don't mean to refuse me the pleasure of another waltz with you!"

Martin, meanwhile, had joined the small group of young ladies whose mamas, like Lady Bolderwood, did not sanction the waltz. If he could have done it, he would have detached Marianne from the fair bevy, but his arrival was greeted with so much delight by a damsel, just emerged from the schoolroom, and whom he had known all his life, that civility obliged him to remain talking to her for several minutes. By the time another gentleman came up to claim her notice, Lord Ulverston, escaping from the clutches of Lady Grampound, was seated beside Marianne, entertaining her with a few of the military anecdotes so much frowned on by the Dowager; and although Martin might hover jealously over Marianne he could not lure her attention away from her more amusing partner. He had had the forethought to engage her for supper, but whatever solace this might have afforded him was banished by the chance which set Ulverston upon her other hand at the table. Besides the long table in the centre of the saloon, several smaller tables had been set up, and it was at one of these that the two couples were seated. Martin, who had adjured Abney to keep the table free for him,

was very soon regretting what had seemed at the time
to be a piece of good strategy. The two parties naturally
merged into one, and it would have been idle to deny
that Lord Ulverston was the life and soul of it. This was
bad, and still worse was it to perceive, a little later, that
his lordship had won Marianne's hand for the second
time that evening. Martin felt quite indignant with her
for yielding to the solicitations of one whom he was fast
beginning to think a confirmed rake; and had the opportunity offered he would have been much inclined to
have told her that her Mama would by no means
approve of her standing up twice with the same gentleman. The ball had become an insipid affair; he
wondered that his partner in the set could have so little
to say for herself; and decided that dancing was a stupid
business after all.

When the next set was formed, he had the happiness
of leading Marianne into it, but no sooner had they
gone down the dance than she had the misfortune to let
her train slip a little from her hand. Lord Grampound,
an energetic if not an inspired performer, lost no time
in setting his foot upon one of its delicate lace flounces,
so that Marianne was obliged to leave the set to effect
a makeshift repair. She assured Martin, who was ready
to knock his brother-in-law down for his clumsiness,
that a couple of pins would set all to rights, and he at
once escorted her to one of the saloons leading from the
ballroom. This happened to be empty, and Marianne,
well-knowing that to go to her bedchamber and to
summon Betty to attend her there would be the work
not of a minute but of half an hour, was content to let
Martin pin up her lace for her. This he did, with the pins

her Mama had warned her to provide herself with for just such an accident. Only a few inches of the lace had been ripped away from the satin, and the task was soon accomplished. Martin rose to his feet, and Marianne thanked him, complimenting him on his deftness, and laughing at the incident. The exercise of dancing had heightened the colour in her cheeks; her eyes sparkled with innocent enjoyment; and she looked so lovely that Martin lost his head, and so far forgot himself as to blurt out a declaration of his passion for her, and to try to take her in his arms.

She was quite unprepared for such a sudden turn, and not a little frightened. Demure flirtations she could enjoy, but the watchful care of Lady Bolderwood had warded off any offers for her hand, and she knew not how to quench the desperate ardour which confronted her. She could only retreat before Martin, saying in a fluttered voice: "No, no! Oh, pray do not!"

It was perhaps not surprising that he should have followed her, and grasped the hands she put out to hold him off; and he would certainly have kissed her, in despite of her faint shriek, had not his sister entered the saloon at that moment, accompanied by their half-brother. He was recalled to a sense of his surroundings by hearing Gervase sharply utter his name, and he swung round, a tide of colour flooding his face, and in his eyes an expression of oddly-mingled shame and fury.

Marianne was quite as discomposed as he, and stood trembling, her face averted to hide the sudden rush of startled tears to her eyes. Lady Grampound's exclamation of: "Good gracious, what's all this, pray?"

did nothing to soothe her agitation. She had no voice with which to speak even such few, disjointed words as rose to her lips; and it was with profound gratitude that she laid her shaking hand on the Earl's arm. He had crossed the room, and was saying in his quiet way: "I came in search of you, for another set is forming, ma'am. I saw the sad accident which befell your gown, and I hope my brother has been of assistance in pinning up the lace."

"Oh, yes! So kind!" she managed to say. "It is of no consequence—the tiniest rent!"

She went with him thankfully to the door, but here they were met by Lord Ulverston, who said, in a rallying tone: "Ger, you are a base fellow, and are trying to steal a march on me! Miss Bolderwood is promised to me for this dance! Unhand her, villain!"

He perceived as he spoke that she was suffering from some embarrassment. One swift glance round the room, if it did not put him in possession of the facts, at least informed him that Martin was in some way to blame for this; and with the ready address which sprang as much from good-nature as from good-breeding he continued to rattle on in his droll style, accusing his friend of treachery, and insisting that he would very likely call him out for it in the morning.

"No, no!" said Gervase, ably seconding his efforts. "*That* would be a great breach of hospitality! If you can be so unmindful of your duty towards your host, *I* at least shall not forget my duty towards my guest!"

"Humdudgeon, Ger! Miss Bolderwood, do not be taken in by these soft words! He played me just such a trick once in France, and was not for a moment at a loss to explain why he should not be punished for it! But, come! We shall find no places if we don't make haste!"

The Earl relinquished her into his friend's care, and she allowed herself to be led back into the ballroom. Gervase turned to look his brother up and down, and to say icily: "Have the goodness to preserve the appearance at least of a gentleman, Martin! These manners may do very well at a Covent Garden masquerade: they are out of place at Stanyon!"

"How dare you?" Martin ejaculated, starting forward a pace. "*You* are not to be the arbiter of my conduct!"

"You are mistaken. I am the *only* arbiter of the conduct of those who live under my roof!"

"Yes! You would like to be rid of me, would you not? You are afraid you have no chance with Marianne while I—"

"We will leave Miss Bolderwood's name out of this. I will not suffer any guest of mine to be insulted, least of all a girl entrusted to our protection! You should be ashamed of yourself!"

Since Martin was, in fact, very much ashamed of himself, this scathing remark made him angrier than ever. His sister then further exacerbated his temper by pronouncing in a pontifical tone strongly reminiscent of her mother: "I am bound to say that St. Erth is perfectly in the right. Such behaviour, my dear brother, is not at all the thing. Grampound would be very much shocked."

"Grampound may go to the devil, and take you and St. Erth with him!" said Martin furiously.

"Now, Martin, do not fly into one of your stupid puckers!" recommended her ladyship. "You had better beg Miss Bolderwood's pardon. I shall tell her that you are a trifle foxed."

"You will do no such thing! I want none of your curst meddling, Louisa, I thank you! I mean to marry Marianne!"

"Possibly," said Gervase dryly, "but before you press attentions upon her which she appears to find unwelcome, you would be well-advised to obtain her father's consent to your pretensions."

"Very true," agreed Lady Grampound. "It is no use to scowl, Martin, for St. Erth's observation is excessively just. When Grampound offered for me, it was not until dear Papa had assured him that he should not dislike the match for me. Indeed, until Mama informed me of it I had not a notion that Grampound was fallen passionately in love with me, for he behaved with the greatest propriety towards me, so that I am sure I thought he cared more for his dinner than for me!"

She laughed heartily at this recollection, but the only effect it had upon her young brother was to make him eye her with acute dislike, and to grip his lips so firmly together that they seemed no more than a thin line drawn across his face.

"I am persuaded that Grampound did just as he ought," said Gervase gravely, but with a twitching lip. "Enough has been said, I think: we had better go back into the ballroom."

"Well, I have not said all I wish to!" Martin shot at him. "You may stop talking to me as though I were a damned rake, just trifling with Marianne! It's no such thing, and if you think I mean to await *your* permission before I ask her to marry me, you will discover your mistake!"

He was interrupted by the entrance of Theo, who came in, looking startled, and considerably shocked. He quickly shut the door behind him, saying: "Gervase! Martin! For God's sake—! Your voices can be heard in the ballroom! What is it?"

"No concern of yours!" replied Martin.

"It is all Martin's fault," explained Lady Grampound. "He has been behaving very badly, and now he will not own it! But so it is always with him! And Mama so much encourages him that Grampound says it is no wonder—"

Gervase intervened hastily: "Grampound is a very good sort of a man, Louisa, but I doubt whether Martin wants to be told of his sayings. Let Theo take you back to the ballroom! It will occasion too much remark if we all go together."

"I think it is you who had better accompany Lady Grampound," said Theo bluntly.

"Nonsense! Martin and I have a little rubbed one another, but we are not going to come to fisticuffs, I assure you! Louisa, oblige me by not mentioning what has occurred to anyone! There is not the least occasion for you to speak of it even to Grampound."

"The person who *should* be told, is Mama," said her ladyship, gathering up her train. "However, I shall not do so, for she will never make the smallest push to re-monstrate with Martin, and so it has always been!"

With these sisterly words, she accepted her cousin's escort into the ballroom, where she proceeded to regale him, without loss of time, with the whole history of the episode.

Left alone with his half-brother, Gervase said in a more friendly tone: "Well, that was all very unfortunate, but it will be forgotten! If I spoke too warmly, I beg your pardon, but to be trying to kiss against her will a girl in Miss Bolderwood's circumstances is the outside of enough, as well you know!"

His sensibilities as much lacerated by Marianne's attempt to repulse him as by the lash of his own conscience, Martin was in no mood to accept an amende. He said in a shaking voice: "Damn you, leave me alone!" and brushed past Gervase out of the saloon.

CHAPTER TEN

IT WAS NOT to be expected that Miss Bolderwood could compose herself for slumber that night until she had poured forth the agitating events of the evening into her friend's ears. Lord Ulverston's kindness and good-humour had done much to calm her disturbed nerves, but these had been shocked, and would not readily recover. Since her school-room days she had almost never found herself alone with a man other than her Papa, for even when the Earl taught her to drive his curricle his groom had always been perched up behind the carriage. The anxious care of her parents had wrapped her about; and although her disposition led her to flirt with her many admirers it had never occurred to her innocent mind that these tactics might lead them, on the first occasion when they found her unprotected, to take shocking advantage of her levity. Her spirits were quite borne down by the discovery; and she was much inclined to think herself a fast girl, with whom gentlemen thought it proper to take liberties.

Miss Morville, however, received her confidences with admirable calm and common-sense. While agreeing that it was no doubt disagreeable to be found in such an embarrassing situation, she maintained that it was no matter for wonder that Martin should have so far forgotten himself. "If you *will* be so pretty, Marianne, and flirt so dreadfully, what can you expect?"

"Oh, I was never so mortified! I had not the least notion he would try to do such a thing!"

"Well, he should not, of course, but he is very young, after all, and I daresay he is ashamed of it now," said Miss Morville consolingly. "If I were you, I would not refine too much upon the incident!"

"How can you talk so? He behaved as though I were—as though I were the veriest *drab!*" She saw that Miss Morville was looking amused, and added indignantly: "Drusilla, how can you be so insensible? *You* must have felt it as I do!"

"Perhaps I might," acknowledged Miss Morville. "I don't *think* I should, but the melancholy truth is that no one has ever shown the smallest desire to kiss me!"

"I envy you!" declared Marianne. "I wish I knew how I am to face Martin at breakfast tomorrow! I cannot do it!"

"Oh, there will not be the smallest difficulty!" Miss Morville pointed out. "It is tomorrow already, and if you partake of breakfast at all it will be in this room, and not until many hours after the gentlemen have eaten theirs."

This practical response was not very well-received, Marianne saying rather pettishly that Drusilla seemed not to enter into her feelings at all, and pointing out that whether it was at the breakfast-table or at the dinner-table her next meeting with Martin must cause her insupportable embarrassment.

"I daresay it will cause him embarrassment too," observed Miss Morville, "so the sooner you have met, and can put it all behind you, the easier you will be."

"If only I might go home!" Marianne said.

"Well, and so you will, in a day or two. To run away immediately would be to give rise to the sort of comment I am sure you would not like; and, you know, you can scarcely continue to reside in the same neighbourhood without encountering Martin."

There could be no denying the good-sense of this remark. Marianne shed a few tears; and after animadverting indignantly on Martin's folly, effrontery, and ill-breeding, turned from the contemplation of his depraved character to dwell with gratitude on the exquisite tact and kindness of Lord Ulverston.

"I can never be sufficiently obliged to him!" she declared. "I am persuaded he cannot have remained in ignorance of my distress, for I was so much mortified I could scarcely speak, and as for meeting his gaze, it was wholly beyond my power! I was ready to sink for fear he should ask me what was the matter, but he never did! There was something so *very* kind in the way he offered me his arm, and took me to drink a glass of lemonade, saying it was insufferably hot in the ballroom, and should I not like to go where it was cooler? And then, you know, we talked of all manner of things, until I was comfortable again, and I do think there was never anyone more good-natured."

Miss Morville was very ready to encourage her in these happier reflections; and by dint of pointing out how sad it would be for Marianne to leave Stanyon before she had become better acquainted with his lordship, soon prevailed upon her to abandon this scheme. If her young friend's artless panegyric left her with the suspicion that an embrace from the Viscount would have awakened no outraged feelings in her breast, this was a thought which she was wise enough to keep to herself.

Marianne was sure that she would be unable to close her eyes for what remained of the night. However that might have been, they were very peacefully closed for long after Miss Morville had left her bedchamber later in the morning. Miss Morville peeped into her room, but Marianne did not stir, and she left her to have her sleep out.

Only the gentlemen appeared at the breakfast-table, but by eleven o'clock most of the ladies had come downstairs from their rooms, including Lady Grampound, who seemed to have risen for no other purpose than to ensure that her sons were given rides by Martin. Upon his not unreasonably demurring at this demand, compliance with which must remove him from the Castle before any of the visitors had departed, she said that to oblige his nephews was the least he could do: an oblique reference to his misconduct which provoked him into replying that if giving rides to her brats would make her departure from Stanyon that day a certainty he would be happy to do it.

By noon, all the ball-guests except the Grampounds had left the Castle, and the Dowager was free to discuss the evening's festivity with anyone so unwise as to approach her chair, to congratulate herself upon the excellence of the supper, and to enumerate all the guests who had been particularly gratified to have received invitations. In this innocuous amusement she was joined by her daughter, who could not conceive of greater bliss for her fellow-creatures than to find themselves at

Stanyon, and who had further cause for complacence in having had her gown admired by the Duchess. The tempestuous entrance into the room of Harry and John, bursting to tell their Mama about the rides they had enjoyed, caused an interruption. Conversation became impossible, for when they had stopped shouting their news in unison to Lady Grampound they fell out over the rights of primogeniture, Harry contending that to ransack the contents of Grandmama's netting-box was his privilege, and Johnny very hotly combating such a suggestion.

"Dear little fellows!" said the Dowager. "They would like to play a game, I daresay. How much they enjoyed playing at spillikins with dear Marianne yesterday!"

"Yes, indeed, Mama, but pray do not put it into their heads to do so again, for I told them they must not tease Miss Bolderwood to repeat her kindness."

Marianne, who was engaged in restoring its contents to the netting-box, took the hint. She insisted that she would be very happy to play with the children, and went away to find the spillikins, while Lady Grampound informed her offspring of the treat in store for them. By the time Marianne returned, peace had been restored, even Johnny's yells at being shrewdly kicked by his brother having ceased at the sight of a box of sugar-plums.

When Martin presently came into the room with Lord Ulverston, Marianne was too much engrossed with the game to accord him more than a brief, shy greeting. He said awkwardly that it was a particularly fine day, so that he thought she might care to walk in the shrubbery before luncheon was served. She declined it, and a moment later he had the mortification of seeing Ulverston join the spillikin-party, and receive a very welcoming smile and blush.

The Grampounds were to leave Stanyon during the afternoon, and while the party sat round the table in one of the saloons, eating cold meat and fruit, Lord Grampound expressed a wish to visit a house in the neighbourhood which he had some thought of hiring for the accommodation of his family during the summer months. This led his wife to explain in detail the extensive improvements which were to be put in hand at Grampound Manor, the fatal effects of Brighton air upon Harry's liverish constitution, and her own ardent desire to spend the summer within reach of Stanyon. The Dowager, loftily disregarding her stepson's claims to be consulted in the matter, at once invited her daughter to come to Stanyon itself, and to remain there for as long as she pleased, an invitation which her ladyship would certainly have accepted had Lord Grampound not intervened to say with great firmness that he preferred to hire a house of his own.

"I daresay it may be best, my love," agreed his wife. "Not but what it would be pleasant for Mama to have the children at Stanyon for a really long stay, and I am sure I do not know where they would be happier. However, I do not mean to be setting myself up in opposition, and it shall be as you wish. The only thing is that I do not perfectly recollect the way to Kentham. Martin, you shall ride with Grampound as far as the house, for I am persuaded you must know how best to reach it, and then we can see it together, and you will be back at Stanyon in time for dinner."

This cool disposal of his time exasperated Martin into saying: "A delightful scheme, Louisa, but I have something else to do this afternoon!"

"Nonsense! what can you possibly have to do?" she replied. "You only wish to be disobliging, and may very well go with us, if you choose."

He was silent.

Lord Grampound cleared his throat. "I should be happy to have Martin's company on the road, but if he does not care to go with us, I shall refrain from pressing him."

Martin was still silent, and Gervase, feeling that he had borne enough, interposed, saying: "If you will accept my escort, Grampound, I shall be glad to go with you. I don't promise to lead you aright, but I fancy I have a general notion of where Kentham lies."

His lordship accepted the offer. Martin was conscious of a feeling of gratitude, which, however, was speedily dispelled by his sister, who read him a homily on conduct, and ended by drawing an unflattering comparison between his manners and those of his brother.

"You may as well stop prosing to me!" he said hastily, thrusting back his chair from the table. "St. Erth is perfection itself, of course! If you toad-eat him enough I daresay he will second my mother's invitation to you to spend the summer at Stanyon!"

"Be quiet, you young fool!" said Theo, under his breath.

"Don't disturb yourself! I'm going!" Martin snapped, and flung himself out of the room.

Marianne could not doubt that his refusal to accompany the Grampounds arose from his determination to engage her in private conversation. He had made two attempts already to detach her from the rest of the party, and since she did not know what to say to him if he offered her an apology, or how to repulse him if he tried to renew his love-making, she was thrown into a flutter of nerves, and so earnestly begged Miss Morville not to leave her side for an instant that Drusilla who had meant to walk across the Park to her own home, to perform some few duties there, was obliged to abandon her design. Until the Grampounds took their departure, everyone lingered in the Castle, but when, not more than an hour later than had been intended, and after only two false starts, the coaches, preceded by the Earl and his brother-in-law on horseback, at last passed under the Gate Tower, and bowled away through the Park, there was nothing to keep the remaining company within doors any longer. Miss Morville suggested the refreshment of a walk in the shrubbery to Marianne, and thither they repaired, enjoying the bright spring sunshine, and talking over such aspects of the ball as Marianne could bear to recall without pain. The painful episode, however, was bound to obtrude, and although a night's repose had to a great extent soothed Marianne's more exaggerated reflections, she confided in Miss Morville that although she had previously thought her Mama very old-fashioned to allow her to go nowhere without her chaperonage, she *now* saw how dangerous it was for a female to be alone with a young man.

After they had been walking about the paths for a little while, they were joined by Lord Ulverston. He had an arm for both ladies, but it was not long before Miss Morville perceived herself to be unnecessary either to his comfort or to Marianne's. She ventured to suggest that she should leave them, to go on her interrupted errand to Gilbourne House. Beyond saying: "Must you go indeed? You will be so tired, after dancing all night!" Marianne made no objection. The dangers attached to finding herself alone with a young man were forgotten; and since Miss Morville had perfect confidence in Lord Ulverston's ability to keep whatever ardour he might feel within the bounds of the strictest propriety, she had no hesitation in leaving him to entertain her friend.

She was met at Gilbourne House by the housekeeper, who had a great many problems to lay before her, and a great many grievances to pour into her ears. Not the least of these was the shocking ingratitude, selfishness, and duplicity of one of the maids, who, having been given permission to spend a night at her own home in the village, had, instead of returning in good time upon the following morning, sent up a message to the house that she had had the misfortune to sprain her ankle, and could not set her foot to the ground. As the village lay a mile beyond Gilbourne House, it was not to be expected that stout Mrs. Buxton could go there to verify the truth of this message; but she informed Miss Morville darkly that she had always suspected the errant damsel of flightiness.

Miss Morville did not share this suspicion, but she promised to visit Kitty's home, for she had a strong sense of duty, and had been bred up by her progressive parents to think the well-being of her dependents particularly her concern.

So after a slight argument with Mrs. Buxton, who, by no means as progressive as her master and mistress, desired her not to go to the village without taking a man-servant with her to act as escort, and to carry her basket, Miss Morville set out to visit the sufferer.

She found the case to be exactly as had been stated, poor Kitty's ankle being very much swollen. Her offerings of arnica, eggs, and a cheese wrested from Mrs. Buxton's jealously guarded storeroom, were accepted with thanks, and some doubt, Kitty's mother being of the unshakable opinion that nothing could do more good to sprains, sores, chillblains, and a variety of other ills, than goose-fat, well rubbed in. But a visit from Miss Morville was at once an honour and a pleasure. She must be taken into the tiny parlour, regaled with juniper wine, and the whole history of Kitty's accident, and thanked again and again for her condescension. The hour was consequently rather far advanced when Drusilla at last left the cottage, and it was beginning to be dusk. She had only a little way to walk, however, before she was able to enter the Park, by one of its subsidiary gates. An avenue led from the gate to the stables, and the kitchen-court, but it was circuitous, and the quickest way was through the Home Wood, by one of the pleasant rides which led to the main avenue.

The wood was full of shadows, and already a little chilly, after the setting of the sun, but Miss Morville, neither so fashionable as to disdain wearing a warm pelisse, nor so delicate as to be unable to walk at a brisk pace, suffered no discomfort. She did not even imagine, when some small animal stirred in the undergrowth, that she was being followed; and was so insensible as to remain impervious to the alarm which might have been caused by the sudden scutter of a rabbit across the path.

A quarter of an hour's quick walking brought her to within sight of the main avenue. The thud of a horse's hooves came to her ears, which led her to suppose, not that a desperate, and probably masked, brigand approached, but that the Earl, having parted from the Grampounds, was on his way back to the Castle. She was right: in another instant, she had a brief vision of Cloud, cantering along the grass verge beside the avenue. Since she was walking almost at right angles to the avenue, Cloud and his rider were swiftly hidden from her sight, as they passed the opening of the ride, and became obscured by the trees and the bushes which bordered the avenue. But although she could no longer see the horse and his rider, she could still hear the thud of the hooves, and when these ceased abruptly, to be succeeded by the unmistakable sound of a fall, followed by the scrabble of hooves on loose stones, and the clatter of a bolting horse, she was not so prosaically-minded as to suppose that these sounds could have been caused by anything other than an accident. It seemed odd that the Earl should have taken a toss on a smooth stretch of turf, but without pausing to consider the improbability of such an occurrence Miss Morville picked up her skirts and ran forward as quickly as she could. Within a very few seconds she had reached the avenue, to be confronted by a startling sight. Of Cloud there was no sign, but his rider lay motionless across the narrow grass verge, his head and shoulders resting on the avenue. This circumstance, as Miss Morville realized, was enough to account for his having been stunned. She dropped to her knees beside his inanimate form, and without the smallest hesitation ripped open his coat to feel the beat of his heart.

The Earl regained consciousness to find himself

lying with his head in Miss Morville's lap, his elaborate Mail-coach cravat untied, and the scent of aromatic vinegar in his nostrils. Gazing bemusedly up into the concerned face bent over him, he uttered, a trifle thickly: "Good God! I fell!"

"Yes," agreed Miss Morville, removing her vinaigrette from under his nose. "I cannot discover, my lord, that any limb is broken, but I might be mistaken. Can you move your arms and your legs?"

"Lord, yes! There are no bones broken!" he replied, struggling up to a sitting posture, and clasping his head between his hands. "But I don't understand! How in the devil's name came I— Where's my horse?"

"I expect," said Miss Morville, "that he has bolted for his stable, for there was no sign of him when I reached your side. Do not disturb yourself on his account! He could scarcely have done so had he sustained any injury! It is, in fact, a fortunate circumstance that he bolted, for he will give the alarm, you know, and since your groom knows in which direction you rode out we may shortly expect to receive succour."

He uttered a shaken laugh. "You think of everything, ma'am!"

"I may think of everything," said Miss Morville, "but I am not always able to accomplish all I should wish to! My chief desire has been to procure water with which to revive you, but, in the circumstances, I scarcely dared to leave your side. I do not *think,* from what I can observe, that you have broken your collar-bone."

"I am very sure I have not, ma'am. I have merely broke my head!"

"Does it pain you very much?" she asked solicitously.

"Why, yes! It aches like the very deuce, but not, I assure you, as much as does my self-esteem! How came I to fall, like the rawest of greenhorns?" He received no answer to this, and added, with an effort towards playfulness: "But I forget my manners! I must thank you for preserving my life, Miss Morville—even though it may have been at the cost of my cravat!"

"I am not, in general," said Miss Morville carefully, "an advocate for the employment of hyperbole in describing trifling services, but I believe, my lord, that in this instance I may be justly said to have done so."

He was engaged, with only slightly unsteady fingers, in loosely knotting the ruined cravat about his throat, but at these words he paused in his task to frown at her in some bewilderment. "I collect that in this uncertain light I must have been so careless as to let Cloud set his foot in a rabbit-burrow. I own, I have no very clear remembrance of what occurred, but—"

"No," said Miss Morville.

He looked intently at her. "No?"

"You have been unconscious for several minutes, sir," said Miss Morville. "When once I had ascertained that your heart still beat strongly, I had leisure to look about me, to discover, if I might, what had been the cause of the accident. I am excessively reluctant to add to your present discomforts, but I must request you, in your own interests, to look at what met my eyes a minute or two ago."

The Earl's surprised gaze obediently followed the direction of her pointing finger, and alighted upon a length of thin, yet stout, cord, which lay on the ground across the avenue, to disappear into the thicket beyond.

"You will observe," said Miss Morville dispassionately, "that the cord is attached to one of the lower branches of that tree upon your left hand. I have been trying to puzzle it out in my mind, and I am strongly of the opinion, my lord, that if the other end of the cord were to be held by some person standing concealed in the thicket to your right, it would be a simple matter for such a person suddenly to pull it taut across the path at the very moment when your horse was abreast of it."

There was a moment's silence; then the Earl said: "Your power of observation is acute, ma'am. But what a happiness to be assured that I fell from no negligence of my own!"

She seemed to approve of this light-hearted response, for she smiled, and said: "I am sure you must be much relieved, my lord." She was then silent for a short space, adding presently: "To be attaching exaggerated importance to trifling circumstances is what I have no patience with, but I cannot conceal from you, my lord, that I do not at all like what has occurred!"

"You express yourself with praiseworthy moderation, Miss Morville," Gervase returned, rising to his feet, and brushing the dirt from his coat. "I will own that for my part I dislike it excessively!"

"If," she said, holding her hands rather tightly clasped in her lap, "I could rid my mind of the horrid suspicion that only my unlooked-for presence here is the cause of your being alive at this moment, I should feel very much more comfortable."

He held down his hand to her. "Come, get up, ma'am! You will take cold if you continue to sit on the damp ground. My case was not likely to be desperate, you know. I might, of course, have broken my neck, but the greater probability was that I should come off with a few bruises, as indeed I have, or with a broken limb at the worst."

She accepted his assistance in rising to her feet, but said with a little asperity: "To be sure, there is not the least reason why you should credit me with common-sense, for I daresay I may never have warned you that although I am not bookish I have a tolerably good understanding! My fault is a lack of imagination which makes it impossible for me to believe that a cord was stretched across your path by some mischance—or even," she added tartly, "by supernatural agency, so pray do not try to entertain me with any of your non-sensical ghost-stories, sir, for I am not in the mood for them!"

He laughed. "No, no, I know your mind to be hardened against them, ma'am! Let us admit at once that a cord was tied to that tree, and allowed to lie unnoticed across the avenue until my horse was abreast of it. There can be little doubt that it was then jerked tight, an action which, I judge, must have brought it to the level of Cloud's knees. That he came down very suddenly I recall, and also that I was flung over his head."

"Who did it?" she said abruptly.

"I don't know, Miss Morville. Do you?"

She shook her head. "There was no one in sight when I ran out into the avenue. I looked for no one, for I had *then* no suspicion that the accident had been contrived, but I think I must have noticed anyone moving by the thicket."

"You could not have done so had he stood behind the thicket. Was it long after I fell that you came up with me? By the by, where *were* you, ma'am? I did not see you!"

"No, for I was walking along that ride, coming from the village, you know," she replied, nodding towards the path. "You would only have perceived me had you chanced to turn your head, and from the thicket I must have been wholly obscured. I heard the fall, and you may readily suppose that I wasted no time in running to the spot—it cannot have been more than a matter of seconds before I had reached the end of the ride. It must have been impossible for anyone to have had sufficient time between your fall and my coming into view to have removed that cord, or—"

She stopped. He prompted her gently: "Or, Miss Morville?"

"Excuse me!" she begged. "I had nearly said what must have given you reason to suppose that I have a disordered intellect! I believe that the shock of seeing you stretched lifeless upon the ground has a little overset my nerves."

"You mean, do you not, that the finishing blow might have been dealt me while I lay senseless, had you not been at hand to frighten away my assailant?"

"I did mean that," she confessed. "The misadventure you escaped at the bridge the other day must have been in my mind, perhaps."

"So you knew about that!"

"Everyone knows of it. One of the servants heard your cousin rating Martin for—for his carelessness in forgetting to warn you. You must know how quickly gossip will spread in a large household! But if it was indeed Martin who brought your horse down, I am persuaded he did not mean to kill you!"

"Just a boyish prank, Miss Morville?" Gervase said.

"It was very bad, of course, for he could not know that the accident would not prove to be fatal. When his temper is roused, there is no saying what he will do. He seems not to care— But I own this goes beyond anything I should have thought it possible for him to do! There is no understanding it, for he is by no means a genius, so that we cannot excuse him on the score of eccentricity."

His head was aching, but he was obliged to smile. "Is it your experience that geniuses are apt to perform such violent deeds, ma'am?"

"Well, they frequently behave very irrationally," she replied. "History, I believe, affords us many examples of peculiar conduct on the part of those whose intellects are of an elevated order; and within my own knowledge there is the sad case of poor Miss Mary Lamb, who murdered her mama, in a fit of aberration. Then, too, Miss Wollstonecraft, who was once a friend of my mother's, cast herself into the Thames, and *she,* you know, had a most superior intellect."

"Cast herself into the Thames!" echoed the Earl.

"Yes, at Putney. She had meant to commit the dreadful deed at Battersea, but found the bridge there too crowded, and so was obliged to row herself to Putney. She was picked up by a passing boat, and afterwards married Mr. Godwin, which quite turned her thoughts from suicide. Not that I should have thought it a preferable fate," said Miss Morville reflectively, "but, then, I am not at all partial to Mr. Godwin. In fact, though I never met him—nor, indeed, Miss Wollstonecraft, either—I have often thought I should have liked Mr. Imlay better than Mr. Godwin. He was an American, with whom Miss Wollstonecraft had an unhappy connection, and although a great many harsh things have been said about him, Mama has always maintained that most of the trouble arose from Miss Wollstonecraft's determination to make him an elm-tree round which she might throw her tendrils. Very few gentlemen could, I believe, support for long so arduous a role."

"I find myself, as always, in entire agreement with you, Miss Morville," he said gravely. "But do you wish me to suppose that a deranged mind was responsible for my accident?"

"By no means. Martin has too little control over his passions, but he cannot be thought to be deranged. Indeed, I cannot account for your accident, except by a solution which I am persuaded is not the correct one."

He smiled slightly. "I have a great dependence on your discretion, Miss Morville. We shall say, if you please, that I was so heedless as to let Cloud set his foot in a rabbit-hole. Meanwhile, I think it would be well if I gathered up this cord, and stowed it away in my pocket."

She watched him do so in silence, but when he had untied the cord from about the tree, and had returned to her, she said: "I think you perfectly able to manage your own affairs, my lord, and I shall certainly not interfere in them. But, absurd though it may seem to you, this incident has made me feel apprehensive, and I do trust that you will take care how you expose yourself while you remain at Stanyon!"

"Why, yes, to the best of my power I will do so," he answered. "But nothing will be gained through my noising this trick abroad: whoever was responsible for it knows that his design was frustrated, and he is not very likely to betray himself. I must suppose that everyone at Stanyon knew that I should return to the Castle by this road. Who, by the way, knew of your visit to the village?"

"No one, and only Marianne and Lord Ulverston can have known that I went to Gilbourne House."

"That is no help at all. I never suspected Lucy of wishing to put a period to my life," he said, smiling.

CHAPTER ELEVEN

THEY BEGAN TO WALK slowly down the avenue in the direction of the Castle, the Earl assuring Miss Morville that apart from an aching skull he had sustained no injury from his fall. They had not proceeded far on their way when they heard the sound of an approaching vehicle, being driven towards them at a furious pace. "If this is Chard, springing my grays, I will very soon give him something else to alarm him out of his senses!" said the Earl.

But the four horses which almost immediately swept round the bend ahead of them were not grays, nor was Chard driving them. He sat perched up beside Lord Ulverston, who had the ribbons in his hands, and was encouraging his team to gallop down the avenue.

The Earl drew Miss Morville on to the grass verge, but the Viscount had already perceived him, and was checking his horses. They pulled up, very much on the fret, and the Earl called out: "If I had guessed this was how you meant to use my bays I swear I would never have sold them to you, Lucy! Four-Horse Club, indeed! The veriest whipster!"

"Good God, Ger, what a fright you have given us!" the Viscount said indignantly. "I had just come in from tooling Miss Bolderwood about the country for an hour, when Cloud came bolting into the yard, in a lather, and with his legs cut about! I thought you must have put him at a regular stitcher, and taken a bad toss!"

"I took a toss, but not at a stitcher. A common rabbit-hole was the cause of my downfall."

"A rabbit-hole? *You?*" exclaimed Ulverston incredulously.

"Don't roast me! We all have our lapses!"

"Where is this famous rabbit-hole?"

"Oh, in the Park! I would not engage to point you out the precise one: there are so many of them!"

"Exactly so! So many that you ride with a slack bridle, and your head in the clouds, and, when you part company, *leave go of the rein!* Gammon, dear boy, gammon!"

"How badly are my horses' legs cut?" interrupted Gervase. "That is the worst feature of the business!"

Chard, who had jumped down from the curricle, and had been listening to him with a puzzled frown on his face, said that he thought the injuries were hardly more than grazes. "I handed him over to Jen, me lord, not knowing what kind of an *embarazo* you was got into, and thinking you might need me more than the horse."

"Nonsense! Is it likely I could be in serious trouble?"

"As to that, me lord, there's no saying what trouble you could be in," replied his henchman bluntly. "All I know is I never knew your horse to come home without you before!"

By this time, the Viscount had turned the curricle about, and was commanding Gervase to climb into it.

"Certainly not! It is Miss Morville whom you shall drive, Lucy, not me!"

"Take you both!" said the Viscount. "You won't mind being a trifle crowded, ma'am? Come, Ger, no playing the fool with me! I don't know how you came to do it, but it's as plain as a pikestaff you took a bad toss! Shaken to pieces, I daresay—your cravat is, at all events! Never saw you look such a quiz in my life!"

Thus adjured, the Earl handed Miss Morville up into the curricle, and climbed in after her. The Viscount observed that it was a fortunate circumstance that they were none of them fat; Chard swung himself up behind, and the horses were put into motion.

"Tell you another thing, Ger, about this precious tumble of yours!" said the Viscount. "Can't see how—" He broke off, for the Earl, who had flung one arm across the back of the driving-seat, in an attempt to make more room for Miss Morville, moved his hand to his friend's shoulder, and gripped it warningly. "Oh, well! No sense talking about it!" he said.

They were soon bowling through the archway of the Gate Tower. Miss Morville was set down at the Castle, but the Earl insisted on driving to the stables, to examine Cloud's hurts. Here they found Theo, also engaged on this task. He came out into the yard at the noise of the curricle's approach, and said, in his unemotional way: "Well, I am glad to see you safe and sound, Gervase! Pray, what have you been doing?"

"Merely coming to grief through my own folly," replied Gervase, alighting from the curricle. "In the failing light I didn't perceive a rabbit-hole, that is all!"

"My dear St. Erth, your horse never cut his knees stumbling into rabbit-holes!" expostulated Theo. "I thought, when I saw him, you must have put him at a stone wall!"

"Are they badly damaged?"

"I hope not. He has done little more than scratch himself. Whether he will be scarred or not, I can't tell. I've directed your man to apply hot fomentations."

The Earl nodded, and went past him into the stable, followed by Chard. Theo looked up at the Viscount with a questioning lift to his brows.

"No good asking me!" Ulverston said, correctly interpreting the look. "He don't want it talked of, that's all I know. Where's that damned fellow of mine? Clarence! Hi, there, come and take the horses in, wherever you are!"

His groom came running up. The Viscount relinquished the team into his care, and jumped down from the curricle. "Where's young Frant?" he asked abruptly.

"Martin? I don't know," Theo replied, a surprised inflexion in his voice.

"Mr. Frant went out with his gun a while back, my lord," offered Clarence.

"Oh, he did, did he? Very well; that'll do!"

"What's this, Ulverston?" Theo said, drawing him out of earshot of the groom. "What has Martin to do with it?"

"I don't know, but if you can believe all this humdudgeon of Ger's about falling into rabbit-holes, I can't! Part company he might; leave go of his rein he would not! No wish to meddle in what don't concern me, but Ger's a friend of mine. Fancy he's a friend of yours too. Don't know what it was, but something happened to him he don't mean to tell us about. Dash it, I haven't spent three days here without seeing that that young cub of a brother of his would do him a mischief if he could!"

Theo was frowningly silent. After a moment, the

Viscount said: "Quarrelled last night, didn't they? Oh, you needn't be so discreet! I walked into the middle of it! Got a shrewd notion I know what it was about, too."

"They did quarrel, but I believe it was not serious. Martin is hot-tempered, and will often say what he does not mean."

"What's the matter with the fellow?" demanded the Viscount. "Seems to live in the sulks!"

Theo smiled faintly. "He has certainly done so ever since St. Erth came home, but he can be pleasant enough when he likes."

"Pity he don't like more often! Does he dislike Ger?"

"He is jealous of him. I think you must have realized that. St. Erth has inherited what Martin has always regarded as his own. I hope he may soon perceive the folly of his behaviour. Indeed, I believe he must, for there is not a better fellow living than Gervase, and that Martin will be bound to discover before he is much older."

"But this is Gothick, Frant, quite Gothick!" objected Ulverston.

"Well, in some ways I think Martin *is* rather Gothick!" said Theo. "His disposition is imperious; his will never was thwarted while his father lived; nor was he taught to control his passions. Everything that he wanted he was given; and, worse than all, he was treated as though he had been the heir, and Gervase did not exist."

"Went to school, didn't he?"

"Yes, he followed Gervase to Eton."

"Well, don't tell me his will wasn't thwarted there!" said Ulverston. "Doing it too brown, dear fellow! I was at Eton m'self!"

"You were perhaps not so much indulged at home. With Martin, the influence of school counted for nothing once he was back at Stanyon."

They were interrupted by the Earl, who, coming up behind them, said lightly: "What treason are you hatching, the pair of you? I don't think Cloud's legs will be marked."

"Gervase, are you concealing something from us?" asked Theo bluntly.

"Oh, so Lucy has been telling you that I have never been known to let my rein go, has he? I thank you for the compliment, Lucy, but it is undeserved. Now I think I should do well to slip into the house unobserved, for if Martin were to catch a glimpse of my cravat in its present lamentable condition he would cease to think me a dandy, and that would be a sad disappointment to both of us."

"Martin ain't in the house," said the Viscount. "He went out with his gun, my man tells me."

"Ah, did he? He is the most indefatigable sportsman! I have not yet seen him riding to hounds—neck-or-nothing, I feel tolerably certain!—but he is an excellent shot. Lucy, I never thanked you for coming so heroically to my rescue! My dear fellow, I could not be more grateful if I had needed you!"

"Bamming, Ger, bamming! I know *this* humour, and shan't be taken in!"

The Earl laughed, kissed the tips of his fingers to him, and vanished into the Castle.

He was received in his bedchamber by Turvey, who palpably winced at the sight of him. "I know, Turvey, I know!" he said. "My coat will never be the same again, do what you will, and I am sure you will do everything imaginable! As for my cravat, I might as well wear a Belcher handkerchief, might I not?"

"I am relieved to see that your lordship has sustained no serious injury," responded Turvey repressively.

"You must be astonished, I daresay, for you believe me to be a very fragile creature, don't you?"

"The tidings which were brought to the Castle by Miss Bolderwood were of a sufficiently alarming nature to occasion anxiety, my lord."

"Oh, so that is how the news was spread!"

"Miss Bolderwood had but just stepped down from my Lord Ulverston's curricle when your lordship's horse bolted past them. I understand that the young lady sustained a severe shock. Permit me, my lord, to relieve you of your coat!"

The Earl was seated at his dressing-table when, some twenty minutes later, Ulverston came into his room. He was dressed in his shirt and his satin knee-breeches, and was engaged on the delicate operation of arranging the folds of a fresh cravat into the style known as the Napoleon. At his elbow stood Turvey, intently watching the movements of his slender fingers. A number of starched cravats hung over the valet's forearm, and three or four crumpled wrecks lay on the floor at his feet. The Earl's eyes lifted briefly to observe his friend in the mirror. "Hush!" he said. "Pray do not speak, Lucy, or do anything to distract my attention!"

"Fop!" said the Viscount.

Turvey glanced at him reproachfully, but Gervase paid no heed. He finished tying the cravat, gazed thoughtfully at his reflection for perhaps ten seconds, while Turvey held his breath, and then said: "My coat, Turvey!"

A deep sigh was breathed by the valet. He carefully disposed the unwanted cravats across the back of a chair, and picked up a coat of dark blue cloth.

"And what do you call that pretty confection?" enquired Ulverston.

"The Napoleon—how can you be so ignorant? Do you think I ought not to wear it?"

"No, but I wonder you don't start a fashion of your own! *Earthquake à la St. Erth!* How's that, dear boy?"

Turvey gave a discreet cough. "If I may be permitted to say so, my lord, the Desborough tie already enjoys a considerable degree of popularity in the highest circles. We are at present perfecting the design of the Stanyon Fall, which, when disclosed, will, I fancy take the *ton* by storm."

"You should not betray our secrets, Turvey," Gervase said, standing up to allow the valet to help him to put on his coat. "Thank you: nothing more!"

Turvey bowed, and turned away to gather up the discarded riding-coat and breeches. The Earl had picked up a knife from his dressing-table, and was trimming his nails, and did not immediately look up. The valet paused, laid the breeches down again, and thrust a hand into the tail-pocket of the coat. He drew forth the coil of thin cord which was spoiling the set of the coat, and in the same instant the Earl raised his head, and perceived what he was doing. A shadow of annoyance crossed his face; he said, with rather more sharpness than was usually heard in his voice: "Yes, leave that here!"

The slight bow with which Turvey received this order expressed to a nicety his opinion of those who carried coils of cord in their pockets. He was about to lay the cord on the chair when the Viscount stepped forward, and took it out of his hand.

"You may go." The Earl's head was bent again over his task.

Ulverston returned to the fireplace, testing the cord by jerking a length of it between his hands. When Turvey had withdrawn, he said: "Saw a whole front rank brought down by that trick once. Mind, that was at night!—ambush!"

The Earl said nothing.

"Stupid thing to do, to leave it in your pocket, dear boy!"

"Very."

Ulverston tossed the coil aside. "Out with it, Ger! That's what happened, ain't it?"

"Yes."

"Martin?"

"I don't know."

"Well, one thing you do know is that he was in the grounds at the time!"

"So you say."

"Dash it, it was Clarence who said so, and what reason had he to say it if it wasn't true?"

"None. I don't doubt it: I fancy Martin generally does take a gun out at sundown."

"Well, what do you mean to do?" Ulverston demanded.

"Nothing."

"Famous!" said Ulverston. "That fairly beats the Dutch! I collect that a little thing like that—" he jerked his chin towards the cord "—don't even give you to think?"

"On the contrary, it gives me furiously to think. My reflections on this event may be false, and are certainly unpleasant, and with your good leave, Lucy, I'll keep them to myself."

"This won't serve!" Ulverston said. "You cannot do *nothing* when an attempt has been made to kill you!"

"Very well, what would you wish me to do?" Gervase asked, laying down the paring-knife. He glanced at the Viscount's scowling countenance, and smiled. "You don't know, do you? Shall I announce to the household that I was thrown by such a trick? Or shall I accuse my brother of wishing to make away with me?"

"Send him packing!"

"On what grounds?"

"Good God, ain't these grounds enough?"

"Yes, if I could prove them."

"There's your proof!" the Viscount said, pointing to the cord.

"My dear Lucy, proof that someone tried to play a malicious trick on me, but not proof that my death was intended."

"Stuff!" the Viscount said explosively. "How can you stand there talking such crack-brained nonsense to me, Ger?"

"Well, I am not dead, am I?" said Gervase. "I am not even hurt, and that I was stunned for a moment or two might be thought a mischance. If I had not fallen with my head upon the carriage-drive, that would not have occurred."

"What the devil are you trying to make me believe now?" demanded Ulverston, staring at him. "Do you take this to have been a schoolboy prank? There is no schoolboy in the case!"

"Oh, don't you think so? I find Martin not a step removed from that state. I own, I do not perfectly understand him, but it is sufficiently plain to me that he thinks I should be the better for a sharp set-down. You heard what passed at the table this morning: 'St. Erth is perfection itself!' was what he said before he flung himself out of the room. Well! It would certainly have afforded him satisfaction had I, the day you came here, suffered a ducking in a muddy stream. I did not do so, so perhaps I had instead to be made to tumble off my horse—such a nonpareil among horsemen am I said to be! By the way, I wonder who *did* say so?"

"It don't matter who said it, or if no one said it!" replied the Viscount, quite exasperated. "This is all a damned hum! Your precious brother ain't such a boy that he didn't know the thing might have had fatal consequences!"

"If he had paused to consider the matter at all," agreed St. Erth. "It is quite a question, you know, whether he *does* pause to consider what may be the outcome of his more headlong actions. Come in!"

A knock had sounded on the door, and this opened to admit Theo. Gervase instantly said: "Oh, the devil! No. Go away, Theo! Lucy has said it all for you!"

Theo shut the door, and advanced into the room. "No use, Gervase! I am determined to know what happened to you this afternoon. Ulverston has already said enough to make me uneasy—and I beg that you won't insult my intelligence with any more tales of stumbling into rabbit-holes, for they won't fadge!"

"All you'll get from Ger is a bag of moonshine!" said the Viscount roundly. "The plain truth is that his horse was brought down by a cord stretched across his path—and there is the cord, if you doubt me!"

"Oh, my God!" Theo said. "Martin?"

His cousin shrugged. He walked over to the fire, and stood staring down into it, his face hard to read.

"What I'm saying is that it's time Ger was rid of that lad!" announced the Viscount.

"Theo will not agree with you," interposed Gervase. "We have spoken of this before today."

"This had not happened then!" Theo said, slightly raising his head.

"Are you of another mind now?" Gervase asked, watching him.

Theo stood frowning. "No," he said, at last. "No, I am not of another mind. If Martin did indeed do this—but do you *know* that?—I am of the opinion that it was done in one of his fits of blind, unreasoning rage. His quarrel with you last night, his sister's teasing today—oh, I know Martin! He was as mad as a baited bear today, and in that mood he would not pause to consider the consequences of whatever foolish revenge he chose to take on you!"

"This," said the Viscount, not mincing matters, "is all fudge!"

"You don't know Martin as I do. But if he had a more dreadful purpose in mind—then I say keep him here, under your eye!"

The Viscount rubbed the tip of his nose reflectively. "Something to be said for that, Ger," he admitted.

"I have no intention, at present, of driving him away from Stanyon," Gervase said.

"Do you mean to charge him with today's misadventure?" Theo asked.

"No, and I beg you will not either!"

"Very well. I certainly did no good by anything I said to him about his conduct over the bridge," Theo said, with a wry grimace. "I wish I may not have goaded him into this. I begin to be sorry that I urged you to remain at Stanyon, Gervase. It might have been better, perhaps, to have given Martin time to have grown used to the thought that it is you who are master here now."

"He had a year in which to grow used to that thought," replied Gervase dryly. "Are you now advising me to retire to London? You are too late: I do not choose to be driven out of Stanyon."

"No, I would not advise that course. Matters must come to a head between you and Martin—but what that head will be, and whether you will be able to settle it without injury, and without scandal, I know not."

"Nor I, but I shall do my possible. Both injury and scandal I should dislike quite as much as you, Theo, I assure you. Meanwhile, there is no more to be said. It must be time for dinner: let us go and join her ladyship!"

They found the rest of the party already assembled in the Long Drawing-room. Martin was standing a little apart from the group near the fire, fidgeting with a pair of snuffers. He looked round when he heard the door open, and coloured a little. He had not encountered his brother since his outbreak of temper at the nuncheon-table, which might have accounted for the slight constraint with which he said: "Hallo, St. Erth! They tell me you have taken a toss. How came that about?"

"Mere carelessness. Cloud set his near-fore in a rabbit-hole."

"He wasn't hurt, was he?"

"A trifle scratched. I hope no lasting scars."

"Lord, that's bad!" Martin said. "I daresay you don't want my advice, but if I were you I would apply hot fomentations. They may bring up his legs like bladders, but *that* won't last, and ten to one you'll never see a mark once the cuts have healed."

"I agree with you, and it is being done."

The Dowager broke in at this point to favour the company with a recital of all the tosses which the Earl's father had taken, coupled with an account of her own sentiments upon these occasions, and some recollections of rattling falls suffered by her dear Papa, a very bruising rider. "Not that my dear father was not an excellent horseman, for I am sure there can never have been a better one," she said. "I am not fond of the exercise myself, but I daresay I should have ridden very well, had I taken to it, for I should have had the benefit of my father's teaching. Indeed, I recall to this day many of the maxims which he laid down for my brother's guidance. 'Hold him steady by the head' was one of them; and if he had been alive when Martin broke his collar-bone at one of the bullfinches in Ashby Pastures, he would have said, 'You should have held him steady by the head.' 'Throw your heart over,' was another of his sayings, and 'Take your own line', as well, and 'Get over the ground if you break your neck'."

The Earl was standing beside Martin, and said in a

soft undervoice: "Were you—er—acquainted with your grandfather, Martin?"

"No, I thank God!" returned Martin, grinning. "I'd be willing to lay you odds he was the kind of fellow who would head a fox!"

"Oh, I wouldn't take you!" Gervase said. "There cannot be the least doubt of it!"

It was fortunate that Abney entered the drawing-room at that moment, to announce dinner, for the sudden crack of laughter which escaped Martin attracted his mother's attention, and she demanded to be told what it was that had amused him. She did not forget that she desired to be admitted into his confidence, for her mind was of a tenacious order, but by the time she was seated at the foot of the dinner-table, and could repeat her demand, he had had leisure to think of a suitable and an unexceptionable answer.

CHAPTER TWELVE

A CERTAIN LANGUOR, which was felt by everyone except the Dowager, hung over the company. After the bustle and the excitement of the ball, the smaller party seemed flat. Between two of the persons seated at the table there was constraint; others had been provided with food for grave reflection; and only between the Dowager and the Chaplain could conversation have been said to have flourished. From the combined circumstances of being largely impervious to fatigue, and not having exerted herself beyond what was strictly necessary during the past twenty-four hours, the Dowager was not conscious of weariness, but enlivened the dinner-table with several more anecdotes about her father, and a recapitulation of the excellence of the arrangements for the ball, and the pleasure evinced at their entertainment by the guests. In this exercise she was assisted by Mr. Clowne, who indefatigably corroborated her statements, laughed heartily at her anecdotes, and generally enacted the role of antistrophe. Her care for his interests had placed Martin beside Marianne at the table, but her absorption in her own conversation prevented her from perceiving that for the first half of dinner, at least, this disposition was not a happy one.

Such laboured attempts at engaging Marianne's attention as were embarked upon by Martin were met by shy,
monosyllabic responses, and it was not until Gervase,
abandoning Miss Morville to his cousin, began to talk
to Marianne, interpolating such leading questions as
must draw Martin into the conversation, that the ice
between these old acquaintances melted. It was with
relief that those who knew him best realized that
Martin's mood was chastened. He seemed to have laid
aside his sulks, and to be determined to conduct himself,
even towards his brother, with a civility that bordered
on affability. His manner to Marianne could hardly have
been bettered, for he behaved as though he had forgotten the events of the previous evening. A lucky remark
of the Earl's enabled him to say to Marianne: "Do you
remember—?" She did remember, and in unexceptionable reminiscence was able to see in him again her favourite playfellow. Her constraint became noticeably
less; and by the time the dessert was set upon the table
she was chatting freely to Martin, and the Earl was able
to turn back to Miss Morville. Since the Dowager had
applied to Theo for the details of a very dull story with
which she was boring the Viscount, she had been neglected for several minutes, but she met the Earl's look
with a warm smile of approval.

"I do beg your pardon!" Gervase said, in an undervoice.

"Indeed, you need not!" she returned, in the same
tone. "It was very well done of you."

When the ladies left the room, Martin did not abate
his good-humour. The cloth was removed from the
table, the port and the madeira set upon it, while he con-

versed with the Viscount; and when the Viscount was drawn into a three-cornered discussion with Theo and Mr. Clowne, he only hesitated for a moment before changing his seat for the vacant one beside his brother.

The Earl regarded him pensively over the top of his wine-glass, but he said nothing. Martin raised his eyes, as though forcing himself to look him boldly in the face, and said: "St. Erth, I— Well— What I mean is—"

"Yes?" said Gervase encouragingly.

"It's only—St. Erth, I shouldn't have done it, of course! I didn't mean to, only—"

"Shouldn't have done what?"

"Last night—Marianne!"

"Oh!"

"The thing was, you see—"

"You need not tell me," Gervase interrupted, smiling. "I know very well what the thing was."

He saw the flicker of fire in the eyes so swiftly meeting his own at these words. He held them in a steady regard, and after a moment they fell, and Martin uttered a self-conscious laugh, and said: "Yes—I suppose! The thing is, ought I, do you think, to say anything to her?"

"On that subject? By no means! Let it go!"

Martin looked relieved. He drained his glass, found the decanter at his elbow, and refilled the glass, saying: "Then you don't think I should beg her pardon?"

"You would only cause her embarrassment."

"I daresay you may be right." Martin sipped his wine reflectively, and set his glass down again. "I wish that gray of yours had not cut his legs!" he said suddenly. "The most curst mischance! Can't think how he came to do so!"

"Or how I came to be thrown so ignominiously?" suggested the Earl, watching him.

"Oh, there's nothing in that! Everyone takes a stupid toss or so in his life! But your gray is a capital hunter! I would not have had him scar himself for a fortune!"

At this moment, the Viscount demanded that the decanter should be set in motion, and the conversation became general.

When the gentlemen presently joined the ladies, there was some talk of getting up a game of speculation, but the Dowager, who did not wish to play cards, said that everyone would prefer the indulgence of a little music, and begged Marianne to go to the piano-forte. Marianne looked very much alarmed, and assured her ladyship that her performance was not at all superior. When the Dowager showed no sign of accepting this excuse, she looked imploringly at Miss Morville, who at once responded to the silent appeal, rising from her chair, and saying: "I am sure Lady St. Erth would like to hear you sing, Marianne; and, if you will allow me, I shall be pleased to play for you."

It was not quite what Marianne desired, but since she had a pretty voice, and knew herself to have been well-taught, it was infinitely preferable to being obliged to struggle through a Haydn sonata. She accompanied her friend to the instrument, and delighted the company with two or three ballads. Not very much persuasion was needed to induce her to join with Lord Ulverston in a duet. Their voices blended admirably; they discovered a similarity of musical taste in one another; and if their combined performance gave little pleasure to one member of their audience, everyone else enjoyed it very much, the Dowager going so far as to beat time with one foot, and to hum several of the refrains.

The party broke up early that evening, the ladies going to bed immediately after prayers. The Earl took his friend off to play billiards, and Martin, to his surprise, went with him. He was so obliging as to mark for them, a kindness which made Ulverston glance rather keenly at him, and say, later, to the Earl: "Your engaging young brother remorseful, eh?"

Gervase smiled. "I told you he was not far removed from a schoolboy. We may go on more comfortably now."

"Shouldn't be surprised if it was all a take-in," replied the sceptical Viscount.

On the following day, both Miss Morville and Miss Bolderwood received missives from their mamas, Miss Bolderwood's having been brought over by a groom from Whissenhurst. Lady Bolderwood was able to leave her room again, and was anxious to have her daughter restored to her; and it seemed, from the contents of two closely-written sheets from Mrs. Morville, that Drusilla too would soon be leaving Stanyon. The Lakeland scenery was very fine, but Greta Hall was rather too full of Coleridges, Mrs. Coleridge and her interesting off-spring having apparently taken up permanent residence with the Southeys. Mrs. Morville wrote that a scheme was afoot to place poor Mr. Coleridge in the care of a gentleman living in Highgate. Mr. Southey had dis-closed that his unfortunate brother-in-law had been con-suming as much as two quarts of laudanum a week over the past couple of years. He gloomily believed that the charge of the children must fall upon his shoulders. He was already paying for Hartley's University career, and had sent Derwent to a private school at Ambleside. Sara, the youngest of the trio, was precocious, Mrs. Morville considered; and there was too much reason to fear that Hartley had inherited his father's instability of character. Mr. Morville, wrote his wife, was grieved to discover how far Mr. Southey had receded from his earlier and nobler ideals; for her part, Mrs. Morville could not wonder at it: she could only marvel at his being able to continue in the profession of author in the midst of such a household.

The Dowager expressed a gracious regret that they must bid farewell to Marianne that very day; at the prospect of soon losing Miss Morville's companionship she evinced a flattering concern, reiterating with unwearied frequency her conviction that Mrs. Morville could not possibly wish for her daughter's return to Gilbourne House.

To all her representations of the superior attractions of Stanyon over Gilbourne House Miss Morville returned civil but firm answers. Lord Ulverston begged to be granted the honour of escorting Miss Bolderwood to her own home, and upon Martin's saying hastily that he had the intention of performing this office, became afflicted with a deafness much more distressing to Martin than himself. Marianne blushed, thanked, and looked uncertain; after allowing the Dowager time to announce that she would herself drive to Whissenhurst with her young guest, Miss Morville said that she would like the drive. The Dowager had no objection to put forward to this, and the end of it was that the two ladies occupied the barouche, while Ulverston and St. Erth rode behind.

Arrived at Whissenhurst Grange, Marianne begged her three companions to enter the house, and to partake of refreshment there. The Earl demurred at this, thinking that the invalids might not wish for such an invasion, but while Marianne was assuring him that Mama would be disappointed if he did not come in to pay his respects to her, Sir Thomas was seen standing at the window of one of the front parlours, waving and beckoning. They all went into the house, therefore, and Lord Ulverston was made known to the Nabob and his lady. Wine and cakes were sent for, and while the Earl enquired after the state of Sir Thomas's health, Marianne, standing a little apart, beside the Viscount, said shyly that she supposed he would be leaving Stanyon very soon too. But it seemed that the Viscount had no immediate intention of leaving Stanyon. Marianne was surprised, and said, looking innocently up into his face: "I quite thought that you stayed only for the ball!"

"No—oh, no!" Ulverston responded. "Don't quite know how long I shall be fixed at Stanyon!"

"Shall you be in town when we give *our* ball?" asked Marianne.

"Yes," replied his lordship promptly. "Will Lady Bolderwood send me a card?"

"Oh, yes! I hope you will be able to come to it!"

"Not a doubt of it, Miss Bolderwood: I shall most certainly come to it! When do you remove to London?"

"I believe, in a fortnight's time—if Papa's illness has not overset our plans."

"A fortnight? Just when I shall be going to London myself!" he said.

"But you said you did not know when you should be going!" she pointed out, laughing a little.

"Quite true! I didn't! You had not told me *then* how long you would be remaining in Lincolnshire."

She looked charmingly confused, her art of coquetry deserting her, and could only blush more than ever, and pretend to be busy with the retying of one of the knots of ribbon which adorned her dress.

Sir Thomas, meanwhile, who had been persuaded to resume both his seat by the fire and the plaid shawl which had been draped round his shoulders, said to the Earl: "Who is this young fellow, eh, my lord? What did you say his name was?"

"Ulverston: he is Wrexham's eldest son, and, like myself, has lately sold out of the Army."

"H'm!" Sir Thomas's shrewd gaze dwelled for a minute on the Viscount and Marianne. "I like the cut of his jib," he decided.

"He is the best of good fellows."

Lady Bolderwood seemed also to like the Viscount, which was not surprising, since he seized the first opportunity that offered of seating himself on the sofa beside her, and making himself agreeable. Upon hearing that he was staying for the present at Stanyon, she very cordially invited him to come to Whissenhurst with the Earl to an informal party she had the intention of giving before leaving for London. He accepted, but he did not feel it to be incumbent upon him to tell her that she might expect to have the pleasure of seeing him at Whissenhurst considerably before this date.

The Stanyon party soon took leave, and Lady Bolderwood went with Marianne upstairs to her dressing-room, in the expectation of hearing every detail of her visit. She did indeed hear that Marianne had enjoyed herself very much, that Lady St. Erth had been kind, and dear Drusilla *very* kind, that the ball had been delightful, and she had had so many partners she could not remember the half of them; but it seemed to her that her daughter was rather abstracted. She supposed that she was tired from so much excitement, and expected her to profit by a long night's rest. But on the following morning Marianne was more abstracted than ever; paid very little need to Mr. Warboys, who called at Whissenhurst on the plausible excuse of wishing to know how Sir Thomas was going on; and was three times discovered by her Mama to be lost in some day-dream: once when she should have been practising her music, once when she had been desired to wash the Sèvres ornaments in the drawing-room, and once when she should have been setting stitches in the sampler destined for her Aunt Caroline. Lady Bolderwood felt herself to be obliged to speak reprovingly to her, pointing out to her that if she allowed herself to be so much affected by one country-ball, a Season in London would transform her into a good-for-nothing miss, never happy except when at a party. Much discomposed, Marianne bent over the sampler, murmuring that it was not *that,* and indeed she did not care so very much for parties.

"Well, my love, you must not let Stanyon make you discontented, you know. I daresay the Rutlands, and their set, may have been very agreeable, but I did not like to see you so uncivil to poor Barny Warboys."

"Oh, *no,* Mama!" Marianne protested, tears starting to her eyes.

"You did not make him very welcome, did you? One should never discard old friends, my dear, for new ones."

"I did not mean—I have the head-ache a little!" Marianne faltered. "*Indeed* I did not mean to be unkind to Barny!"

"No, my love, I am persuaded you would not mean to be unkind," Lady Bolderwood said, patting her cheek. "It is just that your mind is running a little too much on your pleasuring at Stanyon. There! Don't cry! I know I have only to give you a hint."

Marianne kissed her, and promised amendment. She did indeed perform conscientiously such tasks as were given her, but her spirits were uneven. At one moment she would be her merry self, at the next she would be pensive, slipping away to walk by herself in the shrubbery, or sitting with her eyes bent on the pages of a book, and her thoughts far away. The various young gentlemen who paid morning-visits to Whissenhurst found her gay, but disinclined to flirt with them, a change which Lady Bolderwood at first saw with satisfaction, and which soon led her to suspect that Marianne might have got into a scrape at Stanyon. When Martin came to Whissenhurst, and was met by Marianne with unaccustomed formality, she was sure of it, and she begged her daughter to tell her what had occurred. Marianne, hanging down her head, admitted that Martin had tried to make love to her, but she hastened to add that it had not been so *very* bad, and Drusilla had thought it would be foolish to refine too much upon it.

"Drusilla Morville is a very sensible girl," said Lady

Bolderwood approvingly. "She is perfectly right, and perhaps I am not sorry that it happened, for it has made you see what flirting leads to, my dear, and in future you will take better care, I am sure."

She believed that the want of tone in Marianne's spirits was now accounted for, but when she confided the story to her husband he disconcerted her by saying in his bluff way: "Well, Mama, you should know your daughter best, but it's the first time I ever heard of a girl's moping about the house because a handsome young fellow shows himself to be head over ears in love with her!"

"My dear Sir Thomas, I am persuaded she was much shocked by Martin's behaviour—"

"Shocked! Ay, so she might be, the naughty puss! But that's no reason why she should peck at her dinner, and sit staring into the fire when she thinks we ain't watching her. No, no, my lady, if it's young Frant who has made her lose her appetite, you may call me a Dutchman!"

His wife smiled indulgently, and shook her head, but events proved Sir Thomas to have been right. On the very next morning, when Marianne sat in the window of the front parlour with her Mama, helping her to hem some handkerchiefs, a horseman was seen trotting up the drive. Lady Bolderwood did not immediately recognize him, and she was just wondering aloud who it could be when she became aware of an extraordinary change in her listless daughter. Marianne was blushing, her head bent over her stitchery, but the oddest little smile trembling on her lips. In great astonishment, Lady Bolderwood stared at her.

"I think—I believe—it is Lord Ulverston, Mama!" murmured Marianne.

Lord Ulverston it was, and in a very few moments he was shaking hands with them, fluently explaining that since his way led past their house he could not but call to enquire whether Sir Thomas and her ladyship were quite recovered from their indispositions. Lady Bolderwood's astonishment grew, for as he turned from her to take Marianne's hand in his she perceived such a glowing look in her daughter's countenance, such a shy yet beaming smile in her eyes as made her seem almost a stranger to her own mother.

Sir Thomas, informed by a servant of his lordship's arrival, then entered the room, and made the Viscount heartily welcome. To his lady's considerable indignation, he bestowed on her a quizzing look which informed her how far more exactly he had read their daughter's mind than she had.

The Viscount stayed chatting easily for perhaps half an hour, and if his eyes strayed rather often to Marianne's face, and his voice underwent a subtle change when he had occasion to address her, his conduct was otherwise strictly decorous. When he rose to depart, Sir Thomas escorted him to the front-door. No sooner, however, was the parlour-door shut behind them than his lordship requested the favour of a few words with his host.

"Ho! So that's it, is it?" said Sir Thomas. "Well, well, you had better come into my library, my lord, I suppose!"

When Sir Thomas presently rejoined his ladies, and they had watched the Viscount riding away, Marianne asked if he had been showing his Indian treasures to his lordship.

"Ay, that was it," replied Sir Thomas, chuckling. But when Marianne had left the room, he said to his wife, with one of his cracks of mirth: "Indian treasures! It wasn't any *Indian* treasure his lordship came after!"

"Good heavens!" she exclaimed. "You cannot, surely, mean that he has made an offer for Marianne?"

"That's it. Came to ask my permission to pay his addresses to her, just as he ought."

"But he has only been acquainted with her a few days!"

"What's that got to say to anything? I knew *my* mind five minutes after I met you, my lady!"

"She is too young! Why, she is not yet out!"

"Ay, so I told him. I said we could not sanction any *engagement* until she had seen a bit of the world."

She regarded him with suspicion. "Sir Thomas, do you mean to tell me you gave him permission to pay his addresses?"

"Why, I said if my girl loved him I would not say no," he confessed. "It would be no bad thing for her, you know, Maria. Setting aside the title, he's just the cut of a man I fancy for my little puss. He ain't after her fortune: from what he tells me, he's a man of comfortable fortune himself. I can tell you this, I'd as lief her affections were engaged before we expose her to all the handsome young scamps with high-sounding titles and lean purses who are hanging out in London for rich wives!"

"I am persuaded she would never—"

"Maria, my dear, there's no saying what she might do, for she's not up to snuff, like some of the young ladies I've seen, and when a girl is heiress to a hundred thousand pounds every needy rascal will be paying court to her! A pretty thing it would be if she chose to set her heart on a man that only wants her fortune!"

"Yes, yes, but— My dear Sir Thomas, you run on so fast! You do not consider! The Wrexhams might not care for the match, after all!"

He gave a dry chuckle. "There's only one thing could make the Wrexhams, or any other high family, dislike it, Maria, and that's for me to gamble my fortune away on 'Change!" he said.

CHAPTER THIRTEEN

WHILE THE Viscount was pursuing his courtship of Marianne, Martin seemed to be making an effort to get upon better terms with his half-brother. His attempts at friendliness, which were sometimes rather too studied, were tranquilly received, the Earl neither encouraging nor repulsing him, but holding himself a little aloof, and meeting advances that were not unlike those of a half-savage puppy with a serenity which was as unruffled by present blandishments as it had been by past enmity.

Though the Viscount might regard Martin's change of face with suspicion, Theo and Miss Morville observed it with feelings of hope, and of relief.

"I think," Miss Morville said thoughtfully, "that the sweetness of his lordship's temper has had its effect upon Martin. He was at first inclined to see in it a lack of manly spirit, and now that he has discovered how far this is from the truth he begins to respect him—and with Martin, you know, respect must be the foundation of liking."

"Exactly so!" Theo said warmly. "Your observation is very just, Drusilla! For my part, I believe Martin has seen the folly of his former conduct, and means to do better in the future."

"And for *my* part," interpolated Ulverston, "I think your precious Martin has had a fright, and is set on making us all think him reconciled to Ger's existence!"

"A harsh judgment!" Theo said, smiling. "I have known Martin almost from his cradle, and I cannot believe that there is any real harm in him. He is hot-at-hand, often behaves stupidly, but that there is vice in him I *will* not think!"

"Ay, there you have the matter in a nutshell!" said Ulverston. "You *will* not think it!"

"I know what is in your mind, but I believe him to have repented most sincerely."

"Lord, Frant, do you take me for a flat? If he repents, it is because he caused Ger's horse to cut his knees!" He encountered a warning look cast at him from under Theo's brows, and added impatiently: "Nonsense! Miss Morville was with him, and must know the truth!"

"Drusilla, is this so indeed? And you said nothing?"

"I do know the cause of the accident," she replied calmly. "His lordship desired me to hold my peace, however, and I have done so, because I think him very well able to conduct his own affairs without my interference."

"None better!" said the Viscount. "Never knew anyone with a better understanding! He ain't the man to be taken-in by a hoax, and if he don't see that all this brotherly love that whelp is showing him is too smoky by half, he ain't such a deep 'un as I've always thought!"

"Remember, though you may know Gervase, I have reason to know Martin!" Theo said. "I must continue to hold by my opinion! I don't deny that I have been made to feel a greater degree of uneasiness than perhaps you have any idea of, but events have so turned out that I begin to think that I shall be able to leave Stanyon with a quiet mind presently."

"Leave Stanyon? Do you mean to do so?" asked the Viscount, surprised.

"Oh, not for ever! Merely, I ought, a week ago, to have set forth on my travels, and have postponed my journey. I am my cousin's agent, you know, and at this season I, in general, spend some days at his various estates."

"Ay, do you so? And why have you postponed your journey?" demanded the Viscount.

Theo laughed. "Yes, yes, you have me there! But that is to be a thing of the past, if you please! If Martin's passions have led him to play some dangerous pranks on his brother, he will do so no more! See if I am not right!"

Martin himself seemed anxious to reassure his cousin. His reason for doing so was not far to seek, and he stated it bluntly, saying: "You need not spy on me, Theo! I know you think I may play some trick on St. Erth, but I shall not!"

"My dear Martin!"

"Well, you do think it!" Martin insisted. "Merely because I didn't warn him about that bridge! Such a kick-up as you made!"

"Are you surprised?"

"Oh, well! I own I shouldn't have cared if he had fallen into the river, *then;* but I have come to think he is not such a bad fellow—if only one knew how to take him!"

"Is it so difficult?"

"It may not be for you, because he likes you."

"He has given you little cause to suppose that he does not like you," Theo said, in a dry tone.

"You may as well say that *I* gave him cause not to like me, for that's what you mean, I collect!" said Martin rather angrily. "I don't know what you think I may do to tease him, but I wish you will stop hovering about me, as though you were my gaoler, or some such thing!"

"This is fancy, Martin!"

"No, it ain't. Why did you choose to go with us, when I took Gervase round the new coverts?"

"Good God! Why should I not go with you?"

"That wasn't the only time, either!" pursued Martin. "I suppose you thought, when I challenged him to shoot against me, I might fire my pistol at him instead of the mark, unless you were there to watch us?"

"No, Martin: in spite of what occurred when you tried to match him with foils, I did not think that."

Martin flushed hotly. "That was an accident!"

"No accident that you did not get out of distance when you saw that the button was off your foil."

"If you mean to throw it up at me for ever that I lost my temper— Besides, he is a much more skilful fencer than I am! I could never have touched him!"

"I beg your pardon! I had no thought of throwing it up at you, until you began on this nonsense. You had better put it out of your head. You will not be burdened with my presence for a while: I am off to Evesleigh, and then to Maplefield, in a day or two."

When the Earl heard of these plans, he showed how well-aware he was of having been kept under protective surveillance by laughing, and asking, at his most demure, if Theo thought that he would be safe without him. He was playing chess with Miss Morville, in the library, when Theo informed him what his movements would be, and he did not scruple to add: "I go on very well with Martin, and shall go on better still when I have no watch-dog. I am much obliged to you, Theo, but I fancy your care of me has not gone unobserved, and has done little to endear me to Martin. It is your move, Miss Morville."

"I know it, but I *think* you have laid a trap for me," she responded, frowning at the board. "I have noticed, my lord, that whenever you make what seems to me to be a careless move I immediately find myself in difficulties."

"What an unhandsome fellow!" said Theo, smiling. "I had not thought him capable of duplicity!"

"Strategy, not duplicity, Theo!"

"I stand corrected. I wish my own efforts in strategy equalled yours, but they seem to be sadly deficient in subtlety. You are right, Gervase: I have been taken to task by Martin for having accompanied you both on your various expeditions, and will mend my ways."

"Yes, pray do so: I don't need a bodyguard. But must you go to Evesleigh? Can your business there not be done from Stanyon? It is only ten miles distant, is it not?"

"A little more than that. I find it is always better if I spend a day or two on the premises. The question is whether, this year, I should go to Studham. I must ask Martin if he wishes it."

"Ask Martin if he wishes what?" demanded Martin, who had entered the room in time to overhear this.

"Studham. Do you mean to be your own agent, or shall I act for you?"

"Lord, I'd forgotten that! I wouldn't above half mind managing the place myself, if it *were* mine!"

Theo looked amused. "If it were not for *one* circumstance, I should suggest that you accompany me there," he said. "As it is, if you go, you go alone! I shall not readily forget your last encounter with its present occupant."

"Is it possible that Martin does not care for Aunt Dorothea?" asked the Earl, moving one of his knights to protect a threatened pawn.

Martin grinned, but it was Theo who answered: "It is a case of mutual dislike. It has been my unhappy fate to act as mediator in several skirmishes, and it is my firm resolve not to be present at their Waterloo!"

"I'll tell you what, St. Erth!" said Martin. "*You* should go to Studham with Theo!"

"I can perceive not the smallest reason why I should do anything of the sort."

"To pay your respects to my aunt, of course! If you will invite her to live here, dash it, *I* will go and live at Studham!"

"Thank you, Martin, I prefer your company to Aunt Dorothea's."

"Why, how is this? I had thought you liked her! You threatened to bring her here, didn't you?"

"There was really no danger of my doing so, however."

"What a hand you are! I must say, I wish my father had not allowed her to settle at Studham, for she is bound to live for ever, only to spite me."

"You had better give her notice to leave."

"Well, I would, but the thing is that I don't know that it would suit me to live there myself," said Martin ingenuously. "To be at such a distance from Quorndon

Hall! I don't know how I should go on." He paused, and added: "Of course, if you would like to be rid of me—"

"No, not at all. Check, Miss Morville!"

"Black must resign, I believe. You will chase my King all over the board."

"Where is Ulverston?" asked Martin abruptly.

"I fancy he has ridden out."

"Oh!" The lowering expression descended on to Martin's brow. "How long does he mean to remain at Stanyon?"

"I have no idea."

"I thought he meant only to stay for a day or two," Martin muttered.

The Earl made no reply. Theo said: "Well, if I am to do your business for you, Martin, it will be well if I have your instructions. Are you at liberty? Come to my room!"

"Oh, you will manage better than I should, I daresay!" Martin said, shrugging, but following him to the door. "But I wish you will look into what that stupid fellow Mugginton is about! How my father came to appoint such a saphead as bailiff I don't know! Why, the last time I was there, he was talking of putting the Long Acre down to wheat! Now, Theo, you *know*—"

The closing of the door cut off the end of this sentence. Miss Morville said, as she restored the chessmen to their box: "It is a pity that he and Lady Cinderford cannot agree, for he needs occupation, and nothing would suit him so well as to be managing an estate. I believe he knows as well what should be done as your bailiff does."

"I fancy he will never live at Studham. It is extremely profitable, however, so if he chooses to do so he may buy himself a house in Leicestershire."

She considered this, but shook her head. "I think he would not be happy there. I daresay you may not have talked with him very much, or he might be shy of confiding in you, but his thoughts are bound up in Stanyon. He loves it, you know."

"For him it is full of the happiest memories," he remarked.

She raised her eyes to his face. "Do you dislike it so very much, my lord?"

"Why, no! I am learning to like it pretty fairly, I think. I imagine it must have every inconvenience known to man, but it might be made tolerably comfortable, if one cared enough to set about the task."

"Well, I hope you will care enough," she said. "And, if I were you, my lord, the first thing that I would do would be to make one of the saloons on this floor, which nobody ever uses, into a dining-parlour! Then you might not be obliged to partake of dishes that are cold before ever they reach the table!"

He laughed. "An advantage, I own! When I undertake my improvements, I shall certainly come to you for advice, ma'am!"

"I don't suppose that you will," she replied. "You will, instead, place the whole in the hands of some fashionable architect, and he will build you another wing, so that you will find yourself worse off than before."

"Very much worse off, if I am to employ a fashionable architect! Whom have you in mind? Nash? Beyond my touch, I fear!"

"I don't *think*," she said seriously, "that Mr. Nash's style would be at all suitable for Stanyon."

The news that Theo was about to set out, as he had

punctually done for several years, on visits to the Earl's various properties naturally afforded the Dowager with matter for surprise and complaint. She said a great many times that she had had no notion that he had meant to go away; and long before she had reached the end of her objections to the project the uninitiated might well have supposed that Mr. Theodore Frant spent the better part of each year in jauntering about the country, while everything at Stanyon was left at a stand. He met her complaints with unmoved patience, only taking the trouble to answer them when she demanded a response from him. From having looked upon any enlargement of the family-party at Stanyon with bitter misgiving, she had now reached the stage of bemoaning its break-up. It occurred to her that with Theo absent her whist-table must depend upon Miss Morville for its fourth; and this circumstance brought to her mind the imminent return of Mr. and Mrs. Morville to the neighbourhood, and their daughter's consequent departure from Stanyon. "And then, I daresay, you will be going to London, St. Erth," she said. "I am sure I do not know what I shall do, for I have no intention of removing to town until May. London does not agree with my constitution. When Martin goes, he may stay with his sister. She will be very glad to welcome him, I daresay."

"Stay with Louisa, and that prosy fool of a husband of hers?" exclaimed Martin. "No, I thank you! Besides, I may not go to London at all!"

"Not go to London! You will go to the Bolder-woods' ball!"

"I don't know that," Martin said sullenly.

This astonishing announcement set up a fresh train

of thought in the Dowager's mind, even more unwelcome to her audience. She could not imagine what her son could be thinking about, for she was sure that if he had said once that he should go to London when the Bolderwoods left Lincolnshire he had said it a hundred times. No efforts were spared either by Gervase or by Miss Morville to introduce a topic of conversation that would give her thoughts another direction, but they were unavailing: she continued to wonder and to comment until her exasperated son abruptly left the room.

Her egotism did not permit her often to trouble herself with the concerns of others, but Martin was her darling, and if she did not go to the length of putting his interests before her own convenience, at least she grudged no time spent in discussing his welfare. She feared that a lovers' quarrel must have estranged Martin from Miss Bolderwood; and when Miss Morville, to whom she confided this solution, ventured to suggest that whatever Martin's feelings might be Marianne had given no one reason to suppose that she favoured him more than any of her other suitors, she was incredulous. She must think it an absurdity that any young woman should not fall in love with Martin. *She* had signified her approval of the match, so what could be the hindrance, excepting only some nonsensical tiff? Could it be that the Bolderwoods had not presumed to think her kindness to their daughter a hint that she would not object to receiving her as a member of the family? She believed Sir Thomas to be a very respectable man, who would be anxious not to encroach: she had a very good mind to drive over to Whissenhurst to set his mind at rest on this score.

Miss Morville was not easily daunted, and although this suggestion might make her blench she contrived to conceal her dismay, and to argue her ladyship out of a decision which could only lead, she believed, to a painful scene with Sir Thomas.

"Can it be," demanded the Dowager, suddenly struck by a new idea, "that the Bolderwoods are hopeful of drawing St. Erth in? Upon my word, *that* would be a high flight indeed! I had not believed Sir Thomas to be capable of such presumption, for the Earl of St. Erth, you know, may look as high as he may choose for a bride, and had there been the least chance of Martin's succeeding to the title I should not have countenanced the Bolderwood connection for a moment!"

"I do not think, ma'am, that such a thought has entered Sir Thomas's head. He and Lady Bolderwood consider Marianne to be too young to be thinking of marriage."

"Depend upon it, my dear, a girl is never too young for her parents to be scheming to make a good match for her," said the Dowager. "I shall drive over to Whissenhurst, and just drop a hint that an alliance with St. Erth would be most unacceptable to me. I assure you, I should oppose it with my dying breath!"

Miss Morville found no difficulty in believing her; her dependence on the likelihood of this opposition's being attended to, either by the Earl or by Sir Thomas, was less secure, and she renewed her efforts to dissuade her ladyship from a mission which could only end in her discomfiture. By dint of discovering in herself a great desire to see Marianne again, and stressing the propriety of discovering exactly how the

case might be before her ladyship moved in it, she succeeded in persuading her to postpone her visit to Whissenhurst until she had been put in possession of all the
facts. These she engaged herself to discover. It did not
seem to her to be incumbent on her to suggest to the
Dowager that it was an Austell and not a Frant who
had succeeded in capturing the heiress's affections.
The shock would be severe, she knew; and she suspected that nothing less than a public announcement
of betrothal would suffice to convince her ladyship
that any other than a Frant had been accepted by the
Bolderwoods.

Since Theo had formed the intention of riding to
Whissenhurst on the following morning, to take formal
leave of the Bolderwoods, Miss Morville applied to
him for escort. He expressed his willingness to go with
her, and they rode there together, in happy ignorance
that Martin had set out earlier in the same direction.

It was inevitable that Theo should learn from her the
reason for her visit, for he was so much in everyone's
confidence that it seemed the most natural thing to tell
him what had passed between herself and the Dowager.
He was not so much diverted as she had expected him
to be, but said, with a forced smile only: "I have lived
too long with her ladyship to be surprised by her absurd-
ities. It must have been plain to everyone but herself
from the first moment of his clapping eyes on her that
Ulverston was much struck by Miss Bolderwood. The
fact is that she would not readily be brought to believe
that even a Howard or a Percy could be preferred to a
Frant." He was silent for a moment, and then said: "I
must suppose that the Bolderwoods, discovering that St.

Erth had no serious intentions, are anxious to secure Ulverston for their daughter. It is not to be wondered at."

He spoke in his usual quiet way, but she thought that
she could detect an undercurrent of bitterness in his
tone, and said: "You do them less than justice, I think.
Their ambition is merely to see Marianne happy."

"Certainly, but they may be pardoned for believing
that the happiness of a future Countess is more likely
than that of a mere commoner's wife. I do not blame
them: Miss Bolderwood is worthy of the highest
honour."

He said no more, and she did not pursue the subject,
but turned the talk, after a minute's silence, into less
awkward channels.

Martin, meanwhile, had reached Whissenhurst a
little earlier. As he rode in at the gate, he obtained a
glimpse of Marianne through a division in the yew
hedge which screened the drive from the gardens. He
guessed that she was busy amongst the spring bulbs
which had become one of her chief hobbies, and at
once turned his horse towards the stableyard. Leaving
the hack in the care of the head-groom, he made his way
to the succession-houses which Sir Thomas had had
erected at such enormous expense. She was not there,
but just as Martin was standing irresolute, wondering
if, by ill-luck, she had gone into the house again, he
heard the sound of her voice uplifted in a gay ballad. It
came from the potting-shed, and he strode up to it, and
looked in, to find that she was alone there, engaged in
transferring several white hyacinths from their separate
earthenware pots to a large Worcestershire bowl. She
made a charming picture, with her pale golden curls un-

covered, and confined only by a blue riband, a shawl pinned round her shoulders, and a small trowel in one hand. She did not immediately perceive Martin, but went on singing to herself, and carefully pressing down the earth round her bulbs, while he watched her. Some slight movement he made which caught her attention; she looked round, and with a startled exclamation dropped the trowel.

He came into the shed, and picked up the trowel. "You need not jump and squeak!" he said. "It's only I!"

She took the trowel from him, and laid it down. "Oh, no! I did not mean— That is, I was not expecting— You gave me such a fright! Thank you! See, are they not perfect blooms? I am so proud of them, and mean to place them in Papa's book-room, for he would only laugh, when I began my gardening, and said my bulbs would come to nothing, because I should forget all about them in a week. He will be regularly set-down!"

"Marianne," he said, disregarding this speech, "I came because I must and will speak to you!"

"Oh, pray—! Of course I am always pleased to see you, Martin, but I can't think what you should want to speak to me about! Don't look so grave! It is such a lovely day, and when the sun shines I can't be solemn— you must know I cannot!"

He was not to be diverted; he said: "You have not allowed me to come near you since the night of the ball. I frightened you—I should not have spoken to you *then!*—but you cannot have doubted my—my sentiments towards you!"

"I hope we have always been good friends," she said nervously. "Pray do not pain me by speaking of what

happened *that* night! You did not mean it—I am persuaded you did not mean it!"

"Nonsense!" he interrupted, almost angrily. "Of
course I meant it! You know that!"

She hung down her head, faltering: "I am afraid I
have not always behaved as I should. I didn't guess—
but it was wrong of me, if—if my conduct led you to
suppose—that I was in the expectation of receiving a
declaration from you."

He looked at her with a kindling pair of eyes. "It was
not so with you a week ago!"

"I was foolish—Mama said I ought not—"

"It is all since this frippery fellow Ulverston came
to Stanyon!" he interrupted. "You have been flirting
with him, encouraging his advances—"

"It is not true! I won't listen to you! You ought not
to say these things, Martin! You know you ought not!
Pray do not!"

"You think you may keep me on your string with all
the rest, but you are mistaken! I love you, Marianne!"

She made a protesting gesture, and he caught her
hand, and held it in a hard grasp. Words tumbled off his
tongue, but she was too much distressed to listen to his
vows to make her happy, if only she would marry him.
Trying unavailing to free her hand, she gasped: "No, no,
you must not! Papa would not permit me—indeed,
indeed, this is very wrong in you, Martin!"

He now had possession of her other hand as well;
looking up at him, she was alarmed to see so stormy an
expression in his face. She could as readily have
believed that he hated her as that he loved her, and the
knowledge that her own light-hearted coquetry had

roused so much passion filled her with as much peni-
tence as terror. With tears trembling on the ends of her
lashes, she could only utter: "I didn't mean it! I didn't
understand!"

"You thought differently once! Until St. Erth came
home! Is that what it is? First St. Erth, now Ulverston!
You would sing another tune if I were St. Erth, wouldn't
you? By God, I think I begin to value you as I should!"

She was provoked into crying out against this accusation, her tears now falling fast. "It is untrue! Let me
go! You are hurting me! Let me go! Oh, please, please
let me go!"

There seemed to be little likelihood of his attending
to her, but at that moment the Viscount, who had come
out of the house in search of her, looked into the shed.
Two swift strides brought him up to them; his hand
gripped Martin's shoulder; he said authoritatively:
"That will do! You forget yourself, Frant!"

Marianne was released immediately. Martin spun
round, the intervention, coming from such a source,
being all that was needed to fan his passion to a flame.
The Viscount was granted barely more than a second to
read his purpose in his blazing eyes, but he was a quick-
witted young man, and it was enough. He rode the blow
aimed for his chin, countered swiftly, and floored
Martin. Marianne, backed against the wall of the shed,
uttered a little scream of terror, pressing her hands to
her blanched cheeks.

The Viscount stepped quickly up to her, saying,
with a reassuring smile: "Beg pardon! An infamous
thing to alarm you so! Don't cry! No need at all—
word of a gentleman! Will you go into the house?

Miss Morville is sitting with your Mama. You'll find Theo Frant as well—overtook 'em on the road here! Say nothing about this to your parents! Much better not, you know!"

"Oh, no!" she said faintly. "But you won't—you won't—?"

"Lord, no!" he said cheerfully, drawing her towards the door. "Nothing for you to tease yourself about!"

She whispered his name beseechingly, but he said, in a low tone: "Hush! Not now!" and gave her a little push over the threshold.

Martin had picked himself up from among the shattered pots, and was furiously brushing the dirt from his person. The Viscount surveyed him sardonically. "Habit of yours—forcing your attentions on females who don't want 'em?"

Martin's fists clenched, but he kept them at his sides. "You'll meet me for this, my lord!"

"Tomfoolery!" Ulverston said shortly.

"You may name your friends! They will hear from mine!"

"Good God, how can I meet you?" demanded Ulverston. "I'm a guest in your brother's house, you young fool!"

"It is not my house! You've knocked me down: do you mean to deny me satisfaction?"

"Y'know I've no taste for rodomontade!" said Ulverston. "You should be thanking me for having given you the leveller you were standing in crying need of!"

He would have left the shed on the words, but Martin stood in his way. "Will you, my lord, name your friends, or don't you care to pit your marksmanship against mine?"

"Oh, go to the devil!" snapped Ulverston. "Whom would you have me name? Your brother? Your cousin?"

Martin was for the moment nonplussed, but he recovered quickly, and said: "Mr. Warboys will be happy to serve you!"

"Thank you! I shan't call upon him to act for me."

Martin's right hand came up like a flash, and struck him an openhanded blow across the cheek. "Does *that* make you change your mind, my lord?"

The Viscount, curbing his instincts, kept his own hands lowered, but he was by this time very angry indeed. He said: "Yes, that makes me change my mind! If no one else will teach you a lesson, Martin Frant, I will!"

CHAPTER FOURTEEN

IT WAS FORTUNATE for the cordiality of the relations between Stanyon and Whissenhurst that before she had reached the house Marianne was met by Miss Morville, who had walked out to look for her. It was evident that Marianne was much discomposed, her bosom heaving, her eyes full of tears, and her cheeks whitened. She uttered the one word: "Martin!" in answer to her friend's solicitous enquiry, and seemed inclined to fall into strong hysterics. Miss Morville needed no more to prompt her to convey Marianne upstairs to her own room, and to beg her to tell her the whole. The story which was poured into her ears was incoherent, and freely interspersed with self-blame. She unravelled it as best she might, and did what lay in her power to soothe Marianne's fears. When, shuddering, Marianne told her of the brief fight in the shed, she could not help smiling a little, so very much shocked did Marianne seem to be. She apologized for this insensibility by explaining that she had so often seen her brothers at fisticuffs, and had so often applied raw steaks to their blackened eyes, that she no longer felt on this subject as perhaps she ought. She could even hope that the exchange of blows might have gone some way to relieve exacerbated tempers, but

Marianne's description of the scene, and of Martin's mien when he picked himself up from the floor, soon put such comfortable ideas to flight. She knew his temper; she could imagine what his chagrin must be: her only dependence must be on Ulverston's good sense.

"If they were to meet—and *I* the cause—!" Marianne said, wringing her hands.

"Well, they shan't meet," replied Miss Morville. "It would be most improper!"

"Improper! It might be fatal!"

"I cannot suppose that either would be so stupid."

"Not Ulverston, no! But Martin! In such anger! How can you tell what he might do?"

"You are right: I can't tell," owned Miss Morville, dispassionately considering it. "Well, there is nothing for it but to put a stop to a duel—if that is indeed what they intend, and I daresay it may be, for gentlemen have such nonsensical notions that one may believe them to be capable of any folly."

"Oh, if one could but prevent it! But they will tell us nothing, for females should never know anything about such things! They would dislike it so very much, if one attempted to interfere in a matter of honour!"

"I am not in the least concerned with what they may dislike," replied Miss Morville somewhat tartly. "What I am thinking of is how excessively disagreeable it would be for you and the Frants to have such a scandal in your midst. Do let me beg of you, my dear Marianne, not to mention what has occurred to another soul! There will be no duel, if I have to lay an information against them both to prevent it."

Marianne looked as though she hardly knew

whether to be relieved or scandalized. "Oh, that would be dreadful!"

"You need not be alarmed: I am persuaded there will be no need to proceed to such an extreme."

Her air of assurance had its effect. Marianne dried her tears, and was soothed. By the time she had tidied her ruffled ringlets, and folded up her shawl, she was calm enough to descend the stairs to the saloon, where Ulverston and Theo were chatting to Sir Thomas and his lady.

There was nothing to be learned from the Viscount's manner, but Miss Morville thought that Theo was looking grave. Of Martin there was no sign, and since the Bolderwoods did not mention him she supposed that he must have left Whissenhurst without seeing them.

This was soon found to have been the case. The Stanyon party left the Grange together, and while Ulverston was exchanging a word or two with Sir Thomas on the front steps Theo found the opportunity to draw Miss Morville aside, and to ask her if she knew what was amiss between Martin and the Viscount.

"Yes, and so, I fancy, must everyone! Has Ulverston spoken to you?"

"Not Ulverston, but I ran into Martin, and I never saw the boy look so wild! Some nonsense he blurted out to me, demanding if I would act for Ulverston in an affair of honour! He cannot, surely, have been serious!"

"I fear it. What did you reply?"

"He gave me little chance to do more than to say I should certainly do no such thing. If he had not looked as he did, I should have thought him to have been speaking in jest. But Ulverston—! Good God, this cannot be permitted! I'll speak to Martin."

There was no opportunity for more. The horses had been led up, and Sir Thomas was waiting to say good-bye. Miss Morville was handed into the saddle, and the party set off, the Viscount enlivening the way with a great deal of droll conversation, in a manner that would not have led anyone to suppose that he had been engaged in a violent quarrel not an hour earlier.

Upon their arrival at Stanyon, the gentlemen chose to ride on to the stables. Miss Morville dismounted at the foot of the terrace steps, and went quickly up them. She learned from Abney that his lordship was in the library, and went there immediately.

He was engaged in filling a two-colour gold snuff-box, ornamented with grisaille enamel paintings, with some of his special sort, but when he saw who had entered the room he rose at once, and set the jar aside. One glance at Miss Morville's face made him say: "Is anything amiss, ma'am?"

She let the long skirt of her riding-dress fall, and began to strip off her gloves, saying with a slight smile: "You perceive so much more than one might imagine, my lord, that is it almost disconcerting."

"Do I? But what has happened to cause you concern? Sit down!"

She obeyed, but said: "Well, I don't know that I am greatly concerned, but there *is* something amiss, and I believe you are the proper person to be told of it." She then, in the baldest of terms, recounted to him the story Marianne had poured out to her. "I should perhaps not have set much store by it had it not been for what Theo told me later. Marianne was greatly agitated, but that, I think, was largely because she has no brothers, and is consequently unaccustomed to scenes of violence."

"Unlike Miss Morville?"

"Dear me, yes! In fact, I think it a pity that Marianne did not run away at once, for then, you know, they might have had what Jack calls a regular set-to, and I have little doubt they would have enjoyed it excessively, and parted the better friends. At least," she added thoughtfully, "it is what I should expect of most men, but I own Martin is a little different."

"That he tried to force a quarrel on to Lucy I can believe, but that Lucy should let him do it certainly surprises me."

"I do not know, of course, what gentlemen consider to be insupportable provocation, but I imagine Marianne might offer such provocation?"

"With enthusiasm," he agreed. "The devil fly away with that boy!"

"He is very troublesome. But, although you may not like me to say this, I feel that he has not been quite properly treated. He did receive—and Marianne is fully conscious of it—a degree of encouragement which makes him not altogether to be blamed for his intemperate behaviour."

"Oh, I know it! If she were not so innocent, one might call her an arrant flirt."

"I am sure she had never the least intention of causing unhappiness."

"No, the mischief lay in his being too young to rate her pretty smiles at their true worth, and in *her* being too young to recognize that Martin was no man for her playful arts. What a stupid business it is! Are you expecting me to settle it?"

"Certainly I am. If you do not, I shall be obliged to lay an information. Should it be to a magistrate?"

He laughed. "I hope we may not have to go to quite such a length as that! Will you leave it in my hands, and trust me to do what I can?"

"Yes, willingly," she replied, rising, and picking up the train of her dress. "Theo said that he should speak to Martin, but I should not be surprised if you were found to have more influence than he has ever had. At all events, your word must carry weight with Lord Ulverston."

She then left him, and he returned to his task of filling his snuff-box. It was very soon accomplished, and he had just restored the jar to a cupboard when Ulverston strolled in.

The Viscount instantly picked up the gold snuff-box from the table, and inspected it. "That's pretty!" he remarked. "Where did you find it, Ger?"

"Rue St. Honoré—Louis XV. Not really suitable for day-wear, of course."

"Oh, at old Ducroix's? I bought one from him— genuine Barrière, with lapis panels."

"I know you did. He showed it to me, but I thought the marble-enamel displeasing. How did you find them all at Whissenhurst?"

"Oh, in high gig! Lady Bolderwood is full of schemes for their party next week. The devil of it is that I find I can't stay to attend it."

"No, so I apprehend," replied the Earl. "You have received a letter which summons you to town, haven't you?"

Ulverston laid the snuff-box down, and raised a

rueful pair of eyes to the Earl's face. "So you know all about it, do you? Has Martin been with you?"

"No, Miss Morville. I should warn you that she is ready to inform against you to the nearest magistrate, Lucy."

"Meddlesome female!"

"Not at all. She is a woman of remarkable good-sense. What nonsense is this, Lucy?"

"No nonsense of my seeking."

"But you cannot mean to meet Martin, surely!"

Ulverston shrugged. "I told him I could not, but when he chose to slap my face what would you have expected me to do?"

"I can think of several things you might do. They would all of them do Martin a world of good, but they don't include calling him out."

"Boot's on the other leg: he called me out. Of course I told him not to be making such a cake of himself, but when it came to his suggesting I didn't care to face his marksmanship, it was the outside of enough!"

"Oh, here's a high flight!" said Gervase, laughing. "My poor Lucy, you have great need to prove your mettle! I beg your pardon! But you can't prove it against my foolish young brother, you know."

"Don't be alarmed! You don't suppose I mean to hit him, do you?"

"No, I fear he means to hit you."

"I'll take my chance of that."

"Make no mistake about this, Lucy!" Gervase said quietly. "If Martin means to kill you, there will be no chance. He is a very fine shot."

"Is he?" The Viscount looked a little startled. "As good as you?"

"Much better."

"The devil he is! The more reason, then, for not drawing back!"

"Lucy, if you really wish to be reassured, let me tell you that you will earn nothing but praise for withdrawing a challenge to a boy with not one tenth your experience!"

"You're quite out. Not my challenge at all: I had nothing to do but accept a quarrel he was determined to force on to me."

The Earl, who had been twirling his quizzing-glass on the end of its ribbon, now raised it to one eye, and through it surveyed his friend. "You said Martin slapped your face!"

"He did. I gave him a leveller; he asked me for satisfaction, which I refused to give him; he then slapped my cheek, and asked if I would *now* meet him. I call that his challenge, not mine!"

"How very irregular!" remarked the Earl, slightly amused.

"Irregular! The whole affair is quite abominable! God knows I don't want to quarrel with your brother— not but what it's time someone taught him not to persecute defenceless girls with his damned attentions!"

"Forgive me, Lucy, but what is your interest in Miss Bolderwood? I have myself called Martin to book for— unmannerly conduct towards her, but it ought, I think, to be remembered that they are old playfellows, and have not been used to stand upon ceremony with each other."

"Oh, yes! Boy and girl stuff! I know that!" Ulverston said impatiently. He took a turn about the room.

"Well! I imagine you have guessed! Nothing is to be announced until after her presentation, but you may wish me happy, Ger!"

"With all my heart! She will make you a delightful wife, and you will have the felicity of knowing yourself to be the object of a general envy!"

The Viscount grinned, as he grasped his hand. "Is she not beautiful, Ger? Those speaking eyes! So much countenance!"

"Indeed she is!" Gervase responded warmly.

"I can tell you, I think myself fortunate to have secured her affections before *you* had done so!"

"I cannot flatter myself that she ever thought more of me than of Martin."

"Oh—Martin!" the Viscount said, his grin vanishing. "If I thought I had cut *you* out, I should be sorry for it!"

"No, you have cut Martin out."

"I care nothing for that. It ain't true, either."

"I fancy he has been the most fav—prominent—of her suitors," Gervase said, correcting himself hastily.

"Very likely. They are, as you have said, old playfellows. If he chose to think she cared for him, he must be a bigger coxcomb than I knew!"

Gervase let this pass. He picked up his snuff-box, and opened it, and took a meditative pinch. "Will you go halfway to meet Martin, Lucy?"

"To save you annoyance, yes!"

Gervase smiled at him. "Really, you know, Lucy, we cannot have such a scandal! These little affairs always leak out. By the by, was I to act for you?"

"Exactly what I asked the young fool! He told me

Warboys would be happy to act for me! Man I've only met three times in my life!"

Gervase burst out laughing. "Warboys! I wish he may come to offer his services to you!"

But at that very moment, Mr. Warboys was most strenuously resisting all efforts put forward to make him do this very thing. "No, dash it, Martin!" he said. "Don't mind acting for *you*—not but what I think you're making a cake of yourself, mind!—but I'm damned if I'll act for a fellow I don't know!"

"You do know him! He was at our ball!"

"What's that to say to anything? Seen him at Whissenhurst a couple of times too, but that don't mean I know him!"

"What does it signify? The circumstances are peculiar, and—"

"Yes, and that's another thing!" said Mr. Warboys. "No wish to offend you, dear old boy—and it ain't a bit of use trying to call *me* out if you are offended!—but the circumstances are *too* dashed peculiar! Mind, now, I'm not sure, because I haven't been out myself, but I don't think this is at all the thing. I'll ask my father: knows everything, my father!"

"You will not! Do you think I want the whole world to know of this?"

"Precious soon will know of it," commented the sapient Mr. Warboys. "All over the countryside within twenty-four hours! A nice cry-out there will be! You take a damper, dear boy! much the best thing to do!"

"I tell you the fellow knocked me down, and has accepted my challenge!"

"You told me it wasn't till you gave him a facer that

he did accept your challenge. Good sort of a man, Ulverston," said Mr. Warboys thoughtfully. "Withdraw
the challenge. Nothing else to be done."

"No?" said Martin, through his shut teeth. "I'll show
you what else is to be done!"

"Won't show *me*," said Mr. Warboys, in a tone of
strong resolution. "The more I think about it the more
I think it ain't the kind of affair I want to be mixed up
with. Can't call a fellow out when he's staying in your
house."

"St. Erth's house, not mine!"

"Comes to the same thing. Very important to be nice
in all points of honour. Another thing! No business to
have challenged him at all. Quite the thing, when he
knocked you over: nothing to say against that! When
you hit him, his business to ask for satisfaction, not
yours. Damme, you've made a ramshackle business of
it, Martin!"

"I have, have I? Do you think I'll withdraw because
you tell me to?" demanded Martin furiously.

"No," said Mr. Warboys mournfully. "Just thought of
that. Ought to have told you to go on with it. Never
knew such a fellow for going against everyone! Often
crossed my mind you wouldn't have run mad after Miss
Bolderwood if you hadn't seen the rest of us hanging
round her. Nothing would do for you but to carry her
off just to spite us!"

"By God, Barny, if you weren't a friend of mine—!"
Martin said, his fists clenching.

"If I weren't a friend of yours, wouldn't have dared
to say it," responded Mr. Warboys frankly. "Quite true,
though. Dash it, Ulverston did the right thing when he

gave you that leveller! Sorry I didn't see it. Might have tried to do it myself, if I'd seen you frightening that poor little angel! Don't say I'd have succeeded because I never was up to your weight, but there it is: daresay I should have been carried away."

"You would!" retorted Martin, with grim humour.

Mr. Warboys, grappling with deep thoughts, paid no heed to this, but pronounced, after a moment: "Tell you what, Martin! Shouldn't be surprised if there was more to it than we know. Occurred to me the other evening: seems devilish taken with Ulverston, don't she? No sense in putting a bullet into the fellow: might easily give her a distaste for you, and then where are you?"

This eminently reasonable point of view found no favour. Martin said roughly: "I didn't come here to listen to you prosing like the saphead you are! Will you, or will you not, act for Ulverston?"

"No," said Mr. Warboys. He added scrupulously: "That is, not if he don't ask me to. If he does—ask my father!"

"And you call yourself a friend of mine!" Martin said bitterly.

"Dash it, Martin, it ain't the part of a friend of yours to second your opponent! Told you I'd act for you, didn't I? Stupid thing to do, but not the man to go back on my word."

"Barny, if he applies to you, will you act for him?"

Mr. Warboys scratched his chin. "Might have to," he conceded. "But if I act for him, who's to act for you? Tell me that!"

"Good God, anyone! Rockcliffe—Alston!"

"Ay, that will be a capital go!" said Mr. Warboys

scathingly. "Why don't you ask out the town-crier from Grantham, and ask *him* to act for you? Lord, Martin, dashed if I don't think you must be queer in your attic!"

"Very well! I'll have Caversham!" said Martin, a little taken aback, but recovering. "*He* won't talk!"

"No, and he won't hear either!" retorted Mr. Warboys, justly incensed. "You can't choose a man to be your second who has to have everything written down on a slate!"

"It makes no odds to me!" Martin said, picking up his gloves and his whip.

"I know it don't make any odds to you: *you* won't have to fix the arrangements with him! If you want to fight, get your cousin to act for you!"

"He won't do it," Martin said briefly. "The first thing is to tell Ulverston you are willing to stand his friend."

"If Theo Frant won't second you, you *are* wrong!" said Mr. Warboys.

But Martin had already stormed out of the house, leaving his long-suffering friend to search in his father's library for a copy of the *Code of Honour.* Careful perusal of this invaluable work revealed the fact that the first duty of a second was to seek a reconciliation. Mr. Warboys spent the rest of the evening endeavouring to compress into as few words as could conveniently be written on a small slate a moving appeal to his prospective colleague to assist him in promoting this excellent object.

Martin rode back to Stanyon. That a meeting with Ulverston at the dinner-table must be attended by considerable embarrassment he knew, but his temper was too much chafed to permit of his caring for that. He did not even consider it; still less did he consider what must be the unpleasant consequences of killing the Viscount, which he was determined to do. In blackbrowed silence he allowed his valet to help him to change his riding-dress for his evening-coat and knee-breeches; in the same dangerous mood he left his room, and strode along the gallery in the direction of the Grand Stairway. He was checked by the Earl's voice, speaking his name, and looked round to see that Gervase had come out of his own room. He said curtly: "Well?"

"Come into my room! I want to speak to you."

"I have nothing to say to you, St. Erth!"

"But I have something to say to you. Here, if you wish, but I had rather it were in a less public place."

"I know what you mean to say, and you may spare your breath!"

"You don't know it."

Martin stared at him, hostility and suspicion in his eyes. He hesitated, then shrugged, and followed the Earl into his bedchamber. "You mean to try to make me cry off meeting Ulverston. Don't tell me I can't do it, for I can, and, by God, I will!"

"No. It is quite impossible that you should."

"I know of only one circumstance that would make it so! If *he* were to cry off! Is that it? Hasn't he the stomach for it?"

"Ulverston will meet you where and when you will," the Earl replied. "If you are determined on it, he will delope, and so, I think, will you."

"You are wrong!" Martin said, with an ugly little laugh. "If he chooses to do so, the more fool he! Warn him! I shan't miss *my* mark!"

"I have warned him," replied Gervase. "He will take

his chance. It's not for him to withdraw: the challenge was yours."

"It was mine, and you cannot force me to withdraw it!"

"No, of course I cannot," said the Earl, his tranquil voice in odd contrast to Martin's fiery tones. "But you acted under a misapprehension, Martin. He is betrothed to Miss Bolderwood."

"What?" Martin thundered, the colour rushing into his cheeks, and fading almost as swiftly, to leave his face very white.

"There is to be no announcement until after her presentation, but he has been accepted."

"It's a lie!" stammered Martin. "You say it so that I shan't meet Ulverston! I'll not believe it!"

Gervase made him no answer. He was standing before the fire, and he neither looked at Martin nor seemed to attend to his words, but stirred one of the logs in the grate with his foot, and meditatively watched the shower of sparks fly up the chimney. A hasty movement on Martin's part made him glance up, but Martin had only flung over to the curtained window, as though desirous of putting as much space as possible between himself and his half-brother, and the Earl lowered his eyes again to the fire.

"She might have told me!" burst from Martin.

"Yes."

"She knew I—she *knew*—!"

"She is young, and a little heedless."

"Heedless! Oh, no! Not that! A title—a great position! *those* were the things she wanted! She is very welcome to them! If *you* had offered she would have accepted you! If you were dead, and I stood in your shoes, she would take me, and Ulverston might go hang!"

"You would scarcely want her upon such terms."

"On any terms!" Martin declared wildly. "She is the only woman I shall ever love!"

The Earl diplomatically refrained from commenting upon this assertion. If there was a flicker of amusement in his eyes, Martin did not see it.

"Women!" Martin ejaculated, with loathing. "Now I know what they are! I shall never again be taken in!" He took a turn about the room, his restless hands picking up, and discarding, a book that lay on the table, twitching a fold of the curtains into place, tugging at one of the heavy tassels adorning the hangings of the great bed, and finally seizing on an ivory comb from the dressing-table, and bending it savagely until it snapped in two pieces. He cast them from him, saying defiantly: "I've broken your comb! I beg your pardon!"

"It is of no consequence."

"I suppose you have a dozen combs!" Martin said, as though this likelihood added to his hatred of his brother.

A discreet knock on the door made the Earl turn his head. It heralded the entrance of a footman, who said apologetically that he was sent to inform his lordship that dinner awaited his pleasure.

"Desire Abney to announce it in a quarter of an hour's time, if you please."

"Yes, my lord. Her ladyship—"

"Convey my excuses to her ladyship. I have been detained, and have not yet completed my toilet."

The footman cast a covert look from him to Martin, and bowed himself out.

The door had hardly closed behind him before

Martin exclaimed: "Do you expect me to continue to remain under the same roof as Ulverston?"

"He has told me that he finds himself obliged to leave Stanyon. I believe it will give rise to less comment if he remains until Monday, but it shall be as you wish."

"If I must sit at table with him tonight, I may as well do so for ever!" said Martin disagreeably. He took another turn about the room, and fetched up abruptly in front of the Earl, as a thought occurred to him. "After all, he knocked me down! He owed me satisfaction!"

"Would you think so, had your positions been reversed?"

Martin resumed his pacing, reminding his brother irresistibly of a caged wild creature. After a turn or two, he flung over his shoulder: "What should I do?"

"You may meet him, if you choose, and acknowledge the justice of his action by deloping."

"Folly!"

"So I think."

"I'll not beg his pardon! No, by God, that's too much! How could I guess—?"

"I believe him to be sensible of the misapprehension under which you acted. He is not the man to demand an apology from you. If you wish it, I can settle it for you, so that it will be unnecessary for any mention of the matter to be made between you. If you charge me with this office, I shall tell him that I have disclosed to you the secret of his betrothal, upon which you have naturally withdrawn your challenge."

After a moment's inward struggle, Martin said in a choked voice: "Very well!" He cast one of his smouldering looks at Gervase, and said: "Obliging of you!

You think I should be grateful no doubt! I'm not grateful! If it had not been for you, that fellow would never have come here!"

"Why, no! But if she had returned your affection, Martin, his coming would not have injured you," the Earl said gently.

Martin seemed to brush aside these words. "All was right until *you* came here! *You* put the wish to become a Countess into Marianne's head, trifling with her, flattering her with your balls and your distinguishing attentions—to cast my pretensions into the shade! Then you brought in Ulverston, encouraged him to remain here! You set everyone against me! Marianne, Theo, Louisa—even my mother! Yes, even my mother, bemoaning the fact that you are going away to London! She will miss you amazingly! Ay, that is what she says! But there is *one* person you haven't cozened with your soft words, *one* person who will not miss you! I hate you, St. Erth! From the bottom of my heart, I hate you!"

"If that is what you think, I cannot wonder at it," the Earl said, a little sadly.

"Tell my mother I have gone to dine with Warboys!" Martin said fiercely, and flung out of the room.

CHAPTER FIFTEEN

MARTIN WAS TOO MUCH in the habit of dining from home for his absence to be greatly felt by his mother. Beyond saying several times that she had had no notion he meant to go to the Warboys' that day, and supposing that he would drink tea at Whissenhurst, she made no comment. Her mind was engrossed by one of the complicated relationships in which she delighted, for she had chanced to read in the *Gazette* that a son had been born to the wife of a Mr. Henry Lamberhurst, which instantly reminded her that a third cousin of her own had married a Lamberhurst, who, in his turn, was linked by two other marriages with a branch of the Austell family. With the Viscount's good-natured, if not very valuable, assistance, she beguiled the dinner-hour by pursuing through all their ramifications every offshoot of both families until she reached, with the dessert, the apparently satisfactory conclusion that the unknown Henry Lamberhurst could not be connected with the Lamberhursts she knew.

The Viscount was spared her subsequent recollections of some people she had once met at Ramsgate, and whom she rather fancied to have been in some way related to the family, these being imparted only to Miss

Morville, when the two ladies withdrew to one of the saloons. Miss Morville, who had contrived to evade giving an account of her discoveries at Whissenhurst, and who had no wish to be more closely interrogated on that subject, encouraged these tedious reminiscences, and by interpolating a question now and then managed to keep her ladyship's mind occupied until the appearance of the gentlemen turned her thoughts towards whist.

It was not until the party had broken up that Theo was able to exchange any private conversation with the Earl. He detained him then, as he was about to leave the library in the Viscount's wake, and said in his blunt way: "One moment, St. Erth! What happened at Whissenhurst today between Martin and Ulverston?"

"A misunderstanding only."

"Gervase, Martin must not be allowed to call Ulverston out!"

"He will not do so."

Theo looked shrewdly at him. "He seems to have had that intention. Did you scotch it?"

"Not that precisely. He was not fully informed of the circumstances."

"I see. In short, Ulverston has offered for Miss Bolderwood, and has been accepted?"

"The engagement is not to be made generally known yet," the Earl warned him.

"You need not be afraid that I shall spread the news. Well! I guessed as much. I am sorry for Martin. He has not had time to grow accustomed to the knowledge that he is not of sufficient consequence to aspire to the hand of an heiress."

"Really, Theo, I think you wrong Miss Bolderwood!"

"Never. This is her parents' doing. I always knew they had set their ambition high. Oh, don't think I blame them! It was inevitable." He forced a smile. "I fancy *you* raised expectations, trifler that you are!"

"Nonsense!"

"My dear Gervase, you cannot be such an innocent as to suppose that Sir Thomas would not have jumped at the chance of seeing his daughter Countess of St. Erth!"

"You sound very like my mother-in-law," remarked the Earl. "He gave me no encouragement, nor do I think that his wishing not to announce this engagement immediately shows him to be jumping at the chance of seeing Miss Bolderwood the future Countess of Wrexham."

"I daresay not. He had hoped for better. The Frants were Earls of St. Erth before ever the Austells rose to the dignity of a barony!"

"*Very* like my mother-in-law!" murmured Gervase.

Theo was obliged to laugh, but he said: "However you may disregard the difference you may be sure the Bolderwoods do not! Offer for Marianne before her betrothal to Ulverston is announced, and see what Sir Thomas will say to you!"

"My dear Theo, where have your wits gone begging? It was a case of love at first sight with them both! You must have seen that!"

"Did Martin?"

"Oh, Martin—! Does he ever see beyond his nose?"

"No, and for that reason I am more than ever sorry for him. I believe he had no suspicion, and the news must have come to him as a severe shock."

"I am afraid you are right, but he will very soon recover from it. He is at present forswearing women—an excellent sign!"

"Where is he?"

"Unless he did indeed visit his friend Warboys, I don't know."

"I hope he has done nothing foolish!" Theo said, a crease appearing between his brows. "He almost knocked me over when he brushed past me on his way out of the house, and looked as though he would have willingly murdered me, had I dared to address him."

"Poor Theo!" said the Earl lightly. "I'm afraid you were acting as my scapegoat—or possibly Lucy's!"

"Did you quarrel?" Theo asked, the crease deepening.

"It takes two to make a quarrel."

"Evasion, Gervase! Was he—" He broke off, for a quick footstep was heard approaching the library across the Great Hall beyond it, and in another instant Martin had entered the room.

He was looking tired, and pale, his face rather set, and his expressive eyes sombre. He checked on the threshold when he saw his cousin, and ejaculated: "Oh—! You here!"

"Do you wish to speak to Gervase? I am just off to bed."

"It doesn't signify. I have no doubt you know the whole!" He glanced at St. Erth, and then lowered his eyes. "I only wished to say—I was in a rage!"

"Yes, I know," the Earl replied quietly.

Another fleeting glance was cast up at him. "I think I said—I don't know: I do say things, in a rage, which—which I don't mean!"

"I did not regard it, and you need not either."

Martin seemed to force his rigid mouth to smile. "No. Well—mighty good of you to take it so! Of course I know it was not your fault. Good-night!"

He went quickly away, and for a full minute there was silence in the library. The Earl snuffed a guttering candle, and said: "Do you mean to return to Stanyon when you have done all your business at Evesleigh, Theo, or do you go on immediately to Studham?"

"I believe I may postpone my journey," Theo said slowly.

"Indeed! May I know why?"

Theo looked frowningly at him. "It might be best if I were to remain at Stanyon—for the present."

"Oh, are you at that again? I have told you already that I don't need a watch-dog, my dear fellow!"

"And still I should prefer to remain!"

"Why? When you have heard Martin make me an apology?"

Theo met the deep blue eyes full. "In all the years I have known Martin," he said deliberately, "I have never heard him utter an apology, or even acknowledge a fault!"

"My regenerating influence!" said Gervase flippantly.

"I should be happy to think so."

"But you don't?"

"No," Theo said. "I don't!"

"Nevertheless, Theo, you will oblige me by going to Evesleigh tomorrow, as you have planned to do."

"Very well. But I wish this business of Ulverston's had not been disclosed!" Theo said.

The breakfast-party on the following morning was attended, inevitably, by a certain measure of constraint. It was the first time Martin and the Viscount had met since their encounter at Whissenhurst, and even Mr. Clowne seemed to be conscious of the tension. His nervous platitudes filled the gap between the exchange of cool greetings between these two and the entrance of the Earl, who made his appearance in a coat of such exquisite cut that the Viscount exclaimed at it, demanding to be told the name of the tailor who had made it. "Not Scott!" he said.

"No, Weston," responded the Earl. "Martin, what's this I hear of kestrels in the West Wood?"

He could have said nothing that would have made Martin more certainly forget, for the moment, his injuries. The dark eyes lit; Martin replied: "So Pleasley says! He swears there is a pair, and believes they may be nesting in one of the old magpies' nests. I know the place."

"Too early in the year, isn't it?" asked the Viscount.

"I have known them to start breeding as early as March," Martin said. "It is not usual, I own, but it is very possible." He turned his head to address his brother. "I have said I'll ride to Roxmere this morning, to look at some likely young 'uns, but I mean to take a gun out this afternoon, and try for them."

"It is sad that the kestrel, or as I like to call it, the wind-hover, should be so destructive," said Mr. Clowne. "To see them hovering above, as though suspended, is a pretty sight."

"I question whether they are so destructive as people suppose," remarked Theo.

"Good God, if we were to have a pair of them breeding in the West Wood we should not have a pheasant or a partridge chick left!" Martin exclaimed.

"I fancy you would find, if you could observe them

closely, that they subsist mostly on field-mice. Had you said *sparrow-hawks,* now—!"

In refuting this heresy, and in recalling to Theo's memory various incidents which seemed to support his own theory, Martin for a little while forgot his care, and talked with an animation which would not have led anyone to suppose that he was suffering all the more severe pangs of unrequited love. He looked as though he had not slept well, but he ate a large breakfast, and only towards the end of it remembered that his affections had been blighted, and that his arch-enemy sat opposite to him, unconcernedly consuming cold beef. The cloud descended again on to his brow, and he relapsed into silence; but when he rose from the table, and the Earl called after him: "Keep your eyes open for anything that might suit me at Roxmere!" he paused in the doorway, and replied quite cordially: "If you wish it, but I don't think Helston has much to show me but young 'uns."

"I don't mind that. A good three-year-old, Martin, not too short in the back, and well ribbed-up! But you know the style of thing!"

Martin nodded. "I'll see," he said.

He did not return to Stanyon until noon, and by that time the Viscount had driven himself over to Whissenhurst. Martin walked into one of the saloons just as his mother, Miss Morville, and Gervase were sitting down to partake of cold chickens and fruit. He brought with him two letters, which had been fetched up from the receiving-office. "One for you, Drusilla, and one for you, St. Erth. From Louisa," he added. "Lay you a pony she wants you to invite them all to Stanyon in June!"

"From Louisa?" said the Dowager. "Why should Louisa be writing to St. Erth? Depend upon it, you are mistaken! It cannot be from her!"

"Well, it's Louisa's writing, and Grampound franked it," said Martin, displaying the letter, which was directed in large, sloping characters, and stamped Free.

The sight of Lord Grampound's signature, scrawled across one corner, convinced the Dowager that the letter was indeed from her daughter; and after satisfying herself that Martin had not misread The Right Honourable the Countess for the Right Honourable the Earl, she reluctantly allowed her stepson to assume possession of his property. While he broke the wafer that sealed it, and read its two crossed sheets, she maintained an unbroken flow of comment, surmise, and astonishment. "I do not understand what Louisa can mean by sending a letter to St. Erth," she said. "What can she possible have to say to him? Why has she not written to me? Are you sure there is not a letter for me, Martin?"

"Of course I am, ma'am!" he said impatiently. "The rest are for Theo, but he has gone off somewhere with Hayle."

"It is most extraordinary!" she said, in a displeased tone. "I should have been very glad to have had a letter from Louisa."

"My dear ma'am, you might have this one with my good-will," said Gervase, perusing the crossed lines through his quizzing-glass. "In fact, you *shall* have it, for I find Louisa's writing quite baffling."

The Dowager had no hesitation in taking the sheets from him. "Louisa's writing is particularly elegant," she said. "I do not find it all difficult to read. She would have done better to have directed her letter to me."

"Does she want to come here?" demanded Martin.

"No, something about double doors at Kentham, and Pug."

"That creature!" ejaculated Martin, with a look of disgust. "What the devil has Pug to do with you?"

"Too much, I fear. Well, ma'am? What is it precisely that Louisa feels I can have not the least objection to doing for her? I fear the worst, and beg you won't keep me in suspense!"

"You will be very happy to render Louisa your assistance," stated the Dowager, in a voice that did not admit of argument. "Poor Louisa! But I told her how it would be, for I am sure there was never anyone more disobliging than Mrs. Neath, and now, you see, she will not answer above half the questions Louisa has addressed to her. It is all of a piece! She behaved in a very unhandsome way to Mrs. Warboys about a poultry-woman once, and when I heard Grampound had the intention of hiring Kentham I advised him rather to come to Stanyon, for, depend upon it, I said, you will not like to hire Mrs. Neath's house, for she is a very disagreeable woman. You see what has come of it! Louisa cannot recall whether the two saloons can be thrown into one, or how many beds they are able to make up, and so St. Erth is obliged to drive there to discover how it may be! It is a great deal too bad of Mrs. Neath, and I should not be at all surprised if she has neglected to reply to Louisa's questions on purpose to drag St. Erth into her set! She is a very encroaching woman, and I have never invited her to Stanyon, save on Public Days.

If you do not care to put yourself in her way, Gervase, Theo may go in your stead."

"My dear ma'am, Theo is going in the opposite direction to Kentham!"

"It cannot signify to him, if he goes first to Kentham. However, I daresay she will more readily accede to your requests than to his. He is not at all conciliatory—not that I should wish to conciliate Mrs. Neath, but how shocking it would be if she refused to permit poor little Pug to go to Kentham!"

"Are you going all that way to beg favours for Pug?" demanded Martin scornfully.

"I suppose so. Something tells me it would be the wisest course. I may as well drive over to Kentham this afternoon, for I have nothing else to do—unless I go with you, after these kestrels of yours."

"Oh—! If you choose! But I daresay I shan't get a sight of them," Martin replied ungraciously. "You will be wasting your time, I expect—and I may stay out later than you would like, on the chance of a rabbit or two."

"Then I had better go to Kentham," said the Earl placidly. "I will pull up at the Wickton cross-road on my way back, in case you should still be out, and wish to be driven home."

"No need: I'd as lief walk. It would fret me to know that you might be waiting for me."

"As you please," the Earl said, shrugging. "What had Helston to show you?"

"Nothing you would care for. At least, there was one bay I liked. He is not up to my weight, but I daresay he might suit you."

The Dowager, having finished with her daughter's letter, now had leisure to turn her attention to Miss Morville, who was slipping her own letter into her reticule; and to enquire with a regal condescension which almost robbed her question of its impertinence who was her correspondent. Upon learning that Mrs. Morville had written to inform her daughter that she and Mr. Morville expected to return to Lincolnshire in the following week, she fell into a complaining mood, which had the effect of speedily breaking up the nuncheon-party. Martin went off to change his riding-dress for a shooting-jacket; Miss Morville escorted the Dowager upstairs to the Italian Saloon, where she very soon fell asleep on one of the sofas; and the Earl strolled down to the stables, to take a look at Cloud's forelegs.

He found Theo there, giving some directions to his groom, who was to bring his riding-horse over to Evesleigh on the following day, when a cast shoe should have been replaced. He burst out laughing when he heard whither the Earl was bound that afternoon, but said: "You will not go!"

"My dear Theo, I do not dare even to hesitate! Only think how shocking it would be if Louisa were to come down upon us again!"

"True! But to send you running about the countryside on such an errand—! Shall I go in your stead?"

"No, you are not conciliatory, and although my mother-in-law by no means desires to conciliate Mrs. Neath, she has commanded me to perform this office for my sister."

"Humbug! Much you would care for her commands!"

"Why, the truth is," said the Earl, laughing, "I have

not had my grays out for three days, and I can as well exercise them on a drive to Kentham as anywhere else."

"Oh, if that is the case—! But one might have expected Louisa to apply to Martin rather than to you!"

"But I thought I had made it plain to you that a conciliatory manner is what is desired?"

"So you did! Where is Martin?"

"I have no very exact knowledge. He is going off to West Wood, to try if he can get a shot at a kestrel, and has firmly abjured my company."

"Oh, so that holds, does it? He had better leave them alone: they will do little harm!"

"Very likely, but I do not grudge him the relief of being able to slay *something!* Chard, we are going to Kentham. Bring my curricle round in half an hour, if you please!" He looked at his cousin. "When do you set forth on your travels, Theo?"

"As soon as I may. There is a letter from Maplefield I must first deal with, but unless I find another shoe to be loose I hope to be away not much later than four o'clock!"

His groom, wilting visibly, withdrew to the shelter of the harness-room. Gervase murmured: "What a harsh task-master you are! Driving?"

"Yes, a gig, with much of your worldly wealth stowed in the back! What hope I have of visiting the farms I had *intended* to visit, I know not!"

"Peace! Your unfortunate groom is out of hearing! If you mean to shut yourself up in your tower with letters from Maplefield, I'll bid you farewell. Do not allow my tenants to impose upon me!"

Theo took his hand, and gripped it, and held it for a minute. "I won't. Gervase—"

"Well?"

Theo released him. "Nothing. Take care of yourself while I am gone!"

"I always do. Your presence is not needed to keep me safe, I believe."

"No. I think you may be right."

"I am almost sure I am right."

"He has certainly taken it better than I expected—but Ulverston's presence cannot but keep the wound green!"

"He leaves us on Monday, and will certainly be engaged at Whissenhurst until then."

"That circumstance will hardly serve to mollify Martin!" said Theo, grimacing.

Half an hour later, the Earl set forth for Kentham, Chard seated beside him in the curricle, with his arms primly folded. This was one of his few concessions to the etiquette governing the conduct to be expected of a private gentleman's groom, but neither this nor his tall, cockaded hat made him look like anything but a soldier. He had known the Earl throughout his army career, had fought in the same engagements, shared the same discomforts, and was wholly devoted to his interests. He thought it a pity that his master should have sold out, for he had a poor opinion of all but military men (and, indeed, a rather poor opinion of such military men as belonged to any other regiment than his own), but after the first strangeness of riding out in a plain coat, with no accoutrements and no sabre, had worn off he found that he did not dislike his new position. An Earl's head-groom was a personage of considerable consequence, particularly when his master travelled. He might be sure of the best accommodation for his horses at every inn on the road, and excellent attention for himself. More important, this Earl was a good master, who reposed complete confidence in him, and treated him with the easy familiarity Turvey so much deplored. Thus it was that consideration for the Earl, and not the fear of incurring a chilly set-down, held him silent for the first part of the drive. The grays were fresh, and the country lanes both rough and narrow, so that the Earl's attention was fully occupied in handling his horses. It was not until they had covered a couple of miles that Chard ventured to distract him by remarking that he should not be surprised if one of Lord Ulverston's wheelers had a splint forming. Since the Earl knew that Chard and the Viscount's Clarence, who had been his private groom in France, were old foes, he paid very little heed to this, or to several dark strictures on the customs his lordship allowed to be followed in his stables.

"Very reprehensible," he said. "I daresay he washes the mud from the legs of his lordship's horses, too."

"That, me lord, I don't say," replied Chard severely.

"How wretched for you that you cannot! What will you do when his lordship leaves Stanyon on Monday? You will be obliged to turn your attention to the iniquities of Mr. Martin's head-groom."

"Young Hickling," said Chard. "No, me lord, I should call him very *adecuado*—with his horses."

"How do you go on with him?"

"Well, me lord, bearing in mind what you said to me at the outset, we haven't had a *batalla campal,* but that ain't to say we won't, because one of these days

I shall catch him a *bofetada,* and then we'll have a real turn-up."

"Why?"

"Because," said Chard frankly, "it's his idea that everything has got to be the way Mr. Martin wants it, and that ain't by any means my idea. I daresay if I was as meek as what he'd like me to be we should have to stable *our* horses in a cow-byre no one don't happen to be using." Without moving his eyes from the road ahead, he added: "*No se moleste usted!* as they used to say to us in Spain, whenever anything went wrong. I can handle young Hickling, me lord. The trouble with him is he's kind of growed up alongside of Mr. Martin, and, like every Johnny Raw you ever saw, he hasn't got many notions in his silly head that came there natural, as you might say. Put there, they were, though it ain't for me to say *who* put them there."

The Earl did not reply for a minute; when he did speak it was in his usual soft, untroubled voice. Chard, straining his ears to catch a note in it of comprehension, or even of anger, could detect none. "Continue to handle him, Chard—without a pitched battle, if you please."

"No objection to me keeping my eyes open, me lord?"

"None. But don't mistake shadows for the enemy!"

"I *have* been posted as vedette in my time, me lord," said Chard. "They didn't, so to say, *encourage* us to give the alarm when a hare hopped across the path."

The Earl only smiled, so his slightly offended henchman relapsed into correct silence.

The errand on which he had been sent to Kentham might, in St. Erth's judgment, have been despatched in twenty minutes, but in fact occupied him for over an hour. So far from receiving him in a disagreeable spirit, Mrs. Neath almost overwhelmed him with protestations and attentions. She could not conceive how it had come about that she had overlooked any of dear Lady Grampound's questions, and she was excessively shocked to think that his lordship had been obliged to drive over from Stanyon only because she had been so stupid. But none of those vital questions could be dealt with until Mr. Neath had been hurriedly summoned from the Home Farm to receive his distinguished guest; and even when this rather morose gentleman had been hustled into a more suitable coat, and almost thrust into the drawing-room by a servant, primed in a hissing whisper by his mistress, cakes and wine had to be pressed on the Earl before any heed could be paid to the problems which had brought him to Kentham. At last, however, he managed to bring his business to a close, after which he had only to listen to Mrs. Neath's plans for spending the summer months in Brighton before he contrived to make good his escape.

Chard, who had found the entertainment offered him of a shabby nature, remarked, as the Earl gave his horses the office to start: "Have to spring 'em, me lord, if you ain't wishful to be late for your dinner."

"Thank you, I had rather have no dinner at all than lame my horses!" retorted his master.

His grays were a fast pair, and he drove them well up to their bits, but when he reached the cross-road where he had offered to pick Martin up it was a little after six o'clock. Beyond the lane which led to Wickton stretched the West Woods, the Stanyon road cutting through them for rather more than a mile. The Earl checked his horses when the cross-road came into view, but there was no sign of Martin on the road, and he drove on. The scutter of rabbits, fleeing from the road into the undergrowth on either side of it before the approach of the curricle, seemed to indicate that no human presence had disturbed them for some time. The Earl quickened the pace again, saying as he did so: "I wonder if Mr. Martin got his kestrels? He seems to have gone home, so perhaps he was successful."

"Well, me lord," said Chard grudgingly, "if he got a sight of them I reckon it would be enough for him. A very pretty shot is Mr. Martin, that I *will* say!"

The words had hardly left his lips when he was startled by the sound of a shot, fired, as it seemed to him, over the horses' heads. An oath was surprised out of him as the grays bounded wildly forward, and before he had had time to realize what had happened he saw the reins slack, and grabbed at them as the Earl lurched against his shoulder.

The grays were bolting, and although Chard caught the reins he could do no more than hold them, while with his other hand he gripped his master, fearing every instant to see him flung from the bumping, swaying vehicle. For several dreadful seconds he thought him dead, but it was only seconds before the Earl lifted a hand, and rather uncertainly tried to push away the grip on his arm. "Get them under control!" he said faintly. "And get me home, for I think I have it!" He thrust his hand into his coat, over his breast, and withdrew it, and tried to focus his eyes upon it. His glove was wet with blood. "Yes. I have it," he said.

CHAPTER SIXTEEN

THE EARL BECAME aware that someone, from a very long way away, was insistently calling to him. A voice repeated over and over again: "Ger! Ger, old fellow! *Ger!*" Its urgency began to tease him, and a faint crease appeared between his brows. The voice, a little nearer now, exclaimed: "He's alive!" which seemed to him so foolish a remark that he opened his eyes to see who could have uttered it. There was so dense a fog enveloping him that he was unable to see anything at all, but he felt his head being lifted, and was aware of something hard and cool pressing against his lips. A different voice, not urgent, but calm and authoritative, told him to open his mouth. He was disinclined to make so great an effort, for an immense lassitude possessed his every faculty, but the command was repeated, and since it was less trouble to obey it than to argue about it, he did open his mouth. He was then told that he must drink, which irritated him. He was about to expostulate when he found that his mouth was full of some pungent liquid, so he was obliged to swallow this before he could murmur: "Don't be so foolish!"

The urgent voice, which he now recognized as Lord Ulverston's, exclaimed joyfully: "He took it! He's coming round! That's right, Ger! Stand to your arms, dear boy! Not dead this engagement!"

The fog seemed to be clearing away; through it he could hazily perceive the Viscount's face, which seemed, in some peculiar fashion, to be suspended above him.

"That's the dandy!" Ulverston said. "Come, now, old fellow!"

Ulverston appeared to have some need of his instant services, which made it imperative for him to try feebly to respond to the appeal. He found himself to be without the strength to thrust away the hand that was preventing him from struggling to raise himself; and he was, on the whole, relieved to hear the other voice say: "Pray do not talk to him any more, my lord! He will do very well if you let him alone."

He thought this the most sensible remark he had ever heard, and tried to say so. Raising his leaden eyelids again, he found that Ulverston's face had disappeared, and that it was Miss Morville's which now hung over him. She seemed to be wiping his brow with a wet cloth; he could smell lavender-water. It was pleasant, but he felt it to be quite wrong for her to be sponging his face. He muttered: "You must not! I cannot think…"

"There is no need for you to think, my lord. You have only to lie still," replied Miss Morville, in a voice which reminded him so forcibly of his old nurse that he attempted no further argument, but closed his eyes again.

He desired nothing more than to slide back into the comfortable darkness from which Ulverston's voice had dragged him, but it had receded. He was aware of being in bed, and soon realized that it must be his own bed at Stanyon, and not, as he had mistily supposed, in some billet in southern France. He heard Miss Morville desire Turvey to tighten a bandage, felt himself gently moved, and was conscious of pain somewhere in the region of his left shoulder.

Ulverston's voice asked anxiously: "Is it bleeding still?"

"Very little now, my lord," replied Miss Morville.

"How much longer does Chard mean to be?" Ulverston exclaimed, in a fretting tone. "What if that damned sawbones should be away from home?"

The Earl found these questions disturbing, for they made him think that there was something he must try to remember: something that flickered worryingly at the back of his clouded mind. The effort to collect his thoughts made him frown. Then he heard Miss Morville suggest that Ulverston should go downstairs to receive Dr. Malpas. She added, in a low tone: "Pray remember, my lord, that we do not know how this accident occurred, but think it may have been a poacher!"

"Oh, *don't* we know?" Ulverston said, in a savage under-voice. "Poacher, indeed! Chard knows better!"

"I particularly requested him to say nothing more than that," said Miss Morville. "I believe it is what *he* would wish."

A train of thought was set up in the Earl's mind. He said suddenly: "She does not object to Pug, and they can make up ten beds."

"That is excellent," said Miss Morville calmly, sponging his face again. "Now you may rest."

"What happened to me?" he asked.

"You met with a slight accident, but it is of no consequence. You will be better directly."

"Oh!" His eyelids were dropping again, but he smiled, and murmured: "You are always coming to my rescue!"

She returned no answer. He sank into a half-waking, half-dreaming state, aware of an occasional movement in the room, but not troubled by it. Once, a firm, light hand held his wrist for a minute, but he did not open his eyes.

But presently he was disturbed, rather to his annoyance, by a new and an unknown voice, which seemed to be asking a great many questions, and issuing a tiresome number of orders. It was interrupted by Ulverston's voice several times. The Earl was not at all surprised when he heard the strange voice say: "I assure your lordship I should prefer to have no one but Miss Morville and the valet to assist me."

Ulverston seemed to think that Miss Morville could not assist the stranger. He said, in his most imperious tone: "Nonsense! She could not do it"

"Yes, she could," said the Earl, roused by this injustice.

There was a moment's silence, then his wrist was firmly held, and the strange voice said, directly above him: "Oh, so your lordship is awake, eh? That is very well, and we shall soon have you feeling more the thing…. My lord, Miss Morville and I are old colleagues, and I know her to be equal to anything. You need not fear to leave the patient in our hands…. That table, if you please, my man—what's your name? Turvey? Very good, set it there, and the bowl upon it. Now, my lord, I am afraid I must hurt you a trifle—just a trifle!"

It soon became apparent to the Earl that the stranger had grossly understated the case. The hurt he began to inflict upon his patient was considerable enough first to wrench a groan from him, and then to make him grip his underlip resolutely between his teeth. He was just wondering how long he could endure when a pang, sharper than the rest, took from him all power of resistance, and he felt himself to be falling into an upsurging darkness, and lost consciousness.

He came round to find that he was once again being commanded to drink. He obeyed, and was lowered on to his pillows, and heard a cheerful voice say: "There! You have nothing to do now but to go to sleep, my lord. I shall come to see you in the morning, and I expect to find you much more comfortable."

"Thank you," murmured the Earl, wishing that he might be left in peace.

The wish was granted. Silence fell, broken only by the rattle of curtain-rings, drawn along the rods, and the crackle of the fire burning in the hearth.

When the Earl opened his eyes again, it was to shaded lamplight. He saw Miss Morville rise from a chair beside the fire, and cross the room towards him, and said faintly: "Good heavens, what o'clock is it?"

"I have no very exact notion, my lord, but it doesn't signify," she answered, laying her hand across his brow. She glanced towards the door leading into the dressing-room, which stood open, and said: "Yes, his lordship is awake, Turvey. If you will come in, I will go and prepare the broth for him."

"The housekeeper desired me to tell you, madam, that she should not go to bed, and would hold herself in readiness to prepare whatever might be needed."

"Thank you, I will go to her," Miss Morville said.

When she returned to the bedchamber, bearing a small tray, Turvey had raised his master a little against his pillows, combed out his tumbled gold curls, and straightened the bed-coverings. Beyond thanking him for the various services he performed, the Earl said nothing, nor did Turvey encourage him to speak. He was deft in his ministrations, but quite impersonal, his impassive countenance not betraying his opinion of a household in which such shocking accidents could occur. Upon Miss Morville's entrance, he moved away from the bedside, and began to pick up some scraps of lint which had been allowed to fall on the floor. He then bowed, and said that he should be in the dressing-room when Miss Morville had need of him, and withdrew, closing the door behind him.

The Earl watched Miss Morville set down her tray on a table drawn up beside his bed, and said: "I remember now. Who— Did Chard see—?"

"No," she replied, seating herself, and picking up the bowl from the tray. "The horses, you know, were bolting, and by the time Chard had checked them you had lost consciousness, and he knew that it was more important to bring you home than to try to discover who had wounded you. Will you see if you can swallow some broth now? Oh, no! Don't disturb yourself! I am going to feed you."

The Earl, who had tried to raise himself, said ruefully: "I seem to be as weak as a cat!"

"You lost a great deal of blood," she said matter-of-factly. "If I were you, I would not try to talk."

"Yes, but I must know—" He broke off, for she had presented a spoon to his lips. He swallowed the broth in it, and said: "This is absurd! I am sure, if you could thrust another pillow behind me, I could feed myself!"

"I expect you could," she agreed, presenting another spoonful. "You may do so, if you wish it very much."

"I *ought* to do so," he said, smiling, and submitting. "You should be in bed: I am persuaded it must be very late."

"I shall go to bed when you have had your broth. Do not tease yourself! I settled it with Turvey that I should remain with you for the first part of the night."

"Indeed, I am very much obliged to you—and very much ashamed to have put you to such trouble!"

"You need not be. It is no hardship to me. I have frequently helped to nurse my brothers."

He attempted no further expostulation, but after a minute or two said again: "I must know. After I was hit—"

"I am afraid," she interrupted apologetically, "that I can tell you nothing, for I have been almost continually in this room, you know. Chard saw no one, and, as I have said, he dared not stop."

He moved restlessly, frowning. "Yes, but—Lucy must not—I seem to remember hearing him say something! To you, was it?"

"He did say something to me, but there is no need for you to fret yourself, my lord. We are agreed that it would be most improper to give utterance to suspicions for which there may be no real grounds."

A slight smile touched his lips. "You mean that you have prevailed upon Lucy to hold his peace. I might depend on you for good sense!"

"Certainly you might, but it will be better if you think no more on this subject until you are a little stronger," she replied.

"Don't let Lucy quarrel with Martin!"

"He will not do so."

"You don't know him! He must not tax Martin with this, and that is what I fear he may have done."

"I assure you, upon my word, he has not."

"What has Martin said?"

She turned away to put the bowl back on the tray, and answered, without looking at him: "Nothing, my lord."

"Nothing?"

"I have been busy," she reminded him. "I have not seen Martin."

"I daresay you might not, but—"

"I can only tell you that there has been no quarrel with him."

His eyes followed her as she carried the tray across the room. When she turned towards him again she perceived the strain in them, and she said: "I think your wound is paining you, my lord. Dr. Malpas left a sedative draught for you, and if you will take it you will feel more comfortable."

"It is not that. But while I lie here, with no strength even to pull myself up, and quite shut off from the household—"

"Tomorrow you will find yourself a good deal restored, if only you will be quiet now," she promised. "Nothing has happened at Stanyon that you would not wish, and, you know, it is past two o'clock now, so that even if you could rise from your bed there is nothing you could do, for everyone has been in bed these many hours."

He was obliged to acknowledge the justice of this reminder, but murmured with something of his sweet, mischievous smile: "You have always a reasonable answer, Miss Morville!"

She returned the smile, but did not answer, merely going to the door into the dressing-room to summon Turvey to relieve her watch. She stayed only until she had seen the Earl swallow his sedative draught, and then, directing Turvey to remove two of the pillows that were propping him up, bade her patient sleep well, and went away to her own bedchamber.

She had not left it when Dr. Malpas arrived, before nine o'clock, and it was Lord Ulverston who escorted the doctor to the Earl's room. He found the patient, as Miss Morville had prophesied, very much more comfortable, though still very weak.

"Weak, my lord! Ay, no wonder!" the doctor said, taking the Earl's pulse. "A trifle of fever, too, which was to be expected. I shall not cup you, however, for I think you will go on very well. But a bad business! I cannot conceive how it can have come about! There are poachers enough in the district, but they are not in general so careless as to fire across the roads—no, and I have never known them to go about their work in daylight before! I was speaking about it last night to Sir Geoffrey Acton, whom I was obliged to visit—just a touch of his old enemy, the gout!—and he gives it as his opinion that you might have been shot by one of these discharged soldiers we hear so much about. I daresay many of them are great rascals, and, you know, once they are turned loose upon the world, there is no saying what they will be up to."

Lord Ulverston uttered an impatient exclamation, but the Earl engaged his silence by a look, and himself said: "Very true."

The doctor, who had by this time laid bare the wound, seemed to be delighted with it. "Excellent! It could not be better!" he declared. "As clean a wound as you would wish for, and has not touched the lung! I can tell your lordship, though, that it was a near-run thing! Ay, you had bled so freely by the time your man got you home that if it had not been for Miss Morville's presence of mind and resolution, you might well have died before I had reached your side. She is a very good girl, and one that has a head on her shoulders besides. None of your squeaks and swoons at the sight of blood for her!"

"By Jupiter, yes!" the Viscount said. "I don't know what we should have been at without her, Ger, for a gorier sight I've seldom seen, and how to stop the bleeding was more than I knew!"

"Miss Morville is a very remarkable female," replied Gervase. "I am sorry, though, that she should have been confronted by such a hideous spectacle as I must have presented."

"Lord, she made nothing of that! It was her ladyship who went off into a swoon, right at the head of the stairs, when she saw you carried up!" The Viscount gave a chuckle. "There was I, clean distracted, and telling Miss Morville to come to her ladyship, and all she said was that I should call her maid, for she had something more important to attend to! I was ready to have murdered her, for, y'know, Ger, swooning females ain't in my line, but when I saw how cleverly she set to work on you I was bound to forgive her!"

At that moment a gentle knock fell on the door. Turvey moved to open it, and ushered in Miss Morville herself. The Viscount said gaily: "Ah, here she is! Come in, ma'am! I have been telling St. Erth what a stout heart you have! And here is the doctor saying that you don't squeak and swoon at the sight of blood!"

"I believe," said Miss Morville prosaically, "that my sex is, in general, less squeamish than yours, my lord." She then bade the doctor good-morning, observed with satisfaction that the Earl was looking better, and desired Dr. Malpas to visit the Dowager before he left Stanyon.

"Tell her I beg her pardon!" the Earl said, smiling, and stretching out his right hand, in an unconsciously welcoming gesture.

She looked at it, but she did not move from where she stood. In her most expressionless voice, she said: "Certainly, my lord."

Dr. Malpas, having applied a fresh dressing to the wound, and bound up the Earl's shoulder, had only to issue his instructions before announcing that he was ready to go to her ladyship. He made his patient grimace by prescribing thin gruel and repose; warned him that if he should try to exert himself too soon he would end in a high fever; and followed Miss Morville to the Dowager's apartments.

The Earl, who was more exhausted by the doctor's visit than he would own, dismissed Turvey; and, when the valet had withdrawn from the room, turned his head on the pillow to look at his friend. "Now, if you please, Lucy!"

"Dear old boy, no need to tease yourself! All's right!"

"It teases me more to be kept in ignorance. You are hiding something from me, you and Miss Morville!"

"Fudge!" said the Viscount unconvincingly.

"Lucy, whatever may be your suspicions, don't let

anyone say that it was Martin who shot me! This story which the doctor and his gouty patient have set up will do very well! It must not be whispered all over the county that Martin tried to kill me!"

The Viscount was silent, fiddling with the bed-curtains. After a moment, Gervase said more strongly: "Lucy, I'm in earnest! Good God, only think what you would feel yourself!"

"I know that. I wouldn't think of it, if I were you, Ger. No use!"

"What has Martin said?" Gervase demanded, watching him under knit brows. "Where *is* Martin?"

"That's more than I can tell!" said the Viscount, with a short laugh.

"What do you mean?"

The Viscount hesitated, and then said: "Listen, Ger! If I know anything of the matter, it's already all over the county that Martin tried to murder you! Martin ain't here!" He looked up, saw the startled look in the Earl's eyes, and said: "Hasn't been seen since he went off yesterday, saying he would try for a shot at those kestrels. *That's* why your mother-in-law wanted to see the doctor! True she swooned when she saw you carried in, but it wasn't that which upset her."

"Oh, my God!" Gervase said sharply. "Go on! Tell me the whole!"

"Don't think I should, dear boy!" said Ulverston, re-garding him in some alarm. "Ought to be quiet, y'know!"

"You'll tell me the whole, or I'll get up out of this bed!"

"No, no, don't do that! It's only this, Ger!—his gun has been found. Shot-belt, too."

"Who—? Where?"

"Chard. Good fellow, Chard! Rode off to the place where you were hit as soon as he'd fetched the sawbones over last night. Thought he might discover some trace. Well, he did. Found Martin's gun thrust down a rabbit-hole, and his shot-belt in a gorse-bush. Looks as though he had got rid of 'em quickly, because the end of the stock wasn't hidden well. That's all, but everyone here knows you've been shot at, and your brother ain't to be found—and if you think that news won't spread, you're a sapskull, Ger!"

"Martin would not take ball out for kestrels!"

"Daresay he wouldn't. Nothing to stop him loading his piece with ball, if he went for bigger game!" said the Viscount brutally. "No wish to distress you, but he had a couple of rounds in his belt. Seen 'em—not gammoning you!"

The Earl pressed a hand to his brow. "A couple of rounds in his belt.... Yes, and what more?"

"Nothing. No trace of him to be found. Thought he had done for you, of course! Took fright! Just the sort of hothead who would do so!"

"Very well. And then?"

"Got my own notion about that," said Ulverston darkly.

"What is it?"

"Nearest port. If he took fright, dared not stay—only thing to do, get out of the country!"

The Earl's hand dropped. "Yes. I think I see."

Ulverston perceived that he was looking very pale, and said in a conscience-stricken tone: "Shouldn't have told you! Don't put yourself into a fret, dear boy! Only want you to tell me what you wish done!"

"Chard. Send him up to me!"

"Can't. At least, not immediately, Ger! Told him to ride over to fetch your cousin! Seemed to me he's the man we need." He paused, and then, as Gervase said nothing, but only stared frowningly before him, he added: "I know you didn't like it when Frant kept Martin under surveillance. Told him you didn't need a watch-dog, didn't you? Well, it's precisely what you did need, Ger! While Frant was here, and Martin knew he was alive to his little game, he dared not pursue his damned purpose. No sooner was Frant out of the way, and Martin knew he was no longer being watched, than he seized the first chance that offered! Daresay this engagement of mine inflamed him."

The Earl's eyes travelled to his face. "If Martin tried to kill me, it was so that he should inherit my dignities. He could not more surely brand himself as my murderer than by running away!"

"Ay, thought of that myself!" agreed Ulverston. "Stupidest thing he could do, of course; but the more I think about it the more I think he's just the sort of rash young fool who would do it! No head, Ger! No head at all! Might even have repented of it as soon as he'd pulled the trigger. Lord, I haven't been staying here this while without learning a few things about your precious Martin! Done a lot of wild things in his time, because he wouldn't stop to think before he gave way to his passions! Wouldn't surprise me at all if he'd taken fright as soon as he realized what he'd done, and run for it. No, and I'll tell you another thing, Ger! It won't surprise me if he comes back, and tells us all some hoaxing story to account for his having gone off like that. Just as soon as he's had time to get over his fright and see the folly of running away!"

"I must get up!" the Earl said, in a fretting tone. "I must get up!"

Rather alarmed at the consequence of his unguarded talk, Ulverston said hastily: "No, no, what good would that do? Dash it, I wish I hadn't told you!" He looked round quickly, as he heard the door open, and hailed Miss Morville's entrance with a mixture of relief and guilt. "Here, ma'am, come and tell St. Erth he must stay where he is! You won't like it, but I've told him his brother ain't been seen since yesterday, and what must he do but declare he shall get up?"

"It seems to me a great pity," said Miss Morville acidly, "that you cannot be left to bear Lord St. Erth company for a bare quarter of an hour without throwing him into a fever, my lord! I beg your pardon if I seem impolite, but I must desire you to go away!"

"Well, you do, ma'am! Devilish impolite!" said the Viscount indignantly. "Dash it, St. Erth had to know it!"

"If you do not go, my lord, I fear I shall become still more impolite!" Miss Morville warned him.

The Viscount retreated in no very good order, and Miss Morville, after a glance at her patient, went to the table and picked up a glass from it. Into this she poured a dose from an ominous bottle she had brought into the room. Gervase said in a tired voice: "More of your sedative draughts, Miss Morville?"

"It is merely the medicine Dr. Malpas ordered me to give you at this hour," she replied, bringing it to him.

He took it from her, but he did not at once raise the glass to his lips. "Lucy was right. I had to know."

"To be sure, but not now."

He again put his hand to his brow. "I wish I could think! My head feels like a block of wood!"

"Very likely. It will be better when you have recovered your strength, and that you may do by being patient, and doing as you are bid."

He smiled wryly, but lifted the glass, and drank its contents. "Does my mother-in-law know what is being said?"

"She does, of course. It is painful for her, but *you* cannot cure that."

"Poor woman! Assure her I shall not die! Ought I to see her?"

"No, you will see no one but Turvey and me until tomorrow."

He sighed, but even as she uttered the words the door opened, and Theo came softly into the room.

He was looking pale, and very grim. He said in a low voice to Miss Morville: "Ulverston told me I might see my cousin. How is he?"

"He is excessively tired, and would be the better for sleeping," answered Miss Morville.

He came farther into the room, and looked towards the bed. He saw that the Earl was awake and dreamily regarding him, and stepped closer, saying in a moved voice: "Gervase! How is it, my dear fellow?"

"Excellent! I could not wish for a cleaner wound."

"Chard told me the whole, I came at once—knowing I should never have left Stanyon!"

"Not now, if you please!" said Miss Morville.

Theo glanced at her. "No. You are very right! But Ulverston sent me to try what I could do to set his mind at rest. I believe I know your will, Gervase. I will do whatever it is you wish me to do. If you want this affair to be hushed up, I will do my possible, upon my honour!"

"Yes, I knew I could depend upon you for that," Gervase said. "The doctor's story will answer the purpose as well as any other. I have now come to my senses, and I have disclosed to you that I caught a glimpse of a thick-set man in homespuns, skulking in the undergrowth. But Martin must be found!"

"He will be," Theo said soothingly. "Only do not fret, Gervase! I can take care of this for you, and I will."

"Thank you," Gervase said, his eyes half-closed.

Miss Morville signed to Theo to go, and he nodded, and went away without another word. She found the Earl's pulse to be tumultuous, and could only hope that rest and quiet would restore its even tone.

The Earl spent the remainder of the day between dozing and waking. His two nurses found him docile, swallowing the nourishment and the medicine they gave him, and acquiescing in Miss Morville's ban on visitors; but his pulse continued to be agitated, and his brief spells of sleep were uneasy. Towards night, he seemed to be more comfortable; and, rousing himself from his abstraction, he resolutely opposed Miss Morville's scheme to share the night watch with his valet. There was no real need for a watch to be kept, and perceiving that insistence would only tease him, Miss Morville consented to go to bed. It was arranged that Turvey should spend the night on a truckle-bed set up in the dressing-room; and with a silent resolve to pay at least one visit to the sick-room during the night, Miss Morville withdrew to her own bedchamber. She was, in fact, extremely weary, and although her conscience told her that she ought to visit the Dowager before retiring, she felt quite unequal to the strain of a conversation with that lady.

It was ten o'clock when she laid her head on the pillow, and she almost instantly fell asleep, waking rather more than two hours later, within ten minutes of the time she had set for herself. She lit her candle, and got up. She had removed only her dress and her slippers on going to bed, and these were soon resumed, and her hair tidied. Picking up her candle, she stole down the gallery, and round the angle of the court into the gallery on to which the Earl's bedroom opened. The house was very silent, but a lamp had been set on a table outside the Earl's door, and dimly lit the gallery. Miss Morville stealthily opened the door, and crept into the room.

Here too a lamp was burning low, set at a little distance from the bed, that its light should not worry the Earl. He seemed to be sleeping, but the tumbled bed-clothes indicated that he was restless. The sound of heavy and rhythmic breathing coming from the dressing-room informed Miss Morville that Turvey, at all events, was enjoying an excellent night's repose. She saw with displeasure that the fire had been allowed to die down, and went softly to lay more wood upon it. Then she returned to the bedside, and ventured, very cautiously, to draw the quilt, which was slipping off the bed, over the Earl's exposed shoulder. He stirred, but he did not open his eyes, and after standing still for a moment she began to tiptoe towards the door.

She had almost reached it when she was checked by a sound she could have sworn was a footstep. It was

muffled, but even as she decided that she had been
mistaken she heard it again. She was puzzled, for it
came neither from the gallery nor from the dressing-
room, but seemed rather to be located opposite the
dressing-room. It was followed by a sound so like the
brushing of a hand across a door that her heart jumped.
She moved swiftly back to the bed, and stood there,
staring through the dim light at the wall to the right. One
swift, uncertain glance she cast towards the dressing-
room, as though she would have called to Turvey; then
she closed her lips, and again searched with her eyes the
other side of the room.

The wall was panelled, like the rest of the room, the
sections masked by carved pilasters, and the dado and
skirting mitred round in an unbroken line. The light of
the flames, which were beginning to lick round the logs
she had laid on the fire, flickered over the interlaced
arches, and the elaborately carved capitals. The brushing
sound was heard again, like someone groping in
darkness. Then there came the unmistakable click of a
lifting latch. Miss Morville stood rigidly still. Suddenly
she knew that the Earl was awake; she heard him move,
and before she could turn to look at him felt his hand
grasp her wrist warningly. She looked quickly down,
and saw that he too had his eyes fixed on the panelling.
He said, so softly that she scarcely heard him: "Quiet!"

Her heart was beating uncomfortably fast, but she
knew her presence to be safeguard enough, and she had
not meant to raise the alarm.

The woodwork creaked; one of the sections of the
wainscot was sliding behind another, and the lamplight
showed a hand grasping the edge of it.

CHAPTER SEVENTEEN

THE APERTURE WAS widening slowly, but the lamp had been turned too low for its light to be thrown into the cavity revealed by the removal of the panel. There was a moment's pause, which Miss Morville found singularly nerve-racking, and then the silence was broken by a voice, raised little above a whisper, which uttered urgently: "St. Erth!"

The grip was removed from Miss Morville's wrist. "Come in, Martin!" the Earl said calmly.

Martin bent, and stepped over the skirting-board into the room. He started when Miss Morville moved from her station by the shadowed bed into the light, and stammered "I didn't know! I thought—" He broke off, shrugging. "It's of no consequence. St. Erth, I *had* to see you! I beg pardon if I startled you, but I was determined to have speech with you!"

"Where does that passage lead?" interrupted the Earl, nodding towards the cavity.

"It isn't a passage: it's only the secret stair! It leads to the cupboard by the door out to the old bowling-green. You must know it!"

"You are mistaken. I neither knew, nor was I told, that a secret stair led directly to my room."

Miss Morville moved silently to the door into the dressing-room, which stood ajar, and closed it, and then went to turn up the lamp.

"I suppose you were thought to know of it," Martin said. "What's the odds? I want—"

"Who does know of it?"

"Why, everyone!" said Martin impatiently. "There's no secret about it nowadays! No one uses it, of course—"

"That does not seem to be true."

"Well, I mean in the general way! I had to see you!"

Miss Morville had trimmed the lamp, and its golden light grew stronger. Looking up, she now perceived that Martin was looking haggard, and unusually white. She made no comment, but picked up one of the spare pillows, and carried it to the bed. "Let me put this behind you, my lord," she said. "It will be better for you not to support yourself on your elbow."

He thanked her, and leaned back, with a sigh of relief. She glanced at Martin, and said composedly: "Your brother is still weak, and should not be talking at this hour. Pray do not prolong your visit!"

"I've no wish to do him any harm—though I daresay you won't believe that!"

She did not answer, but sat down beside the fire. He scowled at her, but she returned his look with one of her wide, direct stares. Flushing, he turned from her to his half-brother.

"Tell me!" said the Earl. "Why do you choose to enter my room by a secret stair rather than by the door?"

"Choose! They will not let me come near you!"

"Who will not let you?"

"Theo—Ulverston—that damned groom of yours!"

"Indeed! But has a sentry been posted at my door?"

"No! Not at your door, but at mine!" Martin said bitterly. "Chard is sitting outside my room. The only wonder is that he has not locked me in!"

"Dear me! How, may I ask, did you contrive to slip past him unnoticed? Or is there also a secret way into your room?"

"No, there is not! I climbed out of the window. I tell you, I had to see you!"

"Why, Martin?"

"They think I tried to kill you!"

"Have they said so?"

"Not in so many words, but the questions they have asked me—the way they look at me! I'm not a fool! I know what they think! They say my gun and my shot-belt were found where—where it happened, and that I had rounds of ball in my belt! I had not! It is a damned lie, St. Erth! Good God, what should I want with ball when all I went for was an accursed pair of kestrels, and perhaps a pigeon or two?"

"Did you get the kestrels?" enquired Gervase.

"No. I never got a sight of them."

"Or a pigeon?"

"No!"

"Did you not fire your gun at all?"

"Yes, at a rabbit," Martin muttered. "Oh, we have had all that out, never fear! The gun has been fired, and I don't deny it! I bagged a rabbit, but where it is now I don't know! I can't produce it! *I never fired at you!*"

The Earl's head lay back against the supporting pillow; from under drooping eyelids he was watching every change in Martin's face. "Martin, why did you run away?" he asked.

"I didn't run away!" Martin exclaimed.

"Hush! Not so loud! My valet is sleeping in the next room. Where, then, have you been?"

"I don't know!" He saw his brother's brows lift, and added, in a goaded tone: "Ask Chard! He will tell you fast enough! It was some village short of Wisbech where he picked me up: I don't know its name!"

"I hope you mean to tell me what he was doing there, for I have not the remotest guess."

"I'll tell you!" Martin threw at him. "He was set on by your friend Ulverston to look for me on the road to King's Lynn! Ulverston believed I should be found making for the nearest port! God, how I have kept my hands from Ulverston's throat I don't know!"

"Yes, I remember now that Lucy told me that," Gervase said thoughtfully.

"I was trying to get to Stanyon, not to the coast!" Martin said, taking an impetuous step nearer to the bed.

"That, also, he foretold," murmured Gervase.

Martin recoiled. "I might have spared myself the pains of coming to you! You won't believe me any more than he or Theo do! Very well! Have me arrested for murder!"

"But I am not dead," Gervase said, smiling faintly. "What is it that I shan't believe?"

"I was kidnapped!" said Martin belligerently.

Miss Morville, who had been gazing into the fire, apparently divorced from this interchange, raised her head, and looked curiously at him.

"Now tell me you don't believe me! I expect that!"

"Not at all. Where, when, and how?"

Martin cast him a sullen glance. "I don't know when—except that it was not long after I had shot the rabbit, and I've no notion when that may have been, except that it can't have been a great while before you were fired at. I'd had no sport; I thought I might as well try for a brace of wood-pigeons, but you know what they are! There's no getting them, unless you lie-up, once they've been alarmed! I crouched down behind a thicket, to wait. I suppose someone stalked me: I don't know! All I know is that I was struck a stunning blow from behind. I *do* know that, but nothing more, until I came to myself, and how much later that was I've no notion!"

There was a short silence. "And your spaniel?" said the Earl.

"Not with me," Martin answered, colouring. He raised his eyes. "He had run a thorn into his foot, and was dead lame! I would not take him. Ask Hickling if that's not true! Oh, yes! I know what you are thinking! Hickling would tell any lie to oblige me, would he not?"

"I don't know. Would he?"

"I daresay! This is the truth!"

"Very well: go on!"

"I tell you, I don't know what happened! I didn't come to myself till I was being taken off somewhere, in a cart, or something. I couldn't see: I was trussed up, and gagged, and there was a sack over my head—not that I cared, for my head was aching fit to split, and I cared for nothing, *then*, except being jolted so much that I think I went off into another swoon. I don't remember that, but I *do* remember feeling devilish bad. And then

I wasn't in a vehicle, but lying on the ground some-where. It might have been a cow-byre: it smelled like it, but I couldn't see, or move, and I don't know. I don't even know how long I was there: hours and hours, I think! I suppose I slept part of the time. I must have, because I woke up with a start when someone began to haul me up. And then there was more of that curst jolting, and being hauled out of the cart again, and rolling down and down and down!"

"Rolling down where?" asked the Earl.

"It was a sand-pit, but I didn't know that at the time."

"Oh! And who rescued you from the sand-pit?"

"No one. I managed to get free. If I hadn't, I might be there now, for it was miles from anywhere, and disused, I think."

"But how did you contrive to free yourself then, when you had been unable to do so before?" asked Miss Morville, quite mystified.

"I suppose the cord must have frayed," Martin said, hesitatingly. "Or perhaps it worked loose—no, that wasn't it, because when I found I could move my arms at last, I strained and strained, and the cord broke, so I think it must have frayed, or was weak in one place. Look!" He thrust his sleeve up, and showed a bruised and chafed forearm.

"I will give you some arnica for it, if you would like it," said Miss Morville kindly.

He swung round to face her. "I don't want it! You think it's all lies, don't you?"

"Oh, no! Only one should never allow oneself to be carried away by exciting stories, and I am bound to observe that it would not be so very difficult to inflict such a bruise with one's own hands. I daresay it all happened exactly as you have described, but one can readily understand why it was that Theo and Lord Ulverston would not believe you."

"I am much obliged to you! Why don't you say you think I'm a murderer, and be done with it?"

"Martin,' interrupted Gervase, "why were you stunned, kept in durance vile, and finally rolled into a sand-pit?"

"Good God, if I knew that—! I suppose some desperate fellow meant to rob me!"

"And were you robbed?" asked Gervase.

"No, because I had no money on me! A man don't carry money in his pockets when he goes out shooting!"

"Just what I was thinking," agreed Gervase. "It does not seem to have occurred to that desperate fellow. Do you think he may have rolled you into the sand-pit in a pet at finding you so little worth his trouble?"

"No. It wasn't robbery, of course. I see that now, but at the time— Well, I know it sounds smoky, but it's true! I never thought about not having any money until I got out of that sand-pit. *Then* I remembered I hadn't as much as a groat in my pocket!"

"Was that why you decided to come back?"

Martin flushed. "I always meant to come back! It's why I didn't reach Stanyon till past ten o'clock tonight! At least, it is, in part! I can tell you, I didn't feel so stout when I first got free! I couldn't stand, and my head was aching till I could scarcely see out of my eyes, and I had such a thirst—! As soon as my legs would bear me, all I cared for was to get out of that pit, and find some water! Well, I did get out, and I had no more idea of where I was than—than anything, but there was a wood quite close, and I thought very likely there might be a stream near it, and so there was! And then I—I—"

"You?"

"I went to sleep!" Martin said. "I think I must have slept for hours, because it was very little past dawn when I got that sack off my head, and it was past noon when I woke up, judging from the sun. I felt better then, and I set out to get to the nearest village. Such a figure as I must have looked! I could see they took me for a common vagrant, at the ale-house. They had no post there, of course, and the landlord said he had no horse I might hire, but I might be accommodated at Guyhirne, which was not far."

"And were you?"

"No. That is—" Martin stole a glance from his brother's face to Miss Morville's. "I didn't go there. I know this was folly, but—I fell in with some country-fellow driving a waggon, and he took me up, and *that* was when I learned what had happened to you, St. Erth!"

"Learned it from a waggoner?"

"I might have learned it from a dozen such, I daresay! Some carrier who was at Cheringham this morning spread the story everywhere he went! The waggoner told me that you had been murdered and that *I* had disappeared, and was being everywhere looked-for! Of course, I might have guessed it wasn't as bad as that, but—well, I—"

"Took fright?"

"I didn't know what to do!" Martin blurted out. "I thought if anyone recognized me—or guessed who I was—I should find myself hustled off to gaol—*I*, Martin Frant! All I could think of to do was to get back here without being seen, and—and discover how it was, and think what I must do. But that fellow, Chard, was hunting for me, and I *had* been seen, of course, though no one knew me, all that way from Stanyon, and in such a rig! But I suppose when he described me, and what I was wearing, those curst bumpkins set him on my track. He came up with me in that village—driving *my* gig, too!—and—and then I heard how it was, and he brought me home as though I had been a felon, and he my gaoler, bringing me up to the Assize, or something! And after that, there was Theo—*and* Ulverston!—not believing a word I said, and declaring I should not see you! But I had to see you, and *tell* you—!"

Miss Morville, who had been watching the weary face against the pillow, said: "Well, Martin, now that you have done so, I shall be very much obliged to you if you will go away again, and leave his lordship to sleep! There is nothing more to be done tonight, you know, and I daresay, if you wish it, your brother will see you again tomorrow."

She wished then that she had not said this, for the Earl moved his head in a gesture of dissent, and his lips framed the one word: "No."

Martin saw it too, and said sharply: "St. Erth, you can't mean—St. Erth, you'll let me come and see you tomorrow, surely!"

"No. You can have nothing more to say to me. Keep away from this room! When I am on my feet again—we will see."

A frightened look, almost one of panic, came into Martin's face. He started forward involuntarily, exclaiming: "Gervase, you don't mean to accuse me of this? You can't think I would commit *murder!*"

A queer little smile flitted across the Earl's eyes. "You haven't murdered me."

"I never tried to! You must believe me! We're—we're half-brothers! Only think of the scandal!"

"I have thought of it. I told Theo I had caught a glimpse of a thick-set fellow, dressed in homespuns, hiding in the thicket."

Martin drew a shuddering sigh. "I knew you could not—*did* you see such a fellow?"

"I saw no one."

"Are you sure of that?" Martin asked, frowning down at him. "Because— Well, never mind!" He caught Miss Morville's eye, and said: "Oh, very well! I'm going! Only if you are afraid to let me enter your room, and I am to have Chard standing guard over me in this way—"

"You shall be relieved of Chard. Before you go, tell me how that panel works!"

"I wonder you should never have been shown! I remember when my father first showed it to me: I can't have been more than ten years old."

"Very likely. I had not the felicity of standing upon such easy terms with him. How is it opened?"

"Oh, it is quite a knacky thing! It has a queer latch upon the inside, with a stop on it, so that when it is down the panel cannot slide back. You may open it from this side by twisting one of the bosses at the head of that pillar." He stepped up to the wall, and laid his hand on the boss. "This one. It has a device which lifts the latch, if you turn it—like this!"

"Ingenious! May I ask how the panel is secured from this room?"

"It ain't. You may only secure it from the inside.

That's very simply done: you have only to thrust a wedge between the latch and the guard, so that it can't be raised. If that's done, the boss won't move, of course. I daresay that when they came spying out priests' holes, in the old days, they used to try if any of the mouldings on the wainscots could be moved. This would have baffled them!"

"No doubt. Is there no means of securing the entrance at the bottom of the stair?"

"No, but the cupboard is kept locked. We don't use it nowadays."

The Earl held out his hand. "The key, if you please!"

"I was going to lock the cupboard, and put the key back!"

"Thank you, I prefer to keep it in my own possession. Where, in general, is it to be found?"

"In the steward's room. Perran has all the keys hanging in a cupboard there."

"It is not an arrangement which recommends itself to me."

"Oh, as you please!" Martin said, and gave an old-fashioned key into his hand.

"Thank you. Now go back to your own room, and tell Chard I wish to see him, if you please!"

"Very well. And you don't think—you don't believe that—"

"Forgive me! I am too tired to discuss this matter further tonight."

"Then I'll say good-night!" Martin said stiffly. "I beg your pardon for disturbing you!"

Gervase did not answer. Miss Morville waited until Martin had left the room before she said: "I hope, my lord, that you mean Chard to lock that door immediately!"

"Why, yes!"

"I trust I am not one to refine too much upon trifles, but I do *not* like the notion of having a secret stair leading to your room!"

"Nor I," he said, regarding her in some amusement.

"To own the truth," she confessed, "my blood ran cold when I saw that panel begin to slide open!"

"Indeed, I was afraid that you would call Turvey in, which I particularly did not wish."

"No, I had made up my mind not to do that before you grasped my wrist. While I was present you were safe, I knew."

"You are a remarkable woman, Miss Morville."

"On the contrary, I am sadly commonplace," she replied. "I shall say no more to you tonight on what has occurred. I can see it has teased you very much, and I wish you will try to put it out of your mind until you are stronger." She straightened the quilt as she spoke, and after a moment's hesitation said, in a colourless tone: "Your medicine I keep in my own charge, and you may like to know, my lord, that all the nourishment you partake of passes from the head-cook's hands to Turvey's only."

"Yes, I had not considered the chances of poison," he said thoughtfully. "Thank you! This is your doing, I collect."

"By no means. I fancy it was concerted between Turvey, Abney, and the head-cook himself. Whatever may be the sentiments of certain members of your family, sir, you have trustworthy guards in your servants."

"It seems so indeed! I cannot conceive why they should concern themselves with my welfare!"

She said gravely: "There is no understanding it, to be sure, but so it is! And here, I think, comes Chard. I shall leave you now, my lord. Pray do not vex yourself more than you need! You have been frowning ever since you heard Martin's story, you know!"

"Have I? I beg your pardon! He has given me food for a good deal of thought."

"You will be able to think more clearly in a day or two," she said, and went to the door, and opened it. "You may come in, Chard: his lordship wishes to speak with you. You will not keep him wakeful overlong, I know. Good-night, my lord!"

She went out, and Chard approached the bed cautiously. He was welcomed with a smile. "Not dead yet, Chard. What a work you must have had, driving those grays, and preventing me from falling out of the curricle!"

"Well, I did, me lord," Chard owned, grinning at him. "And very much *contra pelo* it went with me not to be able to stop to catch the villain red-handed! But by the time I had them grays under control you was gone off into a swound, and bleeding so that I durstn't do anything but drive home hell-for-leather."

"I am very much obliged to you. You did right, and I doubt whether you would have caught my would-be assassin, even had you been able to stop."

"I would have liked to have got just one glimpse of him, me lord," Chard said. "I know what I know, but it ain't enough. And I'm rare set-about that I let that young—let Mr. Martin slip through my hands tonight, so to speak! What I *don't* see is how he got into your lordship's room without me seeing him at it!"

"He got into it by way of that stair, which you may see, if you turn round."

"Ho!" said Chard, having subjected the panel and the cavity beyond it to a close inspection. "So that's the way it is, is it? Next thing we know we'll be having an *embascado* inside this here Castle, as well as out of it! Well, me lord, that's properly bowled me out, that has! Why, you might have been smothered in your bed, and no one the wiser!"

"I fancy that very nearly did happen to me once," said the Earl reflectively. "I don't mean to be approached by that stair again, so, if you will be so good, Chard, you may take a candle, and go out by the secret way, and when you come out of the cupboard, into which I understand it has access, lock it, and keep the key. Here it is!"

Chard took the key, but said: "Ay, me lord, but that ain't enough! There's someone as is desperate set on stashing your glim, and by what I've seen he won't stop for much. Seems to me we'll both of us be easier in our minds if I was to set here quiet during the night, while your lordship gets a bit of sleep!"

The Earl shook his head. "Thank you, no! I have something else for you to do. I fancy nothing will be attempted against me while I am confined to my bed, with Turvey in the dressing-room."

"Him!" said Chard scornfully. "He *might* wake if you was to sound a trumpet outside his door—there's no saying!"

"He would wake if I called to him. But I have a better answer for a would-be assassin than Turvey. Open the top right-hand drawer of that chest, if you please! You will find my pistol there: bring it to me! Be careful! It is loaded and primed. Thank you!" The Earl took the pistol, and laid it on the table beside his bed. "Now light a candle!" He waited until Chard had obeyed him, and then said: "Don't mount guard outside Mr. Martin's room!"

"Me lord!" Chard said explosively. "Mr. Martin was caught by me the best part of the way to King's Lynn this day!"

"Yes. I know."

"Very good, me lord, but p'raps you don't know what sort of a Canterbury tale he saw fit to tell me!"

"I have heard it. But I do not wish him to know that he is watched. In the house, I think I stand in no danger. But in a day or two I shall be out of this bed, and when that happens, then I want you to watch Mr. Martin, once he is outside these walls. You will not always find it possible to follow him, but discover where he goes, and if he takes a gun out, follow him as close as you may." He paused. "And if I too am outside these walls, Chard, don't let him out of your sight!" he said deliberately.

CHAPTER EIGHTEEN

MARTIN'S RETURN to Stanyon brought about two changes
in the existing arrangements at the Castle: the Dowager
emerged from the seclusion of her own apartments, and
Lord Ulverston postponed his departure for London. No
one was much surprised at this, and although the Earl
murmured that Lucy's presence was unlikely to preserve
him from harm he raised no demur to it, events having
largely banished from Martin's mind other and less immediately important issues. Indeed, it was doubtful if
Martin would now have offered for Marianne, had her affections been disengaged, for when she drove over to
Stanyon with her parents, to enquire after the progress
of its owner, her shocked gaze informed him tolerably
clearly what were her sentiments upon the occasion. That
the story he had told should have met with disbelief,
first, and palpably, from his half-brother, and then from
the lady whom he had intended to wed, struck Martin
with stunning effect, and in some measure prepared him
for his reception at Mr. Warboys's hands. "Doing it rather
too brown, Martin!" Mr. Warboys said bluntly. "Always
said that nasty temper of yours would land you in a fix
one of these days!" He added, with considerable courage:
"Lesson to you! Have to live it down, old boy!"

Instead of issuing the challenge which Mr. Warboys would have had no hesitation in declining, Martin had turned on his heel, and walked off without another word spoken.

The Dowager, resuming her place in the household at Stanyon, soon realized that Martin's return had not, as she had felt sure it must, allayed all suspicion against him. Nothing in her well-ordered existence had prepared her for such a situation as now confronted her. Her egotism happily preserved her from self-blame, but her agitation was, nevertheless, acute, and prompted her to pay her stepson a visit. Miss Morville was powerless to resist this incursion; she could only hope that the Earl's constitution was strong enough to support him through the ordeal. She discovered, as others had done before her, that his apparent fragility and his gentleness were alike deceptive. He received his stepmother with equanimity, and although her visit wearied him it did not, as Miss Morville had feared it must, agitate his pulse. The Dowager harangued him for half an hour, ringing all the changes between scolding, dictating, and pleading. He heard her with patience, and answered her with such kindness that she left his room much tranquillized, and only realized some hours later that her intervention had achieved nothing. He did not banish Martin from Stanyon, but he would not again admit him to his bedchamber; he told her that he should adhere to his story of the man in homespuns, but he gave her no assurance that he believed Martin to be innocent of the attempt upon his life. It was not until Martin questioned her upon these points that the Earl's omissions occurred to her. She had seldom suffered so severe

a setback, and its effect upon her was such that Miss
Morville felt herself obliged to accede to her almost
tearful request to her young friend not to leave her while
her nerves were so much overset.

Thus it was that Mr. and Mrs. Morville, arriving in
the middle of the following week at Gilbourne House,
found that although their daughter was certainly there
to welcome them she had no immediate intention of re-
joining the family circle. Mr. Morville, much astonished, was at once shocked and grieved. He feared that
Drusilla had been led away by grandeur; and, had he
received the least encouragement from his helpmate, he
would have felt strongly inclined to have exerted his
parental authority to compel his daughter to return to
her own home. So far from receiving such encouragement, he was dissuaded, in unmistakable terms, from
expressing even the mildest desire for Drusilla's return.

"It appears," said Mrs. Morville fluently, "that they
are in trouble at Stanyon. If Lady St. Erth wishes
Drusilla to remain with her for the present, I should not
like to be disobliging, you know."

Mr. Morville conceded this point, but observed that
he knew not why his daughter should be required to act
as a sick-bed attendant in a household where as many
as twenty—or, for anything he knew, thirty—servants
were employed.

"As to that," said Mrs. Morville, "it is Lady St. Erth
rather than her son-in-law who depends just now upon
Drusilla. These very shocking rumours have distressed
her excessively. I am sure it is no wonder! And Drusilla,
you know, feels that it would be a shabby thing to desert
her, after her kindness. I own, I cannot but agree that

we are very much obliged to her ladyship for entertaining our daughter during these weeks of our absence; and I should not, for my part, wish Drusilla to be backward in any attention."

Mr. Morville, while he assimilated these words, removed his spectacles, and thoroughly polished them with his handkerchief. He then replaced them, and through them regarded the wife of his bosom with some severity. "When we set forth upon our travels, my love," he said, "it was only at Lady St. Erth's earnest entreaty that we left our daughter in her charge. The obligation was upon her side; and had it been otherwise I should never have consented to the arrangement. I had thought that we were at one on this!"

"Certainly! There can be no question!" Mrs. Morville said, showing a heightened colour. "The thing is—Mr. Morville, I have been closeted with Drusilla this past hour! I will not conceal from you that what she said to me—and, even more, what she did *not* say to me!—has given me food for serious reflection!"

"Indeed!"

"Reserve," announced Mrs. Morville nobly, "is at all times repugnant to me! My dear sir, I beg you will tell me anything you may know of this young man!"

"What young man?" asked her lord, in bewildered accents.

Mrs. Morville had the greatest respect for her husband's scholarly attainments, and for his grasp on imponderable subjects, but she had frequently been obliged to own that on more practical matters he was exasperatingly obtuse. She clicked her tongue impatiently, and responded: "Why, the new Earl, to be sure!"

"St. Erth?" he said. "I have never met him. I believe my brother is acquainted with him, but I do not immediately perceive in what way this can be germane to the present issue."

"I daresay you might not," said Mrs. Morville tolerantly, "for you never perceive what is under your nose, my love! What would you say to it if our daughter were to become the Countess of St. Erth?"

"What?" exclaimed the gentleman, in anything but a gratified tone. "You cannot be in earnest!"

She nodded. "I assure you, I was never more so! I saw at a glance, of course, that Drusilla was changed, but until I had enjoyed an hour alone with her I had no more idea of the cause than you. Though, to be sure, I might have guessed, from the scant references in her letters to his lordship, how the wind blew! He seems to be a most amiable young man, my dear sir! And this accident, shocking though it may be, throwing them together in such a way—!"

"Have I heard aright?" interrupted Mr. Morville. "Do I understand that you—*you,* Mrs. Morville!—would welcome such an alliance?"

"Pray, have you heard anything about the young man which would preclude my welcoming it?" she demanded.

"I know nothing of him. I daresay he is as idle and as expensive as any other of his order."

"I am astonished that a man of your mental attainment, my dear Mr. Morville, should speak with such prejudice!" said his wife. "From all I have heard from Drusilla, he is quite unexceptionable, and blessed with so sweet a temper that I am sure he must make any female a most delightful husband!"

"He may be possessed of all the virtues!" retorted Mr. Morville, "but he must be held to stand for everything which you and I, ma'am, have dedicated our lives to combating! His very rank, I should have supposed, would have rendered him odious to you! Is it possible that I have been deceived? Were we not at one in cherishing the hope that our daughter and Henry Poundsbridge would make a match of it?"

"Well," said Mrs. Morville reasonably, "I have a great regard for Henry Poundsbridge, and I own I should not have opposed the connection; for Drusilla, you know, is not a Beauty, and when a girl has been out for three seasons it is not the time to be picking and choosing amongst her suitors. An excellent young man, but not, you will admit, to be compared with Lord. St. Erth!"

"I cannot credit the evidence of my own ears!" said Mr. Morville. "How is it possible that you should talk in such a strain as this, Mrs. Morville? Is this, I ask myself, the woman who wrote *The Distaff?* Is this the authoress of *Reflections on the Republican State?* Is this the companion with whom I have shared my every philosophic thought? I am appalled!"

"So you might well be, my dear sir, if I were such a zany as to prefer Henry Poundsbridge to the Earl of St. Erth for my daughter!" responded the lady with some asperity. "It is an alliance it would not have entered my head to seek, but if the Earl—I say, *if!*—were to offer for dear Drusilla, and you were to refuse your permission, I should be strongly inclined to clap you into Bedlam! I marvel, my love, that a man of your intellect should so foolishly confuse *theory* with practice! I shall continue to hold by those opinions which I share with you, but when it comes to my only daughter's creditable establishment in the world it is time to set aside Utopian dreams!" She perceived that her husband was looking slightly stunned by this burst of eloquence, and at once drove him against the ropes by adding in quelling accents: "As Cordelia Consett, I must deplore the present state of society; but as a Mother I must deem myself unworthy of that title were I to spurn a connection so flattering to my Child!"

"Am I to understand," asked Mr. Morville, "that the Earl is about to make an offer for Drusilla?"

"Good gracious, my dear, how you do run on!" exclaimed his wife. "For anything I know, St. Erth has no such notion in his head! You may be sure that I was careful not to seem to be in the least conscious when I was talking to Drusilla. *That* would never do! Merely, I suspect that her heart may not be untouched."

"If," said Mr. Morville, asserting himself, "you have reason to suppose that St. Erth has been trifling with Drusilla—"

"Nothing of the sort! From what I have learnt today, I am persuaded that he is by far too great a gentleman to raise expectations he has no intention of fulfilling. Besides, men never do trifle with Drusilla," added Mrs. Morville, in a voice not wholly free from regret.

"It appears to me," said her spouse, pointedly opening his book, "that you are making a piece of work about nothing, my dear!"

"We shall see! Only, if I am right, I do beg of you, my dear sir, that you will not allow a foolish scruple to stand in the way of your daughter's happiness!"

"It would be quite against my principles to coerce Drusilla in any way. Or, indeed, any of my children!"

"Very true, and it exactly illustrates what I said to you about theory and practice! For when poor Jack fell into the clutches of that Female, and would have married her had it not been for—"

"That," interrupted Mr. Morville, "was a different matter!"

"Of course it was, my love, and very properly you behaved, as Jack himself would *now* be the first to acknowledge!"

She waited for a moment, in case he should venture on a retort, but when he became to all appearances immersed in his book she withdrew, to indulge in several delightful daydreams, not one of which could have been said to have been worthy of a lady of her intellectual distinction. She knew it, laughed at herself, and had even the grace to be ashamed of the most attractive of these dreams, in which she had the felicity of breaking the news of Drusilla's triumph to her sister-in-law, not one of whose three pretty daughters was as yet engaged to be married.

Her flights into this realm of fancy would have surprised, and indeed horrified, her daughter, whose own view of her circumstances was decidedly unhopeful. Mrs. Morville had not been deceived: Drusilla's heart was not untouched. Impregnable to the advances of that promising young politician, Mr. Henry Poundsbridge, it had crumbled under the assault of the Earl's first smile. "In fact," Drusilla told her mirrored image severely, "you have fallen in love with a beautiful face, and you should be ashamed of yourself!" She then re-

flected that she had several times been in company with
Lord Byron without succumbing to the charms of a
face generally held to be the most beautiful in England,
and became more cheerful. However, a candid scrutiny
of her own face in the mirror soon lowered her spirits
again. She could perceive no merit either in the freshness of her complexion, or in her dark, well-opened
eyes, and would willingly have sacrificed the natural
curl in her brown hair for tresses of gold, or even of
raven-black. As for her figure, though some men might
admire little plump women, she could not bring herself
to suppose that St. Erth, himself so slim and graceful,
could think her anything but a poor little dab of a girl.

"It is a great piece of folly to suppose that because
his manners are so *very* engaging he regards you with
anything but tolerance!" she told her image. She then
blew her nose, sniffed, and added, with a glance of
contempt at her rather flushed countenance: "Depend
upon it, you are just the sort of girl a man would be glad
to have for his sister! You don't even know how to
swoon, and I daresay if you tried you would make
wretched work of it, for all you have is common-sense,
and of what use is that, pray?"

This embittered thought brought to her mind the
several occasions upon which she might, had she been
the kind of female his lordship no doubt admired, have
kindled his ardour by a display of sensibility, or even
of heroism. This excursion into romance was not
entirely successful, for while she did her best to conjure
up an agreeable vision of a heroic Miss Morville, the
Miss Morville who was the possessor not only of a
practical mind but also of two outspoken brothers could

not but interpose objections to the heroine's actions. To have thrown herself between the foils, when she had surprised the Earl fencing with Martin, would certainly have been spectacular, but that it would have evoked anything but exasperation in the male breast she was quite unable to believe. She thought she need not blame herself for having refrained upon this occasion; but when she recalled her behaviour in the avenue, when the Earl had been thrown from his horse, she knew that nothing could excuse her. Here had been an opportunity for spasms, swoonings, and a display of sensibility, utterly neglected! How could his lordship have been expected to guess that her heart had been beating so hard and so fast that she had felt quite sick, when all she had done was to talk to him in a voice drained of all expression? Not even when his lifeless body had been carried into the Castle had she conducted herself like a heroine of romance! Had she fainted at the sight of his blood-soaked raiment? Had she screamed? No! All she had done had been to direct Ulverston to do one thing, Turvey another, Chard to ride for the doctor, while she herself had done what lay within her power to staunch the bleeding.

At this point, the prosaic Miss Morville intervened. "Just as well!" she said.

"He would have liked me better had I fallen into a swoon!" argued Drusilla.

"Nonsense! He would have been dead, for well you know that no one else had the least notion what to do!" said Miss Morville.

"At least I might have screamed when Martin came through the panel!"

"He was very much obliged to you for not scream-
ing. He said you were a remarkable woman," Miss
Morville reminded her.

"I heard him say the same of his Aunt Cinderford!"
said Drusilla, refusing to be comforted.

Miss Morville could think of no reply to this, but
issued instead depressing counsel. "You would do better
to put him out of your mind, and return to your parents,"
she said. "No doubt he will presently become betrothed
to a tall and beautiful woman, and forget your very existence. However, a useful life lies before you, for your
brothers will certainly marry, and although you yourself
will remain single, you will be an excellent aunt to all
your nephews and nieces."

It was perhaps not surprising that it was Miss
Morville rather than Drusilla, who presently carried his
medicine to the Earl.

He had promoted himself that day to a chair beside
the fire, and was seated in it, clad in the brocade
dressing-gown which had excited his cousin's mockery,
and leaning his head back against the cushions to look
up at Lord Ulverston, who stood warming his coat-tails
in front of the hearth. He was certainly pale, and Miss
Morville thought that he looked tired, but he greeted her
with a warm smile, and spoke with a gaiety at variance
with his rather careworn appearance. "I wish you will
tell me why it is, Miss Morville, that you never visit me
unless you wish to force an evil draught down my unwilling throat!" he said. "And this afternoon you did not
even visit me for that purpose, but left Turvey to be your
deputy! I promise you, I think myself very hardly
used!"

"What an exacting fellow you are!" exclaimed the Viscount, in a rallying tone. "Miss Morville went to meet her parents, and you may think yourself lucky she has returned to you at all!"

"Ah, yes, I had forgotten!" Gervase said, taking the glass, and draining it. He gave it back to Miss Morville, saying: "Does this mean that we must lose you, ma'am?"

"Not immediately. I have promised Lady St. Erth that I will remain with her another week," she replied.

"You are very good," he said, smiling at her. "I wish her ladyship and I may not, between us, have given your parents a great dislike of us!" He added, as she laughed, and moved towards the door: "Oh, no, don't run away so soon! How can you neglect me so? Tell me about Martin's new man!"

She was surprised, and repeated: "Martin's new man?"

"Miss Morville, have you not seen him?" demanded the Viscount. "I've been telling Ger it's a trifle too smoky for my taste! Never saw such a fellow in my life!"

"I didn't know that he had engaged a new man," she said. "Has he turned off Studley, then?"

"That's what I'd like to know. All I can tell you is that my fellow says Studley went off with some tale of being obliged to visit his old father, and this new man walked in. Told me he was a valet, but what *I* thought was that he must have broken out of Newgate! What's more, I caught him hobnobbing with that groom of Martin's this afternoon, and if you can tell me, Ger, what Martin's valet was doing in the stables I'll thank you!"

"Most mysterious," agreed Gervase, rather amused.

"Ay, you may laugh!" the Viscount said. "You haven't seen the fellow! Valet! Good God, one would as lief employ a coal-heaver! No, really, Ger! Give you my word!"

"Martin does not care very much for his appearance," Miss Morville ventured to suggest.

Gervase cast her a mischievous look, murmuring demurely: "*Not* one of these dandified jackanapes! Very true, Miss Morville!"

"I am sure," she retorted, with spirit, "he would never be so foolish as to demand to be shaved when he should rather have been measured for a cerecloth!"

The Viscount would have none of this trifling. He said: "A man don't need to be a dandy to hire a respectable valet! Point is, either he don't hire one at all, or he hires one who knows his work! What I want to know is, why was this Newgate fellow brought in?"

"My dear Lucy, my *very* dear Lucy!" said Gervase, at his most dulcet. "What dreadful apprehensions are you trying to instil into my head? Miss Morville, my pulse is tumultuous! I think you should feel it!"

She was, however, intently regarding the Viscount. "What is it that you fear, my lord?"

"I don't say I fear anything," replied the Viscount unconvincingly. "All I say is that there's something devilish queer afoot! First we have Martin coming back to Stanyon with just the sort of bamming story I warned you he would tell! Now, didn't I, Ger? You can't deny it, and you need not try to fob me off with your story about a man in homespuns! Lord, what a hum! I don't say I blame you: no one wants a scandal in his family! but don't try to bamboozle me, dear old boy! Then you don't die after all, and the next thing we know is that there's a villainous-looking fellow prowling about your damned draughty ancestral halls, saying he's your brother's new valet! I tell you to your face, Ger, it won't fadge!"

"But surely Martin would not—" began Miss Morville, and broke off short, looking from Ulverston to St. Erth, in mute question.

"No telling *what* a young fool like Martin would do!" said the Viscount. "Might not have thought anything of it, if I hadn't seen this Leek earwigging that groom today! As it is—*did* see it! Made me think, Ger! Made me add two and two together!"

"But, Lucy, you know you *cannot* add two and two together!" expostulated Gervase. "Whenever you have computed your debts, you have always reached a false total! Why don't you ask Martin why he has taken this strange individual into his service?"

"Martin and I don't exchange any more words than we need!" replied the Viscount grimly. "Daresay he knows what I think! Don't mind if he does!"

"What a happy party must assemble for dinner each evening!" remarked Gervase, watching the play of the candlelight on his emerald signet-ring.

"You may well say so! And when your cousin has left us, we shall have no one but that prosy parson to keep our conversation alive!" said the Viscount.

"Does Theo mean to leave Stanyon?" asked Miss Morville quickly.

"Why, yes!" answered the Earl. "My affairs, you know, cannot be for ever left at a stand! He returns to Evesleigh tomorrow. Now, if only I could prevail upon Lucy to go to London—not that I wish to appear inhospitable—"

"Spare your breath!" recommended Ulverston. "If he were not assured that I have no intention of leaving Stanyon at this present, your cousin would not stir from here, let me tell you!"

"You have both told me so, and I have nothing to do but to reply that you are very welcome—if mistaken!"

"That," said the Viscount, "we shall see, Ger!"

CHAPTER NINETEEN

THE VISCOUNT WAS not the only person to look askance upon Martin's new valet. Turvey, when he undressed his master that evening, informed him that the Castle had a fresh inmate. His tone contrived to convey the additional information that Mr. Leek was scarcely the type of man with whom he was in the habit of associating. "If I may venture to say so, my lord, a strange Individual for Mr. Martin to take into his service. Very different from Studley, who, although scarcely conforming to Our standards, I have always found to be a most respectable person. Besides having quite a Way with Mr. Martin's boots," he added, as one giving honour where it was due. "Of course, my lord, the same results as We achieve are not to be obtained, as I had occasion to tell him, through the use of mere blacking; but when one takes into account the very meagre means at his disposal he did very well—very well indeed! It is to be hoped Mr. Martin will not be disappointed in his new man. More I will not say."

"Whatever else I may believe, that I do not!" said the Earl.

"I hope, my lord," said Turvey, skilfully rolling the bandage he had removed from about the Earl's chest and shoulder, "that I am not one to cast aspersions upon others; and if Studley's sudden removal from the Castle strikes me as being a peculiar circumstance, I am sure I should prefer to keep my reflections to myself, were I not deeply concerned with your lordship's welfare."

"Thank you. I collect that Studley has gone to visit his father."

"Yes, my lord—his ailing father," said Turvey, dusting basilicum-powder over the healing wound. "Very proper, I am sure—though how he became aware that his parent was in poor health I do not know. I fancy, my lord, that Dr. Malpas cannot but be pleased with the condition of your wound. If your lordship would be so obliging as to raise your left arm a trifle, I will replace the bandages!"

The Earl complied with this request, but he said: "Out with it! What are you trying to tell me, Turvey? Do you suspect that Studley has no father?"

"On that head, my lord, I have no information, and shall keep an open mind. I was merely curious to know how the news of his parent's indisposition reached Studley."

"Possibly through the medium of the post. Not too tight, if you please!"

Turvey slackened the bandage. "I beg your lordship's pardon! I should myself have supposed that Studley must have received a letter from his parent were it not for the fact that when Chard rode to Grantham for the paregoric draught recommended by the doctor, he called at the receiving-office, and brought back to the Castle such letters as were there. There were only two, my lord: one for her ladyship, and one for the housekeeper. I trust the bandage is not now too tight?"

"Thank you, no. It is possible, you know, that, having been turned off by Mr. Martin, Studley sought for an excuse to explain his sudden departure. He might not wish it to be known that he had been dismissed."

Turvey bowed slightly. "Very understandable, I am sure, my lord. Particularly if he thought that no one would have believed it. I am told that Studley has been with Mr. Martin ever since he was a boy. Yes, my lord: remarkably attached to him, I am informed." He then helped the Earl to put on his night-shirt, and turned to pull back the bedclothes. "Your lordship might desire me, before I myself retire to rest in the dressing-room, to turn the key in the lock of this door. Mr. Martin's new man—doubtless bewildered by the many galleries and corridors in the Castle, and anxious to acquaint himself with his surroundings—has, if I may say so, a tendency to prowl. Would your lordship care to have a pillow under the left shoulder?"

"No, thank you," Gervase replied, stretching himself out in the huge bed. "Nor should I care to have my door locked. Where does he prowl?"

"That, my lord, I am not in a position to say," said Turvey, tucking in the blankets. "One of the two occasions when I encountered him, he appeared to be acquainting himself with the bedchambers opening on to this gallery. He explained to me that he was trying to find Mr. Martin's room. Is there anything further I can do for your lordship?"

"Only one thing! Do not alarm the Servants' Hall with this story!"

"Your lordship need feel no apprehension. I should think it most improper to impart my reflections to any but your lordship," responded Turvey, with hauteur. "It would be idle to deny, however, that a good deal of comment has been provoked amongst the staff, no one being able to understand what should have prevailed upon Mr. Martin to have hired this Leek. I need scarcely say that I have discouraged all attempts to discover what may be my opinion. I shall continue to do so. Good-night, my lord!"

He then withdrew to the adjoining room, leaving the Earl to digest his sinister tidings.

Upon the following morning, Theo took his leave of his cousin, saying, with his slight smile: "You are so well-guarded I may abandon you with a quiet mind! Don't over-tax your strength! Ulverston, I rely upon you to remember you are under oath to send me word if— if Gervase should suffer a relapse!"

"Ay, you may depend upon me!" the Viscount said. "As for relapses—pooh! If you had ever campaigned with Ger, you would know he has a stronger constitution than any of us!"

He repeated this observation when, later in the day, Miss Morville tried to dissuade her patient from emerging from the seclusion of his own bedchamber. Her efforts were quite unsuccessful, and the Viscount told her privately that she was wasting her time. "All you'll get is a soft answer, ma'am. Never knew such an obstinate fellow as Ger! He don't look it, and the lord knows he don't sound it, but don't you let him humbug you! Besides, it won't hurt him, y'know. Wouldn't think it to look at him, but the time he got that nasty slash on his arm he had it stitched up, and never told a man-jack of us how bad it was."

"I was not thinking so much of that," confessed Miss Morville. "It may be foolish of me, but while he is confined to his room it must surely be impossible for anyone to hurt him!"

"He ain't going to be hurt," said the Viscount confidently. "Best thing now would be for an attempt to be made on him. Can't leave the thing as it is, y'know. Got to catch our fine gentleman red-handed, ma'am. Now, you ain't the blabbing sort, so I'll tell you this: young Martin can't stir an inch without having Chard on his heels! Good man, Chard!"

"Good God! Is he spying on Martin? Does Martin know it?"

"Lord, no! No one knows it but Chard and me!" said the Viscount. "Except you, of course. The thing is, *I* can't watch Martin, and it must be plain to everyone but dear old Ger that someone ought to. So I set Chard on to it. Good notion, don't you think?"

"Excellent!" said Miss Morville, in rather a hollow voice.

"You see," explained his lordship kindly, "it won't do to let the thing alone. Only let Martin try to do Ger a mischief *now,* and we can spike his guns, ma'am!"

"Yes, but—" She stopped, and closed her lips firmly on some unexpressed thought.

The Viscount, tolerant of feminine weakness, advised her to put it out of her mind. Miss Morville, after a short struggle with herself, again refrained from speech.

The Earl left his room some time after noon. His toilet had occupied him for longer than was usual, since he was obliged to move his left arm with caution, and refused to abate one jot of his meticulous neatness. He bore with patience such suggestions from Turvey as that he should make his appearance in his dressing-gown; but when the valet went so far as to beg him to leave the arrangement of his cravat in his hands, patience failed, and he spoke softly but so very much to the point that it needed only a look from him, some minutes later, to dissuade Turvey from offering to escort him to whichever of the saloons he chose to sit in.

Leaving his henchman the personification of cold disapproval, he strolled down the gallery in the direction of the Grand Stairway. As he approached the door which led to the stair up which Martin had told him he had come, on the night of the storm, it opened, and a portly man, dressed in an ill-fitting suit of black clothes, peeped into the gallery. When he saw the Earl, he gave a start, and seemed to be in two minds whether to advance or to withdraw. The Earl, pausing, raised his quizzing-glass to his eye, and surveyed him with interest.

The dress, if not the bearing, of the stranger proclaimed his avocation, but it scarcely needed this to inform the Earl that he was confronting his brother's new valet. Ulverston's description rose forcibly to his mind. Mr. Leek's homely features were certainly unprepossessing, for besides being muffin-faced, he had small, quick-glancing eyes, and a nose which, having at some time in its owner's career been broken, was now far from straight. Close-cropped, grizzled hair, and a gap in his upper jaw occasioned by the loss of two teeth added little to his charm, and his smile, which, while it stretched his mouth left his eyes mirthless, did nothing to improve his countenance.

"Ah!" said the Earl. "You, I fancy, must be Mr. Martin's new man!"

"Valet to the Honourable Martin," said Mr. Leek, on a reproving note. "Tempor'y! Being, as you may say, retired!" He added, as one tardily recollecting his instructions: "Me lord!"

"I see you know me."

"Properly speaking," replied Mr. Leek, "no! But the other flash—the other gentlemen being accounted for, which is the aforesaid Honourable Mr. Frant, and me Lord Ulverston, I reaches by deduction the concloosion that your lordship is this Earl."

"Which Earl?" Gervase enquired.

"The one as owns this ken," replied Mr. Leek, with a comprehensive gesture.

"I do own it, and as its owner I am a trifle curious to know what precise circumstance could take my brother's valet to a stair that leads only to some storerooms, and to the Fountain Court?"

"Getting me bearings, me lord," explained Mr. Leek. "Which ain't as easy as anyone might think which was reared in this Castle! What I *do* say, and will stand to, is that I never in all my puff see a ken which I'd liefer mill! That is, if I *was* a mill-ken, which, o' course, I ain't. But there are them as I know as would slum this ken—ah, quicker than wipe your eye!"

"Break into it?" asked the Earl.

"Ah!" said Mr. Leek. "Well, look at all them jiggers and glazes, me lord!"

"I beg your pardon?"

"What I *should* say," Mr. Leek corrected himself, with an embarrassed cough behind his hand, "is them doors and winders, me lord! Any prig could open 'em, and no one a ha'porth the wiser!"

"Could you?"

"I *could,*" admitted Mr. Leek frankly, "which ain't, howsever, to say I *would!*"

"You need not, need you?" said Gervase, with flickering smile. "You, after all, are inside this ken!"

Mr. Leek, a little disconcerted, agreed to this, adding: "Besides which, milling kens ain't my lay—properly speaking!"

"No, I fancy I have a shrewd suspicion of what your lay is," said the Earl.

Mr. Leek eyed him a trifle askance. "That's right, me lord: gentleman's gentleman!"

"But only temporarily!" the Earl reminded him.

Mr. Leek was spared the necessity of answering by the sudden arrival of his employer upon the scene. Martin, rounding the angle of the gallery, halted in his tracks, exclaiming: "What the devil brings you here, Leek?" He glanced at the Earl, coloured, and said rather awkwardly: "I am glad to see you out of your room, St. Erth!"

The Earl, on whom the almost imperceptible jerk of the head which dismissed Mr. Leek was not lost, replied amiably: "Thank you, Martin."

"You will find my mother in the Italian Saloon!" said Martin.

"Again I thank you. Add to your goodness by lending me your arm!"

Martin looked very much surprised, but after a moment's hesitation he moved forward, and offered his arm. Striving after a natural manner, he said: "I daresay you feel pretty weak still."

"Oh, no, but it will be well if we are seen to be on excellent terms," Gervase replied, slipping a hand in his arm, and beginning to stroll with him down the gallery.

The arm stiffened. "Considering you would not allow me to set foot inside your room all these days—"

"You must make allowances for the whims of an invalid," said the Earl. "Do tell me what singular merit attaches to your new valet! I feel he must possess some extraordinary attribute, under his rough exterior, which induced you to hire him."

"Oh—Leek!" Martin said with a laugh. "You are as bad as Theo! There's no mystery about it! Merely, Studley asked to be permitted to visit his old father, and I hate to have strangers about me."

"Ah, he is an acquaintance of yours?"

"Why, no, not precisely! He's Hickling's uncle—my groom, you know! Of course, it wouldn't do to keep him for ever, but he does well enough while Studley is away. Besides, he—he keeps my boots in good order!"

The Earl, whose Hessians shone with a mirror-like gloss, for an instant levelled his glass at Martin's top-boots. He let it fall, and said politely: "That is certainly an advantage. Er—what does he use on them?"

"Blacking, I suppose! What does Turvey use on yours?"

"Ah, that is a secret into which I have not been admitted!"

"Champagne, perhaps?" said Martin sardonically.

"I should not be at all surprised."

They had come by this time to the head of the Grand Stairway. Abney, emerging from the Italian Saloon, stared at them for an astonished moment, and then bowed, and said, with a good deal of feeling: "Your lordship! May I say how very happy I am to see your lordship restored to us?"

"Thank you; I am much obliged to you. Shall I find her ladyship in the Italian Saloon?"

"Indeed, yes, my lord!" Abney said, moving towards the door again. "Sir Thomas and Miss Bolderwood have called to enquire after your lordship, and are with my lady now."

The Earl's slender fingers closed on an arm that showed a tendency to withdraw itself. Martin said jerkily: "I'll leave you! I have to go down to the stables!"

"In good time," replied Gervase.

"If you think," said Martin, in a savage undervoice, "that I want to watch Ulverston making sheep's eyes at Marianne, you much mistake the matter!"

By this time, however, Abney had thrown open the door into the saloon, and the Earl, merely saying: "Never mind!" obliged his young relative to enter the room beside him.

Their arrival had the effect of cutting off various conversations in mid-air. Marianne, who had been exchanging sweet nothings with the Viscount in the window-embrasure, exclaimed, and ran forward, saying impulsively: "Oh, how glad I am! Everything is right again, and you are better!" She then blushed, cast a deprecating look at Martin, began to stammer something incoherent, and was rescued by Ulverston, who said cheerfully: "Hallo, Ger! How do you find yourself, dear boy?"

"St. Erth and Martin!" announced the Dowager, having verified this fact through her long-handled glasses. "I am excessively pleased to see you, St. Erth. I said it would not be long before you were upon your feet again. I had no apprehension that it could be otherwise. The Frant constitution is excellent. Someone should set a chair for St. Erth. Ah, Martin has done so! I knew I could depend upon him, for I am sure nothing could exceed his solicitude for his brother."

Martin looked anything but grateful for this testimony, but said roughly: "You had better sit down, St. Erth, or you will go off into a swoon, or something, and I shall be blamed for it!"

Sir Thomas, who was cordially shaking hands with the Earl, said bluntly: "Now, that's enough, young man! Least said is the soonest mended! Well, my lord, I came to see how you did, but little did I expect to find you out of your bed! Ay, you are a trifle pale, but that's nothing! I am heartily glad to see you so stout! Such far-adiddles as we have been hearing! Not that I believe a quarter of what is told me! No, no, I have been about the world a little too much for that!"

"St. Erth was shot by a poacher," stated the Dowager. "I was not at all surprised. I thought that that was how it must have been. They should all of them be transported."

"Well, well, if we could lay them by the heels, so they should be!" said Sir Thomas. "Do you sit down, my lord!"

While everyone was either endorsing this advice, or offering the Earl a cushion, or a stool for his feet, Martin escaped from the saloon, almost colliding in the doorway with Abney, who was on the point of ushering in two more visitors, He fell back, bowing perfunctorily, and Abney announced Mr. and Mrs. Morville.

Mrs. Morville acknowledged Martin's bow with a nod, and a smile; Mr. Morville, who had been dragged unwillingly to render the observances of civility to his daughter's hostess, said: "Ha, Martin!" and surveyed the rest of the company with a disillusioned eye, which the Viscount (as he informed his betrothed in a whisper) found singularly unnerving.

Mrs. Morville, meanwhile, having shaken hands with the Dowager, exchanged greetings with Sir Thomas and Marianne, smiled at her daughter, and wished that the Dowager would be a little more particular in her presentation of the two strange young gentlemen.

"My son-in-law, St. Erth, and Lord Ulverston!" said the Dowager generally.

Both gentlemen were bowing. Mr. Morville answered the question in his wife's mind by staring very hard at the Viscount, and ejaculating: "Ulverston, eh? Well, well, that takes me back a good few years! How do you do? Your father and I were up at Cambridge together. You're very like him!"

Mrs. Morville, bestowing a brief smile upon Ulverston, then turned her attention to the Earl, shaking hands with him, and expressing the conventional hope that he was recovered from his accident. Since Drusilla had not chosen to describe him to her parents, his fair countenance came as a shock to Mrs. Morville, who had expected to confront an unmistakable Frant. She almost blinked at him, found that he was smiling at her, and instantly understood why her staid daughter had lost her heart to him. Her own heart sank, for she was by no means a besotted mother, and while she truly valued Drusilla she could not find it in her to suppose that it lay within her power to engage the affections of one who, besides being a notable *parti,* was more handsome than (she felt) any young man had a right to be.

Nothing of this showed, however, in her manner. The Earl was expressing the sense of his obligation to Drusilla: she replied calmly that she was glad Drusilla had found an opportunity to be useful; and, seating herself on the sofa, made a little gesture to the place beside her, saying: "I am persuaded you should not stand, Lord St. Erth."

The Dowager, who had resumed her own seat by the fire, said: "I assure you, he is perfectly well again, my dear Mrs. Morville. Young men, you know, are amazingly quick to recover from such accidents. I daresay *his* nerves have suffered less than *mine.* I have a great deal of sensibility. I do not deny it: I am not ashamed to own the truth. Dr. Malpas has been obliged to visit me every day, and in general I enjoy very good health. I inherit my constitution from my dear father. You were not acquainted with my father, Mr. Morville. I have often been sorry that you were not, for you would have been excessively pleased with one another. My father was a great reader, though not, of course, during the hunting-season."

Fortunately, the historian was too well-used to having such remarks addressed to him to betray his feelings other than by a satirical look over the top of his spectacles, and a somewhat dryly expressed regret that he had not been privileged to meet the late Lord

Dewsbury. Mrs. Morville began to talk to the Earl about his service in the Peninsula; her husband returned to his interrupted conversation with Ulverston, and the Dowager addressed one of her monologues to Sir Thomas, in which her affection for her son-in-law, her hatred of poachers, and the state of her nerves became inextricably mixed with her conviction that if young persons in general, and St. Erth in particular, had more regard for their elders they would take care not to incur accidents calculated to alarm them. By the time she had recollected two of her deceased parent's moral reflections upon the selfishness of young people, Sir Thomas discovered that he must carry his daughter back to Whissenhurst. The Dowager, although she had observed with displeasure Lord Ulverston's attentions to Marianne, had lately had other things to occupy her mind than Martin's courtship. She said graciously: "Marianne is in very good looks. I am always pleased to welcome her to Stanyon, for she has very pretty manners, and she was most good-natured in playing at spillikins with dear little Harry and John. When I come to London I daresay I shall find her quite the belle of Almack's—that is, if you have vouchers, and if you have not I shall be happy to procure them for you."

"Much obliged to you!" said Sir Thomas, anything but gratefully. "No difficulty about that, however! I hope your ladyship will come to London in time to attend Lady Bolderwood's ball. Don't mind telling such a kind friend as *you* that you'll hear me make an interesting announcement." He observed, with satisfaction, a startled look on her face, and chuckled. "Ay, that's the way the wind blows!" he said, with a jerk of his head towards Lord Ulverston. "We said it must remain a secret until after the little puss's presentation, but, lord! I suppose it must be all over the county by now!"

He then took his leave, and the party broke up. Both St. Erth and Ulverston escorted the visitors downstairs, and while the Morvilles' carriage was waited for, Sir Thomas, finding himself beside his host, shot one of his penetrating looks at him, and said: "So it was a poacher, was it? H'm! Coming it strong, but I don't blame you! I shan't give you my advice, because for one thing it ain't any of my business, for another you young fellows never listen to advice, and for a third I've a notion you'll manage your affairs very well for yourself. Only don't take foolish risks, my lord! Where's your cousin?"

"At Evesleigh," replied the Earl.

Sir Thomas grunted. "Gone back there, has he? Well! You be careful! That's all I've got to say!"

He gave the Earl no opportunity to answer him, but turned away to bid farewell to Mrs. Morville. By the time the carriage had driven off, his own and Mari-anne's horses had been brought round from the stables. Lord Ulverston lifted Marianne into the saddle, good-byes were exchanged, and the Bolderwoods rode away. Ulverston, perceiving that the Earl's thoughtful gaze was following Sir Thomas, said: "Regular quiz, ain't he? Rather wondered at first what m'father would say to him, but I daresay they'll deal famously together. He's no fool, Sir Thomas: in fact, he's a devilish knowing cove!"

"I begin to think you are right," said the Earl slowly. "Devilish knowing!—unless I misunderstood him."

CHAPTER TWENTY

THE EFFECT OF Sir Thomas's morning-call could hardly have been said to have been happy. Its repercussions were felt mostly by the long-suffering Miss Morville, who was obliged not only to lend a sympathetic ear to the Dowager's tedious and embittered animadversions on the duplicity of Lord Ulverston and the Bolderwoods, but also to dissuade her from casting repulsive looks at Ulverston, and from mentioning more than once a day that the task of entertaining her son-in-law's friends at the Castle imposed a strain upon her enfeebled nerves which they could ill support.

Both Martin and Gervase came in for their share of her comprehensive complaints, for she could not suppose that Marianne would have rejected Martin's suit, had he put himself to the trouble of using a little address in its prosecution; while as for Gervase, the more she considered his behaviour the greater grew her conviction that he was responsible for every evil which had fallen upon the family, dating from the shocking occasion when he had permitted a four-year old Martin to play with a tinder-box, and so set fire to the nursery blinds: an accident which would have led to the total demolition of the Castle had the nurse not entered the room at that moment, and beaten out the flames with a coal-shovel.

It was not the Earl's practice to argue with his step-mother, but this accusation was so unexpected that he was surprised into explaining: "But I wasn't there!"

He would have done better to have held his peace. The Dowager very well recollected that he had not been there, for it was what she had been saying for ever: he liked his brother so little that even when they had been children he had always preferred to slip away rather than to play with him. She had known how it would be from the outset; she had not the least doubt that he had brought Ulverston to Stanyon merely to ruin poor Martin's chances of marrying an heiress; and now that she came to think of it, she had never liked Ulverston, besides knowing a very discreditable story about his Uncle Lucius.

"And as for your conduct in not wearing the Frant ring, and causing the Indian epergne to be removed from the Smaller dining-table, I am sure it is all of a piece, and just what anyone would have expected!" she said. "I daresay it is the influence of Lady Penistone, but on that head I shall maintain silence, for although I never liked her, and, indeed, consider her a fast, frivolous woman, I do not forget that she is your grand-mother; and if I am persuaded that her third son was fathered by Roxby, as no one could doubt who had ever clapped eyes on him, I am determined that nothing shall prevail upon me to say so!"

She then startled Miss Morville, as much as the Earl, by bursting into tears; and Gervase, who had stiffened at this all too probable answer to the problem of his

Uncle Maurice's curious likeness to my Lord Roxsby, relaxed again, and only said, in a coaxing tone: "It is very bad, ma'am, but although I had not enough good taste to get myself killed in the late wars, at least you may be sure that I shall never accuse Martin of attempting to put a period to my existence."

Perhaps as much surprised as he by her unaccustomed display of weakness, she dried her eyes, saying: "It is one thing to think you would very likely not survive the war, and quite another to be contriving your death, St. Erth! You may choose to believe that I am in league with poor Martin to kill you, which only serves to convince me that I shall never meet with anything but ingratitude, for it is quite untrue, and I have instead been considering how I might contrive a very eligible match for you!"

He thanked her gravely, and she said: "You may ask Louisa if it is not so! But *one* thing I am determined on! No matter what comes of it I shall not desire her to assist me in the matter, for she has written me such a letter, and about her own brother, too, as makes me excessively sorry to think that she is coming into Lincolnshire this summer!"

After this, she begged Miss Morville to find her smelling-salts, and the Earl made good his escape.

His recovery from the effects of his wound was speedy enough to astonish everyone but the Viscount. Having once left his room, he showed no signs of suffering a relapse; and it was not many days before he was taking the air on horseback. On these gentle expeditions he was invariably accompanied by Ulverston, who refused to be shaken off even when the Earl's intention

was merely to return Mr. and Mrs. Morville's call.
Under these circumstances it was scarcely surprising
that the visit should have passed without the exchange
of anything but civilities. Lord Ulverston rattled on in
his usual style; and the Earl, although primed by his
friend with a description of that one of Mrs. Morville's
novels which he had been obliged by circumstances to
read, and which he said was a devilish prosy book about
a dead bore of a girl who never did anything but struggle
against adversity, and moralize about it, wisely chose
to confine his conversation with his hostess to the
military career of her elder son. Nor did he make the
mistake of attempting to hoax Mr. Morville into believing that he had ever so much as looked between the
covers of one of his interesting histories, a piece of rare
good sense which caused Mr. Morville slightly to
temper his first criticism of him. He still said that he was
a frippery young fashionable, whose exquisite tailoring
bore every evidence of extravagance, but he now added,
in a fair-minded spirit, that he was not such an empty-
headed jackanapes as he looked.

Mrs. Morville fully appreciated the worth of this
tribute, which, indeed, set the Earl considerably above
either Captain Jack Morville, of the —th Foot, or Mr.
Tom Morville, Scholar of Queens' College, Cambridge,
but it did not greatly elevate her spirits. She sighed, and
said: "One cannot wonder at Drusilla, but I dare not
suppose that her regard is returned. I perceive that his
manners are so universally pleasing that I cannot but
dread lest she may be refining too much upon what,
with him, is the merest civility. I do not scruple to say,
my dear sir, that his air, his address, and his person are

all so exactly what must cause any girl in the possession of her senses to fall in love with him, that I quite despair! Do you think, Mr. Morville, that he betrays any decided partiality for Drusilla?"

"No," responded her life's partner unequivocally. "Not that I have given the matter a thought, for I believe it to be one of your fancies, my dear."

Mrs. Morville might have been cheered had she known that she was not quite the only person to suspect the Earl of forming an attachment. Whether because his own thoughts were largely occupied by the tender passion, or because he knew his friend better than did anyone else at Stanyon, the lively Viscount had already cocked a knowing eye in his direction. In a burst of confidence, engendered in him by the Stanyon port, he had even dropped a hint in the Chaplain's ear. Mr. Clowne, much startled, exclaimed: "Indeed, if you are right, my lord, I must think it an excellent thing, for I have often thought that Miss Morville would most worthily fill a great position! But I fear—that is, I am sure!—that her ladyship has quite other plans for her son-in-law!"

The Viscount was amused. "Daresay she has. I wish I may see Ger letting her, or Theo, or me, or—damme, or anyone!—manage his affairs for him! Trouble is, my dear sir, you none of you know Ger!"

"I own, my lord, that that suspicion has once or twice occurred to me," admitted Mr. Clowne.

"Any other suspicions occurred to you?" asked the Viscount abruptly. "You don't say much, but it wouldn't surprise me if you saw more than you're prepared to blab. What about this man Martin Frant has hired?"

Mr. Clowne, feeling that he was being towed out of

his depth, said: "Oh, I feel sure your lordship need not consider Leek! To be sure, he is not to be compared with Studley, but I understand how it was! Mr. Martin, you know, is careless in his dress, but he dislikes to have strangers about him, and I daresay he was glad to hire Hickling's uncle, when it was suggested to him. Truly, a rough fellow, but I have always found him respectful, and anxious to conform to our ways at Stanyon!"

"Well," said the Viscount bluntly, "if I had a valet who was always to be found where he had least business, I'd very soon send him packing!"

"My lord!" said the Chaplain, much perturbed. "Your words rouse the gravest apprehensions in my mind!"

"Try if you may rouse them in St. Erth's mind!" recommended the Viscount. "*I* can't! He will only laugh!"

He spoke gloomily, for he had failed more signally to bring home to the Earl a sense of the danger in which he stood. All Gervase would say was that he found Leek a constant refreshment.

"Ger, it's my belief the fellow spies on you!"

"Oh, so it is mine!" agreed Gervase. "I encourage him, and am daily enlarging my vocabulary. He tells me, for instance, that Stanyon would be an easy ken to mill, and expresses his astonishment that no prig has, as yet, slummed it!"

"That's thieves' cant!" said Ulverston quickly.

"Is it, Lucy? I am sure you know!"

"Stop bamming! This is serious!"

"Oh, no! For, you see, I—I think the expression is, *rumbled his lay!*—within five minutes of making his acquaintance! If it comforts you, let me assure you that I shall get rid of him exactly when it pleases me to do so!"

"Ay, will you so? And of me too, I daresay?" said the Viscount.

"I am sure that would be much more difficult," said Gervase meekly.

He spent the rest of the day (particularly when the Viscount was present) either in attempting to use his left hand, and then, apparently, thinking better of it, or in tucking it into the front of his coat. These tactics very soon brought him under the notice of his friend, who demanded to know if his shoulder was paining him. He denied the smallest feeling of discomfort, and so swiftly turned the subject that the Viscount naturally became suspicious, and said: "I'll take a look at it!"

"You will do no such thing!" retorted Gervase. "Much you would know if you did!"

"I've seen a few shot-wounds in my time, dear boy! I'll know fast enough if it ain't healing as it should! However, we can fetch the sawbones to you, if you prefer it!"

"I don't! For God's sake, Lucy, will you stop trying to cosset me?"

"Don't want to cosset you. Thing is, you may have strained it. Better lie up tomorrow, if a night's rest don't put all to rights again."

"Oh, fudge!" Gervase said.

He appeared at the breakfast-table next morning, but he still seemed reluctant to move his left arm; and he admitted, upon being rigorously questioned by the Viscount, that he had not slept well.

"Then let me tell you this, dear boy! You ain't going to Whissenhurst this afternoon!"

"But if the Bolderwoods are going to town

tomorrow, I think I ought to take leave of them!"
objected Gervase. "After all, you will be driving, not I."

"Don't be a fool, Ger! You'd be fagged to death! I'll
be the bearer of your excuses."

"Well, we'll see," Gervase temporized. He glanced
across the table at Martin. "Do you mean to go?"

"No, I have business in Grantham this morning,"
Martin replied shortly. "I daresay I may be detained
there. In any event, I've no thought of going to Whissenhurst!"

Gervase said no more, but rose from the table, and
sauntered out of the room. Ten minutes later he was in
the stables, inspecting Cloud's forelegs.

"Healed beautiful, me lord!" Chard said.

"They have, haven't they? Chard, presently Mr. Martin
will be going to Grantham. Could you find business to
take you there also? In case he should see you?"

"I could, me lord, of course: nothing easier!" Chard
answered, looking at him intently. "Was your lordship
meaning to go there too?"

"No, in quite another direction. I am going to Evesleigh, and I wish to be very sure that Mr. Martin does
not take that road."

Chard nodded, but said: "I'm thinking it's all of ten
miles, me lord, and the grays pretty fresh."

"I can handle them."

"I don't doubt it, me lord, but—you'll take young
Wickham?"

"Oh, yes!"

"Well—not that you'd ever let him take the reins!"
said Chard gloomily. "If you'll pardon the liberty, me
lord, I wish you'd wait till you are a bit more *robusto!*"

"Bastante!" said Gervase, smiling. "I must see Mr. Theo, and as long as I don't have Mr. Martin on my heels I shall take no sort of harm, I assure you!"

"Does he know your lordship means to go?"

"No one knows but you. My shoulder is thought to be troubling me, and I shall presently retire to my room. Say nothing to Wickham! Just tell him to remain on duty while you are in Grantham, in case I should need him!"

He then returned to the house, dawdled through the morning and by noon had confessed his disinclination to accompany Ulverston to Whissenhurst. Miss Morville rescued him from a renewed threat of having the doctor sent for, by saying that there was no occasion for summoning a doctor if only he would behave with common-sense, and rest, instead of unnecessarily fatiguing himself. He allowed himself to be persuaded to lie down upon his bed; and Ulverston, who had insisted on seeing him comfortably bestowed, was able to report to Miss Morville a few minutes later that he showed every disposition to go to sleep. Ulverston then took himself off to Whissenhurst; and Miss Morville went out into the gardens to take the air. Half an hour later, rounding a corner of the Castle, with the intention of entering through the east door, she found herself confronting the invalid, who had just emerged through that doorway.

The Earl halted, exclaiming ruefully: "Miss Morville!"

Miss Morville, thoughtfully considering his caped driving-coat, the hat on his head, and the gloves in his hand, said in a voice of mild interest: "I expect you feel that a drive will do your shoulder good, my lord."

He smiled. "Forgive me! I would not have hoaxed you, if I could have got rid of Lucy by any other means!"

She raised her eyes to his face. "Where are you going?" She coloured, and added: "I don't mean to be prying and inquisitive, but I cannot help feeling a trifle anxious. If you don't choose to tell me, you need not, of course."

"I will hide no secrets from you," he said lightly. "Indeed, I trust you implicitly, Miss Morville! I am going to see Theo."

"Going to see Theo!" she echoed, staring at him. "Oh, pray do not! It—it is such a long way to Evesleigh!"

He took her hand, and held it. "No, it is not such a long way, nor shall I fall into any more ambushes. That is what you are afraid of, isn't it? You need not be: Martin has gone to Grantham, and, although I trust he may not know it, Chard is watching him. He won't let him out of his sight. Believe me, while Chard is with Martin I stand in no sort of danger."

She swallowed, and managed to speak with very fair composure. "I believe you must be safe at Evesleigh. It is on the road! That is where it happened before!"

"But this time only you and Chard know that I am out."

She was silent for a moment. After staring unblinkingly at a clipped hedge, she brought her eyes back to his face, and said: "It is never of the least use to interfere! I daresay you know very well what you are about. I only wish you may not return to Stanyon in a high fever!"

He laughed, and raised her hand to his lips, and kissed it. "You are a woman in a million!" he told her caressingly, gave her hand a pat, and let it go.

He found his under-groom, a zealous youth rigorously schooled by his senior, polishing a saddle in the harness-room. When he was bidden put-to the grays he looked surprised but pleased, and made all haste to obey the order. A couple of stableboys ran to draw the Earl's curricle out of the coach-house; and while this was being done the Earl strolled away to look at his brother's new hunter. Since he had not been expected to enter the wing of the stables devoted to Martin's horses, Mr. Leek had no time to remove himself from the building, but shrank back instead into an empty loose-box. His nephew, who had been leaning on a broom-handle, began briskly to sweep out one of the stalls.

"Don't be bashful, Leek!" said the Earl. "You were just having a word with your nephew, were you not? Where is Mr. Martin's young 'un, Hickling? I haven't seen him yet: fig him out!"

"Yes, my lord!" muttered Hickling, laying aside the broom, and casting a fulminating look in the direction of his uncle.

This gentleman, emerging from the loose-box, achieved a genteel cough behind his hand, and said that he hoped there was no offence.

"None at all," replied the Earl, watching Hickling lead out a rather rawboned youngster, and following him into the yard.

"Exercising them grays, my lord?" enquired Mr Leek, with another cough.

"A couple of inches too long behind the saddle," said the Earl, disregarding this question.

"Very quick over his fences, my lord!" said Hickling.

"You run him down, Jem, and let his lordship see his paces!" recommended his uncle. "Meself, I'd say his middle-piece was a shade light—*jest* a shade!"

The Earl glanced at him. "You seem to know something about horses."

"Brought up with them, in a manner of speaking, me lord!" said Mr. Leek promptly.

"Do you think you could handle my grays?"

Mr. Leek cast them a dubious look, but had no hesitation in asserting that he would back himself to the extent of a double finnup to do so.

"Well," said the Earl, "Wickham cannot, so as I may need a little help you had better come with me in his stead."

Hickling opened his mouth, and shut it again, as though thinking better of what he had been about to say. Mr. Leek's expressionless eyes met the Earl's rather quizzical ones without a blink. "Very pleased to go along with your lordship!" he said. "*And* to lend a hand with them grays, if and when so desired!"

Wickham had not been admitted into Chard's confidence, but he had a shrewd idea that Chard would by no means approve of the new arrangement. Blushingly conscious that it formed no part of the second groom's duties to expostulate with his master, he yet plucked up enough courage to make the attempt. He was silenced, though not unkindly; and was left, ten minutes later, uneasily wondering what Chard would have to say to him when he returned from Grantham.

The grays were very fresh, but the Earl gave no sign that the task of controlling them was imposing too great a strain upon his injured shoulder. As the curricle bowled along the avenue, Mr. Leek ventured to enquire what was their destination.

"I am going to Evesleigh, to visit my cousin," replied the Earl.

Mr. Leek stroked his chin. "Well, now, is that so?" he said. "Evesleigh! Ah! Unless I'm mistook, which don't often happen, that's all of ten miles, guv'nor. Done to a cow's thumb, that's what you'll be!"

"Oh, no!" the Earl said calmly.

Mr. Leek relapsed into silence, which remained unbroken until the grays turned into a narrow lane, when he was moved to point out to the Earl that this was not, according to his information, the road to Evesleigh.

"Not the most direct road to Evesleigh," the Earl corrected.

"O' course I ain't what you might call familiar with these parts," said Mr. Leek. "I'm bound to say, however, that it queers me why a cove—why a gentleman as come as near to slipping his wind as what you done, me lord, should take and drive down a lane which is as rough as this here lane."

"Why, I have a reason for doing so!" said the Earl amiably.

Mr. Leek, himself far from enjoying the rough surface, said severely: "Nice set-out it'll be if that hole you've got in you was to open again, me lord! Asking your pardon, it'll be bellows to mend with you, if the claret starts to flow."

But the Earl only smiled. Through what seemed to his companion a network of country lanes he drove his horses, never seeming to be at a loss for the way. Mr.

Leek said grudgingly that he must know the country-side very well to be able to take such a roundabout way to his destination. "I do," the Earl replied. "I have lately ridden over every inch of this ground. One never knows when familiarity with the country will stand one in good stead." He began to check his horses as he spoke, and as the curricle rounded a bend in what was little more than a cart-track Mr. Leek perceived that a farm-gate blocked the way. Knowing well who would have to climb down from the curricle to open this gate (and possibly several more gates), he cast an unloving look at the Earl's profile.

The grays came to a standstill. "If you please!" said the Earl.

Mr. Leek alighted ponderously. The gate was a heavy one, and he was obliged to lift the end before it would pass over the cart-ruts. The curricle moved forward, and stopped again a few yards beyond the gate. As Mr. Leek, who, being country-bred, had no thought of leaving it open, was shutting it again, the Earl spoke to him over his shoulder. "You will have to forgive me, Leek," he said. "Really, I bear you no ill-will, and I am quite sure your interest in me is friendly, but, you see, I don't like being followed. You are now midway between Evesleigh and Stanyon: if I were you I would walk back rather than forward."

"Hi!" exclaimed Mr. Leek, abandong the gate, and starting towards the curricle. "*Hi,* guv'nor!"

The grays were already moving. Mr. Leek broke into a run, but his years and his bulk were against him, and he very soon abandoned a hopeless chase, and stood with labouring chest and heated countenance, staring resentfully after the curricle until it vanished round a bend in the lane. "Grassed!" he said bitterly. "Well, may I shove the tumbler if ever I been made to look blue by a mouth afore!" He removed his hat, and mopped his face and head with a large handkerchief. After a moment's reflection, he added, with reluctant respect: "Which he ain't—not by a very long way he ain't!"

Having by this time recovered his breath, he resettled the hat on his head, and turned to find his way back to Stanyon. The deeply rutted lane made walking far from pleasant; and since he was quite lost, and had little expectation of receiving succour, his only consolation lay in the hope that several more cattle-gates stood between the Earl and his goal.

But the luck favoured him. At the end of half a mile, the track joined a rather better road, which led, a few hundred yards farther on, to a choice of three ways. Mr. Leek was doubtful which he should take, for none of them seemed to have a distinguishing feature by which he might have remembered it. A battered sign-post informed him that the ways led respectively to Climpton, Beaumarsh, and Forley, but as he was unacquainted with any of these villages this was not helpful. He stood under the post, considering, and just as he had decided to proceed down the lane which he fancied was the least unfamiliar to him the sound of an approaching vehicle suddenly came to his ears. Blessing himself for his good fortune, he waited; and in another few minutes a gig, drawn by a stout brown cob, came into sight. He hailed it, and it drew up beside him. The round-faced young farmer who was driving it looked down at him in some curiosity, and asked him what he wanted. Mr. Leek, laying a detaining hand on the gig, countered by demanding to know whither the farmer was bound. After staring very hard at him for a moment, the farmer disclosed that he was going to Cheringham, at the mention of which known name Mr. Leek brightened, and said: "If you're going to Cheringham, young fellow, you wouldn't be going so very far out of your way if you was to be so obliging as to set me down at Stanyon. Which I'll thank you very kindly for."

"Stanyon?" said the farmer. "Whatever would you be wanting to go there for?"

"Stanyon Castle," said Mr. Leek, with dignity, "is the place where I live—tempor'y!"

"That's a loud one!" remarked the farmer, laughing heartily.

Affronted, Mr. Leek retorted: "If you wasn't half flash and half foolish, Master Hick, I wouldn't have to tell you as I am a gentleman's gentleman, because anyone as wasn't a looby would know it the very instant he clapped his ogles on this toge of mine! The Honourable Martin Frant's new valet, that's what I am!"

"Mr. Martin!" said the farmer, apparently impressed. "Oh, if you're one o' Mr. Martin's servants that's dif-f'rent, o' course! Up you get!"

Mr. Leek clambered thankfully into the gig, and was gratified to observe that the farmer chose the very lane he had himself decided to explore. They had proceeded along it for nearly a quarter of a mile before the farmer, a slow thinker, suddenly demanded to know what Mr. Martin's valet was doing five miles from the Castle. By this time, Mr. Leek, who had foreseen the question, had provided himself with a glib explanation of this circum-

stance. It was accepted, the farmer merely remarking
that there was no telling what quirks Mr. Martin would
take into his noddle, notwithstanding that, give him his
due, he was a rare one for The Land; and the rest of the
drive passed in an amicable exchange of views on the
eccentricities of the Quality, and the chances of a good
harvest.

While Mr. Leek was being driven back to Stanyon
by a rather less circuitous route than that chosen by the
Earl, his employer was also homeward-bound. He
reached the Castle some twenty minutes later than his
valet, escorted by Chard, who rode behind him, very
correctly, and received with an unmoved countenance
a command to stable his hack. Martin, swinging himself
from the saddle at the foot of the terrace-steps, handed
over his bridle, saying with an unamiable smile, and a
glittering look in his eye: "You may now, and for the
first time today, make yourself useful, and take my
horse to the stables!"

"Yessir!" said Chard woodenly, touching his hat.

He took the bridle, and led the horse off. Martin
watched him go, gave a short laugh, and ran up the
steps towards the open doors of the Castle.

Three minutes later, Miss Morville, passing along
the gallery at the head of the Grand Stairway, on her
way, through the Italian Saloon, to the Long Drawing-
room, was checked by the sound of voices at the foot
of the stair. She paused, for she recognized the unmis-
takably urban accents of Mr. Leek, and could not
imagine what circumstance should have brought him
into this part of the Castle.

"...*so,* thinking as this was the very thing for which

I was, as you may say, brought in, I said as I would be happy to go with his lordship."

"Well?"

That was Martin's voice, lowered, but quite as unmistakable as Mr. Leek's. Miss Morville caught up her demi-train, and stole softly down one branch of the stairway, to the broad half-landing, whence the stair led down, in one imposing flight, to the entrance-hall of the Castle.

"He give me the bag!" said Mr. Leek succinctly.

"What?" Martin's voice was sharpened. "Do you mean that you let him get away?"

"Ah!" said Mr. Leek. "Loped off, he did! Bubbled me! *Me!*"

"You fool! You blundering jackass!" Martin said, such molten wrath vibrant in his voice that Miss Morville let her train fall, and tiptoed to the balustrade, and gripped it, peeping over to look down into the hall.

"You knew I had gone to Grantham! You might have guessed that damned groom of his would follow me! You knew Lord Ulverston, even, was out of the way! And you let him escape you! God, how you have bungled it!"

Miss Morville, looking over the balustrade, saw him turn on his heel, and stride towards the vestibule. Her voice tore itself from her. "Martin, no! Stop!" she called.

Either he did not hear her, or he did not choose to hear her. He had disappeared already from her sight, and only Mr. Leek remained, gazing up the stairway in considerable discomfiture. Miss Morville disregarded him. Bent only upon detaining Martin, she darted to the head of the stairs, and began to hurry down them. Her foot caught in her short train, she lost her balance, clutched unavailingly at the massive, mahogany hand-rail, and pitched forward, tumbling and rolling down the stairs, to land in an inanimate heap at the feet of the dismayed Mr. Leek.

Martin, unaware even of her presence on the scene, was already outside the Castle. He did indeed hear Mr. Leek call to him, in agitated accents, but he paid no attention, making his way swiftly, yet with a certain caution, towards the stables.

The peace of the afternoon seemed to reign over them. There was no sign of Chard in the main yard, nor of any of the stablehands. Martin, after a quick look round, crossed the yard to the wing which housed his own cattle. At the door, he paused again, but he heard his groom's voice say: "Get over now!" and he at once entered the stable.

He found Hickling engaged in rubbing down his hack, already haltered in his stall. He said, in an imperative undervoice: "Where's Chard?"

"Gone off to his quarters, I think, sir. Mr. Martin, his lordship ain't in his bed! He went off in his curricle, and my uncle with him, and—"

"I know that!" Martin interrupted. "Any clodpole would have served me better than your damned uncle! Get my saddle on to the bay! Quick!"

"But, Mr. Martin—!"

A footstep sounded outside, and a not very melodious voice, humming one of the ditties popular at one time with the Army in Spain.

"Chard!" Martin whispered. "Leave the saddle—I'll do it myself! Get that fellow out of earshot!"

"Mr. Martin, I don't like it!" Hickling whispered in

return. "If you're meaning to go yourself, it's too dangerous, sir! Only let *me*—"

"No! Do as I bid you!" Martin said, and thrust him towards the door.

He waited, standing very still, until he heard Hickling speak to Chard.

"P'raps, Mr. Chard, if you *happen* to be at liberty, you'd like to take a look at his lordship's Cloud, which you seen fit to turn into the meadow this morning," said Hickling, with awful politeness. "Of course, it ain't any business of mine, and I'm sure if you're satisfied there's nothing amiss, after all the experience you've had, *I* wouldn't wish to raise my voice. I *should* have thought you'd have noticed it, when you brought him out, but there! You was in such a hurry to get off to Grantham I daresay you wasn't looking at him very particular."

"Now then, my lad, what are you talking about?" demanded Chard. "Anything there was to notice you can take it I noticed all right and tight!"

"Then I'm sure I must be mistook in thinking he's got a spavin forming."

"*Spavin?* What d'ye mean?"

A smile twitched the corners of Martin's mouth. He picked up his saddle, still warm from use, and went softly forward to where Hickling had hung up his bridle while he rubbed down the tired hack. He heard Hickling say that he would be happy to show his colleague just what he meant; listened to the sound of footsteps retreating; and quickly entered the loose-box which housed a good-looking bay.

CHAPTER TWENTY-ONE

IT WOULD HAVE saddened Mr. Leek had he known that the only other gate lying in the path of the Earl's curricle was opened for him by an obliging urchin, who darted out of a nearby cottage in the hope of earning a penny. Half a mile beyond this gate, the Earl was able to turn off the track on to a passable road, which led him eventually to the manor of Evesleigh.

The manor had been bought by the Earl's father some years previously, upon his nephew's advice. It contained two good farms, as well as some smaller holdings; and the manor-house, which, though not large, was respectable, had for some time provided one of his lordship's indigent relations with an asylum. A couple of elderly servants, retired from service at Stanyon, waited on the old lady, and, after her death, which occurred within three months of the Earl's own demise, remained there as caretakers. For the greater part of the year most of the rooms were shut up, their chairs swathed in holland covers, but not the least of the manor's attractions were its excellent coverts, and, during November and December, the house was always in a state of readiness for the entertainment of shooting-parties from Stanyon. At other times, only Theo ever stayed at Evesleigh, although the Dowager had several times asserted, during the lifetime of its late tenant, that she wondered to hear Cousin Amelia complain that the house was damp, since it was in every way so agreeable a residence that she had frequently thought that she would like to live there herself.

The Earl's arrival brought not only his two retainers on to the scene, but Theo's groom as well, who came running from the stables, and went at once to the grays' heads, looking very much surprised to see his lordship, and asking whether he should set out to find his master, and apprise him of this unexpected visit.

"Is Mr. Theo out?" the Earl enquired, casting off the rug from about his legs, and alighting on to the carriage-sweep.

"Yes, my lord. He rode out with the bailiff, a couple of hours ago. I don't rightly know whether it was Dumbleton Farm he meant to visit, or Doebridge, or whether— But I could saddle the cob, my lord, and find him, I dessay!"

"No, I'll wait for him," said the Earl. "If he has been gone for two hours, I imagine he will soon return." He turned his attention to Mrs. Allenby, who beamed, and dropped her third curtsey to him. He was evidently no stranger to her, so he said, if not with truth, at least with the kindliness which endeared him to his dependants: "Surely I remember you? I am very glad to see you again!"

"Oh, my lord!" gasped Mrs. Allenby: "To think you should remember after all this time! And me only third chambermaid when you was sent off to school! Well, I declare!"

The Earl smiled, and glanced enquiringly at her husband.

"Yes, my lord, that's Allenby, which was used to work in the garden, but you wouldn't remember *him!*" said Mrs. Allenby, relegating her spouse to obscurity. "If only I'd known your lordship was coming to Evesleigh! Oh dear, Mr. Theo *will* be put about when he finds you here, and him not ready to receive you!"

Shaking her head over this, she ushered his lordship up the shallow steps to the front-door, and then into a parlour overlooking the carriage-sweep. She almost overwhelmed him with apologies for not having the drawing-room prepared for his reception, with promises of instant refreshment, and with solicitous enquiries after the state of his health. He got rid of her only by accepting her offer of home-brewed ale; and when he had drunk this she showed so marked a disposition to linger that he announced his intention of strolling out to look round the demesne.

It was fully an hour before Theo returned to the house. He came striding from the stables, and met his cousin on his leisurely way back from the shrubbery. At sight of that slim, elegant figure, still wearing a caped driving-coat, but with fair head uncovered, he called out: "Gervase! My dear fellow!" and hurried towards the Earl. "I had no notion you meant to come to Evesleigh!" he said. "If that fool of mine had had a grain of sense he would have fetched me an hour ago!"

"He would have done so, but I thought very likely he would miss you, and so told him not to go," replied the Earl.

"Ay, that's what he has just said to me. Has Mrs. Allenby looked after you? Why are you wandering about the garden? You should rather be resting in the parlour!"

"Oh, I am wandering in the garden because she looked after me only too well!"

Theo smiled. "I daresay! But come inside now! I will protect you from her, I promise you."

The answering smile was perfunctory: Theo said, with a glance at the Earl's face: "You are fagged to death, Gervase! And no wonder!"

"No, not as bad as that," Gervase said, mounting the stone steps beside him. "I am really very much harder to kill than any of you can be brought to believe."

"I know well you bear a charmed life, but to be taxing your strength in such a way as this—!" Theo flung open the door into the parlour. "Go in! Let me speak two words to Allenby, and I'll be with you!"

When he returned to the parlour, some ten minutes later, he found the Earl seated in a chair on one side of the old draw-table, which was littered with papers and ledgers. He shut the door, saying: "Mrs. Allenby is so much vexed that she had no word of your coming that nothing I can say will console her. You mean to remain here for the night, I hope?"

"No, I am returning to Stanyon." The Earl tossed back on to the table a paper he had been reading. "I never knew, until I came home, how much work you did, Theo. I have you to thank for it that I find my inheritance in such good order, haven't I?"

"Why, yes!" Theo admitted. "But you did not drive ten miles to tell me that! My dear Gervase, what can have possessed you to behave with such imprudence? When I left Stanyon you had not quitted your room, and here you are, without even Chard to bear you company!"

"I wanted to see you, and alone."

Theo looked at him with knit brows. "Something has happened since I left Stanyon? Is that it?"

"No, nothing has happened, except that I have regained my strength and my wits. My head still ached abominably when I saw you last, Theo. I found it difficult to think, and impossible to act. I was in doubt, too—or perhaps only trying to believe there was doubt. It is of very little consequence."

"If you wanted me, why could you not have sent me word to come to you?" Theo said roughly. "To have driven all this way, and alone, was madness! I wish you may not have cause to regret such foolhardiness!"

"There are those who could tell you that my wounds heal quickly. Sit down, Theo!"

His cousin cast himself into the chair on the other side of the table, but said: "And what if you had met with another accident on your way here? Good God, you must know the risks you run!"

"I am not afraid of being ambushed today," replied the Earl. "Martin went to Grantham, and Chard with him. Even if he has by now returned to Stanyon, Chard is still watching him. He won't let him out of his sight until he sees me safe home again." He paused, and for a moment or two there was silence, broken only by the sound of a horse's hooves somewhere in the distance, and the measured ticking of the clock on the mantelshelf. "So, you see, Theo, I had nothing to fear in driving over to see you."

The sound of hooves was growing momently more distinct; the Earl slightly turned his head, listening.

"Well! I am glad to know you took that precaution

at least!" said Theo. "But who is watching Hickling? Did you think of that?"

"Why, no!" replied Gervase. "Hickling is certainly devoted to Martin, but I hardly think he would commit murder to oblige him!"

He rose from his chair as he spoke, and walked to the window. The hooves were pounding up the carriage-sweep. "What is it?" Theo asked. "Has Chard come to look for you?"

The Earl's right hand had been hidden in the pocket of his driving-coat. He withdrew it, and his cousin saw that it held a silver-mounted pistol. "No," he said, in an odd voice, "but I seem to have been out in my reckoning! I am no longer safe from the strange accidents that befall me."

"Good God, Gervase, what do you mean? Who is it?" exclaimed Theo, starting up.

"It is Martin," said the Earl, turning, so that he faced the room, his back against the wall.

"Martin! But, my dear Gervase, he would never—"

Theo broke off, silenced by a lifted finger. Martin's voice could be heard in the hall, fiercely interrogating Allenby.

"How rash! How witless of him!" sighed the Earl.

Hasty footsteps were crossing the hall; the door burst open, and Martin came impetuously into the room, and slammed the door shut again with one careless, backward thrust of his hand.

"Don't move, Martin!" said the Earl warningly.

"St. Erth! Don't you see?—don't you understand?" Martin cried. "It's not me you need beware of!"

Then he stopped, for he saw that the Earl was not

looking at him, and the pistol was not being levelled at him.

"Yes, I do understand," Gervase said. "Better than you, it seems! You young fool, what if a shot were to be fired in this room, and Allenby ran in to find me dead, and you struggling with Theo? Do you think anyone would believe that it was Theo and not you who had shot me?"

"Are you mad?" Theo demanded harshly.

"No, I am neither mad nor fevered. See if he carries a pistol, Martin, if you please!"

"By all means! You will find that I am quite unarmed!"

Martin moved away from the door, and went behind him, feeling his pockets. He shook his head. "No: nothing."

The Earl lowered his own pistol. "Then, between us, we will settle this affair," he said.

"Are you, in all seriousness, accusing me—*me!*—of having tried to murder you?" Theo said. "It is preposterous! A sick man's fantasy!"

"I had rather have called it a nightmare, Theo."

"What, in God's name, have I to gain by your death?"

"Nothing, if Martin were not implicated in it. If it could be made to appear that he had murdered me, everything you most care for!"

"If this is not madness, it *must* be fever! Was it I who resented your existence? Was it I who openly wished you had been killed in Spain? Or was it I who took care of your interests, and warned you, when you first came home to Stanyon, to be on your guard?"

"Were they my interests, Theo, or did you see them as your own?"

Martin, who had coloured vividly at his cousin's words, interrupted, stammering a little. "Yes, I did resent his existence! I d-daresay I may have said I wished he had been killed! I don't know! It's very possible! But I never meant—I would never, even *then,* when I scarcely knew him, have tried to murder him!"

"Indeed?" Theo said swiftly. "Have you, as well as Gervase, forgotten what I saw when the button was lost from your foil? Were you not trying to murder him then?"

"No, no! I lost my temper—I *did* try for one moment— But I wouldn't have—Gervase, you made me go on fighting! I had recollected myself long before you disarmed me! I wasn't trying to kill you!"

"My dear Martin, I know very well you would have dropped your point at a word from me. It was mistaken of me not to have spoken that word. But I did not then guess that I was helping you to build up evidence against yourself." He smiled faintly. "You scarcely needed help, did you? If you had had to stand your trial for murder, I wonder if the jury would have reflected that your open hostility to me made it very unlikely that you could ever have had the least intention of killing me?"

"No!" Martin muttered. "*You* suspected me!"

"Yes, after the first attempt, I did suspect you, for that would have seemed to have been an accident, I thought."

"First attempt?" Martin exclaimed. "Was there more than one, then?"

"Yes, there was more than one!" Theo struck in. "There was a broken bridge, Martin, which you knew of, and never mentioned to Gervase, though you knew he would ride over it! It was I who saved him that time! I think you have forgotten that, St. Erth!"

"Nonsense, Theo! Even had you thought I should be drowned, I am sure you would have called me back. Martin could have been accused of nothing worse than carelessness. He neither broke the bridge, nor sent me to ride over it."

"Did I also stretch a cord across your path? If there were any truth in your suspicions, that incident alone must prove my innocence! You yourself have said that it would have seemed an accident! How might that have served my ends?"

"I said that so I thought at the time," replied the Earl gently. "But if chance had not intervened, in the person of Miss Morville, not only should I have been despatched, but I think you would have contrived to supply evidence against Martin. Did you not do so once before?"

"When?" demanded Martin sharply.

Theo uttered a bark of laughter. "You may well ask!"

"On the night of the storm," said Gervase, "when I am very sure that you entered my room by way of the secret stair, and dropped one of Martin's handkerchiefs beside my bed."

"Why—why—*that* night?" Martin exclaimed. "The night I went to Cheringham? I remember that you gave me back a handkerchief! You said I had dropped it. I thought you meant I had done so on the gallery!"

The Earl shook his head. "I found it in my room. I think you meant only to leave it if you succeeded in accomplishing your purpose, Theo. Perhaps you were startled by the slamming of the door which must have roused me. Was that it? Or was it my awakening that alarmed you?"

"Really, Gervase, this goes beyond the line of what is amusing! What possible grounds can you have for assuming that because you fancied you heard someone in your room, and later found a handkerchief of Martin's by your bed, it must have been I who had been there? It is nothing but a wild story imagined by you to lend colour to the rest of your absurd suspicions!"

"Not quite," answered Gervase. "I have an excellent memory, Theo. I recall very vividly what passed between us on the following day. How was it that, although you had warned me to beware of Martin, you did not, when I told you that I believed him to have been in my room that night, warn me that there was a way into the room of which I knew nothing?"

There was a moment's silence before Theo retorted: "Good God, how should I have guessed that you were ignorant of it? That old stair! I never even thought of it!"

"That won't fadge!" Martin interrupted. "If Gervase told you someone had entered his room, you must have thought of it!"

"Perhaps I set as little store then by Gervase's imaginings as I do now," Theo said, with a contemptuous smile.

"Yet it was you who set my imagination to work," said Gervase. He moved slowly back to the chair he had vacated, and sat down, as though he were very tired. "This is all so useless, Theo! Let us make an end! I know that you have three times tried to dispose both of me and of my heir. *My* death can benefit no one but

Martin; if he was not guilty of the attempts on my life, who but you could have been?"

"Yes!" Martin said impetuously. "I knew that, but you did not! That night I *did* come to your room by way of the secret stair—you didn't believe what I told you! You would not allow me to come near you again! How *could* you think I would skulk in some bush to shoot you unawares? I didn't behave well towards you—I said things I ought not to have said!—but, my God, if I meant to kill my greatest enemy it would be in a fair fight!"

"Yes, Martin, I know. I did believe what you told me, but I found it impossible to believe that the one person at Stanyon whom I had thought to be my friend could have all the time been plotting my death." He paused, and for an instant he looked at his cousin, standing rigid and silent on the other side of the table. Then he added, with a slight smile: "Even when I was in no case to think at all, it did occur to me that had it been you who shot me you would not have missed your mark! For the rest, nothing was certain, nothing proved. When I refused to permit you to come near me, I was acting only on a suspicion I would, God knows! have been glad to have seen refuted! But if it was true, both your safety and mine, while I was so helpless, lay in letting it be known that you had never, for one instant, had access to my room. I supposed I had then no doubt of the truth. I hardly know. I would have given so much to have had my suspicions refuted! No, I don't mean that I would have preferred to have known that you were my would-be assassin! Not that! Nothing, in fact, that was possible, or that I could explain to you. I told myself I must wait for some proof that you had told me the truth—something more sure than what Theo has called my imaginings. When I knew beyond doubting that it was not you who had tried to kill me, then I waited until I had decided what was best to be done, and until I should be well enough to settle the affair alone."

"May I know when it was that you knew—beyond doubting—that it was not Martin who tried to kill you?" enquired Theo sardonically.

"When I realized that he had introduced a Bow Street Runner into my household," replied the Earl, with a gleam of amusement. "With instructions to dog my every step!"

"You guessed it!" Martin ejaculated. "How? What made you think it?"

"My dear boy! It was patent! I am aware that poor Lucy darkly suspects of him being a hired assassin, but I could conceive of nothing more unlikely! I am afraid you will have to forgive me: I served him a very scurvy trick today! But if I had not obliged him to accompany me, I am very sure he would have followed me on horseback, and the last thing I desire is to have an officer of the law meddling in this business. I conclude that by some means unknown to me he contrived to reach Stanyon far sooner than I had supposed he could, or you would not have galloped that bay of yours into a lather in your gallant but misguided attempt to preserve me from an untimely end!"

Martin blushed, but said in a brooding tone: "It was Hickling's notion that I should make use of his precious uncle! He *was* a Runner, but he ain't now, of course, and no wonder! Much use he has been to me! To be taken

in by such a child's trick! Good God! The only thing he
did, and I suppose it doesn't *prove* anything, was to find
a button that was torn from my shooting-jacket not five
yards from where I told you I was struck down, that day
when you were shot. If I was dragged clear of the undergrowth, before being hoisted up by—" He paused,
and cast a smouldering glance at Theo "—by *you,* my
dear cousin!—it must have been torn off then! He found
signs, too, that a horse had stood for some time within
the wood. But that don't prove much either! I know it
could be explained away!"

"I don't doubt that it was Theo who hid his gig, when
I had parted from him, and thought him on the road to
this place; waited for you; stunned you; left your gun and
your shot-belt to be found; and carried you off in the gig.
Evesleigh is not so far from Wisbech, and I have discovered that he did not arrive here until evening. You will tell
me, perhaps, that you visited outlying parts of my estates,
Theo, which made you late. Don't! I should not believe
you, and I would so much prefer you to tell me no more
lies! Had you killed me, had there been a hue and cry after
Martin, and he had told that story, it must have been
thought the wildest and stupidest attempt to escape
justice that ever was heard! But you didn't kill me; there
was no hue and cry. The story was told only to us, and
although some of us disbelieved it I did not. Its very improbability made me think it the truth. What a risk you
took, Theo! If some chance wayfarer had discovered him
before he had rid himself of the bonds you so carefully
loosened—! It could have happened, you know. And if I
did not die, surely you must have known that it would not
be long before Martin at least realized the truth!"

"Well, I did, of course, though not quite at once," admitted Martin. "It seemed so impossible that *Theo* could have done such a thing to you! Only, I knew *I* had not, so there was no one else! And when I had had leisure to think about my having been kidnapped in such a way, naturally I began to see how it must have been! I knew it had been done so that I should be blamed for your death, but I never guessed the whole! Not that he would not harm you if I *could* not be blamed! It is the most infamous thing! It was bad enough when I only thought he had kidnapped me to save himself from being suspected! All I thought was that he would kill you, if he could, and very likely me too, but not like that! Later—when all the scandal had been forgotten! That's why I hired Leek—at least, it is in part! I thought he might be able to discover some *proof* that it was Theo, and not me! For what was the use of telling you what I suspected, when you were hand-in-glove with Theo, and seemed not to believe a word I said? I'm not such a gudgeon, either, as not to have known that Chard was spying on me! In fact, I made sure you had ordered him to!"

"I had," said the Earl. "Not, however, for any other reason than to safeguard you in case of accident. From the moment of your return to Stanyon until today, when you seem, very unwisely, to have given Chard the slip, I provided you with a witness who must have testified on your behalf had anything happened to me."

"I never thought of that!" Martin said, much struck. "I must say, St. Erth, it was devilish handsome of you! When that fool, Leek, told me you had come here, and alone, I *did* wonder if I should not tell Chard the whole, and bring him with me. But then I thought he would very likely not believe a word of it, and prevent my coming after you into the bargain, so I gave him the bag. I suppose, if I had had time to consider, I need not have come at all, for Theo would never dare to harm you *here!* The thing was, it gave me the devil of a shock, when Leek told me! I thought you had been hoaxed, like everyone else, and anything might happen to you! Coming here quite alone like this! St. Erth, why *did* you?"

The Earl regarded his signet-ring for a moment. When he raised his eyes, it was at his cousin that he looked, not at Martin. He replied in a low voice: "To tell him that I knew. To put an end to it all, if I could, without divulging the truth to anyone. Here I could say what had to be said without fearing that your Runner's ear might be glued to the keyhole. If I had sent for Theo to come to Stanyon, what a damnable situation must have been created! He could not have remained there, nor would I have wished him to. *You* were already suspicious; so, I fancy, was one other. Lucy, the servants— they would all have thought it an odd circumstance if I were to have sent for Theo only to dismiss him within the hour! Well! You have frustrated a part of my design, but we can still prevent this affair from becoming generally known."

"I don't see that!" Martin objected, scowling.

"I was afraid you would not," said the Earl, rather dryly.

"It's very well for you!" Martin said. "No one thinks *you* have been trying to murder anyone! Pray, what about me?"

"Since the only certain information anyone outside Stanyon has is that I was shot by a man in homespuns,

I fancy the accident will soon be forgotten. If it is seen that you and I stand upon very good terms, it will be concluded that whatever rumours were rife had no foundation in fact. I collect, from Dr. Malpas, that some of the rumours are so wild that already people are beginning to shrug up their shoulders, and to disbelieve the whole. Certain persons must be told, of course: Lucy, Chard, Miss Morville (though I think she knows already), but as for the world at large—let it think what it chooses! It will not long think you had anything to do with my accident."

"But do you mean to do *nothing?*" Martin said indignantly. "He ought to be brought to justice!"

Theo, who had walked away to the fireplace, said over his shoulder: "You have imagined an ingenious story. Does it occur to you that not one word of it can you prove?"

"We'll try that!" Martin flung at him.

"Not if I have my way," interposed the Earl. "What, brandish this abominable affair in a criminal court? Set ourselves up to provide the vulgar with a nine-days wonder to gape at and exclaim over? I thank you, Martin, no!"

Martin was silenced. Theo said, in his usual, level tone: "You feel, then, that it would be possible to have me arrested, do you, Gervase? Does your fancy even lead you to suppose that I could be convicted on this evidence?"

"I could have you arrested. I think you would be acquitted. But it would ruin you, Theo."

"I must suppose that it is your intention to ruin me."

"No, it isn't my intention, or my desire. I would prefer to send you to Jamaica."

"Eh?" said Martin, startled.

Gervase turned his head. "Why not? Let him go out to manage the West Indian property! He himself has frequently said that he believed it to be ill-run; neither of us can doubt his ability to manage an estate."

"But the West Indian property is mine!"

"Yes, and yours must therefore be the deciding voice."

"Well, but— Of course, he can't remain at Stanyon!"

"No."

"I must say, that to be putting him in charge of *anything,* after what he has tried to do to us, seems to me the craziest notion I ever heard! However, if he can't remain at Stanyon—and that he certainly cannot!—I daresay it may be best to send him to Jamaica. It would be bound to create a deal of talk and conjecture if he left us, and was still in England. Everyone would know there must have been something devilish bad to account for it, and I'm at one with you in wanting to hush the business up. Dash it, Gervase, it makes me as sick as a horse to think of a thing like this happening amongst us Frants! You had better do as you choose about it, I suppose!"

"Then will you, if you please, go and tell them to put my horses to, Martin?"

Martin glanced undecidedly at his cousin. "Well—" He caught the Earl's eye, said, rather crossly: "Oh, as you please!" and walked out of the room.

There was a long silence. The Earl was absently studying the mountings of his pistol, a frown between his brows; and Theo continued for a full minute to stare down into the fire. He moved at last, and came back to the chair behind the table. He began mechanically to tidy the papers before him into heaps, saying in an expressionless voice: "I hope my successor will do as well by you as I have done."

The Earl raised his eyes. "It is unlikely. I know that Stanyon has never had one who served it better, or loved it more. Alas, Theo! My father did you an ill turn, did he not?"

Their eyes met. After a moment Theo's dropped to the pistol in his cousin's hand. "Oh, put that thing away!" he said.

The Earl slid it into his pocket. "Go to Jamaica!" he said. "If my father, instead of bringing you up to think only of Stanyon, had given you this place, or some other, to have called your own!—if you would have let me repair his omissions—! But it is all too late!"

"I never wanted anything either he or you would have given me!" Theo said.

"No. I suppose it became an obsession with you, a madness! And lately—forgive me!—there was an added reason, was there not?"

He saw Theo fling up a hand, and was silent. After a pause, Theo said heavily: "And if I go to Jamaica—what then?"

"Oh!" Gervase said, smiling, "you will turn the property into a flourishing concern, and then, I have no doubt, you will yourself become a landowner there, and a prosperous one, for you were born to succeed, Theo!"

Theo gave one of his short laughs. "You are a strange creature, Gervase!"

"No, why? I remember only a cousin who took care of my interests, of whom I was fond. The rest will be forgotten." He got up, as he heard the sound of horses on the carriage-sweep. "I think I had better go, or we shall have Martin coming to fetch me. The West Indian business shall be settled as speedily as I can contrive. Good-bye—and God speed!"

He left the room before Theo could reply. Martin was waiting for him below the steps, seated in his curricle. "I've told Theo's men I'll send over to fetch the bay tomorrow. I am going to drive you home!" Martin announced belligerently. "*I* don't want you laid up again, and you're looking as queer as Dick's hatband, let me tell you!"

"Thank you," said Gervase meekly, climbing into the curricle.

"What did he say to you? Did he admit it?" Martin asked, setting the grays in motion.

"To tell you the truth," said Gervase, "we did not speak of it."

"Good God! Well, does he mean to go to Jamaica?"

"Oh, yes!"

"He may count himself fortunate! And who is to fill his place? What a pickle it all is! He was devilish good at looking after our affairs, you know!"

"I fancy you might become as good."

"I?" Martin exclaimed. "Are you asking *me* to become your agent?"

"No, that would be unsuitable. I shall employ an agent, but Theo was more than that. You could do much that he did—if you chose to!"

"If I chose to! Why, there's nothing I'd liefer do!" Martin said. He added, in a burst of unwonted humility: "Mind, I may make mistakes! But if I do—I mean, *when* I do!—you will just have to tell me!"

CHAPTER TWENTY-TWO

MR. LEEK, when he found himself deserted by his employer, and with an unconscious lady on his hands, became a little flustered. Several agitated shouts for help having elicited no response, he knelt down, somewhat ponderously, beside Miss Morville, and tried to ascertain whether she was alive, or whether she had, as he was much inclined to fear, broken her neck. He was not without experience in such matters, and after he had cautiously raised her head, he felt reasonably assured that this ultimate disaster had not befallen her. He could not discover that she was breathing, but after a good deal of fumbling he managed to find the pulse in her wrist. It was certainly beating, so, heaving a sigh of considerable relief, he rose, puffing, to his feet, and went off to ring the iron bell which hung beside the entrance-doors. So vigorously did he tug at it that its summons brought not only a footman, but Abney also, hurrying from the servants' quarters. It then became manifest to Mr. Leek that although the domestic staff might, if suitably adjured, render assistance, no constructive effort need be expected. Abney was so much appalled that he seemed unable to do anything but wring his hands, and demand distractedly what was to be done; and the footman merely waited for orders.

"The first thing as has to be done," said Mr. Leek, "is to take and carry her to a sofy! You catch hold of her head, young feller, and I'll take her feet!"

"Ought she to be moved?" Abney asked nervously. "Oh dear, oh dear, she's very pale!"

"Well, don't start to nap your bib!" said Mr. Leek, with a touch of asperity. "Anyone would look pale as was gone off into a swound! Her neck ain't broke, that I do know, so that's a comfort, anyways. If you was to lope off and fetch a female to her, you'd be doing more good than what you are now, standing about as like as ninepence to nothing, and asking whether she ought to be moved! O' course she ought! Nice thing it would be if we was to leave a swell mort like she is laying about at the bottom of the stairs for anyone to tread on as wasn't looking where they was going! Now, you lift your end, young feller, and gently does it!"

Thus encouraged, the footman carefully raised Miss Morville's shoulders from the floor. Between them, he and Mr. Leek bore her into the Great Hall, and laid her down on one of the sofas. The footman thought she would be more comfortable if he placed a cushion beneath her head; Abney hovered about, wondering whether he should fetch the housekeeper, feathers, or a glass of water; and Mr. Leek, with great delicacy, smoothed Miss Morville's dress carefully about her ankles. Having informed Abney that persons in her condition stood in more need of eye-water than Adam's Ale, he told the footman to call Mrs. Marple, and made a discovery. Miss Morville had broken her arm.

"Well," said Mr. Leek philosophically, as he disposed the limb across her bosom, "that's what you might call Dutch comfort, because it might ha' been worse."

"I will send a message to the stables at once!" said Abney. "One of the grooms must ride for the doctor! Oh dear, I am sure I don't know what has come over Stanyon! It seems to be one thing after another!"

He then hurried away; and after a considerable lapse of time, during which Mr. Leek first fanned Miss Morville, and then, with some misgiving, wondered whether he ought to cut her laces, the housekeeper, who had been enjoying a nap in her room, bustled in, armed with smelling-salts and sal volatile, and followed by a couple of chambermaids. Mr. Leek would have been glad to have resigned Miss Morville to their care, but after he had watched Mrs. Marple's singularly unsuccessful attempts to administer a dose of sal volatile, and had forcefully dissuaded one of the chamber-maids from moving the broken arm, for the amiable purpose of chafing Miss Morville's hand, he decided that it was not the part of a chivalrous man to abandon his post.

By the time Abney came fluttering back to the Great Hall, several more persons had assembled there, including Turvey; and the housekeeper, alarmed by Miss Morville's prolonged swoon, was threatening spasms.

"I fancy, Mrs. Marple, that she may have sustained a blow on the head," said Turvey. "Pray do not become agitated! It frequently happens, in such cases, that the sufferer does not regain consciousness for some appreciable time."

"Ah! And sometimes, when they *do,* they find themselves dicked in the nob!" said Mr. Leek. "Addled!" he explained, for the benefit of one of the maids, who was looking at him in frightened enquiry.

Mrs. Marple gave a faint scream, and pressed a hand to her bosom. Mr. Leek thoughtfully offered her the sal volatile; and Turvey said, with a superiority his more forthright colleague found odious, that he apprehended no such melancholy sequel to the accident.

"Well, when she does come to herself, what you better do is to keep out of sight!" recommended Mr. Leek. "She'll be all to pieces, and it won't do her no good if the first thing she gets her ogles on is that hang-gallows face o' yours!"

"Miss Morville," said Turvey glacially, "is perfectly familiar with my countenance."

"That don't make it no better!" retorted Mr. Leek. "Nor you don't have to use all them breakteeth words to me, because I ain't the sort as can be gammoned easy! I knew a cove as talked the way you do—leastways, in the way of business I knew him! In fact, you remind me of him very strong. I disremember what his name was. He was on the dub-lay, and very clever with his fambles. He ended up in the Whit, o' course."

Fortunately, Miss Morville, at this perilous moment, stirred, and uttered a faint moan, which distracted everyone's attention from the rival valets. Turvey at once picked up the sal volatile, and skilfully raised her sufficiently to enable her to swallow, while Mr. Leek, not to be outdone, held her broken arm. At first she paid no heed to Turvey's request to her to open her mouth, but he persevered, and after a minute or two she seemed to collect herself, for she whispered something, and opened her eyes. Turvey then obliged her to drink the restorative, and she said, quite distinctly: "Oh, my head hurts me so!"

Turvey laid her down again, and turned away to direct one of the maids to procure a bowl of water, and some cloths.

"Martin!" uttered Miss Morville. "No! Don't let him go!"

"That's right, miss!" said Mr. Leek hastily. "No one won't let him go nowhere! Don't you raise a breeze now!"

She raised one wavering hand to her head, but to his relief, said no more. When the water was brought, and a wet cloth was laid over her brow, it was perceived that she had quite regained her senses, for she murmured a thank-you, and seemed perfectly to understand Turvey when he informed her that she had broken her arm, and must lie still until the doctor arrived to set the bone.

Long before Dr. Malpas reached Stanyon, the Dowager had been made aware of the fresh disaster which had overtaken her, and had descended the stairs to the Great Hall. She expressed concern over her young friend's plight, and said that she did not understand how such a thing could have happened. She then announced her intention of sending a message instantly to Gilbourne House, and of herself remaining beside the sufferer.

"I should not wish Mrs. Morville to feel that any attention had been grudged," she said. "But I do not know why there should be so many persons here. I do not understand how you came to allow it, Marple."

This remark caused everyone except the housekeeper, Turvey, and her ladyship's own maid, to withdraw from the Hall as unobtrusively as possible. The Dowager, seating herself majestically in a chair near the sofa, then recalled the various accidents which had befallen the members of her family, and the remedies which had been applied to their hurts; Turvey continued, unmoved, to renew the wet cloths about Miss Morville's head; and Miss Morville lay with closed eyes, enduring a good deal of pain, but making no complaint.

Both Mr. and Mrs. Morville had arrived at the Castle before the doctor's gig at last bowled up the avenue. Their daughter was able to smile at them, albeit rather wanly; and Mrs. Morville told her, with what the housekeeper thought a distressing lack of sensibility, that she would be better presently, and should be taken home as soon as the doctor had set her arm.

"Not yet!" Miss Morville said, for the first time showing signs of agitation. "Indeed, Mama, I could not!"

"No, my dear," said her mother soothingly. "When you are better!"

The setting of the broken bone tried Miss Morville's fortitude, but she bore it very well, only begging not to be moved for a little while, since she felt too faint to lift her head. The doctor said that the place for her to be in was her bed, but this suggestion was again productive of suppressed agitation.

"I think," said Mrs. Morville, "that if she were to remain quietly on the sofa for a little while it would perhaps be best."

"Ay, that's it," agreed the doctor, packing his bag again. "I have given her something which will make her very soon feel more the thing. No need for alarm, ma'am!"

At this moment, the Viscount walked into the Castle, and, perceiving that a large number of persons were gathered in the Great Hall, very naturally joined the party. He was much surprised to learn that Miss Morville had fallen downstairs, exclaiming, sympathizing, and asking so many questions that Mrs. Morville was provoked into telling him that what her daughter needed most was quiet.

"Ay, I'll be bound she does!" said the Viscount, with ready understanding. "Head aching fit to split, eh, Miss Morville? Don't I know it! Took a nasty toss myself once—forget the name of the place: somewhere near Tarbes, it was. Head didn't stop aching for three days."

"Well, I'll come and see you again tomorrow, Miss Morville!" said Dr. Malpas bracingly. "I know I leave you in good hands."

"Yes, and so many of them!" said Mrs. Morville, with a bright smile.

The doctor then went away, and Lord Ulverston, looking round the Hall, suddenly demanded: "But where's Ger? Not still abed, is he?"

"No, my lord," said Turvey. "His lordship is not, so far as I am aware, within the Castle."

"What's this?" said Ulverston. "He was feeling his wound—said he would rest!"

Miss Morville opened her eyes. "He went to Evesleigh," she said.

"Evesleigh! Good God, why?"

The Dowager, who had been regaling the unwilling Mr. Morville with a long, and apparently pointless, anecdote about a set of persons whom he had neither met nor wished to meet, broke off to explain that if her son-in-law had gone to Evesleigh, it was to visit his cousin.

"I know that, ma'am!" said the Viscount impatiently. "How came you to let him go, Miss Morville? What can have possessed him to undertake the journey? He will be quite knocked up! Who accompanied him? That young groom of his?"

"No. I think—" Miss Morville stopped. "I don't know!" she ended uncommunicatively.

He looked down at her rather narrowly. "Know why he went, ma'am?"

"I— No."

"Well, it sounds a havey-cavey business to me!" he said. He glanced round again, frowning. "Martin not home yet?"

"No," she said, and resolutely closed her lips.

"Late, ain't he?"

She was silent.

"Think I'll ride to meet Ger!" said the Viscount.

"A very excellent idea!" said Mrs. Morville warmly. "If I were you, I would go at once!"

"I will!" said the Viscount, and strode off without ceremony.

He reached the head of the terrace steps in time to see the Earl's curricle come sweeping through the vaulted arch of the Gate Tower. The grays were being driven at a spanking pace, and the Viscount was thunderstruck to perceive that it was Martin who held the reins. He was still standing staring incredulously when the curricle drew up at the foot of the steps, and Martin, whose new-found humility had not deterred him from arguing hotly with his brother on certain of the finer points of driving, said triumphantly: "Now own I have not overturned you!"

"Oh, I do! How thankful I am I didn't bring a high-perch phaeton into Lincolnshire!" said the Earl, preparing to alight.

Martin grinned, but merely said that he would drive the curricle to the stables. The Viscount ran down the steps, exclaiming wrathfully: "I'll teach you to hoax me, Ger! What the devil have you been about?"

"Minding my own business," replied Gervase, with one of his mischievous looks.

The Viscount helped him to descend from the curricle. "You deserve to be laid-up for a week! Let me tell you, I was just about to come in search of you!"

"Unnecessary, Lucy! Martin was before you, and, as you see, has driven me home. I am not in the least knocked-up, I assure you."

"Just as well!" said the Viscount. "There's another on the sick-list now!"

"Oh?" said the Earl, beginning to mount the steps. "Who?"

"Miss Morville. Fell downstairs, or something. Sick as a cushion!"

"Miss Morville?" said Gervase quickly. "Is she much hurt?"

"Broken her arm. Can't think how she came to do it!"

"Good God!" exclaimed Gervase, swiftly mounting the remaining steps.

"They carried her into the Great Hall," said Ulverston, catching up with him. "But what's all this, Ger? Come on, now! No humdudgeon! What tricks has that brother of yours been playing on you? Out with it!"

"None at all. I'll explain it to you presently, Lucy, but not now! Only don't look daggers at Martin! It wasn't he who tried to murder me!"

"I suppose he told you so! Upon my word, Ger—! And what about that Leek of his?"

"Lucy, how can you be such a greenhorn?" demanded Gervase, casting his hat and his gloves on to the settle in the vestibule. "Did you never see a Bow Street Runner before?"

He then strode towards the Great Hall, checked for an instant on the threshold, blinking at the unexpected number of persons assembled there, and then perceived Miss Morville, lying on one of the sofas, interestingly pale, and with one arm in a sling. She had raised herself from her supporting cushions, and was looking towards the doorway, so painful an expression of anxiety in her white face that the Earl forgot his surroundings, and, wholly ignoring everyone else in the Hall, quickly crossed the floor, exclaiming: "My poor dear! Why, what has happened to you, my poor child?"

He dropped on his knee beside the sofa, taking the hand that was trying to grasp one of the capes of his coat, and holding it comfortingly. Miss Morville, equally oblivious of her entourage, gazed worshipfully into the blue eyes so tenderly smiling at her, and said foolishly: "You are safe! Nothing dreadful happened to you!"

"Nothing more dreadful than being driven back to Stanyon by Martin!" he assured her. "But you! How came you to tumble down the stairs as soon as my back was turned?"

"The stupidest thing!" said Miss Morville, despising herself. "I wanted to stop Martin—I thought it was the *one* thing that would put you in danger! Only I tripped over my train, and fell! I cannot think how I came to do such a thing!"

The Earl slipped his arm behind her, and raised the hand he was still holding to his lips. "You guessed it all, didn't you, you most wise and most foolish Miss Morville?"

Miss Morville, finding his shoulder so invitingly close, was glad to rest her head against it. "Oh no! How could I think such a terrible thing? Was it true? I would not tell you the thoughts in my head, because they were so very dreadful! Besides," she added, "it was *not* my business, and I was so very nearly sure that you knew!"

Her overstrained nerves then found relief in a burst of tears. But as the Earl chose to kiss her at this moment, she was obliged to stop crying, the merest civility compelling her to return his embrace. As soon as she was able to speak, she said, however, in a voice meant only for his ears: "Oh, no! Pray do not! It was all my folly, behaving in this missish way! You felt yourself obliged to comfort me! I assure you, I don't regard it—shall never think of it again!"

"My poor dear, you must be very much shaken to say anything so foolish!" said the Earl lovingly. "Never did I think to hear such nonsense on my sage counsellor's lips!"

"You would become disgusted with my odious common-sense. Try as I will, I *cannot* be romantic!" said Miss Morville despairingly.

His eyes danced. "Oh, I forbid you to try! Your practical observations, my absurd robin, are the delight of my life!"

Miss Morville looked at him. Then, with a deep sigh, she laid her hand in his. But what she said was: "You must mean a sparrow!"

"I will not allow you to dictate to me, now or ever, Miss Morville! I mean a robin!" said the Earl firmly, lifting her hand to his lips.

This interlude, which was watched with interest by the three servants, with complacence by Mrs. Morville, critically by the Viscount, who was trying to unravel the puzzle just set before him, and with hostility by the Dowager and Mr. Morville, seemed to break the spell which had hitherto held the rest of the company silent.

"St. Erth!" said the Dowager awfully.

"Take care you do not hurt her arm!" advised Mrs. Morville practically.

"Here!" said the Viscount, addressing himself to the domestic staff. "Nothing more for you to do here! You be off, all of you!"

Mrs. Marple and her ladyship's maid, over-awed by his imperative manner, both dropped curtsies, and withdrew. Turvey, rigid with indignation, ignored him, and asked his master if there were any further service he could perform.

"None, I thank you. Go away!" said Gervase.

Turvey then bowed, and walked with great stateliness out of the Hall; and Mr. Morville, who had been controlling his feelings with a strong effort, said: "No doubt I am sadly behind the times, but it may be of interest to you to know, St. Erth, that in *my* day, it was customary, before making an offer to a young woman, to obtain the consent of her father!"

"Yes, sir, I shall endeavour to do so," said the Earl, carefully disposing Miss Morville against the cushions. "Shall I find you at Gilbourne House, if I ride over to call upon you tomorrow?"

"Good gracious!" exclaimed Mrs. Morville, much amused. "Are we to conclude that you have *not* made Drusilla an offer, St. Erth?"

"Not yet, ma'am," he replied, smiling at her. "But I assure you I mean to do so at the earliest opportunity!"

"Well, by the Lord Harry—!" said Martin, who had walked into the Hall in time to hear this interchange. "Do you mean St. Erth is to marry Drusilla? I must say, I think that's a devilish good notion! And the best of it is it will be a famous set-down for Louisa! She told me she had quite made up her mind to it that you and her particular friend, Miss Capel, would make a match of it, Gervase! I'm dashed if I won't write to Louisa this very evening!"

"Silence, Martin!" commanded the Dowager regally. "This must not be! I have a great regard for Drusilla: indeed, I should be glad to have her to live with me, for she is a very obliging girl, and I shall miss her sadly when she leaves me, but I do not consent to her alliance with my son-in-law!"

"And nor do I consent to it!" said Mr. Morville unexpectedly. "In fact, I forbid it!"

"I have other plans for my son-in-law!" said the Dowager, glaring at him.

"I have other plans for my daughter, ma'am!"

"Nonsense, Mr. Morville!" said his wife briskly.

"No use making plans for Ger, ma'am!" said the Viscount. "Always does as he chooses! Assure you!"

"Besides, if you mean Selina Daventry, Mama, we can't have *her* at Stanyon!" said Martin.

"Daventry!" ejaculated Mr. Morville, deriving some obscure pleasure from this disclosure. "Ha!"

"What, not one of Arun's daughters?" exclaimed the Viscount. "Not the red-headed one who makes such a figure of herself in the Park?"

"Ay! Drives a team of showy bone-setters! Lord, she'd lame every horse in the stables! Gervase, you can't offer for that girl!"

"No, no, I won't!" said Gervase, interrupting a low-toned conversation with Miss Morville to respond to this appeal.

"The Duke of Arun's daughter," stated the Dowager, "would make St. Erth a very eligible wife! I do not say that I have made up my mind to the match, for I do not approve of deciding such matters hastily, and I know of several other young females whom I should not object to see at Stanyon."

"Well, well!" said Mr. Morville, refreshing himself with a pinch of snuff. "Arun's girl, eh? I should not like the connection for either of *my* sons, but I daresay it will do very well!"

"Don't think m'father would either," said the Viscount reflectively. "Bad blood there, devilish bad blood!"

"Your father, Ulverston, is a sensible man!" said Mr. Morville.

As much confounded as it was possible for her to be, the Dowager said, with finality: "I do not desire to discuss Lady Selina. I must decline to enter upon any argument. I cannot think that St. Erth will refuse to be guided by my advice, for although I do not deny he has behaved very selfishly to me upon more than one occasion I do not consider that his disposition is bad."

"How can you? How can you, ma'am, say such a thing of him?" uttered Miss Morville, moved to sit up.

"When he has behaved to you with such forbearance—such patience!"

"Hush, my love! This is not like you!" expostulated the Earl, startled.

"Because I have not spoken, do not imagine that I have not *felt!*" said Miss Morville. "I had no right to speak, but I have very often *burned* to do so!" She added, with resolution: "I trust I shall always behave with propriety towards the members of St. Erth's family, but I will *not* allow him to be scolded, and slighted, and beset, which is something I viewed with the strongest disapprobation, even when I felt no decided partiality for him! Or, at any rate," she amended conscientiously, "not very much!"

"My dear sir, I wish you will give me leave to address your daughter at *once!*" said the Earl, quite entranced by this sudden and unexpected declaration of war on the part of his chosen bride.

"Certainly not!" replied Mr. Morville. "I consider the alliance wholly unsuitable. My daughter has been reared in accordance with principles which I do not doubt are repugnant to you. Even were you to assure me that you regard with sympathy the ideals to the promulgation of which I have devoted my life, I should remain adamant!"

"But I don't regard them with sympathy!" said the Earl.

"You don't?" repeated Mr. Morville, looking at him very hard.

"No, how should I? I have not the smallest desire to live in a Republican state, and if an attempt were made to strip me of my possessions I should resist it to the utmost of my power."

"You would, eh? Well, at all events, you seem to have *some* ideas in your head!" said Mr. Morville.

"Upon my word!" said the Dowager. "I do not know what the world is coming to! I can scarcely believe that my ears have not deceived me! That is not very likely, however, for I have very good hearing: it is a thing I pride myself upon. I should have supposed that if there were no objection to this match on *our* side, there could be none on *yours,* my dear sir!"

"If," said Mr. Morville precisely, "I set any value on such things, ma'am, I should feel myself impelled to inform you that the Morvilles were seigneurs in Normandy when the Frants—if Frants there were at that date—were still in a state of serfdom!"

At this point, Mrs. Morville, who had been conferring with the Earl, interposed, saying: "Mr. Morville, St. Erth and I are agreed that it will not do to take Drusilla home today, while she feels so poorly, so we have decided that she shall go immediately to bed, and I will remain to take care of her, if you, ma'am, do not object!"

"Certainly! I shall be very happy!" said the Dowager. "If my nephew were at Stanyon, Mr. Morville, he would show you the Frant records, which we keep in the muniment room!"

"Yes, yes, ma'am, I have seen them! Nothing earlier than the fifteenth century! My brother has in his possession an interesting charter, granted by Edward III to our ancestor, Sir Ralph de Morville. He was a Garter Knight—one of the Founders, and the son of Reginald de Morville, who— Yes, my dear, what is it?"

"I have been saying, Mr. Morville," explained his wife,

with great patience, "that I am remaining here to nurse Drusilla. So if you will inform Mrs. Buxton of it she may pack a night-bag for me, and Peter can bring it to me."

"In 1474," said the Dowager, "we had the honour of entertaining Edward IV at Stanyon!"

"Ay, had you indeed?" said Mr. Morville. "*My* family, of course, always held by the true line!"

It was now apparent to everyone that battle was fairly joined. Mrs. Morville gave it as her opinion that it would be useless to attempt to distract the attention of either combatant, but when Drusilla was assisted to rise from the sofa, to go upstairs to bed, and stood for a moment, supported by the Earl's arm, Mr. Morville happened to notice this circumstances, and broke off in the middle of what he was saying to the Dowager to address fatherly words of encouragement to his daughter. "Going to bed?" he said. "That's right! You look a very poor thing, my dear! Better let St. Erth carry you, or you will be tumbling down in another faint!"

"An excellent suggestion, sir!" said the Earl, and picked his betrothed up, and bore her off, heedless alike of her entreaties to him to remember his own injury, and of the strongly worded disapproval of Martin and the Viscount, who followed him out of the Hall, urging him to relinquish his burden to one or other of them.

"Well, well!" said Mr. Morville indulgently. "They mean to have each other, I suppose! It might have been worse. I don't dislike your son-in-law, ma'am: at least he isn't afraid to know his own mind, which is more than I can say of most of the young men I meet! But as for this Crusader of yours—! No, no, the Férants were

a Gascony family, which died out before 1500! No connection with the Frants, none at all! I told your late
husband so, years ago! *We,* of course, have Raymond
de Morville, and his cousin Bertrand, both of whom
were twice on crusades, and are buried at Fonthaven,
but I don't consider it anything to boast of!"

Everything you love about romance...
and more!

Please turn the page for Signature
Select™ Bonus Features.

THE QUIET
GENTLEMAN

BONUS
FEATURES
INSIDE

A Regency Glossary—
The Sophisticated and the Slang
by Laura Paquet

The language of the Regency era was romantic, filled with elegant words and phrases. The following are just a few of the expressions popular in Regency novels that are rarely heard today.

4

Abigail: lady's maid

Agreeable: pleasing to one's senses

Ardent: characterized by warmth of feeling

Baseborn: born out of wedlock

Collect: to remember, or recollect

Discordancy: the state of being in disagreement

Ill-favored: objectionable, undesirable

Libertine: a freethinker who isn't restrained by conventional morality

Situation: one's (financial) position in life

Vex: to distress or agitate

Yet, as well as this beautiful language, Regency novels are also full of colorful slang.

Above one's touch: far above one on the social scale

Addle pate: a silly, unkind person

All the crack: the latest fashion

Apartment to let: an empty-headed person

Ape-leader: an old maid

Baggage: a bold, impertinent woman, or a prostitute

Banbury story: a fantastic tale or lie

Barque of frailty: fallen woman

Bit of muslin: promiscuous woman

Blow a cloud: to smoke tobacco

Blue-deviled: depressed

Bluestocking: intellectual woman (*not* a compliment in those days)

Blunt: money

Bosky: drunk

By-blow: child born out of wedlock

(To give a woman) carte-blanche: to make a woman one's mistress

Chit: young girl

Cit (also *city-mushroom*): a businessman or merchant, particularly one who tries to buy his way into high society

Cloth-headed: foolish, not very smart

(To give someone her) congé: to end a relationship with one's mistress

Corinthian: a fine gentleman, particularly one known for athletic prowess

Cow-handed: clumsy

Dandy: a man, usually young, overly concerned with fashion and grooming

Dangle after: to be infatuated with (someone)

Diamond of the first water: lovely woman

Diamond squad: people of quality

Draw someone's cork: give someone a bleeding nose

Dudgeon (sometimes *high dudgeon*): foul mood

Dun territory: debt

Faradiddle: falsehood

(Of the) first stare: finest

Foxed: drunk

Fustian: nonsense, silly talk

Great unwashed: the lower classes

Havey-cavey: odd, unusual or suspicious

Hell (also gaming hell): gambling establishment, particularly a rough one

High in the instep: overly proud or stuffy

Hoyden: wild, tomboyish young woman

Incomparable: beautiful woman

Inexpressibles: breeches

In one's cups: drunk

Ivories: teeth

Land someone a facer: hit someone in the face

(Get) leg-shackled: get married

Lightskirt: prostitute

Make a cake of oneself: appear foolish

Mutton-headed: dull-witted

8

Offer (for a woman): propose marriage

On-dit: juicy bit of gossip

On the shelf: unmarried (used for spinsters)

Peepers: eyes

Pinchpenny: miserly person

Pink of the ton (also *pinkest of the pinks*):
a fashionable, sought-after gentleman

Plump in the pockets: wealthy

Pockets to let: short of money

Rake (also *rakehell*): a fast-living man known for his vices and reckless behavior

Rogue: an unprincipled man, often a liar

Rum: excellent, good

Set one's cap at (or *for*) *someone:* to try to attract the attention of a potential suitor

Stubble it: be quiet!

Swell: rich or fashionable gentleman

Tittle-tattle: gossip or chitchat

Toad-eater: someone who effusively flatters his social superiors

Ton (also *haut ton*): the fashionable world; high society

Top-lofty: pompous, proud, snobbish

Uppish: irritable

Vowels: IOUs, often given out while gambling

Waggish: mischievous

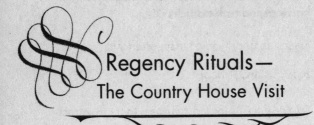

Regency Rituals—
The Country House Visit

During the Regency period, social rituals were very important, especially among the upper classes. One of the most important rituals was the country house visit, which usually included a party or ball.

Often a birth, christening, coming-of-age celebration or wedding would be the reason for a gathering. In other cases, hosts and hostesses arranged a party to help eligible young people meet each other, or simply as a way to enliven long, quiet stays in the country.

These visits took place at large country estates. Due to the difficulties of travel at the beginning of the nineteenth century— railroads had not yet been built, carriages were uncomfortable and most roads were little more than rutted tracks—it didn't make sense for most guests to come for just a day or a weekend. Most people stayed about a week, but some parties lasted longer, if the host and hostess were particularly wealthy or sociable.

These country house visits had four basic elements: relaxing, socializing, gossiping and politicking. Here's how a typical day unfolded for these pampered housguests.

Breakfast

There was no set time for breakfast, which would be set out in the breakfast room early in the morning and might still be available at eleven o'clock. People came and went as they pleased, helping themselves from plates and chafing dishes laid out on a sideboard. A wide range of food was available, usually including at least a few of the following: ham, eggs (shirred, baked or coddled), kippers, porridge, sausages, bacon, cakes (plum, pound or poppy seed), scones and toast, accompanied by butter, jellies, jams, marmalade and honey.

Usually, servants were on hand to refill plates and freshen pots of tea, coffee and chocolate. Tea was the most common beverage, although coffee had been steadily growing in popularity in the decades leading up to the Regency era. Chocolate was similar to what we call "hot" chocolate, although thicker and not nearly as sweet. Instead of sugar, it was often flavored with cinnamon or orange zest. Cold water and milk were rarely served, as they often carried diseases in the days before pasteurization and filtration.

While gentlemen often rose early, ate and then departed to hunt, fish or ride, the ladies might not appear in the breakfast room until around ten o'clock. Their days were less active than the gentlemen's, as well. Acceptable feminine pursuits were largely limited to walking around the grounds, writing letters, playing music, painting, sketching, doing needlework or playing cards. Gossip, of course, was a very popular pastime—the contents of letters were often shared for everyone's amusement and edification.

Midday meals

"Lunch" as we understand it did not really exist in Regency society, since large breakfasts were served late in the morning and dinner took place in the late afternoon. However, people did eat in the middle of the day. Servants usually brought along food to sustain the gentlemen during their outdoor pursuits, and picnics for mixed parties of men and women were popular. Occasionally, particularly if the usual dining schedule was disrupted for some reason, the hosts might offer a light midday meal called "nuncheon," usually consisting of cold meat, bread and fruit. It was also common to serve tea and small cakes in the drawing room in the afternoon, although the custom of an elaborate "afternoon" or "high" tea did not fully develop until after the Regency period.

Dinner

Dinner was served earlier than the meal we now know by the same name—in the country, people usually sat down at the table around four or five o'clock. (In London and other large cities, the hour gradually grew later as the availability and quality of artificial lighting improved, but country people clung much longer to the old custom of eating dinner during daylight hours.) The guests, summoned by a dinner bell, would gather in their finery and proceed into the formal dining room in couples, with the highest-ranking guests first. (Determining just who outranked whom could be a nerve-wracking task for the hostess, involving serious consultation of published etiquette and peerage guides.)

As the main meal of the day, a country house dinner was a long and elaborate affair involving many dishes and copious amounts of wine. If the household was a somewhat conservative one, all the courses but dessert—soup, fish, meat, vegetables, pies and sweet pastries—would be placed in the middle of the table at the beginning of the meal. At more au courant estates, a new style of service called *à la russe* saw servants filling each guest's plate from a range of dishes laid out on a sideboard.

No matter how it was served, the meal showcased the wealth, sophistication and generosity of the host. Rich game and vegetable soups were often flavored with chestnut or artichokes. Fish, usually mackerel, sole or turbot seasoned with herbs, was served at estates near enough to the sea to ensure freshness. There would also be game and roasted meats of all sorts—beef, lamb, mutton, pheasant, quail, partridge, duck, rabbit, grouse and so on—usually accompanied by thick, rich sauces. Hot and cold meat pies were common dishes, and vegetables were becoming more popular, particularly if they were drenched in butter. Sweets such as plum pudding and fruit pies were served with the other main dishes. After this feast, servants would clear the table and bring dessert, usually a pyramid of fresh or sugared fruits, accompanied by marzipan.

Once the meal was finished, the ladies would "withdraw" to the drawing room (hence the chamber's name) for tea, while the men remained in the dining room to enjoy their port. Eventually, if they didn't fall asleep at the table, the men would rejoin the ladies for the evening's entertainment: cards, a musicale or dancing.

Supper

As the evening wore on, the host might offer a light, buffet meal called supper (or, sometimes, a "tea board") around ten or eleven o'clock. It often featured tea or another warm drink, cakes and small savories. If a ball or other large-scale entertainment were in progress, this meal would be a mere break in the proceedings, fortifying guests to return to the festivities. Otherwise, once the supper dishes were cleared away, guests usually retired—initially to their own rooms, but sometimes to a later, secret assignation with an appealing fellow guest.

TO HAVE THE HONOUR
by Georgette Heyer

CHAPTER ONE

YOUNG LORD ALLERTON, a little pale under his tan, glanced from his mother to his man of business. 'But—good God, why was I never told in what case I stood?'

Mr. Thimbleby did not attempt to answer this home question. He perceived that young Lord Allerton's facial resemblance to his deceased father was misleading. There was nothing the late Viscount had desired less than to be told in what case he stood. Three years of campaigning in the Peninsula had apparently engendered in the Fifth Viscount a sense of responsibility which, however welcome it might be in the future to his man of business, seemed at the moment likely to lead to unpleasantness. Mr. Thimbleby directed an appealing look towards the widow.

She did not fail him. Regarding her handsome eldest born with an eye of fond pride, she said: 'But when poor Papa died, you had been wounded, dearest! I would not for the world have distressed you!'

The Viscount said impatiently: 'A scratch! I was back in the saddle within a week! Mama, how *could* you keep me in ignorance of our circumstances? Had I had the least notion of the truth I must have returned to England immediately!'

'Exactly so!' nodded his parent. 'And that, dearest Alan, I was determined you should not be obliged to do! Everyone said the war would so soon be over, and I knew how mortified you would be to be forced to sell out before the glorious end! To be sure, I did hope that directly after Toulouse you might have been released, but it was not to be, and it is of no consequence, except that here we are, with all the foreign notables upon us, and I have the greatest dread that your tailor may not have your evening dress ready for you to wear at my ball next week!'

'That, Mama, believe me, is the least of our problems!'

'Very true, my love,' agreed her ladyship. 'Trix has been in despair, but "Depend upon it", I have said from the outset, "even though your brother may patronize Scott, instead of Weston, who always did so well by poor Papa, you may be confident that *no* tailor would fail at such a juncture!"' Her gaze dwelled appreciatively upon his lordship's new coat of olive-green, upon the pantaloons of delicate yellow which clung to his shapely legs, upon the Hessian boots which shone so bravely, and upon the neckcloth which was tied with such nicety, and she heaved a satisfied sigh.

The Viscount turned in desperation to his man of business. 'Thimbleby!' he uttered. 'Be so good as to explain to me why *you* did not think it proper to inform me that my father had left me encumbered with debt.'

Mr. Thimbleby cast another imploring glance at the widow. 'Her ladyship having done me the honour to admit me into her confidence, my lord, it seemed to me—that is, I was encouraged to hope…'

'To hope what?'

'My dear son, you must not blame our good Thimbleby!' intervened Lady Allerton. 'Indeed, no one is to be blamed, for if you will but consider you will perceive that our case is not desperate!'

'Desperate! I trust not! But that there is the most urgent need of the strictest economy—even, I fear, of measures as repugnant to me as they must be to you, ma'am, I cannot doubt! I dare not think what my own charges upon the estate have been during these months, when I should have been doing what lies within my power to repair what I do not scruple to call a shockingly wasted fortune!'

'No, no, it is not as bad as *that!*' she assured him. 'My dear Alan, there is *one* circumstance you are forgetting!'

He stared at her with knitted brows. 'Pray, what am I forgetting, ma'am?'

'Hetty!' she said, opening her eyes at him.

'I certainly do not forget my cousin, Mama, but in what way my embarrassments can be thought to concern her I have not the remotest conjecture!' said his lordship. A dreadful thought flashed into his mind; he said quickly: 'You are not trying to tell me, ma'am, that my cousin's fortune has been used to— No, no, impossible! She is still under age, and cannot have been allowed— There was another trustee besides my father, after all! Old Ossett could never have countenanced such a thing!'

'Nothing of the sort!' said her ladyship. 'And I must say, Alan, that I wonder at your supposing that I would entertain such a notion, except, of course, under such circumstances as much render it entirely proper! My own niece! I might almost say my *daughter*, for I am sure she is as dear to me as Trix!'

Mr. Thimbleby, who had been unobtrusively engaged in putting up his papers, now judged it to be time to withdraw from a discussion which was not progressing according to hopeful expectation. The Viscount, beyond reminding him rather sharply that he should require his attendance upon the morrow, made no objection to his bowing himself out of the room, but began to pace about the floor, his brow furrowed, and his lips compressed as though to force back unwise speech.

His parent said sympathetically: 'I was afraid you would be a trifle shocked, dearest. It was hazard, of course. I knew no good would come of it when poor Papa forsook faro, at which he had always been so fortunate!'

The Viscount halted, and said with careful self-control: 'Mama, have you realized that to win free from this mountain of debt I must sell some—perhaps all!—of the unentailed property? When I learned that my father had left everything to me, making not the least provision for Timothy or for Trix, I own I was astonished! I see now why he did so, but how I am to provide for them I know not! Ma'am, you have been talking ever since my arrival of the ball you are giving in honour of this Grandduchess of yours, of the drawing-room at which you mean to present my sister, but have you realized that there is no money to pay for these things?'

'Good gracious, Alan, you should realize that if I do not?' exclaimed her ladyship. 'I declare I can scarcely recall when I was last able to pay a bill, and the tiresome thing is that there are now so many of them in that drawer in my desk that I can't open it!'

'For God's sake, Mama, how have you contrived to continue living in this style?' demanded the Viscount.

'Oh, well, my love, upon credit! Everyone has been most obliging!'

'Merciful heavens!' muttered the Viscount. '*What* credit, ma'am?'

'But, Alan, they all guess that you are going to marry dear Hetty, and they know *her* fortune to be immense!'

'Oh my God!' said the Viscount, and strode over to the window. 'So that's it, is it?'

Lady Allerton regarded his straight back in some dismay. 'It has always been an understood thing!' she faltered.

'Nonsense!'

'But it was my dear brother's wish!'

'It can scarcely have been his wish that his daughter should be married to an impoverished— fortune-hunter!' said the Viscount bitterly. 'And it must be very far from Sir John Ossett's wish!'

'Now there you are out!' said her ladyship triumphantly. 'Sir John will raise not the smallest objection to the match, for he has told me so! He knows it is what my brother intended, and, what is more, he has a great regard for you, my love!'

'I am obliged to him!'

'Alan!' ejaculated her ladyship. 'You—you have not formed an attachment for another?'

'No!'

'No, I was persuaded— Dearest, I thought— Of course, she was very young when you went away, but it did seem to me—'

'Mama,' he interrupted, 'whatever my sentiments, you cannot have supposed it possible that I would offer for my cousin in my present circumstances!'

'But it seems just the moment!' protested his mother. 'Besides, she expects it!'

He wheeled about. '*Expects* it?'

'Yes, I assure you she does! Dearest Hetty! If she could have done it, she would have bestowed her entire fortune on me! I never knew a better-hearted girl, never!'

'Oh, good God, then that is why she is now so shy of me!' said the Viscount. 'My poor little cousin! How *could* you let her think it was her duty to marry me, Mama? It is infamous! Have you kept her shut away from the world in case she should meet a more eligible suitor than ever I can be?'

'No, I have not!' replied Lady Allerton, affronted. 'I brought her out two years ago, and she has had a great many suitors, and has refused them all! She is a very well-behaved girl, and would never dream of marrying to disoblige me!'

'She has been shamefully used!' he said.

CHAPTER TWO

THE OBJECT OF the Viscount's pity, Miss Henrietta Clitheroe, was at the moment seated in a small saloon at the back of the house, studying, with her young cousin, the latest issue of *La Belle Assemblée*, and endeavouring to convince Miss Allerton that a dress of gauze worn over a damped and transparent petticoat was a toilette scarcely designed to advance her in the good graces of those august members of the *ton* who were pledged to appear at her mama's party given in honour of the Grandduchess Catherine of Oldenburg. This was not a circumstance which weighed with Miss Allerton, who, at seventeen, was thought by the censorious to have been born for the express purpose of driving her mother into her grave by the outrageous nature of her pranks; but she knew that she would never be permitted to wear such a dress, and so allowed herself to be distracted by the picture of a damsel arrayed in white satin embellished with rose-buds and love-knots.

She was just saying, though disconsolately, that she supposed it was quite a pretty dress, when the Viscount came into the room, and, still holding the door, said: 'The latest fashions? Am I very much in the way, or may I have a word with you, cousin?'

The colour flooded Henrietta's cheeks; she stammered: 'Oh no! I mean, to be sure you may, Alan!'

Miss Allerton, unwontedly meek, obeyed the command contained in the jerk of his lordship's head, and tripped out of the room. The Viscount shut the door, and turned to look across the saloon at his cousin. Her colour rose higher still, and she pretended to search for something in the litter of objects on the table.

'Henry...' the Viscount said.

She looked up at that, a little shy smile on her lips. 'Oh, Alan, no one has called me that since you went away! How nice it sounds!'

He returned the smile, although with an effort. 'Does it? You will always be Henry to me, you know.' He paused; and then said with a good deal of constraint: 'I have been with my mother and with Thimbleby for the past hour. What I have learnt from them has made me feel that I must speak to you immediately.'

'Oh—oh, yes?' said Henrietta.

'Yes. I think I was never more shocked in my life than when I realized—' He broke off, conscious of the awkwardness of his situation. His own colour

BONUS FEATURE

rose; he said with a rueful laugh: 'The devil! I'm as tongue-tied as a schoolboy! Henry, I only wanted to say—I'm not going to offer for you!'

The flush in Henrietta's cheeks began to ebb. 'Oh!' she said. '*N-not* going to offer for me?'

He came towards her, and took her hands, giving them a reassuring squeeze. 'Of course I am not! How could you think I would do so, you foolish Henry? You have been made to believe that you were in some way promised to me, haven't you? Some absurd talk of what your father desired—of what you owed to my family. Well, you owe us nothing, my dearest cousin! It is rather we who owe you a great debt. You have been our—most beloved sister—ever since you came to live with us. I am ashamed that it should ever have been suggested to you that it is your duty to marry me: it is no such thing! You are free to marry whom you please.'

This did not, at the moment, appear likely to the heiress. She disengaged her hands. 'Am—am I?'

'Indeed you are!' With an attempt at lightness, he added: 'Unless you choose someone quite ineligible! I warn you, I should do what I could to prevent *that,* Henry!'

She managed to smile. 'I should be obliged to elope, then, should I not? I—I am glad you have been so frank with me. Now we can be comfortable again!'

'My poor girl!' he said quickly. 'If only you had told me what was in the wind—! There was never a hint in any of your letters. I would have set your mind at rest months ago! No: you could not, of course!'

She turned away, and began to tidy the litter on the table. She said, in a voice that did not sound to her ears quite like her own: 'I own, I had as lief not be married for my fortune!' He returned no answer; after a pause, she added: 'Are your affairs in very bad case, Alan?'

'Not so bad that I shall not be able, with time and good management, to set them to rights, I hope,' he replied. 'I could wish that my mother had not chosen, at this moment, to entertain upon so lavish a scale. I suppose nothing can be done about this party for the Russian woman, but for the rest—the White's Ball, Trix's presentation—'

'Good God, do not tell my aunt she must postpone *that!*' exclaimed Henrietta. 'If she is obliged to wait another year, Trix will very likely run off with a handsome Ensign!' She saw the startled look on his face, and added: 'You don't yet know her, Alan!'

'My dear Henry, at seventeen she can hardly be thinking of marriage, surely!'

'The last man she fell in love with was young Stillington,' said Henrietta thoughtfully. 'To be sure, he was better than that actor she saw in Cheltenham, but still quite ineligible of course.

Fortunately, her mind was diverted by the plans for her first season.'

'It is time Trix was broke to bridle!' said his lordship roundly. He then favoured his cousin with a few animadversions upon the conduct of his lively young sister, and left her to her reflections.

These were not for many moments concerned with the almost inevitable clash between brother and sister. They led Henrietta to the mirror, and caused her to stare long at her own image.

It should have comforted her. Dark ringlets framed a charming countenance in which two speaking eyes of blue became gradually filled with tears that obscured her vision of a short, straight nose, a provocative upper lip, and an elusive dimple. These attributes had apparently failed to captivate the Viscount. The heiress uttered a strangled sob, and dabbed resolutely at her eyes, realizing that she would shortly be obliged to confront Miss Allerton, agog to know whether the date of her wedding had been fixed.

Nor was she mistaken. In a very few minutes, Trix peeped into the room, and, finding her cousin alone, at once demanded to be told what Alan had said to her.

Henrietta replied in the most cheerful of accents: 'I am so much relieved! He does not wish to marry me at all!'

Trix, shocked by these tidings, could only stare at her.

'You may imagine how happy he has made me!' continued Henrietta glibly. 'Had he desired it, I must have thought it my duty to marry him, but he has set my mind at rest on this head, and now I can be easy again!'

'But you have loved him for years!' Trix blurted out.

'Indeed I have!' said Henrietta cordially. 'I am sure I always shall!'

'*Hetty!* When you have been writing to him for ever!'

'Pray, what has that to say to anything? To me, he is the elder brother I never had.'

'Hetty, what a hum! He is *my* brother, and I never wrote to him above twice in my life!'

Before Henrietta could reply suitably to this, they were joined by a willowy young gentleman in whom only the very stupid could have failed to recognize a Pink of the Ton. From the tip of his pomaded head to the soles of his dazzling Hessians, the Honourable Timothy Allerton was beautiful to behold. He was generally supposed to care for nothing but the fashion of his neckcloth, but he showed unmistakable signs of caring for the news which his sister broke to him. '*Not* going to offer for Hetty?' he repeated, aghast. 'Well, upon my soul! Well, what I mean is, might think what's due to the rest of us!

Mind, I don't say I'm surprised he don't like it above half, but the thing is he's the head of the family, and he dashed well ought to do it! What's more,' he said, his amiable countenance darkening, 'if he thinks he can make *me* offer for her he'll find he's devilish mistaken! It ain't that I don't like you, Hetty,' he added kindly, 'because I do, but that's coming it a trifle too strong!'

30

CHAPTER THREE

IF THE VISCOUNT had harboured doubts of his mother's veracity, these were speedily dispelled. His cousin, far from having been kept in seclusion, seemed to him to be acquainted with all the eligible bachelors upon the town, and with far too many of those whom he did not hesitate to stigmatize as gazetted fortune-hunters. She dispensed her favours impartially amongst these gentlemen, whirled about town under the chaperonage of various not wholly disinterested matrons, and in general conducted herself with such frivolity that her perturbed aunt said that she had never known her to be in such a flow of spirits. She raised hopes in a dozen breasts, but the only suitor for whom she betrayed the smallest partiality was Sir Matthew Kirkham; and it was absurd to suppose (as Lady Allerton assured Alan) that a girl with as much good sense as Hetty would for an instant entertain the pretensions of a penniless roué, past his first youth, and with at least two unsavoury scandals attached to his name.

BONUS FEATURE

Alan could place no such dependence on his cousin's good sense. It was rarely that he took a dislike to anyone, but he took a quite violent dislike to Sir Matthew, and warned Henrietta to give the fellow no encouragement: an exercise of cousinly privilege which had no other effect than to cause her to wear Sir Matthew's flowers at the Opera House that very evening.

He was brought to realize that however obnoxious Kirkham might appear in the eyes of his fellow-men he possessed considerable charm for the ladies: Trix told him so. Trix listened with interest to his trenchantly expressed opinion of Sir Matthew, and then disgusted him by talking of the fellow's polished manners, and of the distinguishing attentions he had for so long bestowed upon Hetty.

Sir Matthew was not one of the two hundred guests invited to have the honour of being presented to the Tsar's sister. This lady had arrived in England some time before the various Kings, Princes, Generals, and Diplomats who were coming to take part in the grand Peace celebrations, and was putting up at the Pulteney Hotel. She was neither beautiful nor particularly amiable, but she was being much courted, and had already created a mild sensation by being rude to the Prince Regent, and by parading the town in enormous coal-scuttle bonnets, which instantly became the rage. Trix, giggling over the story of her having abruptly left the party at Carlton

32

House just as soon as the expensive orchestra provided for her entertainment had struck up, because (she said) music made her want to vomit, prophesied that her departure from Lady Allerton's ball would be equally speedy; but Lady Allerton, well-acquainted with the Grandduchess, said, 'No: she only behaved like that when she wished to be disagreeable.'

Trix was not to appear at the ball either. The Viscount had told her that with all the will in the world to do so he was unable at present to find the funds which would enable his mama to launch her into society; and Lady Allerton's sense of propriety was too nice to allow of her consenting to let her daughter attend a ball of such importance before she was out.

Trix bore her disappointment surprisingly well, neither arguing with Allen nor reproaching him. Touched by her restraint, he promised her a magnificent début the following spring, if he had to sell every available acre to achieve it. She thanked him, and said that she had made up her mind to help him in his difficulties.

Such unprecedented docility ought to have alarmed Henrietta, but Henrietta was too much occupied with her own affairs to notice it. It was not until the very evening of the ball, when Trix helped her, in the most selfless way, to array herself in all the elegance of primrose satin and pale green gauze,

BONUS FEATURE

that it occurred to her that this saintly conduct was a suspicious as it was unusual. But Trix, looking the picture of hurt innocence, assured her that she had no intention of perpetrating some shocking practical joke, and she was obliged to be satisfied. Trix embraced her with great fondness, and she went away to join Lady Allerton feeling that she had misjudged her wayward cousin.

In this belief she continued until midnight, when she suffered a rude disillusionment.

CHAPTER FOUR

MR. ALLERTON, seizing a respite from his conscientious labours on the floor, stood in the doorway of the ballroom, and delicately wiped his brow. The May night was very warm, and although the long windows stood open scarcely a breath of wind stirred the curtains which masked them, and the heat from the hundreds of wax candles burning in the wall-sconces and in the huge crystal chandelier which hung from the ceiling was making not only the flowers wilt, but every gentleman's starched shirt-points as well. But this was a small matter. Mr. Allerton, a captious critic, was well-satisfied with the success of the ball. Every domestic detail had been perfectly arranged; his mother did him the greatest credit in a robe of sapphire satin lavishly trimmed with broad lace; his cousin was in quite her best looks; and even his brother, although dressed by a military tailor, did not disgrace him. The Grandduchess was in high good humour; besides the flower of the ton, two of the Royal Dukes were lending lustre to the evening; and, to set the final *cachet* upon a brilliant function, the great Mr. Brummell himself was present.

These agreeable reflections were interrupted. A hand grasped Mr. Allerton's wrist, and his cousin's voice said urgently in his ear: 'Timothy, come quickly to my aunt's dressing-room! I must speak to you alone!'

A horrible premonition that the champagne had run out and the ice melted away seized Mr. Allerton. But the news which Henrietta had to impart to him had nothing to do with domestic arrangements. She was clutching in one hand a sheet of writing-paper, with part of the wafer that had sealed it still sticking to its edge, and this she dumbly proffered. Mr. Allerton took it, and mechanically lifted his quizzing-glass to his eye. 'What the deuce—?' he demanded. 'Lord, I can't read this scrawl! What is it?'

'Trix!' she uttered, in a strangled voice.

'Well, that settles it,' he said, giving the letter back to her. 'Never been able to make head or tail of her writing! You'd better tell me what it is.'

'Timothy, it is the most terrible thing! She has eloped with Jack Boynton!'

'What?' gasped Timothy. 'No, hang it, Hetty! Must be bamming you!'

'No, no, it is the truth! She is not in the house,

and she left this note for me. Dawson has this instant given it to me!'

'Well, I'm dashed!' said Timothy. '*Jack Boynton?* Y'know, Hetty, I wouldn't have thought it of him!'

Too well accustomed to Mr. Allerton's mental processes to be exasperated, Henrietta replied: 'No, indeed! She must have persuaded him to do it: he is so very young! I never dreamed—Good God, I thought that affair had ended months ago! How could she have been so sly? But I might have guessed how it would be! If I had not been so selfishly taken up with my own troub— I mean, *pleasures!*—it could never have happened! Timothy, I must act immediately, and you must help me!'

He blinked at her. 'Dash it, can't do anything in the middle of m'mother's party!'

'We can, and we must! They have fled to Gretna Green, and they must be overtaken!'

'Gretna Green?' echoed Mr. Allerton, revolted. 'No, really, Hetty! Can't have!'

'She makes no secret of it. Besides, where else could they be married, two children under age? She supposed, of course, that I should not receive her letter until too late, but Dawson, good, faithful soul, thought it right to give it to me as soon as she might, and it is not too late! You and I may slip away, and it can't signify to anyone if our absence is noticed. I have thought it all out, and I have the greatest hope of overtaking them before morning! I am persuaded that boy cannot have scraped together enough money to pay for the hire of more than a pair of horses. You and I may hire four, and change them at every stage. The moon is at the full; we shall come up with them before they have gone thirty miles beyond London! Then we may bring Trix home, and no one need know what happened, not even my poor aunt, for I can trust Dawson to keep the secret, and ten to one my aunt won't leave her room until noon tomorrow!'

'Seems to me we'd do better to tell Alan,' objected Timothy.

'Upon no consideration! The Grandduchess is still here, and Sussex too! He at least cannot leave the house! Besides, Trix trusts me not to betray her to him, and however dreadfully she may have behaved I *could* not do so! He would be so angry! Oh, dear, it is all his fault for having postponed her coming-out! I warned him how it would be! Timothy, *you* must know where we can hire a post-chaise and four good horses!'

He admitted it, but entered a caveat. 'Thing is, dare say you're right about Boynton, but I ain't got the ready to pay for a chaise and four either!'

'No, but I have! I drew quite a large sum only yesterday, and I will give it to you,' said Henrietta. 'I will fetch my cloak, and instruct Dawson in what she must say if she should be questioned, and then we may be off. Do not tell Helmsley to call up a hackney! We will creep out by the door into the yard, and find one for ourselves directly!'

'But, Hetty!' protested Mr. Allerton. 'Can't go driving about the countryside in evening-dress! Must change!'

But long acquaintance with her cousin had made Henrietta too familiar with the exigencies of his toilette to allow him this indulgence. Assuring him that his swallow-tailed coat and satin knee-breeches would be hidden by a driving-cloak, she so admonished and hustled him that within a very few minutes he found himself being smuggled out of the house by way of the back stairs and a door leading from the nether regions into the stable-yard.

CHAPTER FIVE

'No,' SAID MR. ALLERTON, some five hours later. 'I won't tell 'em to drive on to the Norman Cross inn! And it ain't a bit of use arguing with me, Hetty, because I'm not going to go another mile on a dashed wild-goose chase, and so I tell you! If you want to go on jolting over a devilish bad road, asking questions at every pike of a set of gapeseeds who wouldn't be able to tell you whether Cinderella had driven by in a dashed great pumpkin, let alone Trix in a chaise, you do it! We've come a cool seventy miles, and never had so much as a whiff of Trix, and I want my breakfast! What's more, when I've had it I'm going back to town! She's hoaxing you; told you so at the outset!'

Miss Clitheroe, who had been ushered by an astonished waiter into one of the private parlours of the Talbot Inn, in Stilton, untied the strings of her cloak and pushed back its hood from her dishevelled curls. Pressing her hands to her tired eyes, she said wretchedly: 'She would not do such a thing! I know

40

she plays shocking pranks, but she would never do this, only for mischief!'

'If I know Trix,' said Timothy, 'very likely told you she was off to Gretna Green to set you on a false scent!'

Henrietta stared at him in dismay. 'You mean she may have fled in quite another direction? Timothy, that would be worse than anything! It may be days before we can discover her whereabouts, and where, in heaven's name, will they find a clergyman to marry them?'

'Exactly so!' said Timothy. He added ghoulishly: 'Won't be a case of taking her home. Have to get 'em married in a hurry to save scandal.'

'No, no, I will not believe it!' cried Henrietta. 'They are ahead of us still! We must go on!'

Mr. Allerton's reply was brief and unequivocal, but when he perceived the real distress in his cousin's face he relented sufficiently to promise that when he had eaten breakfast he would make enquiries at each of the other three posting-houses in the town. With this Henrietta was obliged to be content. The waiter set breakfast before them, listened with polite incredulity to the story, hastily manufactured by Timothy, to account for their appearance in Stilton at eight o'clock in the morning in full dress, of the moribund relative to whose bedside they had been summoned, and withdrew, shaking his head over the reprehensible habits of the Quality.

Mr. Allerton then applied himself to a substantial repast. Henrietta, unable to do more than drink a cup of coffee, and nibble a slice of bread and butter, eyed him in growing impatience, but knew better than to expostulate. He finished at last, and, with a kindly recommendation to her not to expect any good outcome, went off to call at the Bell, the Angel, and the Woolpack.

She was left to await his return with what patience she could muster. The time lagged unbearably; when half an hour had passed she could no longer sit still, but got up, and began to pace about the room, trying to think what were best to be done if he failed to obtain news of the fugitives in Stilton.

42

The sound of a vehicle approaching at a smart pace, and pulling up outside the inn, made her run to the window. The sight that met her eyes was so unexpected and so unwelcome that she caught her breath on a gasp of dismay. Leaning from his own sporting curricle to interrogate one of the ostlers was her cousin Alan, and one glance at his face was enough to inform her that he was quite as angry as she had known he must be, if ever his sister's escapade came to his ears. As she stared out at him, he sprang down from the curricle, and came striding to the door into the inn.

She retreated from the window, wondering how much Dawson had disclosed to him, and what she should say to mollify him. She could almost wish now that the eloping couple had fled beyond recall, for it seemed to her that young Mr. Boynton would be fortunate to escape with his bare life if the Viscount caught him.

The Viscount came in, and cast a swift, searching look round the room. Unlike his brother, he had found time to change his ball-dress for a riding-habit, over which he wore a caped greatcoat with large buttons of mother-of-pearl. He was looking extremely handsome, and singularly unyielding. After that one glance round the parlour, his attention became fixed on his cousin, his pleasant gray eyes so full of wrath that she took an involuntary step backward. Stripping off his gloves, he said furiously: 'How *dared* you do this, Henry? How *could* you?'

It had not occurred to her that any part of his anger would be directed against her. She said pleadingly: 'I suppose it was improper, but it seemed to be the only thing I could do!'

'Improper?' he exclaimed. 'So that's what you call it, is it? The most damnable escapade!'

'Alan! No, no! Imprudent I may have been, but what other course was open to me? I would not for the world tell my aunt, and I dared not say a word of it to you, because—'

'That at least I believe!' he interrupted. 'You knew well I would never permit it! You were right, my girl, very right! Where is the fellow?'

'I don't know. Oh, Alan, pray don't be so out of reason cross with me! Indeed I meant it for the best! *Alan!*'

The Viscount, who had most ungently grasped her shoulders, shook her. 'Don't lie to me! Where is he?'

'I tell you I don't know! And if I did I would not tell you while you are in such a rage!' said Henrietta, with spirit.

'We'll see that! said the Viscount grimly. 'I'll settle with him when I've settled with you! Had you chosen an honest man I would have stood aside, whatever it cost me, but this fellow—! No, by God! If you are determined to marry a fortune-hunter, Henry, let him be me! At least I *love* you!'

Shock bereft her of the power of speech; she could only gaze up into his face. He dragged her into his arms, and kissed her with such savagery that she uttered an inarticulate protest. To this he paid no heed at all, but demanded sternly: 'Do you understand me, Henry? Give you up to Kirkham I will not!'

'Oh, Alan, don't give me up to anyone!' begged Henrietta, laughing and crying together. 'Oh, dear, how *odious* you are! Of all the infamous notions to— Alan, let me go! Someone is coming!'

The door opened. 'Told you no good would come of it,' said Mr. Allerton, with gloomy satisfaction. 'Not a trace of 'em to be—' He broke off, staring at his brother. 'Well, upon my word!' he said, mildly surprised.

'What the devil are *you* doing here?' exclaimed the Viscount.

'Came with Hetty,' explained Timothy. 'Said it was a stupid thing to do, but she would have it we should overtake 'em.'

'Came with Hetty? Overtake—?' repeated the Viscount. 'In heaven's name, what are you talking about?'

Mr. Allerton raised his quizzing-glass. 'You been in the sun, old fellow?' he asked solicitously.

'Timothy, he doesn't know!' Henrietta said. '*That* is not what brought him here! Alan, a dreadful thing has happened. Trix has eloped! I can't think what made you suppose that *I* had! Timothy and I came in pursuit, and oh, I was so hopeful of catching them, but we can discover no trace of them!'

'Quite true,' corroborated Timothy, observing that the tidings had apparently stunned his brother. 'Eloped with Jack Boynton. At least, that's what she said.'

'Are you mad?' demanded the Viscount. 'Trix is at home!'

'Alas, Alan, she is not!' said Henrietta. 'She slipped out in the middle of the party, leaving a letter, which her maid gave me at midnight. She wrote that she had gone with Boynton to Gretna

Green, but I very much fear that she was deceiving me, and that is not her destination.'

The Viscount, who had listened to this with an arrested expression on his face, drew an audible breath. 'Most certainly she was deceiving you!' he said, in an odd tone. 'I see! The—little—cunning—*devil!*'

'He *is* cut, Hetty!' said Timothy.

A rueful smile was quivering at the corners of the Viscount's mouth. He paid no heed to this brotherly remark, but said: 'Let me tell you, my love, that an hour after you had left Grosvenor Square, I also received a billet from Trix!'

'You?' said Henrietta incredulously.

'Yes, I! It summoned me with the utmost urgency to join her in Mama's dressing-room. There she disclosed to me that *you* had slipped out of the house, to elope to the Border with Kirkham. She said that you had bound her to secrecy, but that her conscience misgave her, and she felt it to be her duty to betray you to me.'

'*Oh!*' gasped Henrietta. 'The little *wretch!* She—she deserves to be *flogged!*'

'Well, yes, I suppose she does,' admitted the Viscount. 'You cannot, however, expect *me* to flog her, for she has put me deep in her debt! Besides you must own her strategy has been masterly!'

'Abominable!' scolded Henrietta, trying not to laugh.

'Told you she was hoaxing you,' said Timothy. 'Good notion, as it chances. What I mean is, if you *are* going to marry Hetty, Alan, we shall be all right and tight. The thing that's worrying me is that you must have left home before the ball was over. Dashed improper, y'know! That dishfaced Grandduchess! Half the *ton* invited to have the honour of meeting her, and you walk off in the middle of the party!'

'Well,' said the Viscount impenitently, 'they *had* the honour of meeting her, and *I* have the honour of asking Henry to be my wife, and so we may all be satisfied!' He held out his hands as he spoke, and Henrietta put hers into them.

'Yes, I dare say,' said Mr. Allerton, 'but it ain't the thing. What's more,' he added severely, 'it ain't the thing to kiss Hetty in a dashed inn parlour, and with me watching you, either!'

BONUS FEATURE

**A breathtaking novel of
reunion and romance...**

THE
F RTUNES
OF TEXAS:
Reunion

Once a Rebel

by **Sheri WhiteFeather**

Returning home to Red Rock after many
years, psychologist Susan Fortune is reunited
with Ethan Eldridge, a man she hasn't gotten
over in seventeen years. When tragedy and grief
overtake the family, Susan leans on Ethan to
overcome her feelings—and soon realizes that
her life can't be complete without him.

Coming in February

Silhouette®
Where love comes alive™

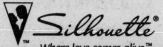